Hidden Bonds

Reforming the Paranormal Council

Book Four

Hidden Bonds

Reforming the Paranormal Council

Book Four

Written by Sheri Eleese

Best wishes
Elizabeth.

Sheri

First Edition August 2021
ISBN 978-1-7775233-4-3

Cover Design:
SelfPubBookCovers.com/Joetherasakdhi

Table of Contents

Acknowledgements vii
Prologue 1
Chapter One 3
Chapter Two 7
Chapter Three 17
Chapter Four 31
Chapter Five 43
Chapter Six 55
Chapter Seven 71
Chapter Eight 89
Chapter Nine 113
Chapter Ten 125
Chapter Eleven 145
Chapter Twelve 165
Chapter Thirteen 185
Chapter Fourteen 201
Chapter Fifteen 213
Chapter Sixteen 233
Chapter Seventeen 247
Chapter Eighteen 261
Chapter Nineteen 279
Chapter Twenty 297
Chapter Twenty-One 321
Chapter Twenty-Two 343
Chapter Twenty-Three 367
Chapter Twenty-Four 387
Epilogue 417
Epilogue Part Two 421
About the Author 427
Other Books by This Author 429

Acknowledgements

First and foremost, thank you to my readers. Your investment in my world and its characters and your hunger for what comes next is truly amazing.

Thank you again to my Alpha and Beta readers for another stellar job. Your feedback is invaluable in turning a draft into a story worth sharing.

A special thanks to my editor, James. Your painstaking attention to detail provides the polishing touch necessary to go to publication. Any mistakes that make it into the final version are all on me for tampering with the finished product.

Thanks to my husband, Mike, for your continued support and constantly firing up the BBQ when I'm too busy working on the book to worry about food.

And to the secret book club at The Crown & Anchor, who don't realize they're a book club, thanks for your support. You guys rock.

Prologue

The slamming door echoed loudly in the early morning air, its turning lock punctuating the end to further conversation.

She glared at the grainy wood, outraged that those who had once curried favor would turn their backs, disregarding debts that were owed. Their rise to power was due solely to her. That they would now deny her claim was intolerable.

Turning away, she gazed upon the empty street, at a loss for her next move. She was out of options.

Or was she?

There was one possibility left; the enemy of her betrayers. Their compassion was a weakness to exploit. She could yet have her revenge. It only required that she put herself in their hands.

A risky move, but to even the scales, she would do what she must.

Decision made, she strode down the sidewalk, the staccato clicking of her heels echoing faintly in the dawn.

It was time to return to her home. And to her sons.

Chapter One

A hidden grotto in the Bayou…

"What is this? Why have you trapped me in this weak vessel?"

Ruth had a brief moment's satisfaction at seeing Zachary die. Then the demon usurped her mind. As it callously tore through her memories with little regard for the damage left in its wake, she had the fleeting thought that Zachary might have been the fortunate one after all. Then all she knew was pain.

Ruth screamed, pulling handfuls of hair from her head as she attempted to fight off the entity invading it. Hands raked down her face, her nails digging grooves into her skin as her mind was shredded, her memories extinguished, and her ordered thoughts scrambled. Blood vessels in her eyes burst from the pressure. The soft tissue of her brain was ripped to tatters when the demon's molten claws raked through her mind, seizing control of all that she was.

Ruth fought, a butterfly against a hurricane, grasping desperately at the torn and ragged fragments, feverishly patching what she could. The overwhelming presence filled the new gaps, expanding until there was only room for one.

Pulling the tiny bits of self that remained, Ruth fled and hid in the farthest corner of her mind. She prayed to the Goddess she had forsaken for deliverance from the demon Ruth, herself, had brought over.

Peter dropped to the ground next to Zachary's body, shouting and grabbing at his head. The hidden part of Ruth watched through red-clouded eyes when Peter tore at his hair, his high-pitched shrieks echoing through the chamber.

"You have failed me. The shifters and vampires yet live."

"Please, Master. Forgive."

"Failure is death."

Ruth sank to her knees, distantly aware of her eardrums bursting when the enraged bellow thundered through the cavern. She struggled for coherence, forcing words from a throat no longer under her control. "For…give."

"One must die."

Feeling the slightest easing of the demon's presence inside her, Ruth began to painstakingly rebuild small sections of her mind, shying away from the blank spots as she worked to restore order.

Her reprieve was short.

Jillian's demon-possessed body slid off the altar and loomed over her. ***"You cannot escape me."***

Ruth recoiled when a hand clamped down on her head, the heated digits branding her skin. Her agonized cry filled the air when the demon surged fully into her mind, ruthlessly squashing her pitiful attempt at freedom as it took total control of her body.

Imprisoned and helpless, Ruth screamed silently in the farthest recesses of her mind when the demon compelled her to walk over and kneel next to Peter, who was thrashing wildly on the ground next to Zachary's body. Her hand pulled the dagger from Zackary's back and set it against Peter's chest. He shook his head and grabbed at her wrist, his mouth twisted as he screamed, but his cries went unheard, muted by the demon who had command of her will.

Ruth renewed her struggles, fighting fiercely for control. The demon's dark laughter rang out as it easily subdued her efforts. Powerless, a slave to the one she'd thought to rule, Ruth drove the dagger into Peter's chest, her last friend and ally dying beneath her hand. Her soul cried when his body stilled and the light faded from his eyes.

Ruth stood and returned to the demon's side, nothing more than a tool awaiting her Master's command.

Dead eyes opened, orbs glowing red in the dim light. The being once known as Peter rose and shuffled across the floor to kneel before the demon. A revenant bowing to its Master.

Chapter Two

Max learns the truth…

My mate-bond with Max is broken and I don't know how to repair it."
"What did you just say?"
Bryan spun around. "Max!"

"Max. Wait."

Afraid of what he might do if he stopped, he kept walking.

"Please. Let me explain."

The persistent tugging on his arm had Max whirling around. "Why now?"

"Because, well…." Bryan pointed back to the office, a sheepish expression crossing his face.

"Because I found out you've been lying to me?"

"I didn't lie to you. Not really." Bryan grimaced. "I didn't mean for you to find out like that."

"No?" Max glared at the man who'd been confusing him since the day they'd met. "How did you plan to tell me you've been lying to me?"

"Damn it, Max. I didn't lie to you. Not intentionally. I was just waiting for the right time."

"You've had months to say something."

"I know. I kept putting it off because I wasn't sure how to tell you."

Max bit back the words wanting to break free. This was his mate after all. "And now you do?"

"Not exactly." Bryan frowned at the floor. A cute dimple popped into existence between his eyebrows.

Max crossed his arms and glowered, refusing to find the sight endearing. Or sexy. Definitely not that. "Then we have nothing to talk about."

"Yes, we do. Just give me a minute to figure out how to explain this."

"You've had plenty of time." Max shook his head and turned to go. "I'm done with this."

Bryan's growl was surprising. But not as much as him grabbing the front of Max's shirt and stopping his escape.

"Listen. I didn't say anything because I thought you'd hate me."

"It's not in me to hate my mate." He held up his hand when Bryan went to speak. "But that doesn't mean I want to hear your excuses. Not right now." Brushing Bryan's hands away, Max strode down the hall, heading toward the training room. Sparring with his enforcers might be enough to keep him from strangling his mate. Maybe.

"Max!"

He kept to his steady pace, refusing to look like he was running away. Even if he kind of was.

"Oh, for the love of…." Footsteps pounded down the hall after him. Bryan yanked on his arm and spun him around. "Would you just listen to me?"

"I think I've heard enough." He yanked his arm free. Bryan grabbed his other one.

"Why are you acting like this?"

Bryan's wounded expression was the last straw. Max lost the slippery hold he had on his control. "You tell me. You're the one who's been avoiding me for months." Max shook off his hand. "I've respected your feelings and given you the space you needed. Even though it physically hurt to keep my distance, the last thing I would ever do was impose myself on you."."

"I didn't realize…."

"And the whole time, you knew we were mates and hid it from me. Nothing you say can excuse that."

"Damn it, Max. What was I supposed to do? Tell you I panicked and screwed up the mate bond? That I didn't know how to fix it?"

"Yes! Exactly that. You tell me. I get mad, we fight, and maybe throw things at each other. Then afterward, we try to fix it. Together. What you don't do is keep it a secret."

"But…."

"A Bloodmate bond is sacred to vampires. You know this." As fresh pain of what he'd lost hit him, Max had to stop. He clenched his fists and turned around, breathing heavily as he counted to ten. Making it only to three, he whirled back. "You know it's importance and you broke it. Then you kept quiet about it for months. Months, where I tried not to force my attention on you. Months, where I despised my lack of pride in wanting you when you clearly didn't want me back."

"I did want…."

"Months where I hated myself for being weak. Months, Bryan, where you could have said something to relieve me of my suffering. But you did not."

"I'm sorry. I didn't realize it was affecting you like that." He turned his head away, muttering, "I thought it was only me."

"Would knowing have changed anything?"

"Maybe. I don't know." He blew out a breath. "I was too cowardly to tell you. I wasn't sure you'd be able to forgive me."

"I don't know if I can."

A strangled cry came from Bryan's throat. "You can't mean that."

Max spoke softly, needing Bryan to truly understand what he'd done. "Because of your silence, I've been distracted for months from my sworn duty of protecting my Prince." He took a step back. "Nothing you say now can make up for my failure. Or my shame."

Bryan's face went white.

Unable to bear his mate's distress, Max raced away. He had to force himself not to turn back when the agonized whisper of his name floated in the air. Damn it. He had the right to his anger. What Bryan had done couldn't be erased just because he was sorry. It would take a lot more than that.

Max sped through the mansion, trying to outrun his instinctual need to protect his mate. Before he faced Bryan again, he needed time to get over his anger. And time to forgive him for breaking his heart.

* * *

"Damn it!" Bryan drove his foot through the wall. Which sucked. It was his wall. "What the hell am I supposed to do now?"

"Give him time. He'll get over his anger eventually."

Bryan banged his head against the paneling. Of course, his brother had been a witness to his humiliation. Could this day get any worse?

"Stop hitting your head. You might knock some sense into it."

Bryan turned and glared at his brother. "This isn't funny. Max hates me. And I can't blame him." He slumped against the paneling. "I screwed up big time."

Lysander snorted. "You really did."

Bryan flipped him off. "This is serious."

"Relax. Max doesn't hate you. He's angry and probably wants to strangle you, but he doesn't hate you."

"You don't know that. You didn't see his face, Sandi."

"He's hurt. And feels betrayed."

"I know. He said he couldn't forgive me."

"He will. One day. But you'll have to earn it." His hand landed on Bryan's shoulder. "It's not going to be easy."

"If you're trying to make me feel better, it's not working."

"I'm being realistic." Lysander tucked his hand under Bryan's elbow. "Come on. You look like you could use a drink."

Giving a last look down the empty hallway, Bryan let himself be pulled back into the office.

"Here." Ice tinkled when the glass bumped into his chest.

Bryan started, then quickly grabbed the glass before it could fall. "Hey. Show some respect. That's top-shelf whiskey."

"Sorry. I thought you saw me."

"I must have zoned out." Bryan took a sip and held it in his mouth, savoring the bite. Swallowing, a slow burn spread through him thawing the cold he'd felt since Max had run from him. Angry eyes flashed into his mind. He tossed back the rest of his drink, hoping to drown out the memory. Lysander's eyebrows went up, but he didn't say anything, just refilled his glass.

Grunting his thanks, Bryan sat on the couch and perched on the edge, holding his glass with his fingertips. "What am I going to do if he doesn't forgive me?"

"You're his mate. He has to forgive you."

"I can hear a but coming."

"Like I said, it's not going to be easy. Or fast. Max is a proud man. And you kept this secret from him for months."

"I know exactly what I did."

"I don't know that you do."

Bryan blinked, surprised by the hardness in his voice. "Then tell me."

"Max is a highly respected warrior who is one of the most honorable and loyal people you'll ever meet. He's responsible for the safety of everyone here, most importantly, Roman. He takes his duty seriously and would give his life for any one of us."

"I know all that…."

"Shut up. He's been respecting your wishes by staying away from you, not understanding why his instincts were driving him closer. It's been painful watching him fight against his opposing needs. The struggle has made him doubt himself. You made him feel weak, Bryan," Lysander's voice could barely be heard when he said, "and unworthy."

Bryan swallowed hard.

"Now that he knows you betrayed him…."

"I did not betray him. I made a mistake."

"Which you compounded by not saying anything. You lied to him. You showed him no respect. Now all the anger he's been feeling towards himself is being directed at you."

Bryan set his glass on the table and dropped his face in his hands, feeling about an inch tall. "Shit. I didn't mean to do any of that."

"Whether you did or did not makes no difference in how Max feels."

"What am I supposed to do now?"

"I'd start by showing him he can trust you. Without that, you can't move forward."

"You're right." Bryan stood.

"And you need to repair your bond. Too much is at stake for you guys to be at odds."

"If anyone knows what's at stake, it's me."

"Then don't screw this up."

"I won't." Angry eyes flashed in his mind again, but this time, he also saw the pain. "My own guilt was why I kept pushing him away. Which was crappy of me. I need to tell Max how I feel. Hopefully then he'll give me a chance to prove I'm worthy of him."

"It is unfortunate you did not think of being honest with him sooner." Roman stalked through the door. Sitting in his leather chair, he turned on his computer, then turned to Lysander. "Prepare yourself for Casey's call. I need to bring Eric back from their trip ahead of schedule, which will inevitably distress his mate."

"Why would you do that? They've been planning this getaway ever since Eric recovered from being poisoned. Couldn't Max look after whatever you need."

"My Second has asked permission to take a leave of absence." Bryan flinched at the anger in Roman's eyes. "Not once in five hundred years has Max needed time away from me or the coven. Until now."

"Oh." Lysander's eyes flicked to Bryan. "What's he going to do?"

"He is insistent on going into seclusion. He is worried that his emotional state is distracting him from his duties. Which it is not, but he will not listen to me."

"Damn. I didn't expect him to leave."

Bryan approached Roman's desk. "Where's he going?"

"I do not believe that is any of your concern."

The frigidness in Roman's voice had Bryan taking a step back before he could catch himself. Looking up, he got caught in the ancient vampire's gaze. The predator lurking near the surface had his lizard brain freezing in terror. But only for a moment. Shaking off his primal fear, Bryan forced himself to hold Roman's gaze. "Max is my mate. Everything about him is my concern."

"You are the only one who thinks that."

"Roman, don't."

"No, beloved." Roman took Lysander's hand. "Max is my Second. But more than that, he is my friend. If Max wishes Bryan to know where he is, I will tell him. Until then, I will protect my friend from further hurt."

"But Bryan and Max need to talk. Otherwise, they won't be able to heal their bond."

"Your brother has had plenty of time in which to speak with him. He will now have to wait until Max is ready."

Lysander huffed out a breath, then turned to Bryan, regret filling his eyes.

Bryan held up his hand. "You don't have to say anything. I get it. I'll wait until Max comes back to try again."

"He has agreed to put off leaving until Eric returns." Roman's words were slightly warmer. "Perhaps you will have time to atone for your mistreatment of him before he departs."

"I'll try my best."

"See that you do."

Lysander jerked, freezing in place.

"Beloved. Are you well?" Roman's hands cupped Lysander's face.

Bryan started around the desk when he didn't respond.

Lysander suddenly groaned and raised a hand to his head. "Zachary's dead."

Roman caught him when his knees buckled and carried him to the couch. Bryan hovered anxiously while Roman got him settled.

"I set him free," Lysander whispered. "Even knowing he would die, I let him go." A tear trickled down his cheek. "But it was the only way to give us a chance. You have to believe me."

"A chance for what?" Bryan sat on the table in front of the couch.

"They brought the demon over."

Ice filled Bryan's veins. No. Not even they would be that stupid. "They couldn't have."

"They did. But something about Zachary's death limited its power." Lysander's watery eyes flicked back and forth between Bryan and Roman. "He knew. Before he died, he reached out to me. He knew what I did." He rubbed his chest. "It hurts. I don't understand. I hated him. I wanted him dead for what he did to our father. Why does it hurt so much?"

"Because you have a gentle soul." Roman gathered him into his arms and tucked them both in the corner of the couch. "Do not take on this burden. You are not to blame for his death."

Lysander twisted towards Roman. "But it's my fault. If I hadn't let him go, he'd still be alive."

"No. You only allowed him to go free. The choice of destination was his own. Responsibility for his death lies with whoever killed him."

"How did he die?" Bryan asked.

Lysander gazed into the distance, his far-seeing eyes disquieting. Long moments passed before he shook his head. "I'm not sure. All I can tell is that something about the way he died weakened the demon. If not for that, we'd all be doomed." Roman's arms tightened around him protectively when he shivered. Lysander closed his eyes and sank into his mate

Bryan stood. Gently squeezing his brother's shoulder, he walked out of the office, leaving Lysander in Roman's care.

Once in the hall, he paused, undecided about whether to pursue Max or continue his work at the Council building. Deciding it might be better to give his mate a chance to cool down, Bryan headed toward the parking garage. A quiet afternoon puzzling out the Elders' records would be the perfect way to fill his time before he tackled Max again.

Chapter Three

The Council building, later that day…

"Sandi, I need you to bring everyone to the Council building? I've got a bit of a situation here." He eyed the gathered crowd warily from his place in the corner.

"Do you need the enforcers?"

"Yeah. Bring Clancy and his team of magic-users too."

"Okay. We'll be there as quickly as possible. Stay safe."

Bryan grimaced as he let his eyes drift over the sea of hostile faces glaring at him. "I'll try my best."

* * *

"Tell me where my daughter is."

Bryan was asking Oliver which one of his daughters he was referring to when an angry voice interrupted him.

"How come my sister's oldest boy was returned to her in a bag? What did you do to him?"

Bryan held up his hands. "I can't answer your questions if everyone speaks at the same time." The noise decreased minutely. Good enough. "We've returned all of the magic-users we've found so far. If you're still missing friends or family, let me know. I promise we'll keep looking for them." Not that he expected it to do any good. If they hadn't found them by now, there was nothing left to find.

"Where's Ruth? I want to speak to her, not you."

Bryan scanned the crowd but missed who'd spoken.

"Yeah. Where is the Council? You're no help. We want to talk to them."

He could only stare in disbelief when everyone took up the chant for the Elders. What the hell? Did none of them read their email?

"You didn't tell me you were throwing a party, Bryan. If I'd known, I would have stopped for pizza." Lysander's forced cheer cut through the angry voices.

Bryan smiled, his muscles unclenching when his brother and Roman walked into the room. They were followed by Carlos, Gideon, Jackson, and Edgar. He strained to see Max, but the assembled magic-users backing away from the new arrivals blocked his view of the doorway.

Lysander and Roman stopped when they reached the center of the room. His brother let out a sharp whistle. "This is not acceptable behavior for a Council meeting. Everyone, grab a chair and sit down. When you're ready to conduct yourselves in an orderly and civilized manner, we'll begin."

"Who do you think you are?"

"We don't have to listen to you."

"Somebody tell me where my nephew is."

Lysander crossed his arms and glared at the angry mob. "Perhaps you didn't hear me. I'll say it again. When everyone sits down and shuts the hell up, we'll answer your questions. Not one second before." He clapped his hands. "Move it, people. We'd like to get started."

Bryan pushed off from the wall and met Lysander halfway, ignoring the sneers and glares being thrown their way.

Lysander leaned in, whispering under his breath, “Are you okay?”

“I’m good. Better now that you guys are here.”

“What’s going on?”

“They came to find out what happened to their magic-users.”

Lysander winced. “What did you tell them?”

“Not much, to tell you the truth. Mostly I let them yell at me.”

“Why would you do that? You should have made them shut up.”

“They need someone to take their anger out on.” Bryan shrugged. “It might as well be me.”

“That’s crap. You’re not to blame for what happened. If they need to yell at someone, they can yell at all of us. But only for so long. We’re not the ones who gave their people to the Elders.”

“That’s another thing. They keep asking for the Elders. They don’t seem to understand they’re not in power anymore.”

“How could they not know?” Lysander squinted at the magic-users slowly sorting themselves out. “Most of the clans were there when you kicked them off the Council.”

“I know.” Bryan looked around and saw many of the magic-users still glaring at them. Soundproofing the area around Lysander and himself, Bryan said, “Someone was trying to break through my shield earlier.”

Lysander’s eyes narrowed. “Excuse me?”

Bryan nodded grimly. “It seems not everyone is happy we’re in charge.”

"They'll have to get over it since we're the ones who are going to save their sorry asses."

Bryan snorted. "I'll tell them that. But maybe not in those words." He sighed. "And I guess we'll have to remind them that the Elders are no longer part of the Council. Hopefully, they'll listen this time."

"Idiots. We should just tie them to their chairs so they have no choice but to pay attention."

"As tempting as that is, we can't use our powers against them."

"I suppose." Lysander glared over Bryan's shoulder. "But some of these assholes deserve it for the way they've always treated me."

"Maybe another day. For now, we'll have a diplomatic discussion and try to resolve this peacefully."

"I'm not going to hold my breath. The more arrogant leaders aren't going to accept the change in leadership easily."

"I know. But we have to start somewhere."

Lysander grunted and crossed his arms.

Bryan bumped his shoulder, then led the way to the front of the room. He looked at the dais where the Elders used to sit and made the decision to stand on the floor. They would not use their positions to force people's submission. Freedom from oppression started today.

Making eye contact with the rest of the men standing with him, Bryan turned to face the crowd.

The questions started immediately.

"What did you do to our kids? My daughter said you attacked her."

"My son's missing. Do you know what happened to him?"

"I told you, I want to speak with Ruth. Where is she?"

He held up his hands for quiet, but the shouting only got louder.

"Enough!"

The room went silent as everyone turned to the doorway.

Max stepped into the room and put his hands on his hips. The enforcers filed in, parting behind him to spread themselves along the walls. Clancy and his team followed them. After a glance toward Bryan, Clancy motioned for his magic-users to join the enforcers.

"Is this intimidation how you took control of the Council?"

Bryan turned to the leader of Clan Ashford. "You know better than that, Helen. The enforcers are here to ensure nobody gets hurt." He paused, making sure he had her full attention. "Specifically, me."

"You were never in any danger." Her statement would have been more believable if her eyes hadn't shifted sideways.

"Of course not," Bryan murmured. At least he now knew one of the magic-users working against him. Clearing his throat, he spoke louder. "The enforcers and magic-users are here for protection." He raised his hand when the muttering started. "For whoever needs it. As long as everyone follows the laws of Hospitality, they won't interfere in the proceedings."

"Who's going to keep us safe from them?" Helen asked. "Everyone knows vampires are nothing more than bloodthirsty, depraved creatures who prey on our innocent young. They're not civilized enough to understand hospitality."

That surprised a laugh out of him. "Vampires are among the most sophisticated and self-controlled of all the paranormal groups."

Helen jumped out of her chair. "They are nothing more than parasites. Monsters who deal in blood and death."

"They are not." Bryan stopped and considered Helen, who kept looking at the enforcers with loathing in her eyes. "Why do you hate them?"

"I never said I hated them."

"No, but it's true, nonetheless."

"They are not fit to be in this chamber." She waved her hand encompassing everyone standing with Bryan. "None of them are. The shifters' instincts run too close to their animal spirits. Their wildness makes them untamable and dangerous. The vampires only care about blood, sex, and fighting. Magic-users are the only ones civilized enough to rule, which is why we're always in charge."

Lysander's laugh echoed off the walls. "You're wrong, Helen. No one is more refined or understands the nuances of polite society better than Prince Roman."

"Where is this Prince?"

"Right here." Lysander rested his hand on Roman's arm. "Let me introduce you all to Prince Roman Greystone, ruler of the North American vampire covens, former ruler of the European Vampire Court." He waited until the whispering died down before adding, "And my fated mate."

"Pfft." Helen waved her hand dismissively. "I should have known you'd end up with a murderer."

Lysander stiffened. "He is not a murderer."

"He's a vampire. Every one of them is a bloodthirsty, murdering bastard."

Bryan elbowed his brother before he could respond. "Helen, you're out of line. Vampires have strict laws forbidding them from harming innocents."

"Lies." Spittle flew from her quivering mouth. "Vampires do whatever they want and relish draining a body until there's nothing left but a husk. I've seen it with my own eyes."

"Madam, I assure you, vampires live by a strict code. It is forbidden to take a life through feeding. To do so is to break one of our oldest laws."

"Vampires break it all the time." Helen sneered at Roman. "Your words are meaningless."

"To the contrary, my words are Law. I will hear your grievance when Council is over. I assure you, if your accusations have merit, justice will be done."

"I don't need your justice." A self-satisfied grin crossed her face. "I took care of the problem myself."

Bryan's mouth dropped open. "That's murder, Helen."

"It's survival. Eliminating it was nothing more than pest control."

"You're wrong. It was murder and a crime punishable by our laws." Bryan turned to Roman. "How do you want to handle this?"

"I would require more information to make a proper ruling. If the vampire in question did drain its donor through feeding, it may have been feral. The only recourse then would have been to destroy it."

"And I did." Helen crossed her arms. "And I'll do it again if necessary."

Bryan glared at her. "You can't kill vampires just because you hate them."

"I'm not doing it because I hate them." Helen's look at Roman said otherwise. "I'm doing it to protect my clan. Ruth explained that bloodlust is something vampires can't control. That it's in their nature to kill." She held out her hands. "If we can't reason with them, then we have no choice but to get rid of them. Not if we're to keep ourselves and our families safe."

"Damn it, Helen. Ruth lied to you." Bryan held up his hand, cutting off her next words. He let his eyes roam over the seated magic-users, many of whom were nodding their heads. "How many of you heard the same information from Ruth or one of the other Elders?" He was appalled by the number of hands that went up.

"Listen up. All life is sacred, no matter which paranormal or human community they're from. Our differences are what make us unique and special. None of what Helen just said is true. It's nothing more than misinformation and lies fed to you by the previous Council." Bryan shook his head. "The Elders brainwashed you to hate other paranormals for their own purposes. I'm disappointed that you let them. I thought you were smarter than that."

Helen glared. "The Council did not brainwash me. They care about what happens to us and want to keep us safe. Unlike those creatures standing next to you. No vampire or wolf would ever protect us from one of their own."

"And yet they did. More than once." Bryan crossed his arms to hide his clenched fists and addressed the crowd. "You were told the previous Council engaged in immoral activities. You were given proof that they created laws to separate and weaken us. Their latest campaigns almost resulted in the eradication of the shifters and the vampires."

"Where is the proof of these accusations?" someone shouted.

Bryan leaned to the side and squinted. "Trudy, was that you?"

The leader of the Driscoll clan stood. "Yes. I want to see proof."

"Copies of the Elder's records and results of our investigations were sent to everyone. Did you not read them?"

"I did. But Helen said it was nothing more than a bunch of lies you were using to trick us."

"Exactly," Helen interjected. "How stupid do you think we are? Telling us our Esteemed Council would poison water supplies and soda, of all things. Complete and utter nonsense."

"They did exactly that and much more. The documentation you were provided proved that."

Helen's eyes narrowed. "You mean, the so-called documentation you fabricated so you could get rid of the rightful Council and could take their place."

"Everything you were given were recorded facts backed up by copies of plans written in the Elders' own handwriting. Nothing was made up."

"According to you. I'd like to hear what Ruth and the others have to say." She smirked. "I'm sure they'd have a different story to tell."

"Helen has a point," said Todd from Clan Whitlock. "We can't just take your word for what happened. I'd like to talk to the real Council and see what explanation they have for the documentation you provided."

Bryan was at a loss for words. Surely, they couldn't be this blind? Praying for patience, he tried again. "You cannot speak to the previous Council. It has been abolished. The Elders' crimes against the paranormal communities were inexcusable and necessitated their removal from power. They are no longer members of the Council or leaders of paranormal society. And they never will be again."

The uproar was immediate. Bryan gave them five minutes before he held up his hand for silence. Nervous glances were thrown to the enforcers as the noise slowly subsided. Once it was quiet enough to be heard, Bryan pointed to the men standing with him.

"We are forming a new Council, a Paranormal Council. One that will have equal representation from all paranormal communities." Bryan used his hand to indicate everyone standing with him. "The six of us, excluding Edgar, will fill the Council Chairs. Our mandate will be to bring the disparate communities together, so that we can live in peace and prosperity. We will offer protection, guidance, and assistance to everyone. We will...."

"But I don't know most of you." a voice shouted.

"Then let me introduce everyone. As you've already been informed, the vampire to my right...."

"I'm not going to let any vampire make decisions for me."

"And what about the Null? Why is that freak standing there?"

Bryan's anger sparked when Lysander flinched.

Todd Whitlock stood and pointed his finger at Bryan. "The Law states only magic-users can be on the Council. Ones that actually have magic. Not vampires, not wolves, and most of all, not Nulls."

That did it. Bryan stormed over to Helen and Todd, peripherally noticing Max move with him.

"Listen up, you fools. Every last person standing in front of you has earned the right to their Council seat. They have given their blood, sweat, and tears to protect the paranormal communities. They have saved numerous lives, including your own families. They deserve your thanks. But more importantly, they deserve your respect." His words reverberated around the chamber.

Todd paled, sinking back in his chair, but Helen was made of sterner stuff. She jabbed her pointy nail at his chest.

"If you shed your blood protecting our children, why was my granddaughter's body returned to me?"

"Why don't you ask your precious Elders?"

"How dare you?"

His head snapped to the side from the force of her slap. Sensing movement behind him, Bryan held up his hand to stop Max. Leaning in, he snarled, "I dare, because the Elders you so staunchly defend summoned a demon into our world. Do you hear me, Helen? Your beloved Ruth brought forth a demon that will destroy all life on Earth." He flung his arm backward. "And these males, these courageous and fearless beings, whom you revile and disrespect, will be the ones sacrificing their lives to keep you and the rest of these idiots safe."

The silence was deafening.

"Hey. What's with all the yelling?" Bryan's best friends, Nick and Alex, rushed into the room. "We could hear you down in the parking garage."

Bryan stepped away from Helen and walked over to greet his friends. "I'm glad to see you." He tipped his head to the seated magic-users. "I take it you were invited to this ambush?"

Nick, leader of the Carlisle Clan in Denver, gripped his hand and gave him a half-hug. "Pretty much. A private message went out to all the clans. Well, except for the Galway clan."

Bryan snorted. "I figured."

"I'd have been here sooner but I wanted to wait for Alex's plane. I thought we could catch up before we got tangled up in this nonsense."

He was bumped aside by Alex Garcia, Clan leader from New York, who grabbed Bryan's hand and slapped him on the back. "Sorry we're late. We ran into traffic. What's happened so far?"

"Other than Helen trying to create anarchy?" Bryan huffed out a laugh. "I've been trying to get these morons to listen to reason. But they're being ridiculously stubborn. They think we made up the accusations against the Elders as an excuse to take over."

"Idiots. They have no idea what we're facing."

"They do now. The problem is they don't believe me." Bryan grimaced. "I don't know how we're going to keep them alive if they won't listen."

Alex cleared his throat, tipping his chin at something behind Bryan. "It looks like Helen and her clan are getting ready to leave."

"Shit." Bryan raced back to the magic-users. "What are you doing, Helen?"

"I refuse to listen to any more of this nonsense. I'll wait until Elder Ruth and the others return."

"I already told you, they won't be returning."

She gave him a sly look. "I think they will. And when they're back, I'll be filing my grievances against you."

"Did you hear nothing I said? They are in league with a demon. Are you trying to get the rest of your clan killed? Haven't you lost enough already?"

"My clan members are dead because you electrocuted the floor of the utility room." Helen's eyes narrowed to slits as she spit out the bitter words. "You, not Ruth, are responsible for those deaths."

Bryan stilled. "How do you know that?"

Her mouth snapped shut. Turning her back, she called out. "Clan Ashford, gather your belongings. We're leaving." There were rumblings from the other magic-users, but many were getting out of their chairs. Too many

"Helen?"

"I have nothing more to say to you." She grabbed a jacket from the back of her chair and put it on.

"Why are you still defending Ruth?" Bryan asked quietly. "You know what she's done. So many of your people have already died because of their involvement with her." Bryan stepped up behind her. "Whatever hold she has on you, we can help you."

"You can do nothing." She spun around. "My loyalty is with Ruth and the others. Until they are reinstated in their rightful places, I refuse to recognize this Council or your claim to it."

"You've known me since I was a boy. You practically raised me with your sons. Why will you not listen to me?"

"Because I no longer trust you." Her next words were barely audible but scored a direct hit nonetheless. "You shouldn't have electrocuted my granddaughter, Bryan Galway. She'd still be alive if not for you."

He could only watch helplessly as her clan and everyone allied to them walked out of the Council chambers.

Nick and Alex walked up to him. "I'm sorry, Bryan. You tried."

"Not hard enough," he said quietly.

"Short of forcing them to stay, there wasn't anything else you could do."

"Maybe that would have been better," Bryan mused. "She blames me for the death of her granddaughter. And she's right. My magic did kill her."

Nick bumped him. "None of that. We're in a war. You had no way of knowing they'd be stupid enough to give their younger magic-users to the Elders. Or that the Elders would use them for cannon fodder."

"I know. But if Helen takes her people to Ruth, they're all going to die."

Alex stared at the doorway, a frown pulling at his forehead. "I don't think everyone went with her willingly. It might be worthwhile for Nick and me to have a chat with a few of them. We might be able to convince them to leave."

"I'd appreciate that." Bryan had never been more thankful these men were his friends. "Let them know we'll offer shelter and protection to anyone who leaves. I don't care who or how many. Nobody will be turned away."

"You're a good man, Bryan," Nick said.

Bryan shook his head. "I'm just trying to save them from themselves. The Goddess knows Ruth and her demon won't show them any mercy."

Chapter Four

The Galway Mansion, later that evening…

Bryan lifted his glass and saluted his two friends. "Thanks for your assistance this afternoon. I was worried we were going to lose more of the clans when Helen left, but the two of you standing with me finally made them willing to listen."

"What the hell was all that about today?" Nick asked.

"Which part? The clans thinking I'm lying to them or that I wrongly usurped power from the Elders?"

"Both."

Bryan shrugged. "I don't know. All I've ever done is try to save them. There's no reason for them to turn on me."

"It's concerning," Nick said. "Last year the majority of the clans were solidly behind you once they found out why the Elders attacked the Estate. They would have followed you anywhere, without question."

"Nick's right. You've always been highly respected by the clans. After the last few months, your credibility should have gone up." Alex frowned. "It doesn't make any sense why none of them believed the evidence proving the Council's corruption."

"If I had to guess, I'd say Ruth was behind it. And more recently, Helen." Bryan grimaced. "I'm praying Helen's blind loyalty doesn't destroy her and the clans allied to her."

"Try not to worry about it. Alex and I will get as many of them away from her as we can."

"Thanks. I appreciate you guys taking that on."

"No problem. If we're going to defeat this demon, we need to be as unified as possible." Nick sat back and crossed his ankles, letting his glass dangle from the tips of his fingers. "While Alex and I are busy subverting Helen's clan, what's next on your agenda of world domination?"

Bryan snorted, appreciating Nick's attempt to lighten the mood. "Right now, I'm saving the Council records to the Cloud. I figure another fifty years or so and it should be done."

Alex snorted. "Better you than me."

"Better anyone than you. Don't forget, I've seen what you call a filing system. We'd be better off doing nothing than letting you have a go at them." Bryan snickered when Alex flipped him off. Grinning, he turned to Nick. "To answer your question, we're trying to undo all the damage the Elders caused. Roman and Jackson are helping the packs with supplies and moving the shifters who are willing to relocate. The packs are slowly recovering but it'll be generations before they're back to full strength."

"We're fortunate Edgar managed to figure out what was going on before it was too late to save them," Nick murmured. "I can't imagine what the world would be like without the packs."

"Me either." Bryan shivered when he recalled how close they'd come to losing Jackson. And Edgar. "Luckily for us, Ruth was too arrogant or lazy to come up with a new method for eliminating the vampires. Edgar and

Lysander put it together quickly enough that only a small number were killed."

"Which was still too many," Alex said grimly. "I lost a couple of friends from the Los Angeles coven."

Bryan reached over and squeezed Alex's hand. "I was sorry to hear about the twins."

"Me too." Alex's lips twisted. "It was a horrible way for two such beautiful souls to die. All I can do is take solace in knowing they were together at the end. It would have been heartbreaking if their souls had been separated." He blew out a breath and gave Bryan a shaky smile. "Hopefully, nobody else will have to die like that."

"That's what we're trying to ensure. Edgar is spearheading the cleanup of the production plant and recalling all the product shipments. If the covens follow Roman's mandate to stay away from live sources of food until we've found and destroyed all the poisoned sodas, nobody else will be at risk."

Nick sat up and set his glass on the table. "That reminds me. Bill called earlier. He did some initial surveillance of the production plant today. He's going to sneak in later tonight to get a better idea of the layout before he does his first official drop-off tomorrow."

"Good. The sooner we neutralize the poison and get the cure distributed to the public, the safer everyone will be." Bryan tipped his head at Nick. "Appreciate you letting us use Bill for this. The rest of us were too well known to pull it off."

Nick laughed. "Bill jumped at the assignment. I don't think I could have stopped him from volunteering if I wanted to."

"He's a good man."

"He is. I'm also pretty sure he wants to move here. For some reason he thinks you all lead more exciting lives than we do."

Bryan rolled his eyes. "Too exciting sometimes. But if he's serious, we'd love to have him."

"Keep your grubby hands off him. You already stole Ted from me."

Bryan snorted. "I think that had more to do with Mary than me."

"Whatever. The point is, you have to stop taking my best men."

"I'll stop as soon as I poach Bill." Bryan grinned at the dirty look Nick gave him. "Come on, Nick. Let me have him."

"I said no."

"But he fits in well with us. And he's good to have around when things go sideways. Which they've been doing a lot these days."

"Yes," said Alex, leaning forward in his seat. "Let's talk about that. I'm tired of waiting for you to get to it."

"Get to what? You know everything that's been going on."

"Not the Council stuff." Alex dismissed that with a flick of his hand. "I want to know what secret you've been keeping."

Bryan squinted. "I'm not keeping any secrets."

"Please." Alex rolled his eyes. "Nick and I both know you're hiding something. You have been for months."

"I have no idea what you're talking about." Bryan tossed back the rest of his drink and got up to refill his glass. A heavy silence followed his words. Damn it. Sometimes your best friends could know you too well. Especially when you were keeping secrets from them.

"You're not seriously going to deny it, are you?" Nick asked.

Keeping his expression neutral, Bryan turned and faced their disbelieving looks. "Sorry to disappoint. There's nothing to tell." Knowing they'd see the slightest flinch, Bryan held up the decanter and tried for casualness. "Do either of you need a refill?"

Nick exchanged a look with Alex. "Does he really think we can't tell when he's lying?"

"Maybe he forgot. He is getting older."

"Excuse me. I'm the same age as you."

"Hush. We're not talking to you." Alex turned back to Nick. "Perhaps he got hit in the head. He has been in a lot of fights lately."

"That might be it." Nick smiled innocently at Bryan. "Did you take any blows to the head recently?"

"You know I didn't." Bryan filled his glass, then turned to see they were still watching him like hawks. "Seriously, nothing's going on."

"Still going with the lying? All right. Let me try again." Alex tapped his lip. "Does it have anything to do with the angry vampire?"

Bryan's eyelid twitched before he could stop it. Knowing grins spread across his friends' faces. Even though he was busted, Bryan still tried for his most innocent look. "What angry vampire?"

"Give it up. You're not fooling anyone with that look."

"Give what up?" Bryan laughed and ducked the cushions thrown at his head. "Okay, okay. It's about the vampire."

"I knew it." Alex held out his hand.

Nick pulled out a twenty-dollar bill and slapped it on his palm. "Lucky guess."

"I can't believe you guys bet on me."

"Like you wouldn't do the same." Alex stuffed the bill in his pocket. "I can't believe you thought you could lie to us."

Bryan snickered as he sat back in his chair. "It was worth a shot."

"So, tell us. What's going on between you and tall, dark, and angry?"

"He's not really angry."

"You could have fooled me."

Taking a deep breath, Bryan blurted out, "Max is my fated mate."

"He is? Congratulations, man." After a hearty slap on the back from Nick, Bryan found himself being squeezed to death by Alex.

"Yeah, congratulations. I'm happy for you. Why didn't you say anything?"

"There was nothing to tell."

"What are you talking about? Finding your mate is huge."

"Normally, it would be. Our mating is a bit…complicated."

Concern replaced the joy on his friends' faces.

"Complicated how?" Alex asked. "Do Nick and I need to have a talk with him?"

"No. Leave Max alone."

"Are you sure Max is your mate?" Nick asked quietly.

Bryan nodded, dreading where the conversation was going. "He's definitely my mate."

"He didn't act like it earlier."

"That's because he's not talking to me." Bryan gulped a large mouthful of his drink, hissing at the burn.

"Why not?"

Clearing his throat, he croaked, "Because until this morning, he didn't realize we were mates."

Silence.

Alex blinked first. "How the hell is that possible? Vampires always know when they meet their bloodmates."

"I know. Somehow I stopped the mate-bond from forming."

Confusion on his friends' faces turned to shock.

"You did what?"

"Just what I said. When we first met, I panicked and put up a block. I did it so fast and so hard, the mate-bond didn't have a chance to form. Max had no idea. And I never told him."

"Until today," Nick whispered.

"Yeah," Bryan gulped. "Until today. He overheard me talking to Sandi."

Alex whistled. "Damn. He must have been pissed."

"And then some."

"I didn't think stopping a bond was possible."

"It shouldn't be," Nick said. "Your magical ability has obviously grown a lot stronger."

Bryan shrugged. "Not that I've noticed."

Alex smacked the back of his head. "What were you thinking? You don't mess with the Goddess' plans. That kind of thing will bite you in the ass."

He rubbed his head, glaring at his friend. "It already did. I can't undo the block."

"There has to be some way to fix it," Nick said. "Maybe we can help."

Bryan shook his head. "I think this is something Max and I are going to have to figure it out for ourselves."

"How are you going to do that if he's not talking to you?"

"I have a plan."

"Great." Nick leaned forward. "Let's hear it."

"For now, I'm going to respect his wishes and stay out of his way."

"That's the dumbest thing I've ever heard you say." Alex smacked his head again.

Bryan batted at his hand. "Stop that."

"Alex is right. That's not a plan. That's you avoiding the issue." Nick plucked Bryan's drink out of his hand and drained the glass.

"Hey. That was mine."

Nick looked at him over the edge of the glass. "You don't deserve it. Not if you're going to be a coward."

"I'm not being a coward. Really," Bryan said when Nick quirked his eyebrow. "I'm only leaving Max alone for a couple of days. Just to give him time to cool down." He grinned. "Then I'm going to start a big fight with him so he has no choice but to talk to me."."

"That's more like it." Nick fist-bumped him.

"Yeah. You had me worried there," Alex said.

"I'm not going to lie. I thought about walking away."

"What? Why?"

"I hurt him pretty badly. I wonder if it wouldn't be better to let him go."

"You're such an idiot." Nick flicked him in the ear.

"Ow. Would you guys stop hitting me."

Ignoring him, Nick said, "You screwed up, brother. The only way to make it right is to fight for him. And if that means you have to fight with him first, then you do it."

"What Nick said. Max deserves to be happy with his fated mate. Even if he's stuck with a dumbass like you. You better not take that away from him."

"I won't. But it's going to take more than a fight. I need your help."

"Now you're talking." Nick rubbed his hands together. "Pour us another drink. We'll come up with a foolproof plan to trap this vampire of yours."

Bryan jumped up to refresh everyone's drinks, feeling better than he had in months. He'd been so worried to tell his friends what he'd done, thinking he'd lose their respect. He should have known they'd have his back. They always did. Just like he had theirs.

He couldn't wait to see what the three of them came up with to salvage the situation and secure Bryan's future with his mate. Whatever the final plan was, it was sure to be creative. And exciting. There was a reason their names were still whispered in awe around the University campus. Their exploits in school had been legendary.

Bryan grinned as he filled the glasses. Max wouldn't know what hit him.

* * *

The vibration of his phone on the desk pulled his attention from the record he was attempting to decipher. Glancing at the display screen, he sighed when he saw it was Lysander. Again. For the fourth time. In the last thirty minutes. Accepting he wouldn't out stubborn his younger brother, he set the document to the side and reached for his phone.

"I'm in the middle of something. Is whatever you're calling about really that important?"

"You tell me, It's about Max."

Bryan's gut clenched. He'd waited one day too long to put his plan into motion. By the time he'd gone looking for his mate, Max had already left. And Roman wasn't talking.

"You still there?"

"Yeah. What about Max?"

"Before I answer, tell me if this is what you're going to do for the next hundred years."

"What are you talking about?"

"I'm talking about you hiding at the Council building instead of facing your mate and fixing your mistake."

"I'm not hiding. You know how important it is to get these records scanned and stored in the cloud. I'm the only one qualified enough to make decisions on what to do with them."

"And it gave you the perfect excuse to avoid Max."

"And I could avoid awkward moments with Max, yes."

"So, I'll ask again. Do you plan on doing this for the rest of your life?"

"No. I'm just biding my time until he comes back. I have a plan."

"Good to hear. What if I said I could help you expedite it?"

Bryan sucked in a breath. "You know where he is?"

"I might."

"Sandi!"

Lysander snickered, then said, "*Max told Roman he was going to someplace secluded so he could work out his anger. He's planning on staying there until he gets to the point of wanting to kiss you more than he wants to strangle you.*"

"He wants to kiss me?"

"No, idiot. Right now, he wants to strangle you."

"Shit."

"But he wants to wants to kiss you. Which is almost the same thing."

Bryan squinted, thinking about it. "Not really," he finally said.

"Close enough. You just need to get him past the wanting to strangle you part, then you're golden."

Somehow, Bryan didn't think it would be that easy. "Just tell me you know where this private place is."

"I have the coordinates right here."

"Give them to me." Bryan carefully input them into his phone. "Thanks, Sandi. I owe you one."

"Don't screw this up. I want you to have your happy-ever-after with Max." He ended the call.

Me, too, Bryan thought as he tucked his phone in his pocket. Glancing at the desk, he shoved the documents he'd been deciphering into a box and shut down his computer. Work could wait. It was time to go after his mate.

* * *

Lysander chuckled as he put the phone in his pocket. Bryan had sounded ready to charge out the door. What he wouldn't give to be a fly on the wall when his brother found Max.

He had a moment of misgiving, wondering if he'd overstepped, then decided, no. Max would be happy to see Bryan when he invaded his retreat. Once he'd finished yelling at him. And possibly punching him. And most likely strangling him. Whatever. Bryan could look after himself.

Whistling a jaunty tune, he strolled down the hallway, wondering when he should let Roman know he'd interfered. It would probably be best to do it when they were in bed. Roman was always in a good mood after sex and feeding. Speaking of, maybe Roman was hungry now. Lysander picked up his pace, eager to see how quickly he could get his vampire naked.

* * *

The linen closet door slowly opened. A kerchief wrapped head poked out. Seeing the hallway was empty, the girl stepped out and hugged the stack of sheets against her chest while she dug out her phone. Dialing one-handed, she nervously shuffled her feet as she waited for her call to be answered.

"Who is this?"

"Miss Charlotte, ma'am. It's Susie, the downstairs maid."

"What do you have?"

"He's going to be leaving the property. I know where you can find him." Susie spoke the coordinates exactly as she'd memorized them. "And you'll send the money today? Thank you, Miss Charlotte." She disconnected the call, blowing out a breath in relief. She could finally buy the medicine her younger sister needed. Hopefully, Mr. Bryan wouldn't be too angry if he found out what she'd done. She couldn't afford to lose this job.

Taking a final look around, Susie rushed down the hallway, in a hurry to get the beds made before anyone started wondering what was taking her so long.

Chapter Five

An abandoned shack deep in the Bayou…

Max leaned cautiously on the rickety, weathered railing and glared at the clouds of mosquitoes covering the water. Their incessant whining made it hard to think. He could handle the alligators no problem, but the miniature bloodsuckers were getting on his last nerve.

Letting his eyes drift to the left, Max zoomed in on the blunt snout and ridged eyes that broke the surface of the brackish water. The alligator had been floating for hours in the spot it had landed when Max had flung it off the deck. He gave it a snappy salute. "Don't worry, big guy. I'll be out of your way shortly."

He might as well head back home. Taking off had proven to be an epic fail. The solitude hadn't done anything to clear his mind. If anything, the extra time to brood was making the tangled mess of his emotions more confusing than they'd been before.

Max rubbed his chest for what had to be the hundredth time that evening. He wasn't sure if it was the ache he always felt when he was separated from Bryan or if it was the pain of betrayal. Not that it mattered.

Whatever the cause, it wasn't going away until he resolved his issues with his mate.

His mate. That had been a shocker. Except…in the deepest parts of his soul, somehow, he'd always known. Still, the confirmation had been a surprise. And the source of his current anger.

Max rested his chin on his crossed arms and blew out a frustrated breath. He was neglecting his duties and all he'd done so far was drive himself half-crazy flipping back and forth between feeling angry and hurt. And the worst of it was, he missed Bryan. Even though Max had been betrayed by him in the worst way possible, he still wanted to be near him. But until he got his anger under control, he didn't dare face the man. The chances of him strangling Bryan were strong.

Hearing a noise that didn't belong, Max was instantly alert, his body coiled in battle readiness. A flock of birds took to the air from the cypress trees to his left, their harsh calls loud in the evening air. Narrowing his eyes, he looked in the direction of the disturbance, then cursed quietly under his breath. He should have expected this. It was his own fault for talking to Roman when his Consort was present. Lysander had to be the biggest meddler Max had ever met.

A quiet "shit" floated across the water from a distant stand of trees. A short time later, the shadow of a man appeared, shaking his leg. Max smirked when globs of mud and grass fell from his shoe.

Waiting until the intruder was within hearing distance, he asked, "What are you doing here, Bryan?"

Bryan jerked and took an awkward step backward, then fell in the mud. "Max? Is that you?"

Max moved along the edge of the porch until he stood in a patch of moonlight. "Who else would it be?"

Bryan climbed to his feet and made an attempt to wipe the mud off his pants. "Out here, anything is possible. There are plenty of stories about people mysteriously vanishing in the swamp."

"The only predator you need to be worried about out here is me."

Bryan grinned. "The only predator I'm not worried about is you."

Max refused to let that grin soften his anger. He folded his arms across his chest when Bryan stepped onto the deck, his extra weight making the rotting boards groan.

Bryan came to a stop in front of him, the smile falling from his face. "You ran, Max. I didn't expect that from you."

"You've been running and keeping secrets for months."

"I had my reasons for not telling you."

"And I had mine for leaving." Max turned to the door. "Go home, Bryan. I don't want to talk to you."

"Too bad. I'm not leaving until you do."

Ignoring him, Max stepped through the doorway, jerking to a stop when Bryan's hand clamped down on his shoulder. Turning quickly, Max twisted one hand in Bryan's waistband and the other in his shirt and tossed him off the deck. He smirked at the creative curses Bryan let out when he hit the water.

Motion to Max's left alerted him to the fact that Bryan's movements in the water had drawn the alligator's attention. When the gator arrowed towards his mate, Max tensed, prepared to jump in and help if Bryan needed him.

"Son of a bitch."

Max's nerves hummed when Bryan used his magic. There was a loud splash near a distant cypress tree when the alligator landed back in the water.

"You asshole." Bryan dragged himself onto the deck boards, glaring at Max as he wiped rotting vegetation off his suit. "What the hell did you do that for?"

Max leaned against the railing, tension draining from his muscles now that his mate was out of danger. "That's how we deal with trespassers out here."

"By throwing them to the gators?

He shrugged. "It keeps them from coming back."

"Not this time," Bryan muttered, pulling off his shoes and socks. He poured the water from his loafers, then slipped them back on. The socks he wrung out and draped over the railing.

Max waited until he was done before saying, "You need to go home."

Bryan ripped his drenched tie from his neck and balled it up before throwing it to the deck. "Not until we talk."

"You already had your chance."

"I'm giving myself another one." Bryan walked across the deck until he stood in front of him. "I'm sorry, Max. I never intended to keep secrets from you. Once I realized I couldn't fix our bond, so much time had passed that I didn't know how to tell you. The longer it went, the harder it got, until it was easier to say nothing at all." He paused and stared into Max's eyes before quietly adding, "Most of all, I'm sorry for pushing you away. My guilt made it difficult to be near you, knowing what I had done."

"And what, the guilt's gone now?"

"No. But I wanted you to know. I couldn't bear the thought of you thinking I didn't want you." He laughed harshly. "Nothing could be further from the truth."

"Now I know. Is that all you came to say?"

"No, it's not." Bryan stepped closer and fisted Max's shirt. "I'm asking for another chance. Come home and let me prove I can be a mate worthy of you."

"No." Max pushed Bryan's hands away and stepped back. "If that's all you had to say, you can show yourself out."

"Damn it, Max. You're my mate. Help me fix the damn bond instead of running away."

"Maybe I don't want to fix it. Did you ever consider that?" Even knowing the words weren't true, his heart twinged at the thought.

Bryan sucked in a breath. "You can't mean that?"

"I don't know if you're the kind of mate I need. I'll have to think about it and get back to you."

"I'm the only mate you've got, so you'd better think fast."

"But since the bond is broken, that's not actually true, is it? Maybe the Goddess will gift me with another mate." That thought did more than twinge his heart. It felt like it ripped it in two.

"You can't have another mate. You're stuck with me."

Not sure why he was being hurtful, but unable to stop himself, Max said, "I guess we'll have to wait and see, won't we?"

"Screw that. You're mine, asshole. Nobody else can have you."

At a loss for how to respond to the bold declaration of ownership, Max shook his head and turned to the doorway. "We're done. It's time for you to go home."

He hadn't taken two steps when he felt the hum of magic. A moment later, he was spitting out brackish swamp water. Flipping his wet hair back, he glared at his mate. Bryan smirked and flipped him off. Max's eyes narrowed further as he considered his next move. A fight with his mate might be just what he needed to get rid of some of his anger at the man. And it wasn't like Max could hurt him. Bryan had proven he could look after himself.

Decision made, Max kicked his feet free from the sucking muddy bottom of the bayou and swam toward the shack, heaving himself onto the deck. He sprang into the air the moment his feet touched the weathered boards and crashed into Bryan, driving him through the rotting wall beside the doorway.

Max grunted when they landed on the floor, Bryan's body taking the brunt of the fall. He was surprised when the magic-user kicked out and rolled, slamming Max to the ground. He quickly reversed their positions, pinning Bryan to the ground. "Nice move, but you're not strong enough or fast enough to beat me."

"No?" Bryan raised an eyebrow. "Guess again."

Before Max had time to realize his mistake, he was flying through the air. His back smashed into the wall, the aged boards cracking under the impact. An invisible force pressed against his chest, pushing him through the rotting timber. A second later, Max was back in the swamp, gaping at the new hole in the wall. Bryan wasn't allowed to use his magic against him like that. Or was he? A dangerous grin spread across his face. Oh, it was on.

He raced through the water, jumped onto the deck and rushed into the shack through the new hole in the wall. He grabbed Bryan and spun in a circle a few times before letting go. Bryan flew into the air and smashed through the hole-ridden roof. There was a distant splash when his body landed in the water.

"Foul move, Max. Let's see how you deal with this."

Max flashed to the doorway and searched the water, but was unable to see any sign of Bryan. He heard a loud crack, then lurched forward when the floor shifted under his feet. The next thing he knew, he was tumbling toward the back of the shack. What the hell? Did Bryan take out the support poles? The answer came a second later when the floor split beneath him, dumping him back in the water. Debris from the destroyed shack landed around him, a broken piece of wood hitting him on the head.

Max treaded water, rotating as he searched for movement. Spying his adversary, he sped through the water, scooped him up, and tossed him toward the shore. Bryan was pushing himself off the ground when Max crashed into him, driving him into a tree.

Birds screeched, bursting into the air to circle its top branches.

Groaning, Bryan lifted his head, then flicked his fingers. Max's body flew sideways with the motion, stopping when he slammed into a distant tree. Before he could react, his feet left the ground. Branches tore at his clothes as he was hoisted up until he was left clinging to a thin branch near the top. The startled birds' shrill noises hurt his ears as they flew around his head.

Bryan shouted. "We can do this all day, Max, but I'd rather we talked."

"Maybe I don't want to talk," Max muttered. Getting his feet under him, he ignored the ominous creaking of the branch and leapt gracefully to the ground, landing in a three-point crouch. He then sprang into the air and landed on Bryan, quickly wrapping his legs around Bryan's lower body and twisting his hands in the lapels of his jacket. If Bryan tried throwing him again, Max wasn't going by himself.

Bryan locked his hands around Max's wrists. "I don't want to keep fighting. I just want you to talk to me."

Max growled. "I have nothing to say to you."

"Oh, you have plenty to say. You're just being stubborn about it." Bryan squeezed Max's wrists gently before letting his hands fall. "We need to deal with this. No more running. For either of us."

Max stared into his eyes, easily seeing his determination not to leave until they'd talked it out. Something Max realized needed to happen. Their fight had burned off most of his anger, bringing clarity to his chaotic thoughts. He knew what he had to do, no matter that it would hurt them both. But it was the only way they'd be able to move forward.

"Max?"

Shoring up his defenses so he could get through the next few minutes, Max asked, "Do you even understand what you did?"

Bryan's eyes narrowed, then he shook his head. "I thought I did, but maybe not."

Max let go of his jacket and sat back. "A vampire searches his whole life but never really expects to find his Bloodmate. Until Roman met your brother, I didn't even know it was possible. For real, not just as a hope. And you stole that from me."

"I can't tell you how sorry I am for doing that."

"Sorry isn't good enough. Every time you had a chance to tell me and kept quiet was a lie. You've been lying to me for months, Bryan. Mates don't lie to each other."

"I know. I didn't mean to. But when I broke the bond, I wanted to fix it before I said anything. When I couldn't, I was afraid to tell you in case you hated me for it. And then, well, I couldn't see a way out, so I said nothing."

"I told you before, I wouldn't have hated you for it. Been angry, without question. But I understand how it happened."

Bryan blinked. "You do"

Max nodded. "When we first met, your entire focus was on saving your brother. You had no time for a vampire you'd never met."

"It sounds bad when you say it like that, but yeah, that's pretty much how it went. I panicked and then it was too late." He smiled at Max. "But I'm sure with your help we can fix it."

Max clenched his jaw and shook his head.

"No? What do you mean no? You just said you understood."

"And I do. The problem is the months of silence afterward. I don't know if I can trust you."

Bryan stilled.

The last of Max's anger drained. His voice was barely above a whisper when he said, "Until there is trust, there can be no mating, whether we find a way to repair the bond or not." Trying not to let the shattered look on his mate's face sway him from his decision, Max stood, then held out a hand to help Bryan up.

Once he was on his feet, Bryan shoved his hands in his pockets and looked everywhere but at Max. "What do we do now?"

"I don't know."

Long moments passed with each of them lost in their thoughts.

Bryan's voice finally broke the silence. "Maybe we could start by spending time together. Give ourselves a chance to get to know one another better." Bryan shrugged when Max glanced over. "It couldn't hurt. We know each other as Roman's Second and Lysander's older brother. Maybe it's time to learn who Max and Bryan are."

Max considered. The idea had merit. Finally, he nodded. "We can do that." He felt a slight crack in the barrier around his heart when Bryan smiled gratefully at him.

"Okay, good." His eyes passed over Max before looking down at himself. "We should probably clean up. We're a bit of a mess."

Electricity hummed over Max's skin. A moment later, his clothes were clean and dry. He ran his hand down the front of his immaculate shirt. "Neat trick."

"It comes in handy." Bryan patted his chest. "Damn it. I lost my favorite tie." He glared at the shack.

Or rather, where the shack used to be, Max thought, looking at the broken boards floating in the water. His lip twitched when he saw the eyes and snout break the surface near what used to be the alligator's home. Poor guy was going to have to find a new place to live. "Nice job on the house. I don't think insurance covers destruction by magic."

Bryan grimaced. "Sorry about that. You made me mad."

Max snorted. "You don't say. I'm used to you being more level headed."

"I don't like losing control, so I try not to let anyone get to me." He shrugged and gave Max a lopsided grin. "You must be a special case."

The idea he could make the cool and composed Clan leader lose control pleased Max for some reason. They looked at the water in companionable silence, broken when Max said, "It was a good fight. You surprised me tonight."

"Me, too." Max could see Bryan's grin from the corner of his eye. "I kind of enjoyed it."

So had Max.

"And I don't know about you, but I feel a lot less stressed now."

Max could only nod.

"Hey." Bryan bumped his shoulder. Max glanced over. "Thanks for being willing to try."

"We're mates, Bryan. Did we have any other choice?"

"Sure. We could not try and be miserable for the rest of our lives. And probably doom the world."

"There is that."

"Besides, if we took too long, Lysander would want to get involved."

"More than he already has?" Max smirked when Bryan's cheeks flushed.

"Umm, he might have told me where I could find you."

"I figured." Max glanced at the stand of trees twenty yards to the left of where the shack used to be. The glint of his bumper shining through the trees was reassuring. "At least you didn't wreck my truck."

"Yeah. About that." Bryan cleared his throat. "I didn't want you driving off on me, so I took your keys from under the driver's mat."

Max's eyes narrowed. "And?"

"They fell out of my pocket." Bryan winced and pointed to the water. "I'm pretty sure they're in there."

Max crossed his arms and glared.

"Sorry. I hadn't planned on going for a swim."

The nocturnal quietness of the swamp was broken as birds took to the air, screeching in warning.

Max turned toward the noise. "Someone's here."

Bryan squinted into the dark. When he saw movement, he cast a binding spell, immobilizing whoever was sneaking up on them. Shock filled him when the intruder shrugged off his bonds. It was quickly followed by anger when he realized why. Stepping protectively in front of Max, Bryan waited tensely for the intruder to come out of the shadows, cursing under his breath when she stepped into a stray patch of moonlight, its beams bright enough for him to see her clearly.

"Hello, Bryan."

"Mother."

Chapter Six

"Why are you here, Mother?"

"I need your help."

"After everything you've done?" Bryan asked in disbelief. "I don't think so."

"This concerns you as well. You must assist me."

"The only thing I must do is put you in the Council dungeon"

"Perhaps you should hear my offer before you attempt to threaten me."

"Trust me, it's not a threat. It's where you belong. Your offer isn't going to change my mind." Bryan stepped toward her.

"I will not allow you to imprison me." Charlotte's hand rose.

Bryan was suddenly looking at Max's back. Thrilled as he was by Max's protectiveness, Bryan didn't hesitate to step around him, expanding his personal shield to cover them both as he did so.

Charlotte's attack slid harmlessly past.

When Max tried to jump in front of him again, Bryan elbowed him back. Ignoring his grumbles, Bryan concentrated on his mother. "Let go of your magic. I may not be able to bind you, but you're not fast enough to stop both of us."

Charlotte's eyes shifted toward Max, then back to Bryan. Her hand slowly lowered. "Will you help me take down Ruth?"

Bryan squinted. "Aren't you allies?"

"We were until I found out she had your father killed. She needs to pay for that."

"And she will when we find her."

"I can give you information to aid in your search." She paused. "For a price."

"We have all the information we need. Nothing you have is enough to keep you out of prison."

"Not even the prophecy?"

Bryan couldn't control his start of surprise.

"I thought as much." Charlotte's smile was victorious.

"Tell me what you know of it?"

"Promise you'll avenge your father's death."

"What do you know about the prophecy, Mother?"

"Promise me you'll kill Ruth." She took a step back.

What did she think she was doing? "Stop right there. I'm not going to let you leave."

"You can't stop me." She took another step back.

Damn it. Knowing it was useless, Bryan tried capturing her anyway.

Charlotte smirked when the binding magic fell away. "Last chance, Bryan. Ruth dies or I take knowledge of the prophecy with me when I leave here."

Before he could respond, a wall of fire lit up the darkness between him and Charlotte.

Gideon arrowed down from the sky with Carlos standing on his back, his hair flying wildly around his head as he waved his arm and shouted. Bryan strained, but couldn't make out what he was saying, his words lost in the wind caused by the fury of their descent. When Gideon touched down, Carlos jumped gracefully from his back and had Charlotte's arms pinned to her sides before Bryan could blink.

"Unhand me, you lout." She gave a twist of her wrist, shock crossing her face when nothing happened.

"Surprise." Carlos' smile was menacing. "My mate would like a word with you, Charlotte."

"I have nothing to say."

"Then I'll do the talking." Gideon stood upright after completing his shift. "Hand over my mating talisman.

"I have no idea what you're talking about."

"It's right here, you thieving bitch." Carlos yanked on the chain hanging around Charlotte's neck, ignoring her cries when the links dug in before breaking.

Bryan immediately trapped her in the magical weaves he'd created to bind a powerful magic-user.

Charlotte's eyes widened. "Release me at once."

Ignoring her demands, Bryan said, "You can let her go now, Carlos. She can't escape."

Carlos immediately stepped back, then peered at the object in his hands. "This is what all the fuss was about?"

"Yes, treasure. That is my mating gift to you." Gideon took the chain and held his finger to the broken links, fusing them before placing it over Carlos' head. When it settled below Carlos's collarbone, Gideon's contented rumble filled the air. "Nothing will be able to harm you now."

"Great." Carlos patted the talisman. "Can we go now? I was finally beating the Consort and don't want him to think I've forfeited."

"Of course, my treasure."

"Before you leave," Bryan pointed to Charlotte, "Mother needs a ride to the prison cells."

"Fuck that." Carlos glared. "Take her yourself."

"I can't. I brought the bike."

"Just strap her to the back."

"Sorry. Max needs to sit there."

"Why doesn't he take his own vehicle?" Carlos' eyes brightened. "Or better yet, why don't we take your bike and you can ride with Max. Just dump her in the back of his truck."

"I lost Max's keys in the swamp."

"You did what?" Carlos' eyes shifted to Charlotte. "Fuck me. You're really going to make me take her, aren't you?"

"I promise to make it up to you."

"You'd better." Carlos stomped over to Charlotte and tossed her over his shoulder. "Shift, dragon, so we can get this crazy bitch locked up. I have a Consort to beat."

"What game are you and the Consort playing?" Max asked as he helped strap Charlotte to Gideon's back.

"Magic."

Gideon's leap into the air drowned out Bryan's laugh.

Gideon and Carlos had just disappeared from sight when Max's phone rang. Pulling it from his pocket, he tensed when "unknown" flashed on the screen.

"How did you get this number?"

"Son. It's good to hear your voice."

Max immediately stood at attention. "General? This is a surprise."

"I'm sure it is."

"How can I help you, sir?"

"I heard from Carlisle. He's going to be in town next month. Maggie thinks we should throw him a surprise party."

"I'm sure he'd enjoy that. When is it?"

"He'll be here on the twenty-third. Maggie's planning it for eighteen hundred hours, but come thirty minutes early so we can get everyone in place.'"'

"Understood. It'll be good to see him again."

"I'm sure he'll be thrilled to see you boys as well."

"It has been a while."

"Make sure you come through the back door. Maggie will be disappointed if Carlisle sees anyone before she can spring her surprise."

"Don't worry, General. I'll make sure I'm not spotted."

"Excellent, son. I look forward to seeing you."

Max frowned as he replayed their conversation, then glanced at the time on his phone. Shit. He needed to get moving. Shoving the phone in his pocket, Max ran toward his truck.

Bryan's footsteps pounded on the ground behind him. "What's going on?"

"Nothing that concerns you." Max had his hand on the door handle when he remembered his keys were lost in the swamp. Growling, he yanked open the door. He'd just have to hotwire it.

Bryan finally reached him. Leaning on the truck as he caught his breath, he asked, "Where are you going?"

"To look after something private. Go home. I'm sure you have important work at the Council building."

"Not as important as helping you." Bryan rushed over to the passenger side door and climbed in the truck.

Max opened his mouth to tell him to get out, then closed it, realizing Bryan's magic might come in handy. "Fine. You can come. But you do whatever I tell you, when I tell you, with no arguments or hesitation."

Bryan blinked, then nodded. "Got it."

Max jumped into his seat. "Can you start this thing or do I need to hotwire it?"

"I'm not sure. Grand theft was never a career choice." His brow creased in concentration.

The air hummed, tickling the back of Max's neck when Bryan released his power. The truck roared to life.

"Sweet," Bryan pumped his arm then clicked his seatbelt into place. "Where are we going?"

"To help an old friend." Max backed out of the grove, then turned the truck toward the overgrown path he'd driven in on.

"This Carlisle you were talking about?"

Max glanced over. "You shouldn't listen in on other peoples' calls."

Bryan rolled his eyes. "I was standing right next to you. It was kind of hard not to overhear it."

Max grunted. It was a fair point.

"So, who's Carlisle? Sounds like someone you knew from your military days."

"Carlisle's dead."

"He is? Then why is Maggie throwing him a surprise party?"

"She's not."

"But the General said she was."

Max could see him frowning from the corner of his eye. "He used Carlisle's name as a warning."

"Why would he do that?"

That was a very good question. "The General will tell us when we get there."

"He knows we're coming tonight?"

"Yes. He's expecting us at ten-thirty."

"But he said the party, that isn't actually happening, is at eighteen-hundred hours. Isn't that six o'clock?"

"It is. But in this case, it was a warning to watch my back."

"Huh. Then I guess the only thing I understood is that we're going in through the back."

"We're sneaking in through the roof."

"Seriously? Did I get nothing right?"

That surprised a laugh out of Max.

Bryan sighed. "Why are we going through the roof and not coming in the back?"

"If anyone's watching the house, they'll have eyes on the doors and windows. Nobody remembers to watch the roof."

"Okay," Bryan said slowly. "That makes sense. Sort of." He looked out the window, his fingers rapping on his leg.

Max had to hold back a grin when Bryan's brows drew together as he tried to piece together the conversation he'd heard.

After a bit, Bryan turned to Max. "How do you know he wants to meet us at ten-thirty?"

"The General said Carlisle was coming on the twenty-third."

"Yeah. Next month. What does that have to do with us meeting him tonight?"

Max frowned, peering into the rearview mirror. Were those lights following them?

"Never mind. I get it. The twenty-third is eleven o'clock. But he told you to come thirty minutes early."

"Yes. We need to hurry so we're not late." Max looked in the mirror again. The lights were definitely coming closer.

"What are you looking at?" Bryan looked in the side-view mirror.

"Someone's following us."

"What?" Bryan spun around in his seat and looked out the rear window. "But we haven't done anything. Why would someone be following us?"

"If I had to guess, a trace was put on the General's call."

"Holy shit. They can do that?"

"Yeah. But they shouldn't have found us that quickly." He glanced in the mirror again, then pressed harder on the accelerator. "Whoever sent them has some serious connections."

Bryan looked out the rear window. "Do you want me to get rid of them?"

Max considered. As tempting as the idea was, he shook his head. "We can't tip our hand just yet. We'll have to lose them without raising their suspicions."

"Okay. Let me think of something."

Max kept one eye on their pursuers and the other on Bryan, who was tapping his leg rhythmically as he stared out the window. Suddenly, he was in a flurry of motion, digging his phone out of his pocket.

"How long will it take to get to the Central Business District?"

"About forty-five minutes. Less if we don't run into any traffic."

"Drive faster." Bryan dialed, speaking as soon as his call was answered. "Nick. It's Bryan. Grab one of the vampire-safe SUVs from the garage and meet us at the theatre on Twelve-hundred Canal Street."

"Okay. When do you want us there?"

"We should be there in thirty to thirty-five minutes. Meet us in the parking lot so we can swap vehicles. Then I need you and Alex to drive to Denver."

"Are you in some kind of trouble"

"I'm not sure."

"What's going on?"

"There's someone following Max and me. It might be nothing. But just in case, you're the decoy."

"All right. Alex and I are heading to the garage now."

"Great. I owe you one."

"Just tell us what's going on when this is over."

"If I can."

"What does that mean?"

"This might have something to do with Max. If it does, I can't tell you anything unless he okays it."

"Fair enough. See you soon."

Max's heart gave a bump when Bryan put his need for secrecy above his best friends' curiosity. He hadn't expected that. Clearing his throat, he asked, "What's your plan?"

"When we switch vehicles, we'll leave our phones with Alex and Nick. Hopefully whoever's following us will chase after them."

"Good idea. We can grab some burner phones after we meet up with the General."

"That's what I was thinking."

"You seem to be experienced at this kind of thing." He turned sideways. "Not something I expected."

Bryan's laugh tickled his nerve endings. "Back in university, there were a few times I needed to fall off the radar." He snorted. "And it was usually because of something Nick and Alex got me into."

"Should I be worried?"

"Nah. We always fought on the side of good."

"Then why the need to disappear?"

"Let's just say not everyone agreed with our methods." Bryan's hand landed on Max's arm. "Nick and Alex will want to know what's going on. You can trust them to keep your secrets if you decide to tell them."

“I might not be at liberty to say anything.”

“Which will make them crazy, but they won’t push.”

“Good.”

Bryan got up on his knees and looked out the back window. “Slow down a bit, would you. I need to see whoever’s chasing us.”

“Why?”

“I’m going to let the air out of one of their tires. Hopefully, that won’t set off any alarms.”

Max lifted his foot off the accelerator, watching Bryan from the corner of his eyes. His skin tingled when Bryan released his magic. Speeding up, he grinned at the rearview mirror when the car chasing them fishtailed before sliding off the road.

“Got ‘em,” Bryan crowed, dropping back into his seat. He grinned at Max as he latched his seatbelt again.

Max sped down the road, his eyes periodically flicking to the side. Bryan had been full of surprises tonight. He was seeing a different side of the responsible Clan Leader he thought he’d known inside and out. It was something to think about.

* * *

Max pulled to the curb, noting the time with a sigh of relief. They’d made it with a few minutes to spare, even after the detour to swap vehicles with Bryan’s friends. He’d been impressed with how efficiently and quietly it had been accomplished. They’d barely pulled into the parking area when their doors had opened and they’d been pushed from the vehicle. It hadn’t taken more than thirty seconds before Max’s truck was pulling onto Canal Street, blending in with the traffic as Alex and Nick began their circuitous drive through the city before heading to Denver.

Now that they were off the radar of whoever had been following them, Max intended to keep it that way. Scanning the quiet neighborhood, he quickly picked out five poorly hidden people watching the General's house. He shook his head in disgust when he saw the van parked halfway down the block. Amateurs.

"How are we going to do this?' Bryan whispered.

Max pointed out the hidden watchers, then indicated the General's house. "That's where we're going. The attic window will have been left unlocked. It's at the rear of the house, so the watchers on the street won't have a clear line of sight."

"Okay." Bryan nodded. "I can get us up there, but I'm not sure how to do it without them seeing us."

"No problem." Max pointed to the Townhouse he'd parked the SUV in front of. "We'll climb up here and travel across the roofs."

Bryan whistled. "That's a long way to fall."

"Fall?" Max's eyebrow lifted. "Vampires don't fall."

"Whatever."

The eye roll was cute. "Will you be able to keep up?"

Bryan nodded. "I'll use magic to levitate."

Max's eyebrow went up, then he smiled. "Like at Christmas?"

"Exactly. Good thing Lysander was insistent on trying it. I'm not sure I would've thought of it myself."

"The Consort's mind is very creative."

"And scary," Bryan said, chuckling.

"That too. If you're ready, we need to go."

"I'm right behind you."

* * *

Bryan slipped into the darkened room behind Max, freezing at the sound of a gun being cocked.

"Who's that with you, Max?"

"Put the gun down, General. This is my mate."

Bryan's eyes widened. Since when did Max call Bryan his mate? He waited, motionless until he heard the sound of a drawer sliding open and the gun being placed inside.

"You know better than to bring a stranger into my house, son."

"He was with me when you called."

"You should have left him behind."

"We might be able to use his help."

"We'll see." There was the sound of another drawer opening. "Nothing else until I turn this up." Static, underscored by other unidentifiable sounds, filled the air.

Bryan whispered, "What's that?"

"Jammer."

"Oh. I can soundproof the room."

"Do it."

Bryan made a weave to prevent anyone from listening in on their conversation, with a small adjustment so their voices could be heard, but not understood. When he was done, Bryan nodded at Max. "We're good."

"Put the jammer away, General. Bryan's protected the room."

The desk lamp clicked on. The General's eyes moved over Bryan. "You're a magic-user?"

"Yes, sir. Leader of Clan Galway."

A soft whistle left the General's mouth. "I've heard of you. And your brother. Quite the mess you boys have been creating lately."

Bryan tensed. How would the General know that? The knowledge shouldn't have gone beyond the paranormal communities.

"Relax. The General knows about most events that happen in the world. He has an extensive information network set up."

"I'd wish we'd have known that. We could have used his help."

Max stiffened but said nothing when Bryan looked at him. The General looked between the two of them, then chuckled. "What makes you think I haven't?"

Bryan blinked. Then he recalled the military-grade equipment Max could procure on short notice. And satellite maps that didn't come off a generic internet site. "Thank you, General. Your assistance has been invaluable."

"No need to thank me. It's the responsibility of everyone to keep the world safe."

"True. Hopefully, I'll be able to return the favor one day."

"That might be sooner than you think." The General turned to Max. "Stephanie's been taken."

"How?"

"They took her when she was leaving work. Her boss witnessed the grab and called me."

Bryan frowned. "Why you and not the police?"

"Because he's ex-military and can spot a well-trained team when he sees one. Bringing in the police would have only led to their deaths."

"Your witness could have warned them to be careful. Having the police involved will get your daughter back faster."

Bryan didn't understand the look the General gave him, but he knew he'd said something stupid. "Don't you want the police to help?" he asked slowly, looking between the General and Max.

"The General has a lot more resources at his disposal than the police do."

"And calling in the police will alert whoever took her that I'm aware of her abduction. I'm hoping if they think I'm in the dark, it will help keep Stephanie safe until we find her."

"Oh. I didn't realize." Bryan looked around. "When is everyone else getting here?"

"Everyone else?"

"Yeah. The rest of the guys coming to the party." Bryan emphasized party with finger quotations.

"Nobody else is coming. Max is all I need."

Bryan looked at his mate in surprise. He knew Max was skilled, but if the General was putting all of his hope in Max to save his daughter, he was even better than Bryan thought.

"And I have you," Max said to Bryan. "Between the two of us, we should be able to handle anything." He turned back to the General, leaving Bryan with his mouth hanging open in surprise. "Do you know who's behind it?"

"I assumed it was a terrorist cell looking for leverage to free one of their own, but nobody's contacted me and I haven't heard any chatter over the lines." He tipped his chin toward the covered window. "The poorly trained spies make me think this is personal."

"We're probably looking at a mercenary group then."

"That was my thinking, yes."

"Whoever's behind this is well connected. We picked up a tail after your call."

"Damn it. How'd they find you so fast?"

"That's a good question. You might want to check how they're tracing your calls."

The General picked up his phone and tore off the back. "Those bastards," he said, plucking out a small electronic device. He handed it to Max who crushed it in his fist.

"I don't think they knew it was me they were following, but just in case, we sent them after a decoy."

"Good call. Whoever is behind this has a wide net in place to find you that quickly." The General sat at his desk and booted up his computer. "I'll put some feelers out on the dark web. See if I can find anything. How do I reach you??"

"You don't. I'll call when I can arrange for a secure line."

"Understood. Thank you. And you as well, Bryan. I realize you have your own battle, but Max is the only one I trust to bring my daughter back alive."

"I'm glad to help. Until we can find the Elders, we're mostly just cleaning up anyway."

"I'll keep my ears open and let you know if I hear anything."

"Thank you."

"I'd like to help more, but there's only so much I can do. There are some who oppose human interference in the paranormal world. This isn't the time to draw their attention."

"Any help you can provide is greatly appreciated."

The General nodded, then flicked his eyes up at Max. "The equipment you'll need is in the secondary spot. The first has been compromised."

Max's eyes went flat. "Only my old team should know about them. You've got a leak."

The General's mouth tightened. "It would appear so."

"You need to plug it."

"I'm working on it."

"I won't bring Stephanie back until you do."

"Good. She needs to be kept safe."

"She will be." Max glanced at the clock on the wall. "We should leave before your watchers get suspicious."

Bryan followed Max to the door, glancing at the General over his shoulder. The man's rigid control was the only thing keeping him together. That and his absolute faith in Max. Something Bryan could understand.

Chapter Seven

A dingy bar somewhere in the French Quarter…

"I need information, Trux."

The large man chuckled. "You know I don't give nothing away for free, kid."

"You owe us. I've come to collect." Max crossed his arms. "I'm looking for a girl."

"I didn't think girls were your thing."

"Special case. What do you know?"

Trux pulled the cigar from his mouth and studied the tip for a moment before looking at Max. "Does Roman know you're collecting on his behalf?"

"He knows."

He chuckled again. "You'll understand if I don't take your word for it. The last thing I need is the Prince coming after me for closing out his account without his knowledge."

"I thought you might feel that way." Max reached into his jacket pocket and held out his phone. "He's waiting to talk to you."

Trux glared at the device, his jaw clenching when he saw the open line. He fixed a death glare on his bodyguards. "Would someone like to explain how an active phone was allowed into my private meeting?"

Both men paled. Visibly swallowing, the one on the left said, "We frisked them, Boss. They didn't have nothing on them when we let them in."

Trux grabbed the phone from Max's hand and shook it at them. "This says differently."

The men eyed Trux nervously, neither taking a breath until Trux looked away and put the phone to his ear. "Roman."

"Theodore."

Trux made a pained sound. "You know I don't go by that."

"It is your name."

"Could you just call me Trux? I don't want the boys thinking I'm soft."

"If that is your wish."

"It is." Trux cleared his throat. "Your boy here is making promises in your name. Does he have permission to cash in your marker?"

"He does. Give him whatever he needs."

"Are you sure?"

"Everything you know, Trux."

"Of course."

"That means no holding back."

"Your credit may not be enough to cover his request. Perhaps another twenty-five G's?"

"You should know better than to haggle with me." The annoyance in Roman's voice came clearly through the speaker.

"A small joke. No harm intended." Trux laughed nervously as he wiped a blunt hand across the back of his neck. "You and me go way back. You can trust me to keep my end of the bargain."

"To do otherwise would cause me distress, which neither of us wants."

"No, we definitely don't want to do that." Trux cleared his throat. "This will clear our debt, yes?"

"It will."

"Okay. I'll give your boy what he needs."

"Thank you. It is good we have trust between us."

"It is. Good night, Prince." Trux handed the phone back. His finger waved between the two guards. "You two, out. You're both being reassigned to Mimi."

"Boss, please. Not Mimi. Give us another chance."

"Yeah, Boss. I promise we checked them over good." The second bodyguard glared at Max and Bryan. "They hid that phone from us somehow. We'd never risk your safety like that."

"I said out." Trux pointed to the door. "Mimi will be expecting you within the hour."

"Yes, Boss." Both men hung their heads and shuffled to the door. "We'll let Booth and Tony know they're being reassigned."

"Tell them to give me fifteen minutes before they come in."

"Yes, Boss." The door closed quietly behind them.

"Mimi?" Max asked, raising his eyebrow.

"My wife." Trux let out a loud belly laugh. "She's a bit, how do you say it, high maintenance. It's always the punishment assignment."

Max snorted and exchanged an amused glance with Bryan before turning back to Trux. "Tell me what you know about someone collecting girls."

The desk chair creaked when Trux leaned his considerable weight back and braced his elbows on the armrests. "You sure you want to get involved in this?"

Max crossed his arms. "I'm waiting."

"Okay. It's your funeral." The big man leaned forward, resting his elbows on the desk. "There's a new player in town. Word is he's collecting merchandise for some buyers overseas."

"Tell me where I can find him."

Trux shook his head. "It won't do you any good. He and the ones surrounding him have the same abilities you do. He also has himself a pet magic-user." Trux eyed Bryan speculatively. "Something you might have in common."

"I want an address."

"I have another option you might want to consider."

"Which is?"

"There's going to be a private auction in three days. I can get you an invitation." He tapped his thick fingers on the desk. "There's just one small problem."

"And that is?"

"He won't let you in. Your friend is going to have to attend instead."

"Why?"

"He doesn't deal with vampires. Which is ironic considering he is one."

"What's his name?"

"Goes by the name Master Robertson."

"Baxter," Max hissed.

Trux's eyebrow went up. "I see you've heard of him."

"We've met." He snapped his fingers. "I'm still waiting for that address."

"You're not going to be able to get through his security shield. His barrier is like nothing I've ever heard of before."

"I have access to a special key. I'll get in."

Trux eyed him for a moment, then shrugged. He pulled a pen from his inside jacket pocket and scribbled on the notepad on his desk. Tearing off the sheet, he held it out to Max. "Where can I contact you when I have the invitation?"

"You can't. I'll be back tomorrow."

Trux frowned. "I might not be able to get one that quickly."

"Have it ready by tomorrow." While Max might not have the ancient power that Roman wielded, he wasn't a youngling either. He leaned on the crime boss with the power he did have, pressing his point home.

Trux flinched, then held up his hands, palms out. "I'll get it for you, Max. No need to get testy."

Max grunted, turning to Bryan. "Let's go." He headed for the door calling over his shoulder. "Tomorrow, Trux. Don't let me down."

"It'll be here."

Max nodded at the guards waiting outside the door.

"Who's Pr…?" Bryan started to ask.

"Not here."

"Sorry."

Max made a beeline for the door, his mind spinning furiously. Baxter. What the hell was that bastard doing in North America?

* * *

The shadow watched the two men walk away, his glowing red eyes a window for his Master to observe the enemy. Sensing movement, he turned toward the fat man standing in the doorway. Sniffing the air, he shuffled forward, drool dripping from his lips.

"Stop."

He jerked to a halt.

"Hide until they return."

"Hungry."

"Hide now. Feast later."

"Yes, Master." The shadow licked his lips, keeping his eyes locked on the big man, the emptiness in his gut more compelling than his Master's command. Pain abruptly seized his body. Falling to the ground, he thrashed wildly as fire became his world.

"Obey."

A moment later, the burning presence left. Released from its hold, Peter faded into the night, hiding as his Master had ordered.

* * *

Back in their room, Bryan barely caught the duffel before it hit him in the face. "What do you want me to do with this?"

"Put on the protective vest."

"I don't need to wear that." Bryan tossed the bag to the ground. "I have my shield up."

Max crowded him, pushing him against the wall. "Don't argue with me." He leaned over and rummaged in the bag, then stood, slamming the vest against Bryan's chest. "Put it on."

"Why are you being so insistent? You know I can protect myself."

"Because something was following us."

"Something? Or someone?"

Max's brow furrowed. "I'm not sure."

Bryan pushed him back. "Whatever it was, my magic will keep me safe."

"Your brother would want you to wear it."

Bryan started to argue, then stopped. Max was right. If Lysander was here, he would push Bryan to wear it. "Fine. I'll wear the damn vest. But I think you're being overcautious."

"Better that than dead." Max strode across the room to the bag they'd filled with an assortment of weaponry and miscellaneous items from the General's hidden cache. He spent a moment rifling through the contents before coming up with a box which he tossed at Bryan, who deftly snagged it out of the air.

Looking at the contents, Bryan raised his eyebrow at Max. "What's this?"

"It's a wire. Can you conceal it with your magic?"

Bryan studied the tiny earbud and miniature microphone. Touching the electronics with his fingertip, he nodded. "Yeah. I can make it so nobody can see them."

"Good." Max waved him off when Bryan went to hand it back. "Keep them. I want you to use them the night of the auction."

"What do you think is going to happen there?"

"I don't know, but I'd rather be overprepared." Max bent back to the bag, this time coming up with a couple of burner phones. He flipped one toward Bryan. "Call your brother and let him know what we're doing. You'll also want a suit for the auction. You need to look like you come from money."

Bryan smirked as he tapped out Lysander's number. "That shouldn't be too difficult. I do come from money." It took him a moment to realize Max had stopped moving. Holding his finger over the call button, Bryan lifted his eyebrow. "What is it?"

"You can't go to that auction."

"What? Of course, I can?"

"You're too well known. We'll have to find someone else."

"What are you talking about? I'm rich, I can act entitled. The role is tailor made for me."

"No." Max shook his head. "Anyone who knows anything about you will realize you don't belong there. We'll have to come up with another plan."

"People can change, Max. My mother trying to kill me and being at war with the Elders have obviously driven me into making some questionable life choices." He shrugged, pressing the call button. "People are always ready to believe the worst. Especially when they have their own skeletons to hide."

He turned his back and began speaking as soon as Lysander came on the line. "Hey, baby brother. I need you to pack up my best suit. I'm going on an undercover mission." He walked toward the bathroom, ignoring Max when he growled at him to come back.

Bryan exited the bathroom a few minutes later when the private part of his conversation was done. "Yes, send it to the Seventh Level Hotel."

"Couldn't you have found a nicer place to stay?"

"We're trying to keep a low profile."

"Did you have to go that low?"

"It's only for a few nights."

"A few nights of hell."

"Stop being such a snob. It's perfectly acceptable."

"If you say so." Muffled noises came over the speaker then Lysander was back. *"Roman says Gideon and Carlos will be there tomorrow. Why do they get to help and not me?"*

"Because you and Roman need to stay away from this situation. Gideon is our key to get in and Carlos is, well,

Carlos. He's handy to have around when things don't go as planned."

"Be careful, Bryan. I don't have a good feeling about this."

Bryan stilled. "That kind of feeling?"

"Maybe. I'm not sure. Just keep an extra eye out."

"Max is making me wear Kevlar."

"Good. Keep doing what Max tells you to do."

Bryan grunted.

"I'm serious. He's got more experience with this sort of thing than you"

"I know, but…."

"You can't assume your magic will keep you safe. Look what Zachary did to Gideon."

Bryan grimaced. "Point taken. I'll do what Max says."

"Good. Call me as soon as you're done."

"I will." Ending the call, Bryan turned and ran into Max who was right behind him. He took a hasty step back. "Sorry. I didn't realize you were there."

Max put out his hand. "Give me your phone."

Startled by the abrupt tone, Bryan handed it over, his eyes widening when Max tore the back off of it. "What are you doing?"

"I'm getting rid of it in case your call was traced."

"Traced by who? Nobody even knows we're here." Bryan shook his head. "Don't you think you might be going a bit overboard?"

"No." Max removed the battery, then pulled out the SIM card and snapped it in half before crushing the phone in his hand. He put the pieces in his pocket.

"What are you going to do with those?"

"I'll scatter them on the way."

"On the way to where?"

"Baxter's place. We're going to check out his security. If he's holding the girls there, we might be able to get them out before the auction."

"And if we can't?"

"Then you'll attend the auction as planned. I'm hoping Trux was wrong about Baxter's security. It would be safer for everyone if we could rescue the girls when Gideon and Carlos get here tomorrow."

"Okay. Let's go see." Bryan opened the door, stopping when Max pulled on his arm.

"This is where things get serious. You do whatever I tell you out there. No questions. No hesitation. Got it."

"Loud and clear." He just managed to stop himself from giving Max a snappy salute.

Max scowled like he'd seen it anyway as he stomped through the doorway muttering under his breath.

Bryan waited until Max was out of sight before grinning. He'd never expected him to be such a worry-wart? And while Bryan was secretly thrilled by his protectiveness, he still thought Max was being ridiculously overcautious. After all, they were only going to look over Baxter's place. What could possibly go wrong?

* * *

They were sneaking down a narrow alley a block away from the address Trux had given them when they ran across a gang of thugs. Bryan instinctively wrapped a protective shield around Max, which was all he had time for before he was grabbed and shoved into a nearby alcove. The next thing he knew, Max had him pressed against the wall and his mouth was being savaged by a wet, heated kiss.

Shock held him still. For a moment. Then he got with the program and wrapped his arms around Max's neck, biting at the lips attacking his own. Mewling sounds escaped as he tried to climb Max's body. Hands clamped on his shoulders, holding him down as their positions were reversed, with Bryan leaning into him as Max's hot mouth feasted on his. A fang scraped across the delicate flesh of his inner lip. Bryan groaned when Max started sucking at the small wound.

Raucous laughter sounded nearby, the discordant sound tearing Bryan from the passionate fog he'd been drifting in. Bryan bit back the denial that tried to escape when Max pulled away and protectively placed his body between Bryan and the gang of thugs approaching them. He glared at the leader over Max's shoulder when the jackass swaggered up to them, wondering if sexual frustration would be an allowable defense if he lit the man on fire. He let his magic rise, tempted to find out.

Max's body bumped him, bringing Bryan to his senses. Shit. They were supposed to be keeping a low profile, not setting random strangers on fire. He pulled back on his power and scowled at the asshole who was now standing in front of Max.

"Look what we found, boys? A couple of treats just waiting to be sampled." He flicked his tongue at Max. "Isn't that right, sweetheart?"

"Jazz, Mr. B's expecting us." A muscular, no-neck thug stepped forward and grabbed the leader's arm. "We don't have time for this bullshit."

Wrenching free, Jazz stepped closer to Max. "These boys shouldn't be here. We have enough time to show them what happens when they come into our territory uninvited." Laughing, he put his meaty hand on Max's neck, squeezing hard enough his fingers turned white.

Bryan's magic surged to the surface. Before he could blast the asshole, an elbow drove into his chest, stealing his breath. Gasping, he leaned his head against Max's back as he tried to force air into his lungs.

"Looks like something is wrong with your boy."

"Get your hand off of me."

"Or what? You going to make me?"

"If I have to."

Bryan lifted his head, his nose and eyes watering, finally able to take short, wheezing breaths. He glared at the strange hand still squeezing Max's neck. Before he could decide if he should blast the asshole, discretion be damned, the thug shoved Max backward, knocking Bryan's head into the wall. He then slammed his fist into Max's stomach with enough force to bend him in half. Magic exploded.

Max shouted and threw himself at the man, tackling him to the ground. Bryan's blade of air passed harmlessly over their heads, cutting halfway through a garbage bin on the other side of the alley.

The gang members dropped into battle ready-stances and drew their weapons against the unseen threat. Shit. This wasn't a street gang. These guys were trained soldiers.

The sounds of fists hitting flesh drew his attention to Max and Jazz rolling on the ground exchanging blows. Silenced bullets peppered the area around their bodies.

Jazz, who had his arm cocked, glared at no-neck. "What the hell, man? You could have hit me."

"Enough screwing around already. It's time to go. Mr. B's waiting."

Jazz drove his fist into Max's face, then stood up. Slamming his heel down into Max's thigh, he spit on him before pointing a finger at Bryan. "Get the hell off these streets or you'll be buried in them." He wiped a hand across his face, smearing blood from nose to cheek, then took point, leading his group down the alley in the same direction Bryan and Max had been headed.

Bryan ran to Max and slid to his knees, ignoring the squelching sound of whatever he'd landed on as he ran his hands over Max's body. "Are you okay?"

Max's eyes popped open. "I'm fine." He pushed Bryan off him, then sprang to his feet, looking up and down the alley.

"How come you let that asshole hit you? We could easily have stopped them."

Ignoring him, Max peered around the corner before coming back to Bryan. "We can't take another chance of being discovered. We'll go the rest of the way by rooftop."

"Damnit, Max. Answer me. Why didn't you pound that guy into the ground?"

"What do you think Baxter would do to those girls if he knew someone strong enough to take out his team was sniffing around?"

"He'd just take them somewhere else, wouldn't he?"

"It's possible. Unless he felt he needed to move quickly. Then it would be easier to dispose of them and have his men grab new ones in his next location."

Bryan blanched. "You mean he'd kill them?"

"Yes."

"Why would he do something like that?"

"Because they're nothing more than a commodity to him."

"But they're…that's…that's horrible. I don't understand how anyone could be like that."

Max's gaze filled with compassion. "That's because your mind doesn't work that way. To you, all life is precious."

"It should be like that for everyone."

"But it's not. You need to prepare yourself for what we might find so the shock doesn't immobilize you when it's time to act."

Bryan swallowed. "Like when Carlos told Lysander he needed to know what his enemies were capable of so he wasn't puking in the bushes while someone was stabbing him in the back."

"Exactly like that. Carlos might be an asshole, but he knows what he's talking about." Max scanned the alley. "We've been here too long. We need to get moving."

Bryan felt ill thinking about what could happen if their presence drew the wrong kind of attention. Like it almost had earlier, except for Max's quick thinking. Which reminded him. He touched his puffy lips. "You kissed me."

Max looked back from the wall he was preparing to scale. "I needed a way to study them. They weren't moving the way a street gang would."

Bryan's heart clenched. "That's the only reason?"

"It also gave us a good excuse for being in the alley."

Bryan flinched, then laughed uncomfortably. "Of course. We wouldn't want them to be suspicious." Swallowing his disappointment, he walked over to the wall and levitated to the top.

As Max watched him disappear over the edge, he cursed himself for being an ass. It wasn't until he'd seen Bryan flinch that Max realized he'd wounded his mate. Which hadn't been his intent. As he'd told him, the kiss had merely been a means to study how the enemy approached. It hadn't crossed his mind Bryan would think it was real. Which made him an idiot.

Max quickly scaled the building and rushed after Bryan, grabbing his arm to pull him to a stop. "Listen, about that kiss…."

"It's fine. I get it."

"I don't think you do. I didn't…."

"It's okay, Max. I've seen you in action. I know that you focus one-hundred percent on the task at hand." Bryan's understanding smile stung for some reason. "It's my fault for getting caught up in the moment and forgetting that. And your kiss was damned convincing." Bryan chuckled ruefully and tugged his hand free, bumping his fist against Max's shoulder. "Don't worry about it. We're good."

Max studied him, not knowing if he should try to explain again or accept that Bryan really did comprehend how Max's mind worked. Seeing only calm acceptance on his face, Max nodded, deciding to take him at his word.

He stared after his mate in wonder as Bryan walked away. Non-military people rarely grasped the absolute single-mindedness that was required to run a successful mission. That his mate did was astounding. But the next time Max kissed him, he would make sure Bryan had no doubts about it being real. The thought made him grin.

"Hey. We going or what?"

Thankful there wasn't going to be any awkwardness between them, Max nodded. "Yeah. Race you there."

Bryan's "asshole" faded in the wind as Max sped across the rooftops, slowing just enough for his mate to keep up.

* * *

Max crawled to the edge of the rooftop he'd chosen as the best surveillance point. Handing Bryan a set of long-range night vision binoculars, he narrowed his eyes as he surveyed Baxter's set up. Trux had been right about the elaborate protective measures that were in place. Even with Gideon's help, getting in would be a challenge.

"I see a couple of the guys we ran into earlier," Bryan whispered.

Max grunted, not surprised to get confirmation that Mr. B was Baxter. Especially since he'd recognized one of the street gang. When Ian had flashed a discrete signal, Max had realized Bryan and he were stepping into someone else's covert mission. Which was unfortunate. He'd try not to mess it up, but Max wasn't leaving until they'd rescued the General's daughter and the other girls.

"He's got quite a few layers of protection built up. I'm pretty sure I can get through the barrier, but it'll take some time." Bryan pulled the binoculars away from his eyes and looked at Max. "Unfortunately, they'll know we're here the moment I break through the first layer."

"Then Gideon will have to get us in. Our biggest concern is the number of armed guards. There are too many to take out at once. If one of them gets a sniff of us, those girls will be dead before we can reach them."

"We have to find a way to save them."

"We'll figure it out." Max spent a few more minutes scanning the property before turning his attention to the neighboring streets and houses. A glint on a rooftop three streets over caught his attention. Narrowing his eyes, he caught a glimpse of a scope being pointed in their direction.

"Son of a bitch." Max threw himself sideways and covered Bryan's body, rolling them away from their surveillance spot. Shots peppered the area they'd been lying in. He held Bryan tightly and kept rolling until they were safely behind the raised stairwell to the roof.

"Was that someone shooting at us?"

"Yeah." Max peered around the corner of the rooftop exit. Bullets sprayed the cinder block next to his head, sending up a cloud of dusty cement fragments.

Bryan yanked him back. "What the hell, Max? Are you trying to get shot?"

"It's okay. They missed on purpose."

"Missed? They almost took your head off."

"That was just a warning. We've stumbled into someone else's op."

"What should we do?"

"We carry on as planned."

"What if we mess up their mission?"

"We'll try not to, but it changes nothing." Max pulled Bryan to the far side of the roof. "Our primary objective is to rescue the girls. If we screw up their op, they'll have to deal. Let's go. We're done for tonight." Max jumped across the gap and waited for Bryan to join him before leading him back to their hotel.

Ian had better warn his team to keep out of their way. Max would hate to take out any of the good guys by accident.

Chapter Eight

Max reached for the doorknob, then froze, his instincts warning him of the presence of another vampire.

"Why'd you stop?"

"There's someone in our room."

"It's probably just Carlos and Gideon."

Max blocked Bryan when he tried to open the door. "They're not supposed to be here until tomorrow."

"They must have decided to come early." Bryan elbowed him aside and went into the hotel room.

If he hadn't felt the buzz of Bryan's magic, Max would have yanked him back. That didn't mean he wasn't going to remind his mate yet again that he needed to be more cautious. The wrong assumption could get both of them killed.

"Hey. It's about time you guys got here. We've been waiting for hours." Carlos swaggered through the doorway of the adjoining room and flopped onto Max's bed. He propped his head on his hand and crossed his ankles, his leather boots leaving smudges on the comforter.

"Get your feet off my bed."

Carlos laughed, then stood and made a production out of wiping off the spot his boots had made before smoothing out the wrinkles where he'd been laying. He patted the bedspread. "There. All better now."

Max rolled his eyes. "What are you even doing here? We weren't expecting you until tomorrow."

"The Consort wanted us to come early." Gideon walked through the connecting doorway and handed Bryan a garment bag. "He asked me to give you this."

"Thanks." Bryan hung it in the closet, looking at Gideon over his shoulder. "I wonder why Lysander thought we needed you sooner. Nothing's really happened. Well, other than running into a squad of mercenaries pretending to be a street gang and looking for a way to break into a secured mansion."

"Mercenaries?" Gideon turned to Max. "Where did you see them?"

"In an alley a couple streets over from Baxter's place."

"Did they seem suspicious of your presence there?"

"No. We managed to distract them."

"Is that right?" Carlos asked, looking between Bryan and Max. "How'd you do that?"

Bryan's cheeks burned. "None of your business."

Carlos laughed. "Like that, is it?"

Bryan flipped him off, which only made him laugh harder. Asshole. Ignoring him, Bryan said, "The important thing is Baxter doesn't know we're here."

"Which is good." Gideon sat down on the couch. "What's the plan for tomorrow?"

"Bryan and I are meeting with Trux to get the invitation and location for the private auction. After that, we're going to run more surveillance on Baxter's house." Max pulled his duffle out of the closet. "We didn't find any weaknesses in his security. I'm hoping you might see something we've missed."

"Did you guys see any sign of the girls being held there?" Carlos asked.

"No."

"If they are, can we get them out before the auction?" Gideon asked.

Max shook his head. "Not without putting them in more danger. There are too many guards to take out at once. I think we're better off waiting for the auction so Bryan can protect them from the inside."

"Okay. Then that's what we'll do unless another option presents itself."

Unzipping the duffle, Max pulled out a couple of boxes and tossed them to Carlos and Gideon. "Communications devices. We'll wear them when Bryan goes in."

Gideon put the box in his pocket. "Is there anything else we need to know?"

"Yeah." Max frowned. "I felt something watching us when we were at Trux's. Somehow, it managed to keep itself hidden from me."

"That's concerning," Gideon said, his eyebrows drawing together. "Carlos and I will keep a lookout for it."

"Appreciate that. I don't like not knowing what it is."

"Do you think it might be someone working for the demon?"

"It's possible. It would explain why I couldn't find it."

"This is probably why Lysander sent you guys early." Bryan dropped onto his bed. "If it is something to do with the demon, Max and I can't handle it on our own."

"Well, now that we're here, that fucking demon stalker doesn't stand a chance."

"No, it doesn't." Bryan's laugh turned into a yawn. "Sorry. It's been a busy day."

"On that note, why don't we get out of your hair?" Gideon took Carlos' arm and pulled him toward the door.

"Okay. See you guys tomorrow."

The turning lock was loud in the sudden quiet.

Bryan yawned again as he got up off the bed and walked across the room. "I don't know about you, but I'm done for the night. Give me a few minutes and then the bathroom's all yours."

Max kept one ear on Bryan's bedtime preparations while he organized his duffle, searching for items that might be useful against whatever was following them. If it was something under the demon's control, he didn't have much.

He looked at the connecting door, thankful Carlos and Gideon were here early. They'd be able to help Max watch over Bryan. No matter that Bryan thought he could look after himself, when it came to his safety, there was no such thing as too much protection.

* * *

The following evening…

"Is all this protective gear really necessary?" Carlos sneered at the Kevlar vest he was holding.

"Lysander wants everyone to wear it," Bryan said.

"He's not even here. I don't see why I have to do as he says."

"Because I'll tell him if you don't." Bryan grinned when Carlos gave him the finger.

"Why the hell would you do that?"

"Because if I have to wear it, so do you."

"You're an asshole." Carlos jerked the vest over his head and adjusted the Velcro straps. "This is stupid.

Nothing can hurt me so the damn thing's completely unnecessary." His shoulders twitched as he settled the vest into place. "And it itches."

"It will please the Consort if you wear it, treasure."

"Like I care." He smacked his vest and glared at Bryan. "Happy now?"

"You have no idea how much." Bryan snickered as he pulled on his own vest.

"I'll remember this, jackass."

"You do that." Bryan looked up from adjusting his straps. "I was too tired to think of asking last night. What did you end up doing with Mother?"

"We locked her in the Council dungeons. The Consort is waiting until we all get back to interrogate her."

"She's not going to like that."

"Too fucking bad. The only reason she's still alive is the knowledge in her head."

Bryan flinched.

"Shit. Sorry. Sometimes I forget she's your mother."

"No. I get it. She needs to pay for the harm she's caused. It's just…I can still remember her being a good mother. Back before my father died."

"It sucks when your parent lets you down." Carlos smacked him on the shoulder. "At least you had your brother. I know if it wasn't for Missy, I would have ended up being just like the old man."

"I don't think so. Lysander said your heart was good. You probably saved yourself as much as Melissa did."

"Good thing we'll never know for sure, isn't it?" Carlos grinned. "I'd hate to be fighting against you boys."

"We'd kick your ass. Again." Bryan laughed, ducking Carlos' fist.

"If you're both ready, it's time to go," Max barked before storming out the door.

Bryan's eyebrow lifted at Max's abrupt exit. What the hell was his problem? It was nearly as baffling as Carlos' laughter.

Max knew it was ridiculous to be annoyed because Carlos was joking around with Bryan. They did it all the time. But Max still was. Which irritated him even more. He made himself stop pacing when Gideon stepped into the hallway and closed the door behind him.

"You're agitated because your unclaimed mate is interacting with another man. It will be that way until you claim him."

"How do you know we're mates? Has the Consort been talking?"

"Max. You know better than that." The censure in Gideon's tone stung.

He huffed out a breath. "My apologies. That was out of line."

"It's okay. I understand how difficult this is for you. But rest assured, once you claim him, the irrational anger will ease."

"How did you know?"

"About your connection?" At Max's nod, Gideon answered, "I can see where the line between you both starts and where it is blocked."

"Why didn't you say something before?"

"It was not my place."

"And it is now?"

"Something has changed. Where the lines were previously dormant, they now strain toward each other. But something is blocking them." The look he gave Max indicated he knew exactly what the problem was.

Growling, Max stalked partway down the hall, then came back. "I don't know why I feel this way. I didn't even know we were mates until a few days ago."

"Just because the bond is hidden doesn't mean it doesn't exist. You've probably always been aware, but the signs may have been subtle enough to overlook."

Max frowned. "Like the way I've always been drawn to him, even when I fought against it?"

"Exactly."

"Or how I can feel his magic."

Gideon's eyebrows went up. "You can feel his magic? Interesting."

"Why do you say that?"

"It's unusual for one who doesn't have magic to feel another's. Your connection might not be as broken as you think."

Max crossed his arms, trying to decide if that was a good thing or not.

"I'm sure once you learn to trust each other, your link will be whole."

Before he could respond, Bryan and Carlos came out of the hotel room. Bryan eyed him questioningly. "Is everything okay?"

"Fine. You guys ready?"

"Yeah. We can leave anytime."

Max nodded, then strode down the hallway, his mind for once not on the upcoming mission. Gideon thought it came down to trust. Which was a problem. Trust didn't come easily once it had been broken. At least not for Max.

* * *

Gideon's steps slowed as they neared the club's entrance. He whispered to Max, "Something's watching us."

"I know. Can you see where it is?"

"No. You?"

Max shook his head.

"Is this the same feeling you had last night?"

"Yeah. But I can't tell what it is."

"Me either. It shouldn't be able to block itself from me." Gideon looked at him sideways. "You know what this means?"

Max grunted. "Demon."

"Yes. Carlos and I will stay out here during your meeting. We'll try to get a look at what's following you."

"Thanks."

"Be careful, Max. If anything seems off, don't hesitate to call us."

"We won't." Motioning to Bryan, who was walking with Carlos behind him and Gideon, he led the way into the smoky club.

* * *

Max blew past the guards and planted himself in front of Trux's desk. "Did you get it?"

"Was there any doubt?" He opened the desk drawer and pulled out a black envelope that had a stylized B.R. engraved in gold on the front and handed it to Max.

Opening the envelope, Max pulled out a black metallic disc and held it up.

"That's the invitation?" Bryan looked enquiringly at Trux.

"Yes. That's one of the requirements to gain admittance."

"What are the rest?" Max asked, putting the disc back into the envelope.

"There's a secret word."

"Of course, there is." Baxter had always been prone to theatrics. "What is it?"

"Xanadu."

Max squinted. "Excuse me?"

"You heard me."

"I don't think I did."

Trux looked pained. "Please don't make me say it again."

Max snorted and let it go. "What else is there?"

"There's also a secret knock."

"A secret knock?" Max asked flatly.

"Yes." Trux demonstrated.

Max looked at Bryan. "Did you get that?"

"I'm not sure. Could you demonstrate it again?" His innocent look didn't fool Max. Or Trux for that matter, judging by the scowl he gave Bryan. "Please."

Max bit back a grin when Trux banged out the secret tempo on his desk, glaring at Bryan the whole time.

When he was finished, Max asked, "Is that it?"

"Almost." Trux pulled a cell phone from his desk drawer. "The location will be texted to this phone sixty minutes before the auction begins."

Max stretched out his hand but Trux pulled the phone out of his reach.

"Trux," Max warned. "Don't screw with me."

"Just to be clear, once I hand this over, my debt to Roman is done."

"It is."

He started to hold out the phone, then hesitated, watching Max with narrowed eyes.

"You have my word. The debt between you and Roman will be paid in full."

"Good." Trux flipped the phone to Max, who snatched it out of the air. "Now get the hell out of my office." He pulled a gun from his drawer and pointed it at them.

Max grabbed Bryan by the arm when he felt his magic rise. Shaking his head, he dragged his angry mate from the room.

Max was thankful Bryan waited until they were outside before he exploded.

"That bastard pulled a gun on us."

"Leave it. We need to get out of the area before Trux does something stupid."

"Like what?"

"Like sending his guys after us."

"What? That's crazy? He has to know Roman will go after him if he does."

"He'll try to make it look like we were killed in some freak accident."

"I'd like to see him try." Bryan glared back at the bar. "We can take out whoever he sends after us."

"Not without making a lot of noise. Which we don't want. The last thing we need is to draw the attention of the police."

Gideon stepped out of the shadows. "Whatever is watching the place hasn't moved since we got here." He frowned as he scanned the alley. "I expect it will follow us when we leave."

"Let's find out."

The four of them ran off into the night.

* * *

Peter held his breath as he waited for the men to run past his hiding spot. Once they were gone, he asked, "Now?"

"Now."

Receiving his Master's permission, Peter scuttled across the alley from his hiding place and crept in through the back door. Scurrying down the hallway, he grinned menacingly when the guards stepped forward to intercept him. Jumping into the air, he landed on the first guard, his sharpened teeth biting deep into his neck. As he feasted, he fixed his red eyes on the remaining guard, who froze with his weapon partially raised when Peter's Master took control of his mind.

When he was finished eating, Peter let the body drop to the ground and turned to the other guard. Terrified eyes stared at him as he climbed the torso, his mouth open wide with blood dripping from his pointed teeth. He bit through the man's face, the eye popping like a succulent grape. He held on tight when the man fell to the ground, chewing ravenously as he gorged, desperately trying to fill the black emptiness in his core.

When he was done, Peter rose to his feet and wiped his hand across his mouth, then licked the crimson smears from his palm. After he'd sucked the last bit of blood off his finger, he opened the office door and stepped inside. It closed behind him with a soft click.

"Hey. Who the hell are you? Guards."

A sharp cry filled the air. The sounds of something crashing against the wall and furniture breaking went unheard. As did the firing of a gun and the growling slurps of an animal as it fed.

Redness seeped under the door and blended with the sticky pools of crimson that darkened the faded hallway carpet.

* * *

Bryan glanced over his shoulder as they raced down the alley and caught a glimpse of a shadow going into the club. He came to a stop. "Hold up, guys. Something just went in the back door."

"It's probably just one of the staff," Carlos said.

"What if it's not?" Bryan frowned at the door. "I think we should check it out. Just in case."

"Bryan's right," Max said. "If it's our secret watcher, Security won't be able to handle it. Not with the demon powering it."

Bryan jerked. "You know for sure it's the demon?"

Max nodded. "It's the only thing that would be able to hide from Gideon's magic."

"Shit." Bryan started running back down the alley. "Hurry. We need to find it before it hurts anyone."

Bryan burst through the door, Max hot on his heels.

Max hissed. "We're too late." He rushed past Bryan down the hallway toward Trux's office.

Running after him, Bryan cursed when he saw the bodies lying on the floor.

Carlos appeared beside him. "Fuck me. Those poor bastards never had a chance."

"Max," Bryan called out, unable to tear his eyes away from what was left of the guards. "Is Trux okay?"

"No." Max closed the office door with a sharp bang. "We'd better check out the rest of the club."

As they raced toward the club's main area, Bryan prayed to the Goddess that nobody else had been killed.

* * *

Bryan escorted the last patron out the side door to the waiting cab, wished him a good night, then locked it behind him. Leaning his head against the wood, his shoulders slumped in exhaustion. The last couple of hours had been a grueling battle to empty the club of inebriated patrons, so he needed a moment to center himself before heading back to the other room and whatever was still left to be done.

When they'd run into the club's main area, he'd been expecting the worst. Seeing the room filled with laughing patrons drinking and dancing had been a huge relief. Until they'd tried to send them home. Then the happy partiers had turned into angry, uncooperative assholes who'd refused to leave and threatened to call the cops. The last thing they'd needed was a riot to break out, so Bryan and Gideon had pasted smiles on their faces and freely used Trux's name to encourage everyone to clear out while Max and Carlos checked over the rest of the building. It had all been worth it in the end when they found no other signs of the minion's presence.

Bryan roused himself after a few minutes and walked back into the main room just as Gideon was finishing his call. "All the customers are gone. What's next on our agenda?"

Gideon put his phone in his pocket. "We need to speak with the authorities. They're on their way now."

"I hate dealing with cops," Carlos said, walking through the kitchen door.

"We're only reporting a crime, treasure. They have no other interest in us."

Carlos snorted. "You're naïve if you think that. The NOPD takes an unhealthy interest in everything I do."

Gideon put his arm around Carlos. "I'm sure it will be fine."

Carlos shook his head. "Trust me. This isn't going to end well."

"Well, well, well. If it isn't my old pal, Carlos Rossi."

"Sanders."

Bryan was surprised at the amount of loathing Carlos managed to put into one word.

The NOPD officer grinned when he pulled his handcuffs free. "I should have known you were involved when dispatch said the victims' bodies had been drained. You know the drill, Rossi. Hands behind your back."

Carlos mouthed, I told you so, to Gideon before turning and crossing his wrists behind his back. "You're making a mistake, Sanders. I didn't do anything."

"That's what you always say." He snapped the cuffs around Carlos' wrists then grabbed his arm and started walking towards the door.

"Aren't you going to read me my rights?"

"Scumbags like you don't have any rights. Now shut up before I add resisting arrest to your charges."

"Excuse me, Officer." Gideon stepped in front of Sanders, forcing him to come to a stop.

"Who are you?"

"Gideon Carmichael III, Red Dragon, Clan Taren" He crossed his arms. "Why are you arresting my mate?"

"Rossi's your mate?" Sanders snickered. "Poor bastard."

"I'd like you to release him."

"I beg your pardon?"

"Carlos hasn't committed a crime. Please let him go."

"Are you telling me how to do my job?" Sanders drew himself up.

"Not at all. But you have no cause to arrest him. He hasn't done anything."

"He's a person of interest."

"For what?"

"For whatever happened here tonight. I'm sure once our investigators have gone through the crime scene, we'll have proof of Mr. Rossi's involvement."

"That's ridiculous," Gideon snarled, smoke wafting from his nostrils.

"I'd watch your tone, Mr. Carmichael. I'm a duly appointed Officer of the Law. You will speak to me with respect."

"Of course, Officer." Bryan winced at the coldness in Gideon's voice. "I assume you were not advised that Carlos and I are the ones who called about the murders."

Sanders waved his finger back and forth between Gideon and Carlos. "You saying you were together?"

"Yes. Carlos has been with me all night."

"Big mistake, dragon," Carlos muttered.

"Is that so?" Sanders snapped his fingers at his partner. "Chauncey, cuff Mr. Carmichael. He's just confessed to being an accessory to Rossi's crime."

"I did no such thing." Gideon yanked free of Officer Chauncey's hold. "What kind of moron are you? You're supposed to be getting our witness statements, not arresting us."

"Don't tell me how to do my job."

"Somebody has to. We're innocent bystanders reporting a crime, not criminals."

"Give it up, Gideon. The idiot's too stupid to listen to reason," Carlos called out.

Sanders grabbed hold of Gideon's arm with both hands and held it out to Officer Chauncy, who quickly snapped a handcuff on it. "Add resisting arrest when you book them." Sanders glared at Carlos. "And slander."

"It's only slander if it's not true, asshole."

Sanders pulled a baton off his utility belt and cracked Carlos across the knee."

"Fucker. You'll pay for that."

"Hey. Stop hitting my mate." Gideon pulled free from Chauncy's hold, the handcuff dangling from one wrist.

"I'd stop moving or the vampire gets it again." Sanders smacked the baton across his palm. "I've always wanted to know how many hits it would take to knock Rossi out. Shall I find out?"

Smoke wafted from Gideon's nostrils as he glared at Sanders, but he allowed Officer Chauncey to pull his wrists behind him. The click of metal on metal was loud in the silence as the handcuffs were securely fastened.

"Get them out of here," Sanders barked.

Bryan stared in shock as the officers began hauling Carlos and Gideon away. Then he headed over to Sanders. He needed to stop this madness before it went any further. "Excuse me, Officer. I think there's been a slight misunderstanding."

"Who are you?"

"Bryan Galway." He held out his hand. "I'm leader of the Galway Clan."

Sanders squinted. "You're one of the magic-users in the big mansion?"

"I am."

"I'm sorry if these men were bothering you. I'll have them out of your way shortly."

"That's what I wanted to talk to you about."

"You can speak with one of the other officers if you want to press charges." He turned to leave.

"You don't understand. I don't want to press charges."

"Then what do you want?" Sanders snarled, before smoothing out his expression. "I'm kind of busy here."

"I think you've made a mistake." Bryan faltered momentarily when Sanders' eyes bulged, then plowed on gamely. "We're the ones who reported the crime. The officer we spoke with asked us to wait so we could give our witness statements. That's the reason we're here."

"To report a crime?"

"Exactly." Bryan smiled politely. "I understand how confusing this must be, but I can assure you, you're arresting innocent men."

"Let me guess, you're with these two?" At Bryan's nod, Sanders shouted to the officers standing outside. "Michaels. Keaton. Get in here and cuff him. We'll take all of them in."

"But we didn't do anything," Bryan said, stunned than anyone wearing a uniform could be so stupid.

"And once the crime scene investigators finalize their reports, you'll be free to go if they find no evidence of your involvement."

"But that could take days." Bryan dodged the officer reaching for him. He wasn't going to let himself be arrested. Lysander would never let him live it down. He stilled when the other officer, Keaton, pulled his weapon. Shit. He couldn't take the chance of a bullet ricocheting off his shield and hitting some innocent bystander outside.

Glaring at Sanders, he didn't resist further when the handcuffs were locked around his wrists.

"It won't be days." Sanders' grin was unnerving. "It will take at least a week to investigate the scene. Who knows what could befall Mr. Rossi in the vampire cells during that time?" Sanders turned to Carlos. "Or would you miss being with your friends? If you'd like, I could put you in general population where there's plenty of sunlight to brighten your day."

"Sanders!" barked a voice from the door. "Did you just threaten a private citizen?"

Sanders spun around. "Chief. What are you doing here?"

"I came to see why my officers were arresting innocent men." The Chief of Police walked into the room, followed by Roman and Eric.

"Sir. These are known associates of Rossi, a person of interest in this crime."

"These are Prince Roman's men. Release them at once."

"But sir…"

"Now, Sanders. And report to me back at the station. It's obviously time to schedule you for another round of sensitivity training."

"But this is Rossi. He's a piece of garbage vampire who's always up to no good."

"Sanders, if you want to keep your badge, you'll shut your mouth." The Chief's scowl was turned on the officer holding a gun on Bryan. "Keaton, harness that weapon immediately. Expect to face disciplinary action for drawing on an unarmed civilian."

"But he was resisting arrest."

"And why were you arresting him?"

"Sanders told me to."

"Is he the Officer in Charge?"

"No, sir. Davenport is."

"And where is Davenport?"

"Investigating the bodies."

"And what were the rest of you supposed to be doing?"

"Interviewing the witnesses dispatch said were on-site." The officer shrank back from the Chief's glare.

"And why haven't you done that?" the Chief of Police growled.

Office Keaton swallowed audibly, then said, "We haven't found them yet."

"That's because you idiots were too busy arresting them," he thundered at his officers, who cringed from the fury on his face. "If you morons have messed up this investigation, you will be relieved of duty, without pay, until I have time to forget your idiocy of today."

"Sir, you can't discipline us because of Rossi's actions. You know he's at the bottom of whatever happened here."

Bryan was worried the Chief broke a tooth with how hard he clenched his jaw.

"Michaels, arrest Mr. Sanders. I want him booked for assault, interfering in an active investigation, perpetuating a hate crime, and whatever the hell else I can come up with to keep this idiot out of uniform. I'll write up my report when I get back to the station."

"Sir?"

"Now, Michaels.".

Bryan felt the cold metal fall from his wrists when the officer removed the cuffs. He brought his hands from behind his back and rubbed the indentations marking his skin with a sigh of relief.

Carlos smirked at Bryan when he snapped the chain holding his arms behind his back and then popped the metal rings off his wrists. Gideon snorted and followed Carlos' example. Bryan flipped them both off.

"Thank you, Chief." Roman came to stand beside Bryan, putting his hand on his shoulder. "I appreciate your assistance in clearing up this misunderstanding."

"No thanks are required, Prince. I'm grateful you let me deal with my men instead of taking matters into your own hands. Their families would have mourned their loss." The four men in question jerked, their eyes flashing to Roman.

"Indeed." Roman's cold eyes landed on Sanders. "Be advised I plan on pressing charges against one of your officers."

"Understood. I'll have the arrest report ready for your signature whenever it's convenient for you to come to the station."

"Thank you, Chief. I'll be there first thing in the morning."

The Chief's eyebrows went up. "The morning?"

Roman grinned. "Yes. First thing."

The Chief nodded. "It will be waiting for you." He pointed at Michaels, who had locked a sullen Sanders in handcuffs, then at Keaton. "You two dumbasses can escort the prisoner to the car and drive him to the station. I'll expect your written reports of what happened here to be on my desk when I get there."

"Yes, Chief."

"Chauncey, you follow them and have your report waiting as well."

"Yes, Chief."

Bryan waited until the officers had left the room before whispering to Roman. "How'd you know we needed help?"

"Max called and asked me to contact the Chief."

"Good thing he thought of that. If he'd tried to stop Sanders, he'd probably have been arrested too."

"Officer Davenport suggested it once he realized what was happening with Carlos. He felt having the Chief here to straighten it out would be faster than trying to get all of you released once you were at the station."

"Good call. I imagine our paperwork would have gotten lost if they'd managed to book us." He glanced over to Roman. "How did you manage to get here so quickly? That only took a few minutes to escalate."

"I'm a fast runner."

Bryan snorted. "True. And the Chief?"

"He was just around the corner following up on another case. I met him out front."

"Luckily for us."

"Indeed. You realize Lysander will not let you live this down."

Bryan sighed. Wasn't that the truth.

"Prince Roman."

Roman turned. "Yes, Chief."

"If your men are agreeable, Davenport would like to speak with them when he's finished with the victims."

"We'd be happy to, Chief," Carlos said, dropping the broken handcuffs into the Chief's hand. "As a law-abiding citizen, I consider it my duty to assist the police in any way possible to help them in their ongoing mission of maintaining law and order."

Bryan rolled his eyes. Roman's body shook with silent laughter.

* * *

"And what did we learn tonight, dragon?"

"That you know what you're talking about. And I should listen to whatever you say." Gideon chuckled. "Though I admit to finding the whole experience rather interesting. I've never been arrested before."

"Meh. It's not that exciting. And the food sucks. Maybe next time you'll pay attention to what I tell you before the cuffs go on."

"Yes, treasure."

Bryan left the couple to their teasing and joined Max at the window that overlooked the empty parking lot of the club.

"Did you and Davenport find any more clues around the bodies?"

"No."

"What are we going to do now?"

Max turned to him. "Nothing changes. After we're done here, we're running more surveillance on Baxter's house. Gideon and Carlos need a chance to become familiar with the layout."

"Do you think that's where the auction is going to be held?"

"No." Max crossed his arms and leaned against the window. "It'll be in another location."

Bryan frowned. "Then why are we worrying so much about Baxter's house?"

"Because we're going in there after we're done rescuing Stephanie and the other girls. With the amount of security he has on the place, Baxter has a lot more going on than just one slave auction."

Bryan's stomach twisted. He hoped whatever captives they found were still alive when they got there. And unharmed.

* * *

"Are you aware someone's watching us?" Gideon whispered from his place on the rooftop.

"Yeah," Max said, glancing toward the window where yesterday's shots had come from. "We've stumbled into someone else's operation."

"Is that something we need to worry about?"

"No. We'll proceed as planned and hope they stay out of our way."

"Good enough."

"At least they're not shooting at us this time?" Bryan muttered.

Carlos snorted. "They shot at you. Did you get hit?

"No. Max said they weren't being serious about it." Bryan shook his head. "It felt damned serious to me."

Carlos snickered. "Maybe we'll get lucky and they'll shoot at us tonight."

"Lucky?" Bryan stared at the insane vampire. Carlos had the audacity to wink. "You're an idiot."

Both of them snickered until Max hissed at them to be quiet. Carlos glanced at Max, then for some reason began to laugh harder.

He really was an idiot."

Chapter Nine

The night of the auction…

Bryan settled the jacket on his shoulders, adjusted his tie, then tugged on the cuffs of both sleeves. "How do I look?"

Max looked up from the listening device he'd been fiddling with for the last thirty minutes and shrugged. "Fine."

Bryan narrowed his eyes then turned back to the mirror. Even with having to wear the protective vest, his quickly altered suit jacket had been cut in such a way that he looked sleek and refined. And rich. Which was exactly what he'd been going for. "I think I look better than fine. I'm sure many would agree."

Max tossed the black box to the bed. "What's wrong with fine? I like fine. Fine is great. You look fine. Nobody else needs to weigh in."

Bryan's eyes widened. "Are you okay? You seem a bit tense."

"I'm fine." The snap in his tone said otherwise.

Bryan studied Max's reflection, trying to figure out what was wrong with him. Max had been getting increasingly snarlier the last couple of days. And if his shoulders got any tighter, something was going to break.

Max snatched the box off the bed and marched over to Bryan, shoving it in his hand. "Put these on. We're leaving soon."

Bryan accepted the pieces of technology. "You have the address?"

"Yes. It came in about five minutes ago."

"Did you tell Gideon and Carlos?"

Max glared at Bryan. "This isn't my first mission."

"Sorry. I'm a little wired."

"I'd rather you be worried. A lot could go wrong."

"I trust you, Max. I know you'll keep me safe."

Max fumbled and almost dropped the empty box Bryan handed back. Holding back a grin at so easily flustering his mate, Bryan turned to the mirror to put on the devices.

Bryan trusted him? Max had been nothing but a right surly bastard for days and he had the nerve to say he trusted him. Max wasn't sure he trusted himself at this point. He tossed his backpack over his shoulder and stormed out of the room, hoping the other two were ready. They needed to get moving if they were going to make it to the auction on time.

* * *

When Bryan reached for the door handle after they pulled up to the curb, Carlos cleared his throat. He quickly snatched his hand back, remembering he was supposed to wait for Carlos to open his door. Shit. He wasn't even out of the vehicle and he'd already made his first mistake on this undercover assignment.

"Sorry," he muttered under his breath.

"It's fine," Max said. "I know this goes against your nature, but you have to remember to act entitled and indifferent."

'Okay." Bryan drew a deep breath and held it for a few seconds before blowing it out. He was the Galway Clan leader. All he had to do was act like his mother. He had this. Nodding his readiness at Carlos, he waited for the vampire to come around and open his door.

"Are you wearing the listening device?" Max asked.

"Yes."

"Show me."

Bryan dutifully turned his head so Max could look in his ear, then pulled his jacket open to show Max the tiny microphone pinned to his shirt pocket.

"Good. Now make them disappear."

Bryan rolled his eyes but did as Max had asked.

Max's eyes narrowed. He turned Bryan's head back and forth and looked at his shirt pocket from multiple angles.

"Do I pass inspection?"

"I feel a slight buzz from the magic, but I don't see anything." He pulled Bryan's jacket back in place. "You'll do."

Max felt a buzz? What was that about? Before he could ask, Carlos opened the door.

"We've arrived at your destination, sir." A white-gloved hand reached into the vehicle.

"Wait." Max gripped his bicep "I need you to be sure you're ready for what you'll see in there."

"We've already gone over this, Max. I'll be fine."

Max shook his arm. "Listen to me. Even with everything you've experienced recently, you're still remarkably untouched. I don't think you truly understand the evil people are capable of. Especially a vampire like Baxter. What you find inside may leave a mark not easily erased."

"Is it going to be worse than anything the Elders or the demon have done?"

"It's possible."

Really? What could be worse than the demon? For a moment he was filled with misgivings, then he pushed them aside. "I have to do this, Max. We can't let them sell those girls."

"I know. Just remember, whatever you see in there, we'll be getting them out."

Bryan swallowed hard and nodded.

"You probably won't be able to talk freely once you get inside. If you need assistance, I want you to do whatever is necessary to let me know."

"What if it puts Stephanie in danger?"

"I mean it, Bryan. Whatever you have to do." Max's intense gaze burned.

"Okay." Bryan pulled his arm free and climbed out of the vehicle. Carlos took a step back, allowing him room to move past. Bryan met his gaze and tipped his head minutely in acknowledgement of Carlos' silent encouragement. Squaring his shoulders, he strode confidently toward the non-descript metal door Max had said was the entrance to the auction.

Bryan looked for a buzzer, but the only things breaking up the smooth surface of the door were the small hole at eye level and a miniature speaker set just below it. Eyeing the speaker, he waited for whoever was manning the door to say something, but it remained stubbornly silent. He was thinking he'd have to find another way in when he remembered the special knock.

Bryan dutifully rapped out the rhythm Trux had demonstrated. When nothing happened, he realized the doorkeeper was probably waiting for the secret word. Trying not to feel stupid, which was difficult with Carlos laughing in his ear, he said, "Xanadu." The speaker finally crackled to life.

"Identification."

Bryan frowned. They'd received clear instructions that all personal identification and electronic devices were to be left behind. His pockets were empty except for the black disc Trux had given them. Shit. The black disk. Pulling it from his pocket, he held it up to the tiny hole. A moment later, a lock clicked and the door opened with a low whoosh. Forcing himself not to look back, Bryan stepped inside.

* * *

Following the steward who had greeted him at the entrance, Bryan glanced around the dimly lit hallway lined with doors. There was no sign that anyone was there.

"Am I the first one to arrive?"

The steward slowed and glanced over his shoulder. "Not at all. In actuality, you are among the last to arrive."

"I'm surprised I don't see anyone. I'd hoped for an opportunity to study my opponents."

The steward's sharp intake of breath alerted Bryan to his error. When the man turned to face him, the withering look he gave Bryan almost made him take a step back. "One does not attend a premier event such as this to study one's opponents. Each guest must decide for themselves the value they place on the incomparable merchandise being offered. A connoisseur of the rare and exotic will intrinsically understand that no price is too high to attain their greatest desire."

"Of course. Please acc…."

"Furthermore, all who attend are given assurances that every measure will be taken to preserve their identities. Master Robertson has a reputation for complete discretion, which our esteemed guests have come to rely on." His eyes narrowed suspiciously. "Something you should know."

Damn it. Not two minutes in and he was already under suspicion. Forcing his body to stay relaxed, Bryan said, "I mean no insult to Master Robertson. His reputation precedes him."

"Yet you enquire about the others?"

"I've found in these situations, knowledge of one's opponents can mean the difference between victory or defeat."

The steward looked down his long, patrician nose and sniffed. "You will not have that advantage this evening."

"Which is unfortunate."

Disdain filled eyes raked over Bryan. "The Master has exacting standards. Available spots for those eligible to attend are in high demand and unattainable to any but a select few. I am most curious how one such as yourself received one?"

Shrugging carelessly, Bryan brushed an invisible speck of dust from his jacket sleeve. "When one has a flawless pedigree, unlimited funds to use as one wishes, and knows the right people, anything is possible." Bryan cocked an eyebrow. "Wouldn't you agree?"

"Indeed." Sniffing, the steward continued down the corridor, coming to a stop before a plain black door adorned by a stylized golden eight. "This will be your private room for this evening. Once everyone has arrived, the curtain on the far wall will retract to reveal the treasures being offered. On the table is a tablet on which you will make your offers. If you are fortunate enough to place the winning bid, you will use the tablet to arrange for immediate payment. When Master Robertson has confirmation that the funds have been received, then, and only then, will the transfer of ownership take place. Do you have any questions?"

"No. That seems pretty straightforward to me." Bryan tipped his head at the manservant before walking into the room, drawing a relieved breath when the door closed, leaving him in solitude.

"You're in. Nicely done."

Was Max out of his mind? He'd almost screwed up the entire mission.

Max continued. *"When you sit down, I want you to carefully look around for hidden cameras. Don't say anything if you find them. They're likely to be outfitted with highly sensitive microphones."*

Drawing on centuries of breeding, Bryan undid his jacket and casually sat in his chair, portraying an air of entitled ennui. He cast out a delicate web of magic. Five spots immediately pinged. Fainter signals came from the rooms to either side of him, confirming that all of them were under surveillance. He just needed a way to let Max know.

"If you've found them, cough."

Bryan brought his fist to his mouth and quietly cleared his throat.

"You're going to need to be extremely careful of your body language. It'll be the thing that gives you away if you don't pay attention."

Right. Bryan slouched in his chair and folded his arms across his chest as he stared blankly at the floor to ceiling curtain. After a few minutes, he shifted restlessly in his seat. Time passed slowly. After another few minutes, Bryan leaned forward in his chair and tapped his fingers rhythmically on the table, wondering how the other "guests" were passing the time.

"Two more people have arrived. Things should get started soon."

Finally. Bryan slid the tablet over and scrolled through the screens, which didn't take long. There was a window for him to place his bids and a portal to arrange for payment. Nothing more. Huffing out a breath of impatience, Bryan pushed the tablet to the side and leaned back in his chair.

After what he estimated to be about thirty minutes, a hidden speaker came to life. "Welcome, honored guests. We have amazing delights in store for you this evening. For those who are decisive and fearless, tonight may provide an opportunity to walk away with your greatest desire. Be bold, so you don't leave emptyhanded."

The black drape slowly moved to the side, revealing a spotlight-lit pedestal.

A pained mewl crawled up his throat.

"Steady, Bryan. Remember. We're going to get them out."

"Our first lot on offer is a lovely rose recently imported from England. As you can see, this delicate bud has yet to bloom, the dew of innocence still fresh on the petals. Handled with care, this particular blossom should provide years of pleasure before its natural beauty fades. Opening bid will be fifty thousand, increasing in increments of twenty-five."

"Holy fuck. How young is she?"

Bryan could barely hear Carlos' voice over the thundering of his heart as he stared into the terrified cerulean blue eyes of the girl on the pedestal. She couldn't have been more than twelve. What kind of monster would kidnap and sell an innocent little girl? He couldn't imagine anyone would actually bid on someone as young as her.

It didn't take long to find out how wrong he was. Bile rose in his throat when the offers quickly reached one hundred and fifty thousand. Then two-fifty. The bidding continued furiously until it reached four hundred thousand. Spots appeared before his eyes.

"Shit. He can't do it. We need to get him out of there."

A whimper fell from Bryan's mouth before he could stop it.

"Bryan. Bryan. Listen to me, damn you. We're going to save them."

Bryan sucked in a breath, remembering why he was here.

"Going once, going twice, sold to the gentleman in room number nine. Bidding on lot number one is now closed." A whirring sound filled the air when the drapes closed, covering the window in a wall of black.

The man in the next room had bought that beautiful young girl? Bryan's magic flared as he glared at the partition between him and the person about to die.

"Stop whatever you're planning on doing. You need to control yourself."

Fine. If Max wouldn't let him put an end to the bastard next door, he'd shut this place of horrors down. Clenching his fists, Bryan gathered his magic, preparing to unleash a ball of energy that would fry every electrical component in the building.

"Bryan Galway. You will stop right now!" Max's bellow hurt his ears, shocking him out of his madness.

Whirring sounded as the drapes began to move.

Counting to ten, Bryan had himself under control and ready to view the next victim by the time the curtain pulled fully to the side. Vibrant green eyes, burning with anger, moved from one viewing window to the next as the naked goddess on display glared with scathing fury at all of the participants. Bryan silently applauded the way she cursed the invisible watchers, first with her eyes and then with her mouth, if he was reading her lips correctly.

"Our next lot is a magnificent emerald that has been harvested locally. As you can see, the raging flame at the core of this spectacular gem has been left intact. Care must be taken with this dangerous treasure lest its fire consumes the unwary. Only the bravest of hearts would dare to add this untamed jewel to their collection. The starting bid is seventy-five thousand."

"That must be Stephanie. Wait until the initial bids are made, then join in when it starts to slow down."

Bryan watched as Stephanie put her hands on her hips, her proud body language daring them to bid on her. If any of these fools thought they'd be able to tame her, they were grievously mistaken. She had the look of someone who would fight to the end. Prepared to break before she could be made to bend.

Bryan reached for the tablet and entered in his bid. It held steady for a moment before a higher bid came in. Not caring how reckless it might appear, he doubled his original bid. When it was topped, he doubled it again. It held steady on the screen for a full thirty seconds before turning red.

"Going once, going twice, sold to the gentleman in room number eight. Bidding on lot number two is now closed."

Bryan waited for the drapes to close but they remained open. He jerked in surprise when three large men entered the display area and dragged a kicking and screaming Stephanie off the pedestal and out the exit. What the hell?

He jumped out of his chair when the door to his room opened, revealing the steward standing in the hallway.

"Come with me please, sir."

Bryan frowned. "Is there a problem?"

"Master Robertson would like a private word with you."

Chapter Ten

Bryan followed the steward, his stomach in knots as he wondered which mistake had given him away. And there was no doubt he'd been found out. The curtains not closing had been a big clue.

As was the fact that the steward refused to answer any of his questions as he led Bryan on a circuitous route through the place, backtracking down numerous corridors. An obvious delaying tactic since the place wasn't that big. When they passed the same fake Ming vase displayed on an authentic Queen Anne table for the third time, he began to worry about why Baxter needed so much time to prepare for him.

Damn it. He should have listened to Max and bid slower, but the thought of dragging out the bidding on Stephanie had made him physically ill. His only hope now was to play off his aggressiveness as determination to win.

After a few more minutes of aimless walking, the steward stopped in front of a set of mahogany doors. Bodyguards stood on either side. Shit. The guard standing on the right was Jazz, the mercenary who'd fought with Max a few nights earlier.

Bryan quickly lowered his head so that his bangs dropped forward and covered part of his face.

The moment Bryan stepped into the room he was surrounded by four guards. Two of them grabbed his arms and held him in place, while the remaining two stood between him and the only way out.

"Well, well, well, who do we have here? If it isn't the powerful and fearless leader of Clan Galway." A vampire dressed in a maroon velvet tuxedo jacket trimmed in black glided toward him.

Bryan tensed. "Master Robertson, I presume?"

"Yes." The vampire came to a stop before Bryan. "I've been given some rather disturbing news about you." He tapped a finger on Bryan's chest. "You've been a bad boy, coming here under false pretenses."

"I have no idea what you've been told, but I'm here for the same reason as your other guests."

"That's not what I hear. You were described as a man of honor. A defender of the innocent. One who upholds the law and makes accountable those who break it."

Bryan waved his hand airily. "That's yesterday's news. You should find another source for your information. Perhaps someone more aware of current events."

"Is that right? You're saying you're not a champion of the downtrodden, a protector of the helpless, the savior of innocents?"

"That becomes tiresome after a while." Bryan made sure his voice held nothing but boredom. "Recently, I've discovered a passion for the darken pleasures. Something to fire up the blood."

"I wonder." Baxter tapped his lip. "I find it intriguing that a person of your distinction managed to come into possession of an invitation to my little event? You don't seem the type to covet the treasures I have to offer."

"There's nothing mysterious about it. The mundane becomes boring after a while. One should sample all the pleasures life has to offer. Wouldn't you agree?"

Baxter called over his shoulder. "What do you think of that, Mr. Frone?"

Bryan's stomach dropped when Jillian's father, Richard, stepped around the corner.

"He's lying. No way would Galway ever participate in a slave auction."

"Silence." Baxter's hand flashed out and slapped Richard across the face. "You do not refer to my collection of succulent blooms and sparkling gems in such a vulgar manner. To compare the delights I offer to those astute enough to appreciate their singular beauty to something as unrefined and common as a slave auction would cost you your head if my esteemed guests overheard. Know that I am considering it anyway."

"My sincerest apologies, Master Robertson." The scarlet handprint on Richard's cheek stood out in sharp contrast to his ashen skin.

After another withering glare at Richard, Baxter turned back to Bryan. "What were we discussing before we were so rudely interrupted? Ah, yes," he said, snapping his fingers. "My pet magic-user has accused you of being a fraud. Explain your intentions in coming here."

"I'm here for the same reason as your other invited guests."

"You're a liar, Galway." Richard shook his finger at Bryan. "You're all about lost causes and protecting the weak. The only reason you'd be caught dead in a place like this is if you were up to no good."

Bryan put as much condescension in his voice as possible when he said, "Don't pretend you know anything about me, Richard. We rarely crossed paths."

"I know enough to know you're lying."

"You know nothing. While you've been playing mundane power games to rise above your standing, I've been exploring new avenues of entertainment."

"Let's see, shall we?" Baxter snapped his fingers. Three guards dragged a still struggling Stephanie into the room. "You seemed quite taken with my Louisiana Emerald."

Bryan kept his muscles relaxed. His and Stephanie's lives depended on how well he played his part. Tipping his head, he examined her from head to toe, stopping at strategic points en route. The scornful glare she gave him would have made him falter in any other situation. In this case, it gave him hope she would come out of this experience mostly unscarred.

Finally finished his perusal, Bryan allowed a lecherous smile to cross his face. "I like her fire. She will add an element of excitement to my life."

"Interesting. I took you for the sort who would rather hide from conflict."

Bryan barely controlled his flinch when the vampire's insight hit his most vulnerable point.

Baxter shook his head. "No. She's not for you. I doubt you would be able to handle her fire."

Bryan laughed. "I'm the only one who would be able to tame her. Your other guests would end up snuffing her flame and destroying everything that makes her unique."

Richard took a step toward him, stopping when Baxter raised his hand. "You're full of shit, Galway. Everyone knows you like boys. You wouldn't know what to do with a real woman."

Bryan raised his eyebrow. "As I said before, I'm trying new things. Unlike yourself, who's still crawling at the feet of those more powerful than you."

Richard rushed him, punching Bryan in the jaw. "Watch what you say, asshole. I'm giving Master Robertson access to my magic in return for his help in finding Jillian. But tonight, I'm earning a special bonus, because I'm giving him you, Galway. We'll see who's crawling at whose feet now."

"What are you talking about?"

"This." Baxter nodded to the guards surrounding Bryan.

Before he could react, a metallic cuff locked around his wrist. The moment it snapped shut, pain flooded his body. Bryan screamed and reached for his magic but it fled from his grasp. Panicked, he tried again to grab it, but the golden wisps pulled free from his hold and floated just beyond his reach.

"My magic. What did you do?" Bryan shouted again as fire burned through his system. His knees buckled from the agony of his magic being leached from him, cell by burning cell, as his power was stolen from him.

"Bryan." Max's voice was loud in his ear. *"Talk to me. What's happening?"*

"It's my magic now," Baxter mocked. "The bracelet on your wrist gives me total control over it. You'll only be able to access it at my behest."

"Fuck. He's a sitting duck without his magic. We need to get him out of there."

"No!" Bryan yelled. They couldn't risk the girls' safety because of him.

"Oh, yes," Baxter said gleefully.

"Hold on, Bryan. We're coming."

He tried to tell Max to stay away but new pain racked his body. His shrieks of pain drowned out anything else that was said. By the time it receded, only the guards' holds on his arms was keeping him upright. He glared at Baxter through tear-clogged eyes.

"Get this thing off me."

"Why would I want to do that after all the effort I took to put it on?" The cruel twist in Baxter's smile chilled Bryan to the bone. "I have the great Bryan Galway exactly where I want him."

Bryan screamed when fire lit up his system again. This time it seemed to last for hours before finally fading. Bryan groaned when the last spark left his body, his limbs twitching as he hung limply in the guards' hold, his sweat-drenched head flopping forward. When he was finally able to lift it, Baxter's grinning face filled his vision.

"Did I forget to mention that I also control your pain?" He tapped Bryan's wrist. "This cuff was designed for the sole purpose of controlling a magic-user's power. One of my ancestors commissioned a set of them." His laughter boomed through the room. "I'm sure you'll appreciate the irony in knowing the first magic-user to ever wear them was none other than the man who created them. He served my family for centuries."

"Centuries?" The thought of the vampire having control of his power for mere minutes made him nauseous. Centuries would drive him mad. And praying for death.

"In my family, we believe that the safest magic-user is the one you control." He snapped his fingers. "Speaking of which." He nodded to the guard standing next to Richard. Before Richard understood the threat, a matching cuff was fastened around his wrist. When he fell screaming to the floor, Baxter grinned at Bryan. "You see. Why would I settle for one magic-user when I can control two?"

Richard cried out from where he lay curled on the floor. "Why are you doing this? We're supposed to be partners."

Baxter looked at him with contempt. "My family does not work with magic-users. We control them. Or we kill them." His fervor when he said kill was chilling. But the way he licked his lips when his eyes locked on Bryan filled his veins with ice.

"I'm sorry, Max," Bryan whispered, praying that his death didn't kill his mate.

* * *

"We need to get to him now." Max threw open the door of the vehicle and started running down the street toward the auction house.

Carlos tackled him to the ground. "Stop. You can't just go running in there. Not if we want to keep the girls safe."

"Damn it." Max pushed him off and got to his feet, feeling like he was being torn in two. His head was telling him to remember the mission but his heart was screaming louder to save his mate.

Gideon rushed up to them. "Give me a chance to nullify the magical shield. Once it's gone, I'll get the two of you past any other magical obstacles. Then we…."

They froze, staring at each other in horror when they heard Baxter discover Bryan's earpiece. His mate's scream of agony almost drove Max to his knees. Every instinct he had was telling him he needed to get to Bryan before it was too late. Praying to the Goddess he'd get there in time, he rushed toward the building, only to be pulled back by Carlos.

"Get your hands off of me," he hissed, slashing at Carlos, who dodged back. "I need to get in there before he kills Bryan."

"Wait until Gideon nullifies the shield."

"Shit." Max squeezed his eyes shut as he tried to get his head in the game. His mate's screams were making it hard to think. Opening them, he pleaded, "Hurry, Gideon. Please."

"I'm going now."

Carlos slipped something over Max's head. He shoved it under his shirt, not taking his eyes off Gideon as he flew to the rooftop.

Carlos tracked his mate's flight. A moment later, he nodded to Max. "He's in. Let's go rescue your mate.

* * *

Sharp nails plucked the earbud from Bryan's ear, slicing his eardrum in the process. His breath locked in his lungs when the new pain hit his system.

"Tell me who Max is?"

Bryan blinked watery eyes as Baxter's face flickered in and out of focus. Claws raked down his chest, but he felt no pain.

"What's this?"

He felt a tugging, then heard the tearing of cloth as his shirt was ripped from collar to waist.

"Kevlar? You wore body armor into my place? What were you planning on doing here?"

Spittle dribbled from Bryan's mouth when he tried to answer. Then pain exploded in his face when his cheekbone shattered from the force of Baxter's hit.

"Get that fucking thing off of him right now."

Bryan fell to the floor when the mercenaries let go of him to pull the vest off his limp body. He was hoisted back up before he had time to catch his breath. This time, he screamed when Baxter's claws slashed his chest.

"Answer me before I strip the flesh from your bones. Who is Max?" A clawed hand latched onto his chin and wrenched his head back. Red tinted eyes locked on Bryan's. The hand slowly closed, Baxter's long nails puncturing Bryan's cheeks as his jaw bone crumbled beneath the pressure.

A cough sounded from the mercenary to his left. "Mr. B. If you break his face, he won't be able to answer your questions."

"An unfortunate truth." Baxter's fingers slid from Bryan's cheeks with soft sucking sounds when his nails pulled free. He stepped back, licking the blood from the tips as he studied Bryan through narrowed eyes. Then he smiled.

Bryan screamed, red bubbles spilling from his mouth when a clawed forefinger stabbed above his collarbone and sliced down to his abdomen, opening the skin of his torso as easily as pulling down a zipper. When it reached the bottom of his stomach, the claw stopped, the tip still embedded deeply in his flesh.

"Tell me who sent you before I finish gutting you." Baxter's finger twitched when he leaned closer, the emotionless cruelty in his voice paralyzing Bryan with fear. "I will have my answers, magic-user. Speak now before I decide I only need one pet."

"Get your hands off of him, Baxter, before I tear them from your body."

Baxter swung around, his claw slicing across Bryan's abdomen. Black rolled across Bryan's vision when something slithered from the opening.

"Max," Baxter shouted, charging across the room.

"Oh, fuck," whispered the mercenary to Bryan's left.

He was lowered to the floor. Hands shoved his insides back through the slit. Then he felt pressure as something was placed over his injury. Bryan sank into the darkness before he thought to ask why they were helping.

Baxter slashed at Max as they circled each other, trying to draw him out. Max waited, then feinted left, his nails swiping at Baxter when he rushed him. Too late, he saw the blade attached to Baxter's elbow. It sliced across Max's ribs, slitting his shirt from front to back.

"Kevlar? What the fuck is with everyone wearing Kevlar today?"

"Better that than a vampire who uses knives," Max sneered. "What's wrong? Afraid you'll chip a nail?"

"Fuck you, Max. At least I'm not a coward wearing a vest."

"You know I'm no coward." Max darted in and slashed Baxter's face before the vampire could move out of his reach.

"I know the old Max wouldn't have worn one." Baxter's clumsy counterattack was easily avoided.

"It keeps my Consort happy."

"Your Consort must think you're weak."

Max laughed, knowing that couldn't be further from the truth. His reaction startled Baxter. When he dropped his guard, Max rushed in and scored a hit across his chest.

Baxter hissed and moved further back. "Why are you even here? You have no cause to attack my place."

"You took something of mine."

"That's a lie. I have nothing of yours…." His voice faded as his eyes flicked toward Bryan. "Him? That's who you're talking about?"

"Never again will I let you harm one of mine."

"Fuck you!" Baxter yelled, taking a wild slash at Max's face. "You know I loved your sister."

"Jenny's dead because of you."

"It was a misunderstanding."

"It was murder." Max charged at Baxter, curling his hand when his claws ripped through his side to maximize the damage. Max tossed away the chunk of flesh he tore free, planning to go after the exposed ribs next. Shouting to be heard over Baxter's cries of pain, he asked, "Where's your wife? Did you bring her with you?"

"You leave Celeste out of this." Holding a hand to his healing side, Baxter almost took Max by surprise when he came in low.

At the last minute, Max somersaulted over him and raked his claws down Baxter's unprotected back when he landed. "She's dead once I've ended your little operation."

Staggering to his right, Baxter sneered. "My little operation spans the globe, asshole. My partners will ensure you can't get near Celeste."

"They can't stop me if they're dead." Max circled, waiting for his moment. There. Satisfaction filled him when Baxter's rib bones snapped like twigs in his hand. The claws that dug into his shoulder blade were a small price to pay when Baxter stumbled back and fell to one knee, blood pouring from the gaping hole in his side.

Moving in for the kill, Max aimed for Baxter's neck. A groan from Bryan distracted him just enough for Baxter to dodge the lethal blow, Max's claws tearing through his shoulder instead of his throat.

"Fucker. You'll pay for that." Baxter rolled to the side, then lurched to his feet. He pulled a twelve-inch dagger out of his boot, gleefully brandishing an ebony blade with a brilliant red ruby inset into the pommel. Its razor-sharp edge glinted in the light, silver sparkles glittering at the pointed tip.

Instinct had Max diving to the side. He rolled to a stop ten feet away, a klaxon warning of danger sounding in his head.

"Smart move," Baxter slid closer. Max stepped back, keeping distance between them. Baxter flipped the blade to his other hand. "This little beauty can cut through anything. Let's see how your Kevlar holds up against it." He lunged forward. Max easily evaded his move.

Keeping his eyes firmly locked on Baxter, Max watched for the tell signaling his next attack. When it finally came, Max was already in motion. He dashed behind Baxter and slashed his nails down his spine before moving out of reach.

Baxter turned awkwardly, pain distorting his expression as he waved the spelled dagger wildly in the air. His eyes flickered to something behind Max.

Too experienced to fall for such an obvious ploy, Max kept his attention focused on Baxter. A set of arms wrapped around him, holding him in place for the second needed for Baxter to leap toward him and plunge the dagger into his chest.

Or rather, he tried to. Instead of sinking into Max, the dagger hit something hard enough to snap the blade in half.

"What the fuck?" Shocked eyes lifted to his.

Max wrenched free of the arms holding him and slashed his claws across Baxter's neck. Baxter dropped the broken blade and grabbed for his throat. Before he could back away, Max grabbed his head and twisted it off, then turned and smashed it into the face of the guard behind him.

He raced across the room to his mate, ignoring the thud of the guard's body falling to the ground. Once he reached Bryan, he stood protectively over him, daring the other guards to come closer. Any who were foolish enough to accept his challenge were quickly dispatched.

Carlos darted through the doorway and caved in the side of the nearest guard's head. He dismembered three others as he worked his way over to Max.

As one, the mercenaries moved out of reach. One of them touched a button on his watch. "Team, fall back. We're pulling out."

"What the fuck are you talking about, Jazz? We won't get our money if we walk on the assignment."

"B is dead. The contract is void. Everyone, move out."

Carlos stepped forward to block the withdrawing mercenaries.

"Let them go, Carlos."

"Fuck that," Carlos grabbed one of the departing men by the arm.

Max pried his hand free and yanked him backward. Then had to duck the punch thrown at his head. Pushing Carlos back, Max nodded imperceptibly at the signal Ian flashed him before he ran after his team.

"What the hell was that?" Carlos' overly observant eyes flicked between Max and the empty doorway. "What the fuck, Max? Do you know him?"

"Don't worry about it."

"Like fuck. They're part of the reason Bryan was injured."

"There's more…oomph." Max's body folded around the punch to his stomach. He threw himself forward and took out Carlos' legs then scrambled up his body to pin his arms before Carlos could hit him again. "Stop. There's more going on than you know."

"All I know is that you're a prick for letting the guys who tortured your mate leave." Carlos bucked his hips, throwing him off. "You'd better have a damned good reason for letting them get away or the Consort will have your head. And I'll help."

Ignoring him, Max rolled to his feet and hurried to Bryan, who was lying too still. Dropping to his knees, his pants were instantly soaked by the pool of blood spreading around him. Shit. Bryan wasn't going to make it if Max didn't do something fast.

He slashed his wrist and held it over Bryan's mouth. Blood pooled before spilling down the sides of his face. Max swore and tore open the newly healed skin on his wrist, holding it over Bryan's mouth again. This time, Max massaged his throat, forcing him to swallow. It took what seemed like forever before the puncture wounds in his cheeks sealed over and the broken bones in Bryan's face moved back into position.

Max then removed the makeshift dressing covering Bryan's abdomen, sucking in a harsh breath when he saw the severity of his wound. Max's blood had helped slow the bleeding, but the damage Baxter had inflicted might be more than his blood could heal.

"Fuck. That bastard really messed him up." Carlos knelt on the other side of Bryan's body. "Do you want me to heal him?"

Max shook his head, not wanting to put Carlos out of commission unnecessarily. "Let me try first." Max spared him a glance as he again slashed his wrist and let his blood pour over Bryan's abdomen. "Shouldn't you be dealing with the guards?"

"Gideon took out the last of them."

Max looked up. "All of them?"

Carlos glared. "Don't worry. I told him to let your friends go."

"Thanks." The blood dripping on Bryan slowed to a stop when Max's arm healed. He looked over the wound, worried by how bad it still looked. He sliced across his wrist for a fourth time, letting the fresh blood fall to Bryan's abdomen. He anxiously watched as the wound slowly closed. Max frowned. Even with as much damage as there was, Bryan should be healing faster than this. His eyes landed on the cuff attached to Bryan's wrist. "Get that thing off of him."

"Shit. I forgot about that." Carlos slid his fingers under the band and pulled until the lock snapped. He yanked it free, then crushed the metal into a small ball before putting it into his pocket.

Max opened his wrist again and let more blood fall onto the wound. The flesh quickly pulled together, until the only sign that Bryan had nearly been eviscerated was a faint pink line running down his chest.

"Thank fuck," Carlos whispered "I don't know what the Consort would have done to us if he'd died. He's going to be pissed enough that we let his brother get hurt."

He really was. Something Max wasn't looking forward to. He sat back on his heels and pressed his palms to his eyes, trying to scrub the memory of how close Bryan had come to dying from his mind.

Carlos hissed.

Max's head snapped up. "What is it?"

In answer, Carlos pulled the torn edge of Max's shirt to the side and plucked something from his vest, holding it up between his thumb and finger.

Max's eyebrows went up when he saw it was the tip of the black dagger embedded in a small red disc that was attached to the chain hanging around his neck. Max looked down and saw the puncture in his vest above his heart. Holy shit, that had been close. He squinted at the object Carlos was holding. "What is it?"

Carlos lifted the chain over Max's head and dangled the disc in front of him. "This is one of Gideon's scales. It's supposed to protect whoever wears it. I never had a chance to test it out." He grinned at Max. "I'm glad it worked."

Max took the chain and gently touched the broken edge of the dagger's lethal point, pulling back quickly when it stung the tips of his fingers. "How'd you know I'd need it?"

"Just a feeling. Any asshole who had a way to imprison a magic-user wouldn't stop there. I knew he'd have more nasty surprises up his sleeve."

"You have no idea," Max said, thinking of the blades strapped to Baxter's elbows. He shoved the chain in his pocket, looking up when Gideon stepped into the room.

"I called Roman. He and the Consort are gathering the troops. They should be here shortly."

"Did you find the girls?"

Gideon nodded. "And boys. They were being held in separate rooms. The bastard had a second auction scheduled tomorrow."

"Son of a bitch. I didn't realize he'd kidnapped boys as well." But he really should have. "What did you do with them?"

"I put them in a couple of suites so they could shower. The Consort is bringing fresh clothes for everyone."

"Gideon, call Roman back and tell them to come in quietly. We don't want anyone to suspect there's been a change in management." Carlos smirked when Max lifted an enquiring eyebrow. "Want to help capture tomorrow's clients when they show up?"

Max looked at his unconscious mate. "It depends on how Bryan is doing." He brushed Bryan's matted hair back from his forehead and tucked it behind his ears, then pulled the torn edges of his shirt together. Sliding his arms under him, Max stood, holding his limp body close to his chest. "Help me find somewhere to lay him down. I don't want to leave him on the floor."

"I know where you can put him." Gideon exited the room and started down the long hallway, Max and Carlos following. "Care to explain why we let the mercenaries leave? Were they not partially responsible for the hurt done to your mate?"

"In a way."

"Then why let them go?"

"I can't say."

"You'll have to do better than that for the Consort. He'll be out for blood once he sees his brother. Don't let it be yours."

Max nodded, wondering how much he could reveal. The secrets were not his to share.

Gideon stopped in front of a door and pushed it open. Max brushed past him and laid Bryan down on the navy bedspread. He listened to his heartbeat for a moment, pleased to hear it was stronger. Making sure his mate was as comfortable as possible, Max stood protectively between Bryan and the door. He'd failed his mate once. He wouldn't let anything harm him again.

Muted banging sounded in the distance. "What's that?" Max asked

"I sealed the doors to the bidding rooms to keep the buyers trapped until we can have time to deal with them."

"Good," Carlos said. "We don't want any of those fuckers getting away."

"No. They will learn the penalty for buying people." Smoke drifted from his nostrils. "I'm sure the Prince and Consort will be happy to instruct them."

"Don't forget about me. I have a few lessons to pound into them as well." Carlos cracked his knuckles.

"You will have to wait your turn, treasure. The former captives also want a piece." Gideon laughed. "I had to set up protective barriers over the doors to keep them away from the buyers." He grinned at Max. "Your girl, Stephanie, was looking for an axe when I left them."

Shit. Stephanie. Max had caught a glimpse of her earlier during his fight with Baxter but had lost track of her. Afterward, he'd forgotten all about her. His entire focus had been on Bryan.

"Is she okay?"

"She's fine. Angry, but she was unharmed."

"Thank you for helping her."

"Don't thank me." Gideon smirked. "I did nothing. She managed to get free on her own."

Max's eyebrows lifted. "How?"

"By beating down her guards."

"Stephanie?" That seemed unlike the sweet girl Max remembered

"Yes. I came down the hall just in time to see her in action." He grinned. "She moves fast for a human. When they tried to shove her in the room, she smashed her head into the face of the man holding her, then kicked the other between the legs. Before they could recover, she'd pulled free and banged their heads together before kneeing them both in the face. The double-fisted chop over the backs of their necks was probably overkill, but she was pretty mad."

Max whistled. "Her dad must have taught her how to defend herself."

"Whoever it was did a great job." Gideon's head lifted. "It sounds like the cavalry has arrived. I'll go let them in. You figure out how you're going to explain this to the Consort."

Touching his mate's cool cheek, Max's heart clenched. He didn't think there were enough words in the universe to explain how he'd let Bryan get hurt. He doubted he'd use them if there were.

Chapter Eleven

Back at the Galway Mansion…

Bryan gasped and lurched forward, reflexively reaching for his stomach.

"It's okay, Bryan. You're back home."

"Max?"

"No. It's Lysander."

"I know." Bryan's lids fluttered open. "Where's Max?"

There was a rush of air and then Max appeared next to his brother.

Bryan smiled. "I thought I felt you."

"Felt me?"

He nodded. "I always know where you are."

"Interesting." Lysander's voice held nothing but amusement.

Tuning him out, Bryan kept his gaze on his mate "Thank you for saving me."

Max's face closed off. "Don't thank me for that. It was my fault you got hurt."

"No, it wasn't. It was Baxter and his mercenaries who hurt me."

"But I let you go in there. I knew something like this could happen."

"You didn't let me go anywhere. I made my own decision to go in."

"But I knew what Baxter was capable of."

"You couldn't have known how bad it would get."

"I still should have anticipated it."

"Max, stop. Even you can't control everything. I survived. That's all that matters."

"But you almost didn't. I'm sorry I didn't get to you sooner."

Bryan reached for his hand. "You got there in time to save me." An evil laugh echoed through his mind. He had to force his next words through the tightness in his throat. "Baxter is dead, right? You did kill him?"

"Yes."

Bryan blew out a breath and sagged back against the bed, his pulse settling to normal. "And the girls? Did you get them out?"

"Yes. Everyone is safe."

"Thank the Goddess for that." Bryan closed his eyes, then quickly opened them when the sadistic vampire's face filled his mind. "Sandi," he whispered, "how long do the nightmares last?"

"I'm not going to lie. It takes a while." Lysander put his hand on Bryan's arm. "Roman helped me get through them." His eyes slid sideways. "Mates help with a lot of things."

"I know." Bryan smiled at Max, then blinked and looked down at the comforter. He picked at a loose thread, wondering if he should ask, then decided to go for it. "What's wrong?"

"Nothing."

"That's not true. I can tell you're hiding something."

Max's eyes narrowed. "How?"

"I just can. What is it? Did I do something wrong?"

"No. You were amazing. And brave."

Bryan snorted and shook his head. "I made so many mistakes."

"You were brilliant. Unlike me. If it wasn't for Carlos and Gideon, it could have gone a lot worse."

Bryan didn't believe that for a minute. He touched his stomach again, surprised he'd healed so quickly. Max's warm hand landed over his, pressing against his abdomen.

"You were seriously injured. I didn't know if I could save you. But I had to try."

The penny dropped. Bryan turned his hand over and locked his fingers with Max. "You gave me your blood, didn't you?"

Max nodded.

"Thank you." He looked down at their linked hands, then up. "Are you okay with that? I know you have doubts about bonding with me."

"Do you feel any different?" Max's watchful gaze stayed on his face.

Bryan took a moment to analyze. Other than a faint soreness in his abdomen and a slight ache in his jaw, he felt remarkably well. "Not really?"

"Nothing's changed at all?"

Why did Max sound disappointed? "No. I feel pretty much the same as always."

"Then my blood didn't trigger a bond between us."

Bryan swallowed hard, then shook his head. "I don't think so, no."

"It didn't for me either."

"I'm so sorry, Max."

"We've gone over this already. It serves nothing to do so again."

"I know. It's just…I wish I could fix it."

"Perhaps we're not ready."

Bryan eyed him speculatively. That didn't sound like Max was still refusing to bond with him. If anything, it sounded like he wanted it. Which would explain his earlier disappointment. Bryan tried to tamp down the joyful hope that rose in case they didn't manage to fix their bond, but it was no use. The idea that he could one day claim Max as his true-bonded mate filled his mind, pushing aside the memories of Baxter and his torture.

Realizing Max and Lysander were waiting on his response, he murmured, "Perhaps not." Bryan cleared his throat. "So, what now? We go on as before?"

Max nodded and kept his eyes locked on Bryan's, who didn't quite understand the message they held. But what he saw gave him even more hope.

Lysander bumped the bed, breaking up the moment. When Bryan glared at him, he winced. "Sorry. I didn't mean to interrupt." He waved his hand in the air. "Carry on with what you were doing."

Bryan looked up to see that Max's expression held only his normal attentiveness, the secret message gone. He sighed. "We're done. What did you want?"

"When you feel up to it, we have some prisoners to see."

"Mother?"

"Yes. We've kept her waiting long enough. It's time to find out what she knows."

Bryan tossed back the covers and climbed shakily to his feet, taking hold of the steadying hand Max held out to him. Once he was sure he could stand on his own, he let go and smiled at Lysander and Max. "I'm ready to see her now."

"We have a debrief in Roman's office first." Max set his hand on Bryan's arm and squeezed, the warmth of his palm branding Bryan's skin. "I'll meet you and the Consort there."

Bryan rested his fingers on his tingling skin, unable to tear his eyes off his mate when Max stepped from the room and strode down the hallway. Not even to punch his idiotic brother who wouldn't stop laughing.

* * *

"Bryan. It is good to see you back on your feet."

"Thanks, Roman. Things went a little sideways on our rescue mission."

Lysander snorted. "A little?"

"Shut it."

Bryan grinned when Lysander flipped him the bird. His relationship with his brother was dependable and unchanging, bringing him balance. His eyes shifted sideways to his mate, who was standing on Roman's left. His relationship with Max, which often left him unsettled, was starting to bring him the same feeling of balance. He felt something deep inside settle at that acknowledgement.

He started to head toward the window where he always stood when Mrs. Davies' warning to take it easy flashed in his mind. He abruptly switched directions and sat on the overstuffed chair that was angled to the couch. Once he'd settled into its depths and arranged his feet on the footstool, he realized nobody was speaking. Looking up, he shook his head when he saw everyone watching him, varying degrees of concern on their faces.

"I'm fine. Just a little worn out from yesterday's events."

"Getting eviscerated will do that," Carlos teased.

"I don't recommend it." He looked over at Max and Roman. "What did you do with the girls?"

"And boys," Lysander said.

"He had boys too? Trux never mentioned that."

"He did not," Max growled. "Which makes me wonder what else he held back."

"Shit. Do you think there were more captives?"

"Not with Baxter, no."

"Then there could be others we haven't found yet." The thought made Bryan ill. Especially since there was no way to know for sure.

Max frowned, then slowly shook his head. "I don't believe so. Baxter wouldn't have left any competition alive."

"Something to be thankful for, I guess."

"Which will make tonight's auction interesting," Carlos said.

"There's an auction tonight? But there's nobody to bid on." His eyes shifted to Max. "Right?"

"Correct. We rescued the prisoners and turned the buyers over to the authorities. What was left of them." He raised an eyebrow at Carlos.

"I told you, my hand slipped."

"Uh, huh."

"I don't understand." Bryan frowned. "If Baxter's dead and there's nobody to bid on, how can there be an auction tonight?"

Carlos laughed. "Because the buyers aren't aware it's been cancelled. We thought we'd let them into the building and then show them the error of their ways."

Blue eyes filled with fear flashed in his mind. He clenched his jaw as he thought about the beautiful young girl who'd been bought by the bastard in room number nine. He hardened his voice. "I'll help."

"Settle down, tiger. You're sitting this one out."

"I am not." Bryan struggled to get out of the chair, but the cushions kept sucking him back down.

"Stop, Bryan, before you hurt yourself. Mrs. Davies threatened us if we didn't let you rest. Do you want to make her mad?" Lysander asked.

"Of course not." Letting gravity have its way, Bryan sank back into his chair, barely holding back his sigh of relief. He crossed his arms. Mostly to hide their trembling. Trying to get out of the damned chair had tired him more than he wanted anyone to know. Feeling eyes on him, he glanced at his mate, who wasn't fooled if Bryan was reading him correctly.

Turning away from his knowing look, he smiled at Roman, "You were about to tell me what happened to everyone."

Roman's expression showed he hadn't been fooled either. Damned vampires and their super senses. "We are in the process of getting them settled. Either by making arrangements to return them to their families or by providing them with accommodations."

"Good. I hope you told them they could stay here if they have nowhere else to go?"

"Max said that would be your wish. Twelve of them are currently being situated in the guest wing."

"Twelve? How many did Baxter kidnap?"

"Thirty-two. Fifteen boys and seventeen girls."

"So many," Bryan whispered.

"There will always be those willing to exploit others for financial gain," Roman said.

"At least Baxter's gone." He swallowed, his mouth suddenly dry and looked at Max. "Was he working on his own or did he have someone helping him?"

"There were others working with him. His files were extensive and contained full details of buyers' names, dates of previous auctions, locations where they grabbed their victims." Max paused. The sound of his teeth grinding was loud in the silence. "We also found records identifying the others directly involved in running the trafficking operation."

"You recognized one of the names, didn't you?" Bryan asked quietly.

He nodded curtly. "It's someone close to the General."

"Do you think they're responsible for Stephanie's kidnapping?"

"I know he is. He's a close friend of the family, so he would've been aware of her daily routine."

"Shit. What did the General say when you told him?"

"I haven't yet."

"Did you want me to come with you when you do?"

Surprise flashed in Max's eyes, before he nodded. "I'd like that."

"Okay. Let me know when you want to go."

"I will."

"Good." Bryan sat back, pleased he'd be able to support his mate with this difficult task. He turned to Roman. "What did you do with the guards and Richard?"

Carlos spoke up. "Baxter's personal guards were all killed. We let Max's mercenary friends walk away."

"You let them go?" Then the other thing he'd said registered. Bryan's head snapped to his mate. "Why did Carlos call them your mercenary friends?"

Max's eyes swam with emotions Bryan couldn't read but he stayed silent.

He turned back to Carlos, who shrugged. "Max told us to let them go. That's all I know."

"I don't understand," he whispered. "They kidnapped everyone. They held me when Baxter cut me open." The betrayal withered his happiness, anger taking its place.

Bryan pushed out of his chair, the body-sucking cushions no match for his fury, and stormed over to Max. "Why would you let them go free?"

Max ground his jaw. "I'm not at liberty to say."

"What the hell does that mean?" He crossed his arms, the pain in his heart almost too much to bear.

"It means that Max is legally obligated not to divulge any information about the men and their actions."

The lightbulb went off. "Because they're the ones who were on the undercover mission." He saw confirmation in Max's eyes, but again, he refused to speak.

"Bryan." His eyes shifted to Roman. "I trust Max and his reasons for letting the men go. Will you do the same?"

Bryan stared at his mate, his mind whirling with everything that had happened weighed against what he knew about Max. When he pushed his hurt feelings to the side and considered only the facts, the decision was easy. "I trust him."

"Then ask no further questions he is unable to answer."

"I won't." He read the relief in Max's eyes. Along with thankfulness. Giving him a nod of acknowledgment, Bryan walked back to his chair and sank gratefully into its plush cushions. "And Richard. What happened to him?"

"We put him in the cell next to Mother," Lysander said.

"I bet she's not pleased about that."

"Not even a bit. You feel up to seeing her later?"

"Sure. We need to get it over with. Besides, I'd like to have a chat with Richard."

"That should be interesting. Since we tossed him in the cell, he's done nothing but complain about us infringing on his rights."

Bryan sat up. "What rights? After working with that bastard, he has no rights. Especially since he's the reason I was discovered." His words triggered a memory. Bile rose when he glanced at his bare wrist. Swallowing hard, he choked out, "What happened to the cuff?"

"I destroyed it," Carlos said.

"And the one on Richard?"

"Destroyed as well."

"Thank the Goddess." He shivered. "I can't believe we didn't know they existed."

"Yeah. About that."

Bryan looked over when Lysander's voice faltered. "What?"

"Baxter's journal said there's another set. His father used them to capture a magic-user a few centuries back. A couple hundred years ago, he gifted the magic-user to one of his friends. Roman knew the recipient."

"Knew?"

"He's dead. We don't know what happened to the magic-user or the cuffs."

"We have to find him and destroy those cuffs." He wiped a trembling hand across his mouth. "You have no idea how it felt to be stripped of my magic. And Baxter had full control of it."

"I know, Bryan. We're already looking."

"Good."

"Roman might have a lead on them. We're just waiting for confirmation. They'll be destroyed as soon as we find them."

Bryan nodded, his heart aching for that poor nameless magic-user, imprisoned and at someone else's mercy for centuries. He would be broken and probably insane by now. Unless he was dead. For the magic-user's sake, Bryan hoped he was. The alternative was unthinkable.

Squeals of laughter floated through the open French Doors. Bryan closed his eyes and let the joyful sounds wash over him, the bright notes of laughter soothing his soul and lightening the grim direction his thoughts had gone. Opening his eyes, he smiled at his brother. "Hearing the pups' happiness helps to put everything into perspective."

Lysander nodded. "It does. But it's not just the pups. The boys and girls you rescued are playing with them." He snickered. "And Stephanie's standing guard."

"She's okay after her experience."

"She's amazing. And fierce. Nobody will be able to get near them without going through her." He grinned. "She'd make a great enforcer. I'm hoping we can convince her to stay."

Bryan expected Max to disagree, so he was surprised to see him considering the idea. Even Roman looked intrigued by the thought.

"I'll talk to her after I report to the General," Max said. "Though he might not want that for her."

"You should ask her anyway," Carlos suggested. "That girl is a fearsome fighter. If she wants to be an enforcer, I have no doubt she'll make it happen."

Bryan was thrilled that the fire he had seen in Stephanie at the auction was backed up by training. He couldn't wait to meet her in person. Once somebody told her that he was one of the good guys, that is.

* * *

The Council building dungeons, later that day…

"Mother."

"It's about time you showed up." Charlotte gracefully rose from the battered chair and dusted the front of her skirt before making her way to stand before Bryan.

He let his gaze drift to the adjoining cell where Richard was raging and pacing like a trapped beast then back to his mother who looked like she was waiting for tea to be served.

"Tell us what you know of the Elders' plans."

Her perfectly shaped eyebrow rose in an arch. "I beg your pardon."

"He said to tell us what you discovered when you were with the Elders." Lysander moved closer to the bars of her cell. "We know you gathered a great deal of information. It's time to share, Charlotte."

"How dare you speak to me in this manner? As your mother, I deserve your respect."

"You are not my mother. You are nothing more than the harpy who made my life hell."

"What did you expect me to do when your father brought home another woman's child to raise? Dance for joy? I think not." Charlotte took a step back. "You have no idea of the shadow your presence cast on my life. You were an embarrassment, proof that the man I loved and committed myself to had dallied with some floozy. The insult was more than I could bear." She walked back to the table and sat gracefully on the rickety seat.

Bryan tugged on Lysander's sleeve, pulling him away from the bars. He left his hand on his brother's trembling arm, offering what comfort he could. "I don't believe Father betrayed you."

"How can you say that? The proof is standing next to you."

"Lysander's heritage is greater than that of Father and another. He has a genetic makeup that encompasses all paranormal groups. How this was accomplished is still a mystery. The one thing I know for sure is that Father was faithful to you. It was not in his nature to be otherwise."

Charlotte got up from the table and neared them, her laser-sharp vision locked on Lysander as though looking for proof of Bryan's words. After a long moment, her gaze settled on Bryan.

"You truly believe your father was faithful?"

"I do. There is more going on in this world than we know. Lysander is part of a larger plan."

"I see." She looked over Bryan's shoulder. "What are they doing here?"

Bryan motioned for Carlos and Gideon to join them. "They are here at my request. You harmed both of them when you stole Gideon's mating talisman."

"I did no such thing. That amulet was bought and paid for in an honest exchange."

"There's no honor among thieves, Charlotte. So whatever back alley transaction you obtained it through had nothing honest about it," Carlos said. "Unless I have that reference wrong." He looked at Gideon for confirmation.

"You have the right of it, treasure." Flinty eyes locked on Charlotte. "You should be thankful you didn't kill yourself in your use of it. It has inherent protections to punish those who take ownership of it through deceitful means."

"As I said, I procured the amulet in a mutually profitable business arrangement."

"How you obtained it matters not. It was stolen and in your possession. One, possibly two, more uses of its power to attack would have resulted in your death."

Charlotte blinked. "Is that why some of the attacks did not work as intended?"

"Yes. Only my true-mate can control the magic of the talisman."

"I see." She brought her hand to her face and rested her fingers on her lips. Bryan saw the slight tremble she sought to hide. Pulling herself together, Charlotte's eyes returned to Bryan. "If you want my information, you will agree to release me."

"What about me?" Richard yelled. "You have no right to hold me like this."

Lysander stalked over to the bars and flicked his hand. Richard shouted as his body slid along the floor until he was pressed against the far wall. "You almost getting my brother killed gives me every right to do what I want. You should be thankful you can still breathe, asshole."

"You wouldn't really kill him, would you?" Carlos whispered from beside him.

"Of course not. I'm channeling you."

"Good call. Except he'd already be dead if he'd hurt Missy. You're a lot more civilized than I am."

Lysander snorted then turned and glared at Richard. "Stay there, shut up, and think of how you're going to explain your imprisonment to Jillian."

Richard gasped and rushed toward the bars, stopping when Lysander raised his hand. Rocking back on his heels, he asked, "You're going to look for her?"

"Yes. Which you'd have known if you'd bothered to ask for our help instead of making a deal with a corrupt bastard who kidnapped and sold innocent people." Sparks flashed from his fingertips.

Richard shrank back from Lysander. When he stumbled back into the wall, he slid down its surface until he sat on the floor. He didn't say another word.

Bryan bumped his brother's shoulder when he rejoined him. "Do you feel better now?"

"Little bit. You?"

"Yeah. I enjoy seeing you in action."

Lysander snickered and bumped him back.

Charlotte's fingernails tapping on the bars brought their attention back to her. She regarded Lysander with interest. "You've become more powerful since I saw you last."

"I have."

"And will you challenge your brother for leadership of the clan?"

"Not even if you paid me," Lysander scoffed. "Why would I want that headache? I have enough to do being a Consort."

"Consort?"

"Yes. While you were trying to marry me off to Jillian, I true-mated with Roman, Prince to all the vampire covens in North America."

Charlotte looked like she'd swallowed a bug.

"You greatly underestimated my brother," Bryan said. "Be thankful he gets his honorable nature from Father. Otherwise, he'd have cause to demand justice for the harm you've done to him."

She nodded, finally tearing her eyes off of Lysander to address him. "Do we have a deal? I will tell you all I have learned. In return, you will release me."

"I have my own condition. You tell me everything you either know or suspect and I will let you go free. Once I've bound your magic."

"No. I will not allow that."

"It is the only way you will be allowed out of here." Bryan locked eyes with his mother in the most intense stare-down of his life. The longer it went on, the more concerned he grew that she wouldn't back down. Even though he held all the cards, Charlotte always played to win. When the tension in the air rose to the point it started to crackle, she finally conceded.

"Agreed. I have one further condition. You and your brother will promise to get justice for your father. Ruth must pay for what she did."

"Deal," Bryan said.

"Deal." Lysander echoed.

"And done. The pact is struck," Gideon said. Dragon magic swirled around the room, coalescing around Charlotte in a spinning torrent, encasing her body in an opalescent glow that covered her from head to toe. It pulsed once, then the magic sank into her skin.

"What have you done?" Charlotte shrieked, running her hands frantically over her arms.

"Bound your powers as was agreed."

"Him," she said, pointing at Bryan with a quivering finger. "It was supposed to be him. Not you."

"I don't recall that stipulation. But not to worry. You will be unable to break the dragon magic and thus less likely to get up to mischief." Gideon snapped his fingers. The cell door opened. "You are free to leave, madam."

"I am completely defenseless now and I have many enemies." Charlotte's eyes darted to Lysander and Carlos. "How am I to protect myself?"

"You will be safe from your enemies. The estate is well guarded."

"And what of my enemies who live on the estate? How will I protect myself from them?"

Carlos suddenly jerked and made a noise that would be considered a whine if it came from anybody else. Then he began cursing.

Bryan's eyes widened when Carlos' feet slowly slid across the floor toward Gideon. What in the world?

Carlos scowled at Lysander. "Why doesn't this bullshit ever happen to you? You're the Chosen One. You should be dealing with this crap."

Lysander started laughing. "It's probably because you're so stubborn you need to be bludgeoned over the head. I listen when the universe speaks to me. You should try it sometime."

"I fucking hate being told what to do. And she bloody well knows it."

"What is it, treasure?"

"You're not going to like it."

"I'm sure it will be fine."

"It's really not."

"Anything you need, you have only to ask."

"Remember, I tried to warn you." Carlos's eyes flicked toward the cells. "I need one of your scales."

"For what?" Gideon's brow creased, then understanding flashed across his face. Smoke billowed from his nostrils. "You must be joking."

"I wish I was."

"You want to give one of my precious dragon scales, a piece of me, to that, that harridan who has been the cause of so much destruction and sorrow."

Bryan sucked in a breath as understanding hit him. Holy shit. He glanced at his brother who looked as surprised as him. "I take it you didn't see this."

"No. And I don't think Gideon's going to cooperate. Not with something that personal."

And he probably wouldn't have until Carlos smoothed his hand down Gideon's face. Which was a surprise to Bryan. Carlos never allowed anyone to see his softer side. He hadn't even been sure the vampire had one. But he was seeing it now. And it looked good on him.

Lysander bumped him. "I told you he had a good heart. He just hides it well."

Bryan couldn't tear his eyes away as Carlos kept stroking his mate's face. "I know it's invasive. And cruel to ask this of you. But I think you need to do it." Carlos glared at the ceiling again. "Otherwise, she wouldn't be so damned insistent."

"Treasure, please." Gideon's cry of distress hurt Bryan's heart.

"I'm sorry. I promise to get it back as quickly as I can."

The Dragon Prince's anguished eyes flashed to Charlotte before they closed. His fists clenched and his body trembled.

So did the ceiling.

Bryan quickly magicked up a protective barrier in case Gideon brought the building down on them. His shield meshed perfectly with the one Lysander also created.

Carlos stretched up and placed a surprisingly sweet kiss on Gideon's lips before reaching under the neckline of his shirt and removing a glistening red scale. "Thank you. I promise. As soon as I can return it, I will."

"I know, treasure. It just hurts to know who will benefit."

"In the end, it might benefit us all." Carlos again kissed him softly and smoothed a hand over his chest before he pulled back and walked over to Charlotte. He looked into his cupped hand for a long moment, gently stroking the scale, before closing his fist over it. Glaring at Bryan's mother, he said, "I give this to you freely, that it may offer protection from those who would harm you. Do not betray our trust in you." He held his fist out to Charlotte, then turned his hand over and slowly opened his fingers, dropping the scale into her waiting hands.

Bryan gasped when the scarlet disc pulsed, alive with Gideon's magic. No wonder he'd been so reluctant to give it up.

Charlotte cradled the scale close to her chest, the child's wonder in her eyes pushing aside their usual icy coldness. "Thank you for this magnificent gift." Clutching it tightly, she turned to Bryan. "I will tell you everything you need to know."

Bryan hoped the information she had was worth the price.

Chapter Twelve

Charlotte's steps faltered when she walked into her old office and saw Roman seated behind the desk. She recovered quickly, the tightening of her lips the only indication of her annoyance at having her former seat of power usurped.

Gliding gracefully across the room, she stopped beside everyone's favorite overstuffed chair and frowned. Bryan bit back a smile at the thought of his elegant mother trying to push herself out of its body-sucking cushions. She must have thought the same thing. Choosing appearances over comfort, Charlotte chose a hard backed chair that nobody, including Jinx, ever used. Moving it closer to the desk, she sat on the wooden seat, her back as rigid as the stark piece of furniture.

Folding her hands primly over her crossed knee, she nodded regally to Roman. "Prince. I see you have made yourself at home."

"To the contrary, madam. What I have done is made it a home. Something it never was under your purview."

Bryan's eyebrow lifted. Damn. Roman was ready to throw down.

Charlotte brushed off the cuff of her blouse. "Home is what you make of it. I found its streamlined elegance comforting."

"If by streamlined elegance you mean impersonal and lifeless, then yes, I imagine you did find that comforting. It was the perfect accompaniment for your cold, barren heart."

Bryan flashed his hand at Lysander. *"Do something about your mate."*

Lysander flipped him the bird. *"You do something. I'm enjoying this."*

Bryan made his eyes as big as possible. *"We don't have time for this. Make him stop."*

Lysander rolled his eyes. *"Fine. But you owe me for ruining my fun"*.

Bryan squinted. *"In your dreams, baby brother."*

Lysander's nose wrinkled. *"Asshole."*

Bryan crossed his arms and leaned back against the window, grinning smugly when his brother put his hand on Roman's arm, ending his icy confrontation with Charlotte. Feeling his cheek burning, Bryan looked to his right and found Max's cobalt blue eyes locked on him.

He raised his eyebrow in challenge. *"Can I help you with something?"*

Max stuck out his chin. *"You're both assholes."*

Bryan straightened. What the hell? He turned to his snickering brother. *"Did you show him how to do this?"*

Lysander tilted his head. *"No. He must have figured it out on his own. Probably from all the time he spends watching you."*

Bryan slumped against the window. *"Son of a bitch."*

Max snorted, his eyes sparkling. Bryan flipped off the too-pleased-with-himself vampire. While part of him was annoyed that Max had broken their brotherly code, the rest of him was thrilled he'd paid close enough attention to figure it out. Bryan's lips suddenly curled up. Max knowing what Lysander and Bryan were secretly saying could be a lot of fun. Especially if he participated. Maybe even more if he couldn't.

Lysander cleared his throat and arched his eyebrow. *"It's time to question Mother."*

Bryan tipped his head. *"Okay. Try to keep your mate under control."*

Lysander winked. *"No promises."*

Bryan snorted and turned to Charlotte. "Mother. What…." He stopped when Roman held up his hand.

"Forgive my interruption. There is one more thing I would know before we begin." Roman turned his piercing gaze on Charlotte. "How did you know where to locate Max?"

"I am not acquainted with any Max."

"Let me rephrase. How did you know where to find Bryan?"

She arched a fine eyebrow. "Since he lives on the Galway estate, it wasn't that difficult."

"Do not play games with me, madam. How did you know Bryan's location in the swamp?"

"One of the maids told me."

"Which one?"

"How am I supposed to know?" Charlotte fluttered her fingers. "They are staff. Names are irrelevant."

"Not to me."

"Then perhaps you should interview them and find out."

"Perhaps I shall." Roman's fierce gaze landed on Bryan.

"I'll have Alfred set up meeting times with all the staff. There's no telling how many of them have been compromised by Mother."

"Thank you, Bryan." Roman turned back to Charlotte. "Your spies will be found and punished for their betrayal."

"Do what you will. It is of no significance to me." Charlotte looked at the tips of her nails and rubbed off a nonexistent smudge before tilting her head at Roman. "Was there anything else?"

The sound of the vampire's teeth grinding was loud in the silence. Shit. If they wanted answers, they needed to get them before Roman tossed her back in the dungeon. Bryan stepped forward.

"Mother. What can you tell us of the Elders' plans?"

Charlotte kept her icy blue eyes locked on Roman for a moment longer before turning to Bryan. "Which plans in particular? They have developed numerous strategies."

"We stopped their campaigns against the shifters and the vampires. What else were they working on?"

"Were you aware they possess a power source that is enhancing their abilities?"

"Yes. They are in league with a demon."

Charlotte froze. "A demon? Then that is what has corrupted them."

"You knew about the demon?"

"Not as such. Zachary mentioned they had a power source that was changing them. It apparently exacerbates their darkest traits. I did not realize it was a demon." Her mouth pursed. "They are more foolish than I realized. Especially Zachary. He should know better than to consort with a demon."

"Zachary is dead," Lysander said flatly.

Charlotte's eyes widened marginally. "I wasn't aware. How did he die?"

"I'm not sure. All I know is that it had something to do with Ruth."

"He was a fool to go near her again." She leaned back and set her clasped hands on her lap. "That leaves only Ruth and Peter. They won't be able to stand against a demon."

"No, they won't. Which is why we need to send it back," Bryan said.

Charlotte gasped, leaning forward. "It has already crossed over?" Fear replaced her normally haughty expression, making his emotionally distant mother seem more approachable.

"Yes." Bryan walked closer to her. "And it will kill everyone unless we find a way to stop it. Do you know how we can do that?"

Holding his gaze, she slowly nodded. "There might be a way."

"Tell us."

"There is a prophecy that speaks of a shadow that would consume the Earth. The only safeguard against it is a relic handed down from the Goddess."

Lysander gasped. "What else does it say?"

"That the liberator would save them."

Bryan exchanged a discrete look with Lysander. "What is this liberator supposed to do?"

"I am unsure. Ruth hadn't finished deciphering it."

"Damn it. I knew that would be too easy." Lysander sat back with a thump.

"What can you tell us about the relic then?" Bryan asked. "Edgar overheard Ruth talking about it, so I'm sure you know something."

"Edgar? Who is…oh. The vampire in the ceiling. He was one of yours."

"Yes," Roman said. "Thank you for sparing him. It was an unexpected act of kindness I did not think you capable of."

"The vampire was an inconvenience I didn't have time to address." Charlotte's cool tone would have withered a lesser man. But not Roman. "Kindness is for the weak. I would never allow such an emotion to dictate my actions."

"Kindness does not make one weak. To the contrary, it takes great strength of character to show compassion for others."

"One does not rise to the top by showing compassion. That is yet another weakness I would not fall prey to."

"Then I shall retract my thanks and give them to the Goddess for preserving my vampire."

"As you should."

"Mother, as much fun as it is watching you spar with Roman, what can you tell us about the relic?" Lysander grinned when Charlotte turned her annoyed gaze on him. "You did agree to help. Or do you miss hanging with your old pal, Richard? By now, he probably wants company badly enough he'd be happy to see you."

"Do not threaten me. I have already agreed to tell you what I know."

"Then do so." All amusement fell from Lysander's face. "The longer we delay, the more likely we are to fail. Tell us what you know about the relic."

* * *

Bryan waited until Charlotte left the room, followed by Eric, her silent shadow. "What a colossal waste of time." He turned to Gideon. "I'm sorry you were forced to give up one of your scales for so little."

"We now know there is a weapon to use against the demon. The hope that information brings is worth any price."

"But all we know is that it's made of stone and hidden somewhere in New Orleans. It could take us years to find it. We don't have that much time."

"You and Max had better start looking for it then. We don't want to go up against the demon empty-handed."

Bryan's head snapped around. "What did you just say?"

Lysander blinked, then turned to Roman. "I said that out loud, right? It wasn't just in my head?"

Roman's lip twitched. "Everyone could hear your words."

"Was I speaking English?"

"Yes, beloved."

Bryan sighed. Younger brothers were a real pain in the ass sometimes.

"I thought as much." Lysander turned back to Bryan. "When was the last time you had your ears checked?"

"You're such an asshole." Choked laughter erupted behind him. "Shut up, Carlos. You're an asshole too."

"At least I don't have to look for a needle in a haystack."

"No," Gideon interjected. "Luckily for you, we're going to New York. It's time for you to meet Father."

"Fuck that. I'm going to help Max and Bryan find that needle. You can see your father by yourself."

Bryan grinned. The panic in Carlos' voice made him feel a lot better. Even if Lysander had given Max and him an impossible task to complete against an unknown, yet urgent deadline.

* * *

The Dragon Court, New York, meeting the parents…

Carlos yanked at his neck, convinced the stupid tie was going to strangle him before the evening was through.

"Stop fidgeting. We're being presented to the King shortly."

"You promised I wouldn't have to wear a stupid suit." He glared at his grinning mate. "I look like an idiot."

"You look amazing."

"And what about this bullshit ritual we have to do? You said I wouldn't have to follow any. I'm disappointed in you, dragon."

"Don't be like that, treasure. It's tradition to have a formal ceremony when the Consort is introduced to the King and Queen. To not follow custom would be disrespectful and set the wrong tone for the future." Gideon brushed Carlos' hands away from his tie and smoothed out the mess he'd made. "Wear it this one time when you are formally presented to my father. After this, I promise you can dress as you wish."

Carlos narrowed his eyes. "This better not be a trick."

Gideon winked and took hold of his hand. "Come. It's time."

At some signal he didn't catch, the guards to either side of a pair of huge oak doors pulled them open to reveal a large ballroom filled with elegant people who were not very subtly watching the doorway.

Carlos squinted, partially blinded when the light from the massive chandeliers reflected off the ridiculous amounts of jewelry the men and women were wearing.

"What the hell, Gideon?"

Gideon snickered. "Behold. The Dragon Court in their full regalia, come to meet my Consort."

Blinking to clear the spots from his eyes, Carlos looked around, his eyes widening when he noticed the men wearing tuxedo shirts with collars so high they could barely move their heads. He brushed his fingers over the top of his much lower collar, realizing he'd been provided with a stylish, comfortable version of formal wear.

"Thanks for not making me dress like those idiots."

"No need to thank me. I would never do anything that made you uncomfortable."

"Is that so?" Carlos gave him a sideways look.

Gideon chuckled. "After this initial presentation, of course."

"Of course." He looked back at the ridiculous finery of the assembled men and women. "Do they have any idea of how stupid they look?"

Gideon let out a long suffering sigh. "Unfortunately, they all think they are the height of fashion."

"Seriously? Do you not have mirrors around this place?" Carlos shook his head. "I mean, look at them. The men can't even move their heads. They look like waddling penguins when they turn to speak to the person next to them."

Gideon barely covered his laugh.

"And that man there. The one with the pointy shoes. Why would he wear something like that? If he's not careful, he's going to trip someone or gut them. Probably both." He blinked. "Unless he's some kind of assassin? Is that it? Is he actually part of a secret guild? Because that would be kind of cool."

"Sorry to disappoint you. The shoes are simply to garner attention."

"Why would he want to advertise that he's a moron?"

Gideon chuckled. "Dragons bore easily. The latest diversion making its way through the Court is trying to outdo each other with over-the-top clothing and accessories. They all hope to be the one who will start a new fashion trend."

"That's the stupidest thing I've ever heard of."

"I agree. All they're doing is making themselves look absurd." Gideon's arm settled around Carlos' waist. "I've always followed the example of my parents, which is to dress with timeless classical elegance."

Gideon led Carlos to the other side of the ballroom where the King and Queen were seated. The crowd flowed around them like water, parting when they neared then closing in behind them. The whispers about the new Consort filtered through the crowd as Gideon and Carlos worked their way across the room. Carlos let a hiss escape when he heard a couple of vampire slurs better suited for the docks. It wasn't something he'd expected to hear at a formal gathering.

Gideon cocked an eyebrow in enquiry.

"No matter how pretty they dress, your dragons are still a bunch of assholes."

"Don't forget, treasure. They're your dragons as well."

"Fuck."

An amused snort overlaid with feminine laughter came from the dais before him. Grinning ruefully at Gideon's parents, Carlos bowed with an elegant precision worthy of any pure-blooded noble. "Your Majesties."

"Carlos. How lovely to see you again." The Queen stepped from the dais and pulled him into a hug, ignoring the gasps from the crowd around them. Her eyes twinkling, Sophia hooked her arm through his. "May I present Gideon's father, King Edmund."

Keeping up the charade of a first meeting, since he and Gideon had met privately with the King and Queen the previous day, Carlos bowed again, being careful not to unbalance Sophia who hadn't let go of his arm.

Grinning broadly, the King stepped off the dais. The crowd immediately exploded with noise.

"What's happening?" Carlos whispered to Sophia.

"It is standard protocol that all must approach the King. He's breaking centuries of tradition by leaving his throne to greet you."

"Why would he do that?"

"I believe he is sending a message to the Court."

Before Carlos could ask further, the King stood before him with his hand held out. His kind, emerald eyes danced with amusement when the Court lost their minds.

Carlos took the man's hand in his and bowed his head. "Your Majesty."

"Carlos. It's good to finally meet the man I've been hearing so much about. Welcome to the family, son."

That was too much for the lady standing next to them. At the King's words, she shrieked in apparent distress, then collapsed in a faint, her overly large tiara tinkling and clinking as she fell to the ground. Concerned men and women immediately surrounded her. In their attempts to revive her, her elaborate headdress was knocked off and crushed underfoot.

Carlos turned to Sophia. "Why on earth would she faint? Shouldn't dragons be more robust than that?"

"It's nothing but an act," Sophia whispered. "Darla has always had a flair for the dramatic."

Carlos raised an eyebrow when someone waved a vial under her nostrils. "She's faking it? Why?"

"Darla had hopes of matching Gideon with her son. She was most put out when she learned he'd found his mate." A spark of amusement lit her eyes. "We may have neglected to mention you were a vampire."

"They're going to hate me, aren't they?"

"Yes, dear." Sophia patted his arm. "But they'll get used to it."

Carlos grunted, not believing that for a second. He sneered at the dragons around the downed woman who were all glaring at him. "I'm probably not supposed to call them assholes, am I?"

"You do whatever you like, dear. You outrank them. If they annoy you, you can always banish them from Court."

"Is that so?" Carlos looked at the recovering lady dragon and waggled his eyebrows. She promptly collapsed again.

The King grinned when his Queen's joyous laughter filled the room.

* * *

Carlos barely held back a snort when the fool with the long pointy shoes, who regrettably was not an assassin, bowed hastily at Gideon while studying Carlos from beneath his floppy bangs.

"Randal." Gideon tipped his head. "I hope your mother is feeling better."

"Pfft," he said dismissively, flapping his hand. "You know what Mother's like. She's perfectly fine." He held a hand out to Carlos. "Randal Welsman, Green Dragon, Clan Spurway. Perhaps you've heard of me?"

"I can't say that I have." Carlos smiled at Gideon. "Weren't you supposed to introduce me to everyone of importance." His hand dropped heavily on the man's shoulder. "Did you accidentally forget my new pal, Randy?" Randal couldn't control his wince when Carlos' hand squeezed.

"An oversight. My apologies, treasure."

"No harm done." Carlos tightened his hold when Randal tried to pull away. "Stay, Randy. Gideon and I were just having a conversation regarding the evolution of vampires. I understand you're quite an expert on the subject."

"Er, I wouldn't go so far as to say that." Randal's eyes flicked nervously around the room, obviously hoping for rescue.

"Nonsense. I heard it from a very reliable source." He pulled Randal back when he tried to step away, this time draping an arm around his shoulders. "We're having a difference of opinion regarding the procreation of the species and could use your insight. You were giving a bit of a lecture on it earlier, I believe."

"Ah, that might have been someone else."

Carlos spoke over him. "What was it you said again? Something about vampires being the offspring of a bat and a harpy, wasn't it?"

"I think it was a leech, treasure. A bat and a leech."

Carlos tilted his head. "How would that work exactly? I can't imagine the lady leeches would want to step out with a bat. It would probably eat them."

"A valid point. It must have been a harpy."

"Luckily, we have Randy here." Carlos slapped him on the back. "He can clear it up for us. Isn't that right?"

Moving out of reach, Randal stammered a reply. "I was, uh, only commenting on my surprise about the Consort being a vampire. The King and Queen didn't mention that part."

"But that's not a big deal in this enlightened age, right?" Carlos closed in and thumped him on the back again, holding back a grin when Randal stumbled forward a few feet before catching himself. "After all, we no longer carry the prejudices of our ancestors who didn't know any better."

"No, of course not." Randal pulled at his ridiculously high collar. "It's just, there's never been a vampire at Court before. It's unprecedented."

"I see." Carlos nodded. "You must be friends with Reid and Noah."

At the confusion on Randal's face, Gideon said, "Clan Gavyn."

Randal's face screwed up with distaste. "Those two. Never."

"Interesting. You share a similar attitude."

"You are mistaken." Randal shuddered. "They lower themselves enough to work like any commoner."

"And you don't?"

"Of course not. One with my excellent lineage would not be caught dead doing menial labor. That is what the common bloodlines are for."

"Is that right?" Gideon's anger could not be missed. "You might recall that I, too, worked for a living. I believe my pedigree is beyond reproach."

"Your work was nothing more than a requirement all Royals must go through in order to understand the common person. Your real function is being a Prince."

Carlos's eyes narrowed. "And what does a Prince do?"

Randal twirled his hand. "Princely things, of course."

"I see. And what do you do?"

"I work on my elocution, etiquette, and rules of State. During my spare time, I dabble in the arts. And of course, I am a leader in setting the latest fashions." He gestured from his high collared shirt to his ridiculous shoes. "One must be prepared when marrying into Royalty."

"Marrying into Royalty?" Carlos turned to Gideon. "You didn't tell me you had a sibling."

"I'm an only child, treasure."

"I see. Is there another dragon court?"

"This is the only one."

Carlos did a slow pan to Randal. "Then you had plans for the Prince?"

Randal flinched at whatever he saw in Carlos' eyes, then drew himself up straight. "We all did, at one time. That he has mated beneath himself is unfortunate, but that can always be rectified."

What the fuck? How stupid was this guy?

"Tell me you didn't just threaten my mate, Randal." Icy blue smoke swirled around Gideon's head.

"Of course not, Your Highness. It was merely a casual observation."

"There was nothing casual about it." The blue smoke thickened.

"There's no need to get excited. Once you've finished playing with your new toy, I'm confident you'll remember your duty." Randal smiled indulgently. "Do not worry, Prince. I promise not to hold your experimental phase with the leech against you when it's time for you to select a dragon of appropriate breeding for your mate."

Carlos turned to Gideon. "Are all green dragons stupid or is it just this one?"

"Unfortunately, a sense of entitlement is a failing among the green clans. My father has been trying to fix that, but it's an ongoing struggle."

"Then there's no point in killing him," Carlos said, grabbing Randal by the collar before he could get away. "The lesson would be lost on the rest of them."

"Kill me?" Randal squeaked.

"It would, treasure," Gideon said, talking over him. "Plus, it would distress my mother to get blood on the carpets."

"We wouldn't want to upset Sophia."

"I demand you let go of me." Randal stomped his foot.

Carlos turned to him. "Did you say something, Randy?"

"Do not call me that. We are not friends." The dragon pointed his nose in the air. "The dragons will never accept you. I will be the one cheering the loudest when you are tossed aside for one better suited to be Consort."

"Too bad it won't be you, Randy." Carlos grinned, being sure to display his fangs. "You and your mother are no longer welcome at Court." He snapped his fingers at three guards standing nearby. "Please escort this gentleman and his mother from the premises. They are to be barred admittance until further notice."

"Yes, Consort."

"Stop. You can't do this," Randal screamed when two of the guards grabbed his upper arms and started pulling him toward the doorway. "You'll pay for this, vampire. Mark my words. Clan Spurway will rule Dragonkind one day. When I sit on the throne, I'll have you torched. And drawn and quartered. And staked in the sun." He shook his fist at Carlos as he was dragged from the room. "You haven't seen the last of me."

Carlos blinked at the overly dramatic exit, then turned to Gideon. "Did that just happen or did I have too much to drink?"

Gideon sighed. "The Welsman's are all prone to theatrics. It becomes tiresome over the centuries."

"Centuries? Fuck that. I'll banish them permanently first."

Gideon looked around. "It would certainly make these affairs much more enjoyable."

"I don't think anything can do that." Carlos shuddered at the thought of eons of unending social gatherings. "I'm done. Let's pay our respects to your parents and get the hell out of here before I start another fight. Otherwise, your Court will be empty of dragons by morning."

Gideon's laughter echoed through the ballroom.

* * *

Randal sucked the last of the bourbon from the glass, then slammed it on the bar top. "Bring me another. In fact, keep them coming until I say stop."

The bartender set a fresh glass in front of him. "You seem troubled, dragon. Want to talk about it?"

Randal picked up his glass and tossed the double-shot back in one go. He put the glass down, ready to ask for another, but the bartender was already exchanging his empty for a fresh drink. He burped and picked up the new glass. Staring into its amber depths, he mumbled, "Unless you know of a way to eliminate the Consort, there's no sense talking about it."

The bartender's eyes went wide. "Did you say Consort?"

Randal blinked. "Did I?"

"I think so, yes."

"Huh. Maybe I did." Randal took a large mouthful, sucking it through his teeth. "I hate Consorts. Especially this one. I wish he was dead." He squinted at the bartender. "Know anyone who could help with that?"

The man smiled. "I just might. Give me a minute. I need to make a quick call."

The bartender pushed away from the bar, pulling out his phone as he walked around the corner.

Randal sipped his drink and listened to his conversation.

"Hi, granny. I have a dragon who's having trouble with a Consort. Yes, I think it's that one. This should help with the debt, shouldn't it? Okay, I'll give him your number and tell him to call tonight. Love you too, Grams."

The bartender came back and handed Randal a slip of paper. "My Grandma Helen is going to introduce you to her friend, Ruth. She'll be able to help you with your Consort problem."

Randal frowned. This was too easy. Wasn't it? "What debt were you talking about?"

The bartender smiled and winked conspiratorially. "You know how old ladies are. They never can resist a good wager." The paper was waved in front of Randal, who snatched it out of his hand. "She's expecting your call, dragon. Don't disappoint her."

* * *

Randal swayed on his feet, looking through bleary eyes at the warehouse in front of him. He blinked at the paper in his hand, checking the number against the one on the building. This was the correct address but it seemed like a strange place to meet with an old lady. The first stirrings of unease rose, but he pushed them aside. If this Ruth could help him get rid of that Prince-stealing vampire, he'd meet with her wherever she wanted.

He stumbled his way to the door and pushed it open, the rusty hinges screeching in the silence. His steps faltered when his dragon spirit screamed a warning. The bourbon-induced fog covering his mind started to clear.

"Come, dragon. We've been waiting for you."

Randal stumbled backward. "Uh, thanks, but I've changed my mind."

"Stay."

An older woman stepped from the shadows, the reflection of the lights from the street had the strange effect of making her eyes appear to be red.

"You must be Ruth. Sorry for wasting your time. This was a mistake." He took another step back. "I have to go." Randal turned, then promptly fell to his knees when a crushing weight grabbed hold of his mind, stealing into his thoughts and pushing him aside. Screaming, he curled on the ground and wrapped his arms around his head, using his last moments of clarity to curse the vampire who'd gotten him into this mess.

After a final wrench that broke something inside, he got jerkily to his feet and walked past the woman in the doorway. His vision filled with red, Randal dropped to his knees and gave himself over to his new Master.

Chapter Thirteen

The Galway Mansion, the same day Gideon and Carlos fly to New York…

Bryan pushed open the gym door and scanned the room for Max. Not seeing him, he was about to leave when he caught sight of Stephanie sparring with one of the enforcers. He slipped quietly into the room and leaned against the wall to watch.

He winced when Stephanie caught a roundhouse kick to the ribs that sent her to one knee. That had to hurt. His eyes widened in surprise when she sprang up and knocked her opponent back with a flurry of kicks and punches before taking him to the ground with a leg sweep. Stephanie then twisted the vampire into an elaborate hold he was unable to break free of. Bryan whistled softly. Damn. The woman was fierce.

"Did you need something or are you just here to ogle my trainees?"

Bryan grinned at the teasing words. "Ogling the enforcers, of course." He nodded toward Stephanie. "She's pretty good."

"The General trained her well."

"Think she'll want to stay?"

"It's hard to say." Max watched the sparring for a minute before turning to Bryan. "Why are you really here?"

"To see what time you wanted to leave."

"We'll head out as soon as it's dark."

"Okay. I'm ready to go whenever."

"Good. I'll…." Max's phone rang, cutting him off. When he looked at the screen, he cursed and grabbed Bryan by the arm, dragging him into the nearby change room before answering the call.

"General."

"Max. I need your help. Stephanie's missing. The police think she's been kidnapped."

Bryan gave Max a puzzled look. "The police?" he mouthed.

Shrugging his shoulders, Max asked, "What happened?"

"They have video of her being pulled from her car."

"How long has she been missing, sir?"

"Five days, Max. They've had my baby girl for almost a week now."

"I'll be there as soon as I can."

"Thank you. I knew I could count on you." The General ended the call.

"I thought he wasn't involving the police," Bryan said. "And why's he's talking about it openly? Does that mean the spies are gone?"

"I suspect it's because now that the police have discovered she's missing, he's acting like a scared father."

"Which isn't really an act. Or were you able to let him know Stephanie's safe?"

"He knows, but I couldn't give him any details."

"Okay. As long as he's aware. I know what it's like when someone you love goes missing."

A shadow passed through Max's eyes. "Me too."

* * *

Bryan scratched his nose to disguise his words. "Why are we going to the front door? Shouldn't we be going through the roof?"

"Not this time. Remember, they know we're coming."

Bryan forced himself not to look, no matter how much his skin crawled. "I can feel their eyes on me. It's making me twitchy."

"Try to act natural." Max grabbed his hand and smiled lovingly. Bryan almost tripped over his feet in surprise.

"Warn a guy next time," he grouched.

Laughing eyes met his. "Or not. You need to be prepared for anything."

"Asshole."

Max chuckled, then got serious. "It's good your instincts are attuned to danger. It'll help keep you safe."

"I suppose." Bryan rolled his shoulders, trying to get rid of the itch he'd felt between his shoulder blades ever since they'd gotten out of the vehicle. "I wish I was more like Lysander and could accidentally light someone on fire. Having to be the responsible one sucks sometimes."

Max snorted, nudging him with his shoulder. "You wouldn't do it even if you could." They walked up the few steps to the front door. "Ready?"

At Bryan's nod, Max knocked. The door opened before he could knock a second time.

"Max. You're here."

"Maggie." Max pulled the tear-streaked woman into a hug. "I'm sorry to hear about Stephanie."

"Thank you for coming so quickly. I know how much George depends on you."

"Whatever help I can give, it's yours."

"I know, dear. You've always been such a blessing." Patting his back, she pulled free and smiled graciously at Bryan. "Who is this with you?"

"This is Bryan, my blood-mate."

Bryan startled at hearing Max refer to him again as his mate. Then he grinned at Maggie and reached for her hand, trying not to give away that his insides were having a happy dance party.

Maggie's next words brought an end to the celebration.

"It's about damn time, Max. Maybe now you'll finally be happy and can stop worrying about that horrible Baxter."

Say what? Bryan let go of Maggie's hand and turned to glare at his mate, who'd apparently known Baxter better than he'd let on. And hadn't said anything.

* * *

"Here you go, dear." Maggie put her hand on the door to the General's office. "Just go right on in. He's expecting you."

"Thank you, Maggie. I'll try and find you before we leave."

"Don't worry about it, dear. I suspect you'll get caught up in one of George's schemes." She patted Max's cheek. "Just promise to visit when you're done with this nasty business." Her hand slid down Max's chest to rest over his heart. "Thank you," she whispered, a tear trickling down her cheek as she turned and walked down the hall.

"Baxter?" Bryan hissed.

"Not now."

Bryan fumed but held his silence. Until Max opened the door and he saw who was speaking with the General.

"You!" Bryan called up his magic as he ran into the office. With a twist of his hand, he pinned the man high up on the wall. A flick of his fingers muffled the man's mouth with a band of air. Glaring into the surprised eyes staring down at him, Bryan snapped his fingers and called up a ball of flame. He would finally get to light someone's ass on fire.

"Bryan, stop." Max jumped in front of him, blocking his view. "You can't. He's a friend."

Bryan froze, the pain of betrayal crushing. He looked between his lying mate and the bastard stuck to the wall. The man he knew as Jazz.

* * *

Max's stomach twisted when Bryan moved away from him but the betrayed hurt in his mate's eyes slashed his heart. "It's not what you think."

"Really? So you're saying this isn't the mercenary who let that asshole Baxter slice me open? Or the one you fought in the alley? Is this his twin brother then?"

"Yes, well, no." He held up his hands when Bryan took another step back. "Let me explain."

"What's there to explain, Max? He kidnapped people. Kidnapped Stephanie. He helped Baxter torture me. He's obviously the one betraying the General. And you just called him a friend." Bryan's eyes hardened with a look Max hadn't seen before. "Get out of my way or you'll be eating fire along with him." The ball of flame hovering above Bryan's hand flared brighter.

Shit. He needed to act quickly before Bryan really did set Ian on fire. Max rushed forward and knocked him to the floor. Before he could try and explain, he was flying backward, his body slamming into the wall next to Ian's.

"Son." The General came out from behind his desk, holding his hands out in front of him. "You need to listen to me before anyone gets hurt."

"There's your betrayer, General. Give me a second and I'll take care of him for you." Bryan brought his arm back in a throwing motion.

"Stop! He's my brother."

Bryan's eyes rounded in surprise. The fire above his hand flickered, then died. Ian and Max dropped like stones, landing on the floor with a loud crash.

Ian groaned as he pushed himself to his feet. "Damn, Max. Is your mate always that trigger happy?"

* * *

Bryan glared at the door of the General's office, wondering how rude it would be if he walked out. Then decided he didn't care. Finding out Max had a personal history with Baxter had been bad enough. But to learn that Jazz, no, make that Ian, was his brother and Max hadn't said a freaking word was the last straw. Bryan was done.

He stomped to the door, cursing when Max cut him off. "Get the hell out of my way."

"If you give me a chance, I can explain everything."

Sidestepping Max's reaching hand, Bryan flicked his fingers and sent Max crashing into the wall, where he stuck him firmly in place. "Screw your explanations, Max. I don't want to hear any more of your lies."

"Bryan, please. You don't understand."

"What I understand is you've been keeping secrets. Which is bullshit after being mad at me for the same damn thing." Bryan tilted his head and squinted. "I just can't figure out if hiding we were mates is better or worse than you having a relationship with the vampire who tortured me. Or that your own brother helped him and you didn't say a damn thing! So much for trust."

"This is different."

"Different this." He lifted his middle finger at Max then covered it with fire. Bryan looked at his fiery appendage and smirked. He was going to call it a flaming bird. Liking that, he flipped Max off with his other hand, giving him a double flaming bird. With a final scowl, he stomped the rest of the way to the door.

Laughter filled the room. Bryan turned his glare on Ian, who was slouched against the wall. The idiot only grinned at him. "I like your mate, Max. When were you planning to introduce us?"

"Not the time, Ian."

"I'm just saying. If you had, it could have prevented all this excitement." He gave Bryan a thumbs up. "I'm glad you survived, man. Sorry I couldn't do more to help."

Bryan gave Ian a flaming bird too, which only made the idiot laugh harder.

"Bryan, listen to me. I would have told you, but I couldn't say anything."

Bryan turned from the door and stormed over to Max. "That's a lie. Ian might have been on a mission, but Baxter wasn't. What was he to you?" The flames on his hand flared higher.

"Ookay," Ian started sliding along the wall. "I'll just wait with the General."

"You stay right there." Bryan flung out a hand, freezing Ian's shoes to the ground while keeping his eyes locked on Max. "Why didn't you tell me?"

"It wasn't important to the mission."

"Are you kidding me? He was the damned mission."

"Ian? He was just peripheral clutter."

"Hey. There's no need for name calling."

"Not him, you jackass. Baxter. What's your deal with him?"

"It's nothing."

"You're lying again."

"It's old business, which no longer matters."

"It matters to me. And to you as well. I can see that. Who was he?"

"It's family business that doesn't concern you."

Bryan saw red. "I'm your mate. Everything about you concerns me."

"But that's just it. You're really not."

"Yes, I am," Bryan yelled. "And you bloody well know it."

"I don't recall agreeing to that. I'm pretty sure I said we wouldn't be mates until I could trust you."

That did it. "You're the one keeping secrets, asshole. And lying about it. I'm not the one in the wrong here."

"You'll always be in the wrong for breaking my Bloodmate bond and destroying my greatest hope. More so for hiding it from me."

Bryan's anger sputtered out as guilt filled him. He licked his suddenly dry lips. "You said you were willing to try. That we'd learn to work together. You told me you understood."

"I was wrong." The lack of emotion in Max's eyes stopped Bryan's breath. "I'll never understand. Just like I'll never be able to forgive you."

"Max, don't," Ian whispered harshly.

Bryan's eyes flicked to him, then back to his mate, whose face had hardened into rigid lines, his shuttered expression blocking Bryan's attempts to find any sign of leniency. Seeing nothing to give him hope, his heart shattered in a million pieces.

Bryan turned and walked blindly to the door. He blinked furiously, refusing to give in to tears where his deceitful mate could see them. He wrenched the door open but froze on the threshold, unable to step through. Everything about this felt wrong. This wasn't like Max. He was never intentionally cruel. Something else was going on.

Bryan's mind spun, weighing what he knew against Max's hateful words. The light suddenly came on. Max was such an idiot. And so was Bryan for believing him. Even if only for a minute.

Stalking back to his mate, he grabbed onto his waistband and dragged him down the wall. Once they were on the same level, he fisted his hands in Max's hair. "You asshole. You think driving me away will save you from having to tell me. Here's a news flash. You're not getting rid of me that easily. Tell me who Baxter is right now or I'll tell Carlos how you keep beating him at poker."

"You wouldn't."

"Wouldn't I?" Bryan pressed his forehead to Max's. "Whatever history you have with Baxter won't change what I think of you. You should know that."

Max slumped against the wall, soft puffs of breath tickling Bryan's jawline. "I didn't want you to hate me. I hate myself enough for both of us."

"More than I'd hate you for breaking my heart?"

"Yeah."

"Tell me."

Agonized eyes lifted to his. "It's because of me that my sister's dead."

"You have a sister?" Bryan shook his head. "Never mind that. What does she have to do with this?"

"Her relationship with Baxter killed her. And I'm the one who introduced them."

"Start at the beginning, Max," Ian said. "Your mate should know everything."

"You know I can't do that. Some of it is privileged information."

"Son," the General said gently, "if this is truly your mate, you can tell him. A mate bond trumps need to know."

"Yes, sir." Sighing, he turned to Bryan. "There was a time when Baxter was one of my closest friends. We trained together, hunted together, and fought together. We had similar interests, so we spent most of our young adult years enjoying the many entertainments offered in that century. One summer, I took him to my family home." He stopped, remembering the day everything changed.

When the silence went on too long, Ian took up the tale. "Baxter took one look at our sister, Jenny, and that was it. They were instantly smitten. For the next few decades, they were inseparable. Sometimes, Max and I joined them in their adventures, but they mostly kept to themselves, having fun and being in love. Until Baxter got bored and decided he wanted a change."

Max took up the tale. "I came to see Jenny one evening and found her packing her things. She'd decided to move out of the family home and in with Baxter. I knew he wouldn't want that so I told her to talk to him first." The sadness in Max's eyes almost broke Bryan's heart. "Baxter wasn't one to be tied down. He wanted the freedom to sample everything life had to offer. Jenny knew that about him but was determined to be with him anyway. She said she could keep him satisfied, so disregarded my warnings." He closed his eyes and whispered, "I should have tried harder."

"You couldn't have known what would happen, Max," Ian said quietly.

"No. But Jenny might still be alive if I'd forced her to listen."

"Force our baby sister?" Ian shook his head sadly. "Once she'd made up her mind, nothing could have stopped her. Not even you, Max."

"What happened?" Bryan asked,

"She showed up at Baxter's house with all her belongings. Rather than let her in, his manservant had her wait in the garden while he went to get Baxter." Max stopped to blink away the moisture in his eyes. Time had not dulled the loss of his carefree, effervescent sister. "Jenny was dead by the time he came looking for her."

"How?"

"Baxter's wife."

"He was married?" Bryan frowned. "I don't understand. You just said he wasn't the kind to settle down."

"And he wasn't. Unless there was something in it for him. His new wife, Celeste, brought a fortune with her."

"What a bastard."

"He was," Ian agreed. "What's worse is that none of us knew."

"How is that even possible?"

"He'd secretly wed Celeste the month before. We don't know if he intended on stringing Jenny along or if he was waiting for the right time to tell her. Either way, while Jenny was making plans for forever, Baxter found himself a wife from an influential family who enjoyed the same debauched pursuits as him, something that Jenny never really had." Max's expression darkened. "His new wife took exception to Baxter's lover showing up uninvited to her marital home. She and one of the guards cornered Jenny in the garden. She never stood a chance. Our baby sister had the gentlest of souls and trusted everyone. She wouldn't have seen the threat until it was too late."

Bryan grabbed Max's hand. "I'm so sorry. I can't imagine what it would have been like to lose your sister that way."

Max swallowed visibly and squeezed Bryan's hand. "When we went searching for her, Baxter and his wife had already fled. They left the guard behind to try and appease us." Max's voice flattened. "It didn't work."

"They were stupid to think otherwise."

"I've been searching for them ever since, but they've always managed to elude me."

Bryan frowned. That couldn't be right. "But Ian knew where he was."

"My team had only recently been contracted to him," Ian said. "I hadn't had a chance to let Max know until we caught you in the alley." Ian winked at Bryan. "Thanks for not taking off my head."

Bryan blinked when he realized how close he'd come to doing just that. If not for Max's "accidental" elbow to his sternum, he could have seriously injured Ian. Then he scowled. "How could you even work for Baxter after what he did?"

"I had no choice." Ian grimaced. "We were on an undercover mission. What I was doing was too important to break cover. Besides, Baxter wasn't the one I really wanted. Now, if I ever find Celeste, that will be a different story."

"Shit. You were after the traffickers too, weren't you?"

"Yeah. One of the girls taken a couple of months back is the daughter of a highly placed government official. We managed to find her, but discovered the trafficking ring has been operating for a few years. Our mission is to identify and eliminate everyone involved, then locate and rescue all their victims. That was far more important than tearing off Baxter's head." Ian tipped his head at Max. "I hear you took care of that."

"Yes. He'll never hurt anyone ever again."

"Good. I, uh, had a chance to get into his private room before you and Bryan infiltrated the auction. I found details of some of the other members of the operation."

"Did you inform the General about Jakobson?"

"Yeah. Just before you came in."

"Did you find anything on Celeste's whereabouts?"

Ian shook his head. "Not yet. But there may be something in his house."

"Let me know. I'd help you search but Bryan and I have a new assignment."

"Oh."

"I'll tell you about it another time." Max turned to his old Commanding Officer. "I'm sorry about General Jakobson, Sir."

"Me too, son. More than you know." The General's eyes burned. "That son of a bitch was here for dinner two weeks ago. He sat at my table talking to my wife and daughter, after arranging for Stephanie to be kidnapped and sold."

"You need to be careful, General. With all the surveillance he had on you, he must be making a move to eliminate you."

"I'd like to see him try."

"I'd prefer it not come to that," Max said. "How do you want me to take care of him?"

"I don't. I'll handle him myself."

"Do you think that's wise?"

The General's steely eyes filled with determination. "Wise or not, I will handle this personally. However, you do have my permission to deal with his nephew, Kyle."

"He's your traitor?"

"Yes. He started working as my assistant a few months ago."

Max's eyes narrowed. "That would have given him the opportunity to tamper with your phone and the rest of your equipment. And explains how they tracked your call to me so quickly."

"Yes. He'll need to be thoroughly interrogated before he's eliminated. It's imperative I plug all of the holes he created in my network."

"I'll take care of it," Ian said. "My team needs to wash away the taste of the last couple of weeks before we report to Baxter's partners. Kyle's blood should help."

"His partners?" Max's eyebrow went up. "They contacted your team?"

"Almost immediately." Ian grinned at Max. "Your guys missed a couple of guards. They had a lot to say about the crazy vampire who attacked Baxter's compound and tore off his head. They think you had a vendetta against him."

"Which I did."

"Which you did. They're worried you'll come after them next so they hired my team to protect them."

"How helpful of them."

"Right." Ian laughed. "I can't wait until they realize their mistake."

"You need to be careful, Ian. Jakobson may recognize you and your men."

"We'll stay out of his way. And if he does recognize us," Ian shrugged, "we'll just take him out."

"You and your boys had better keep a low profile. I want to deal with Jakobson myself."

"Of course, General. The sooner you do that, the less chance there is of our cover being blown."

"Rest assured, it will be dealt with immediately."

"As will Kyle."

And so would Celeste, Max thought. He was getting closer. Jenny's death would soon be avenged.

* * *

Bryan waved goodbye to Maggie then closed the door of the SUV. "What's our next step?"

"To find the relic." Max put the SUV in gear and pulled away from the curb.

"Of course. How difficult could it be?" Bryan leaned against the headrest and turned to Max. "All we know is that it's made of stone and will help us fight a demon. I'm sure we can walk into any occult shop in the city and they'll know what we're looking for."

"Exactly what I was thinking. I know just the place to start."

"You really need to learn how sarcasm works," Bryan muttered. "We've got zero chance of finding anyone who'll know what we're looking for."

Chapter Fourteen

"I know exactly what you're talking about." The gray-haired shop owner held up her finger. "Give me a minute and I'll be right back with the information you want."

Bryan waited until she disappeared through a beaded doorway. "Are you freaking kidding me? How in the hell does she know what we're talking about? We don't even know what we're looking for."

"I told you I knew where to start." Max smirked when Bryan glared at him. "Marie comes from a long line of psychics and witchcraft practitioners. I figured if anyone knew about the relic, it would be her."

Bryan grunted and glanced around the shop, taking in the assorted candles, books, voodoo dolls, tarot cards, crystals, and every other curio and occult item a person could want. "How do you even know about this place?"

"Roman and I once did a favor for her great-grandmother. We've kept tabs on the family ever since. Besides, I had a feeling."

"A feeling?" Bryan's head swiveled. "Like a Lysander feeling?"

Max stilled, then nodded slowly. "Yes, exactly like that. I've never been influenced by a Goddess before. I didn't even realize it was happening."

"She's getting damn good at it," groused Bryan, feeling out of sorts at Max being manipulated. "It's probably from all the practice she's been getting lately with Carlos."

Max choked back a laugh. "He definitely doesn't make it easy for her."

Before Bryan could respond, Marie pushed aside the beaded curtain and hurried toward them. She was carrying a large, leather bound tome edged with gilt, its title written in a stylized font Bryan struggled to make out.

When Marie got closer to him and Max, Bryan's magic flared, agitated by the power emanating from the book. Whoa. This was much more than an old family journal. He reached for the volume but Marie motioned him back. "Before I share what is written on these pages, I would like to know why you are searching for the binding stone."

Binding stone? Is that what it was called? Bryan squinted at the book Marie was holding against her chest, his eyes drawn to the sinuous loops of the title and the magic bound in them. He got lost in the golden winding trail as he strained to read the magical weaves. Words echoed in his mind, a soft whisper flowing on a silvery golden stream, fading before he could catch their meaning. He fell deeper, straining to understand. An opalescent glow filled his vision, holding the answers he needed. He stretched with his mind, brushing the edges of understanding, the knowledge almost in reach. He reached further, then a bit more. Almost there. Warm laughter curled around the edges of his mind.

"Bryan." Someone nudged him. "Bryan!"

He jerked, blinking around in confusion. "Why are you yelling?"

"You zoned out. Are you all right?"

"I'm fine." He looked around the shop blankly. When did he get here?

"I was telling Marie why we were looking for the relic."

"Who's Marie?"

The man frowned and pointed to a lady standing in front of him.

Where had she come from? Bryan held out his hand. "My apologies, ma'am. I didn't see you there." He carefully shook the frail hand held out to him.

"If you could excuse us, Marie. I think my friend needs some fresh air."

"The ancient magic can be a bit overwhelming for those strong in their power." She patted the book with a fond hand.

He let himself be pulled from the shop and down the sidewalk, blinking as the brightness of the streetlights and the marquis on the buildings made his eyes water. Partway down the block, he was shoved into a narrow alcove between two buildings. A large body stood in front of him, blocking most of the annoying brightness. Strong hands cupped his face and tilted his head back. He stared into brilliant cobalt blue eyes.

He ran the tip of his finger under one of the orbs. "So pretty."

His hand was grabbed and pinned to the wall beside his head. He tugged but was unable to free it. That was okay. He had another. He reached out and stroked down the long aquiline nose before trailing his fingertips across the sharp cheekbones. His thumb brushed over full red lips. "So firm. I wonder if they taste as dangerous as they look?"

"Bryan, snap out of it."

He grinned at the beautiful man standing in front of him. "Bryan. I like that name."

"That's because it's yours."

"It is? Cool." He ran his hand down the firm chest covered by a tightly stretched t-shirt. "What's your name?" He batted his eyelashes

"What in the hell's the matter with you?"

"Nothing." He yanked his hand free and grabbed both sides of the man's leather jacket so he could pull the sexy man closer. He rubbed his nose along his jawline before taking a small bite. "Delicious."

Both of his hands were suddenly pinned to the wall. "Ooh, bondage." He yanked but was unable to get them free. "I don't think I like this game."

"It's not a game, damn it."

He pulled again at his hands, then began straining forward with his body, overcome with a burning need to touch the beautiful man. A hard body pressed him into the wall, sending his senses into overdrive. Perfect. He began writhing against it.

"Knock it off."

"Don't want to." He rocked his hips, groaning when his hardness rubbed against another. "Yes. Stay just like that." He picked up his pace, groaning loudly when the man's hips bumped forward.

"Shit." The body pulled away.

"Why'd you do that?" He glanced up, his hips stopping their frantic motions when he saw the worried eyes.

Strong hands settled on his shoulders as thumbs tilted his head back. "Tell me what that book did to you."

"Book? What book?" Suddenly realizing his hands were free, he grabbed onto the muscular arms, rubbing soothingly over the protrusions on the man's wrists. "Beautiful, tell me what's upsetting you."

"There's something wrong with you."

"No, there isn't. I've never felt better." He leaned forward and rested his head on the man's chest, breathing deep. "You smell so good," he murmured, snuggling in. "Like you're mine."

Strong arms wrapped around him as the man let out a loud sigh and buried his face in his hair. "What am I going to do with you?"

"Just keep holding me." He snuggled in more, thinking he could stay like this forever.

One arm dropped free. "Maybe Gideon will know what's going on."

Bryan closed his eyes and let the man's velvety rich voice flow over him when he started talking. "Gideon, it's Max. Something's happened to Bryan."

Max. What a wonderful name. He repeated it in his mind, until all he could hear was an endless echo of Max, Max, Max.

He blinked. Wait a minute. He knew that name. How? The mists slowly cleared from his thoughts. "Max?"

"Hold on a minute. He's coming around." Hands cupped his face. "Do you know me?"

"You're my mate," Bryan whispered. "I always know you."

"You're back. Thank the Goddess." Arms pulled him in tight. "I'll call you later, Gideon."

"Please do. I'd like to know what happened." Max shoved the phone in his pocket

"Why were you calling Gideon?"

"To ask for his help. Something is wrong with you."

"No, there isn't." He shook his head, then grabbed it when stars began swirling around him. "Whoa. I feel dizzy."

"Shit." Max picked him up and rushed toward the SUV. Bryan barely had time to realize he was in Max's arms before he was sitting on his seat with Max crouched in front of him. "Bryan, what's the last thing you remember?"

"I don't understand."

"Just answer my question."

Bryan squinted at him. "Are you okay? You're acting a little strange."

"We're not talking about me. Tell me the last thing you can remember."

Bryan squinted at him before nodding and closing his eyes, ignoring the small bit of vertigo the action caused. "We went into a shop and met with the owner. You knew her." His eyes snapped open. "She had a book. A powerful book."

"Yes." Max's voice sounded tense. "What do you remember about the book?"

"It had extraordinary writing on the cover. I couldn't figure out what it said." He pressed his palms to his eyes as memories floated through his mind. "Max, don't laugh, but I think the book was talking to me."

"Trust me, I'm not laughing. I think the book did a lot more than talk to you."

Bryan dropped his hands. "You do? What?"

"I don't know, but I intend to find out." Max stood. "Wait here while I go have a chat with Marie."

"I'm coming with you."

"Damn it, Bryan. You can barely stand."

"I can stand just fine." Bryan pushed Max back and climbed out of the SUV, locking his knees when the sidewalk shifted under his feet.

"I saw that."

"I don't care. I'm still going with you." He took a wobbly step forward. "Give me your hand." Bryan pretended not to hear Max call him a stubborn idiot. He just grabbed onto the hand held out to him and walked beside his mate into the shop.

"Where is she?" Bryan's head swung back and forth, but other than them, the shop was empty. "Maybe she's in the back."

Max's eyes focused on the beaded doorway. He shook his head. "She's gone."

"What? No. She has to be here."

"The building's empty. She must have left the minute I took you outside."

"How are we going to find the Goddess' Platter of Unification without the information in that book?" He waved his arms in the air. "We need to find her."

"What did you just say?"

"I said we need to find her."

"No. The other thing you said."

"What other thing?" Bryan touched Max's shoulder. "Are you sure nothing's wrong? You're still acting weird."

"I'm fine. Please repeat what you said."

Bryan shook his head in exasperation. "If you insist. I said we need to find Marie and the book so we could see what it says about the Goddess' Plat…," his words strangled in his throat. "Max," he whispered, "how do I know what it's called?"

"I don't know, but I want you out of this shop." He glared at the beaded exit to the back rooms, shouting,

"You better have a good explanation for what you've done to my mate, Marie."

"You said she wasn't here." Bryan looked around but didn't see any sign of the missing proprietress. "I don't think she can hear you."

"She may not be here but I'm sure she heard every word. Didn't you, Marie?" Max's teeth flashed when he hissed at the beaded curtain before he took Bryan's hand and led him out the door.

Bryan looked over his shoulder as he was pulled from the shop and caught a flash of movement. He opened his mouth to say something when Max pulled on his hand and hurried him into the shop two doors down. Once they got inside, Max pushed him behind a large display cabinet, before crowding against Bryan's back and whispering in his ear, "Someone's following us."

Bryan peeked around the cabinet but didn't see anybody who looked out of place. "Are you sure? I don't see anyone."

"Me either. But I know someone's there. Close your eyes and feel with your magic." Max pressed in tighter, his breath stirring Bryan's hair when he leaned forward to look out the window.

Bryan swallowed from a mouth suddenly gone dry. Hardly daring to breathe, he waited for Max to realize how close he was and move back. Instead, Max somehow squeezed in closer, his vibrant energy surrounding Bryan and bringing a tingling awareness to his entire being. Black spots floated across his vision. He staggered sideways. A hand fell to his hip.

"Hold still."

Gasping, Bryan sucked in a lungful of air. The black spots receded. His breath stuttered when the hand slid off his hip and wrapped around his stomach. Did Max not realize the effect he was having on Bryan? His eyes narrowed. Of course, he knew. He had to be doing this on purpose. Bryan shoved backward, stilling when he bumped into Max's hardened length. Then he grinned. Good to know he wasn't the only one affected.

Behind him, Max stiffened. "Got you, you little bastard."

What the hell? Bryan was considering head butting him when Max whispered, "Look to the far left. The alley next to the flower shop."

Bryan squinted, scanning the darkened alley. He gasped, jerking back when he saw two glowing red spots. "I see it." His eyes flicked to the side when a door opened behind them. When he looked back, the red spots were gone. "Where'd it go?"

"I'm not sure. I couldn't see where it went."

Footsteps walked up to them. "Can I help you boys?" asked a laughing voice. "Or should I give the two of you a few more minutes?"

"We're good," Max growled.

More than one set of footsteps moved away, muffled giggles filling the air until they faded behind a closing door.

Bryan waited for Max to let him go. When he didn't, Bryan asked, "Are we still looking for whatever is following us?"

"No." A second arm wrapped around Bryan's waist.

"Umm, what are you doing?"

"Holding my mate."

"Oh." Bryan swallowed past the lump in his throat. "Why?"

"Because I want to. It feels nice." The arms squeezed tighter. "Better than I ever imagined."

"Yeah." Was that gravelly sound his voice? Bryan relaxed into Max's hold. This did feel good. Really good. Something he could have had all along if he hadn't messed up when they first met.

Taking full advantage of the moment, Bryan pulled in a deep breath of his mate's clean, cedar fragrance, and rested his weight more fully against Max. The small, empty place in his core slowly warmed, a spark flaring to life, flickering gently as it began to grow. Bryan's breathing slowed as his heartbeat synced with Max's, their souls, for the first time, in harmony.

Sooner than he was ready for, Max eased back. He clasped Bryan's hand and led the way to the exit. "We need to get moving. If that thing is following us, we should go to a less populated area."

"Right." Bryan cleared his throat, then raised his voice loud enough to be heard in the back. "We're leaving now. Thank you and have a good night."

Muffled laughter followed them out of the shop. He turned to see what was so funny, freezing when he saw the sign on the door. That couldn't be right. He blinked, but the words remained the same. Freaking unreal.

"Why'd you stop?"

Bryan pulled his hand free and pointed to the discrete sign advertising that the shop they'd just left carried the finest selection of adult sex toys to be found in New Orleans.

Max snorted. "I wonder what they thought we were doing?"

Bryan choked. "We weren't doing anything."

"They don't know that."

"But…we were in the middle of their shop?"

"I'm sure they've seen worse." Max took one look at his shocked expression then began laughing. He started walking toward their SUV, calling over his shoulder. "Are you coming?"

Asshole. His face on fire, Bryan followed, trying to ignore the laughing eyes that watched from the shop's window.

* * *

Marie held out the pentacle with a trembling hand, knowing it was far too late to run. She watched the demon's minion come closer, praying she could delay it long enough for her granddaughter to escape with the Book.

Calling upon the Goddess, Marie gathered her power and hurled it at the oncoming creature. It screamed when flames engulfed its body before falling to the ground, its limbs thrashing wildly. Marie took one step backward, then another. As she took a third, hope that she might survive this night sparked to life.

The flames covering the minion's body flickered then died. It crawled to its feet and shuffled toward her, stalking her movements with relentless determination.

Seeing her fate approaching, Marie used the last of her strength to send her formidable powers to her granddaughter, Angela, who would need the advantage in the days to come. Completely defenseless except for her faith in the Goddess, Marie held her head high as the revenant drew nearer.

Red filled her vision, then became her world.

Chapter Fifteen

Bryan buckled his seat belt and waited patiently until Max pulled away from the curb and merged into traffic.

"So, the red eyes in the alley pretty much confirm that whatever is following us is under the demon's influence."

"Yes." He looked over at Bryan. "Not that I needed confirmation."

"I don't like that my magic can't detect it. How do you and Gideon know when it's around?"

"Decades of fighting teach you to know when someone is watching you." Max glanced sideways. "You felt a bit of that yourself at the General's house."

Bryan nodded. "I suppose. I just wish there was a way to know for sure when it's near."

"All we can do is be vigilant."

Bryan grunted. Easy for the vampire with the super powerful senses to say. Bryan needed to up his game if he was going to be any help to Max in watching for the minion. He stared out the window for a few minutes, then asked the question that was weighing most heavily on his mind. "What do you think Marie's book did to me?"

Max hesitated, then haltingly said, "As strange as it sounds, I think it dumped information into your head."

"There's nothing strange when it comes to magic." Bryan leaned back against the headrest and massaged his temples "I can't believe it got past my shields." He shivered at the thought of foreign magic crawling through his brain.

"How do you feel?"

Bryan took a moment to consider. Once he got past the stomach-twisting thought of outside magic invading his mind, he didn't feel any different. "I feel the same as always. Which is worrisome. I can't tell what the book did."

"I don't like it either." Bryan's breath caught when Max dropped his hand on his leg and squeezed. "But I don't believe Marie would have done anything that would cause you harm, so try not to worry about it."

"Easier said than done."

"Do your best. Worrying unnecessarily will only distract you and make you careless."

"I know." He stared out the window, barely noticing the passing lights. Contrary to his words, he kept probing at his mind, searching for any lingering signs of the book's magic.

Max's hand on his leg tightened. "Hey, I thought we agreed we weren't going to worry about it."

"I know. It's just…the thought of something messing with my head is freaking me out."

"Whatever it might have done, I promise, we'll deal with it together."

Bryan gave him a weak smile, then made a determined effort to push it to the back of his mind. Knowing Max had his back made it easier than he'd expected.

"There's another place I'd like to check out tonight if you feel up for it."

"I'm good."

"Are you sure?" Max asked doubtfully.

Bryan nodded. "We have to find the relic, so we should spend every available minute looking for it." He reached over and touched Max's arm. "I'll be okay. I promise."

"As long as you're sure." Max drove another block, then frowned before signaling and pulling over to the curb.

"Why are you stopping? We just said we'd keep searching."

Max put the SUV in park then turned to Bryan. "We will. I need to talk to you about something first."

"What?"

"I don't think we should go back to the mansion to wait out the day. Not with the demon's minion watching us. We can't take a chance of it getting to the kids."

"Holy shit. I didn't even think of that." Bryan's heart almost stopped at the thought of the children being in danger. He shook his head. "We definitely can't go home. Not until we get rid of it." He sucked in a breath as a horrible thought crossed his mind. "Do you think it knows about everyone?"

Max hissed. "I have no idea."

"I'll call Sandi and tell him to watch out for it." Bryan pulled out his phone. His eyes flicked to Max. "It seems to be following us, so there might be nothing to worry about. If we keep moving, maybe it'll stay away from the estate."

"Let's hope so." Max put the SUV back in drive and merged into traffic while Bryan made his call.

As they drove, Bryan ran through different scenarios to destroy the minion but hadn't landed on anything that felt right when he felt the SUV slow when Max turned right and crept down a dark and dirty alley, complete with overturned garbage cans and an assortment of rusted appliances. The vehicle came to a stop in front of a battered metal door bare of any signage.

Bryan pressed his face to his window. "What is this place?"

"One of the least reputable pawn shops in town."

Letting his eyes pass over the garbage strewn everywhere, he muttered, "That I can believe." He turned to Max. "Why'd we come here?"

"Hank has a sideline dealing in one-of-a-kind items and rare collectibles. Most of his clients come to him because he doesn't worry about things like provenance or procurement methods."

"Stolen goods?"

"For the most part. This is a long shot, but I'm hoping he might have heard some chatter about the relic."

"Can he be trusted?"

"Not even a bit. But he knows not to cross Roman, so he'll tell us if he's heard anything."

"If you say so," Bryan pushed open his door and climbed out of the vehicle. His nose wrinkled when the scents of the alley were carried to him on the slight breeze. Dear Goddess. Had something died out here? He looked around for the body that had to be the cause of the overpowering smell.

"Come on. We don't have all night."

"How can you stand it?" Bryan asked, tucking his face into his elbow. "Your sense of smell is much better than mine."

"I only focus on what's important." He grabbed Bryan by the elbow. "Come on. Hank knows we're here."

Bryan squinted, sure there'd been a message in Max's words. He'd try to decipher it later. When he could breathe without gagging.

Bryan stepped gratefully through the doorway and dropped his arm to take a deep breath of the fresh air inside the shop. And promptly heaved. He clapped a hand over his mouth and nose, swallowing frantically to keep everything down. What the hell? It smelled even worse in here.

"Max. What brings you to my fine establishment?"

"Hank."

Bryan squinted at the old man approaching and knew he'd found the source of the smell. Hank's dirt encrusted overalls hung on his wiry frame by one button and looked to have at least a year's worth of food and other mysterious substances smeared on them. His long, greasy hair was matched by an equally dirty beard that reached halfway to his navel. When Hank scratched his armpit before holding out a black-stained hand to him, Bryan quickly shoved his own into his pockets.

"That's mighty rude of you disrespecting a man in his own place of business." Yellowed eyes glared balefully at Bryan.

"Sorry. I don't mean to be rude. It's just that…uh…I have a slight skin infection." Bryan grimaced. "Very contagious."

Hank yanked his hand back in horror and took a step back. "You stay by the door. Or better yet, go outside. There's no telling what other filthy diseases you've brought into my place." He grabbed at his neck. "I think I might be coming down with something. Max, are my glands swollen?" He opened his cavernous mouth, exposing his brown, rotted teeth. Bryan held his breath thankful he wasn't any closer to the rancid smell coming out of it.

Max's eyelid twitched. Bryan held back a smile when he stepped back. "You know there's nothing wrong with you. When you're done messing around, we have some business to discuss with you."

Hank cackled. "Why didn't you say so? Let's go to my office and talk." He pointed a dirt encrusted fingernail at Bryan. "Not you though. You stay right there. And don't touch anything. You've got a shady look about you."

Bryan's eyebrows went up. He looked shady? Then he thought about being trapped in a room with Hank and nodded. "I won't move from this spot."

"See that you don't." Hank wove his way through the boxes strewn over the floor and shelves filled with assorted junk until he reached a piece of rotted material nailed to the door frame. Pushing it to the side, he gestured Max through and glared at Bryan as if making sure he hadn't moved any further into the shop. Bryan shuddered at the thought.

A few minutes later, Max exited the office. It took only one look at his face to know he'd had no luck.

"See you around, Max. Next time, leave that other fellow at home." Cackles, followed by choked hacking sounded from behind the rotted curtain.

Bryan followed Max to the vehicle, wondering if he should feel insulted or not. But since he never planned on coming back, he guessed it didn't really matter. Bryan climbed into the SUV and closed the door with a sigh of relief at escaping the worst of the stink of the alley.

"Pass me the hand sanitizer in the glove box, would you?"

Bryan snickered and dug around in the glove compartment until he found the miniature bottle. Flipping it at Max, he asked. "I take it Hank didn't know anything?"

"No." After slathering his hands liberally with the sanitizer, Max put the vehicle in drive and crawled down the alley. "He did suggest another place we can try. It's still open so we might be able to talk to the owner tonight. Once we're done there, we'll need to find a hotel to wait out the day."

"Sounds good." Bryan yawned, then leaned his head back and closed his eyes. "Let me know when we get there."

* * *

Hank stashed the money Max had given him into his hidden safe, idly scratching his belly. The new amount added to the day's take meant he had enough to justify closing the doors early. He might even ring up his old friend, Ed, to see if he wanted to meet him for a drink.

A crash of falling metal sounded from the outer shop. Glancing at the security monitor, he frowned when he didn't see anyone on the screen. "Those idiots probably let in some damned alley cat. I'd better get rid of it before it pisses on everything and stinks up the place."

Spinning the dial on the safe to lock it, Hank stepped around the stacks of papers and magazines covering the floor and pushed aside the curtain, gazing around the gloomy interior of his shop. Seeing no sign of the stray cat, he stomped over to the rusted fridge in the corner and pulled out the tuna sandwich he'd planned on eating later.

Shoving half of the sandwich into his mouth, he held out the remainder and crooned, "Here kitty, kitty. Come get this nice sandwich." Walking behind one of the shelving units, he almost knocked over a man standing there. "How the hell did you get in here?"

The man turned his head, revealing eyes filled with flames.

Shouting, Hank scrambled backward, his heel catching on a stack of magazines. His arms windmilled as he fell to the floor with a bone-jarring crash.

The red-eyed man slunk toward him.

"Stay back." Hank brandished the wilted sandwich like a weapon as he pushed himself backward, his feet scattering magazines in all directions. "Get out of here before I call the cops."

The red-eyed man opened his mouth, exposing razor sharp teeth.

"Shit. What in the hell are you?"

The devil-thing crouched, then leapt forward, landing on Hank's chest.

"Get off of me." Hank threw the sandwich at its head, then tried to push it off. Red filled his vision.

The loud crunch startled the tabby slinking between the shelves following the scent of tuna. It hissed, then streaked out of the building, slurping noises filling the air behind it.

* * *

Bryan opened his eyes when the car came to a stop. Sitting up, he looked out his window at the brightly lit shop Max had parked in front of. From what Bryan could see through the sparkling glass of the display area, the furniture was high-end, organized, and polished until it glowed. He grinned. Now this was his kind of store. "Nice place."

"Derek's a dealer in fine antiquities and ancient artifacts. It's possible he might have heard of the relic."

Bryan opened his door. A hand clamped onto his arm before he could get out. He looked back at Max. "What?"

"Perhaps you should wait in the vehicle." Max's eyes danced. "Unless, of course, that highly contagious skin infection has cleared up."

"Shut up." Bryan yanked his arm free. "You're just jealous because you didn't think of it first."

Max laughed and got out of the vehicle. Grinning, Bryan followed suit.

The bell tinkled merrily when they stepped through the door. Bryan's attention was immediately captured by a Queen Anne desk sitting in the far corner. Walking over to take a closer look, he absently noted the sturdier Chippendale replica tucked behind it, then did a double-take, stumbling to a halt when he felt the energy emanating from the rich mahogany piece. It couldn't be.

Hurrying around the Queen Anne, he bent for a closer look, breathing in the scent of the ancient wood that still teemed with life. Growing excited, he ran the tips of his fingers over the grain of the wood, sparks flickering to life and following the path of his fingers as he stroked the gleaming surface. He sucked in a breath. Dear Goddess. This really was a genuine Thomas Chippendale, lovingly crafted by the master's hand and imbued with his magic to keep the spirit of the wood alive. His fingers twitched with the need to touch it further.

"Max. Come and look at this. I've never seen such a remarkable piece."

A deep baritone laugh interrupted his love affair with the exquisite desk. "I see you've found my pride and joy."

Bryan stood and smiled at the smartly dressed man who'd joined them. "It's amazing. Wherever did you find it?"

"My great, great, a few more times great, grandmother had it commissioned for her husband-to-be. It's been passed down to the oldest surviving heir since his death." He rested his hand on the shiny surface.

"Oh. It's not for sale then," Bryan said, disappointment running through him as he ran his eyes over the rich, smooth curves. It would have looked amazing in his office

"Sorry. I'm saving it for someone." A fleeting look passed through his eyes.

"They must be very special."

"He is. And when I find him again, I'm going to make sure he knows it." Derek ran his hand over the desk, murmuring, "Todd will understand when I give this to him." He shook off his mood and gave Bryan a wistful smile as he gestured to the other desk. "Perhaps I can interest you in this lovely Queen Anne instead."

"No, thank you. I wasn't really looking for a desk. But I would have made space for the Chippendale." Bryan regretfully ran his hand over the beautiful surface one last time. "If you ever change your mind or come across another like it, please let me know." He held out his hand. "Bryan Galway."

"Derek Chambers. I'm pleased to meet you, Bryan." He chuckled when Max tensed. "Don't worry, vampire. I won't poach your man."

Max grunted and moved closer to Bryan, who raised an eyebrow at him. What was up with the possessiveness? Turning back to Derek, he said, "We actually came to see if you could help us locate something."

"I'll do my best. What is it you're looking for?"

"An ancient stone relic. Do you deal in items like that?"

Derek nodded. "I do. I've recently acquired a few new pieces. Were you looking for something specific?"

"Yes. The one we're searching for is sometimes referred to as the binding stone."

"Hmmm. I don't recall anything specifically by that name, but I might have something similar." Derek walked over to a large glass-fronted cabinet against the wall and pointed to a stone disc inscribed with four elements. "This piece is called the Unifying Stone. Perhaps this is what you're looking for."

Bryan exchanged a surprised look with Max. Surely, it wouldn't be this easy. Stepping closer to the case, Bryan asked, "Could I have a closer look at it?"

"Of course." Derek unlocked the case and lifted the stone off its mount, then handed it to Bryan.

He looked the piece over carefully, running his hands over the surface and using his magic to search for an energy signature. Disappointment filled him when he couldn't find any signs of it being anything more than an ordinary stone.

"Is that what you wanted?"

Bryan shook his head and handed it back. "I don't think so, no."

"That's too bad." Derek put it back in the display cabinet. "Do you have some information about it? I have contacts overseas who might recognize it and can advise you where to look."

"All we know is that it's a stone relic. We've found out recently it might be called the Goddess' Platter of Unification."

Derek gasped.

"You've heard of it?"

He nodded. "I've seen that name. Recently too." Derek put a hand to his forehead, eyes narrowed in concentration. Then he shook his head. "I'm sorry. I can't recall where. I think it might have been in some journals I received last week. I'll have to look through them again to be sure." He walked briskly to the sales counter and pulled out a mobile phone. "Give me your number. I'll call you if I find anything."

Bryan quickly gave Derek his number, getting his in return, hope sparking that Derek might actually have the information they needed.

* * *

Bryan walked into the hotel suite and collapsed on the nearest bed. "Did it seem a little too convenient that every place we went today provided a solid lead on the relic?"

"Yes. But if it gets us results, do we care?"

Bryan propped himself up on his elbow. "I suppose not. But it would be easier if the relic just fell from the sky instead of leading us around like this." He flopped back and covered his eyes with his arm. "I'm starting to understand Carlos' hatred of being manipulated."

"I believe there are rules against the Goddess taking direct action."

"Tugging our strings and sending us to the exact place we need to go seems pretty direct to me. For crying out loud, she physically moves Carlos to ensure his compliance."

Max frowned. "Our situation may be more dire than we realize if She's disregarding the rules that maintain balance."

"Which is a terrifying thought."

"Yes. But until we know more, there is no sense looking for trouble."

"True." Bryan yawned, then rubbed his eyes, blinking to alleviate their grittiness. "Sorry. I'm done for the night." He shoved a pillow under his head, then grabbed another and tucked it into his chest. Rolling to his side, he let out a deep breath and sank into the mattress

"Don't you at least want to change your clothes?"

"Nope."

A moment later, soft snores filled the air.

* * *

"Wake up!"

Bryan bolted upright, heart pounding in alarm. "What?" He looked around frantically. "What is it?"

"Come here. You need to see this." Max grabbed him by the arm and hauled him off the bed before he was completely alert. His foot tangled in the comforter, pitching his body forward. Max caught him before he could fall and held him close until Bryan could get his feet under him.

"What is so urgent you had to…?" Bryan's eyes fell on the television screen. Shaking off Max's hold, he stumbled closer to the television and rested his hand on the screen.

"Why is Marie on the news?"

"Because she's dead."

"She can't be. We just saw her earlier today." He looked at his watch. "Or rather, yesterday." He turned to Max. "Somebody made a mistake."

"There's no mistake. Someone called in an anonymous tip. When the police followed it up, they found her body."

"Someone killed her? But why? She was a harmless old lady."

"She was killed the same way as Trux and his bodyguards."

"No," Bryan shook his head, not wanting to think of that sweet old lady facing that kind of horror. "You can't possibly know that. The police wouldn't release those kinds of details to the news station."

"I spoke with the lead detective on Trux's murder while you were sleeping. He told me what happened to her."

"Damn it. Why Marie?" The news switched to live feed reporting on a fire. Frowning, Bryan leaned closer to the screen. "Is that Derek's place? Holy shit, it is. Max, Derek's shop is on fire."

Max's phone began to ring. Picking it up from the dresser, he said, "It's Roman."

Max's conversation with Roman faded into the background. Bryan's eyes were glued to the screen as he watched the fires greedily consume Derek's store and the fabulous one-of-a-kind wonders inside. His heart wept, knowing the amazing Chippendale he'd fallen in love with was gone. Never again would he be able to see or touch its magnificent beauty. Max's loud exclamation tore his gaze away from the conflagration filling the screen.

"What is it?"

"Roman just got off the phone with the Chief. A couple of his officers were sent to deal with looters at Hank's shop. They found his body in the back." The look in his eyes stole Bryan's breath. "He died the same way as Marie."

Bryan blinked, then looked at the fire raging on the television screen, his eyes going wide with realization. "That thing's killing everyone we talked to yesterday. Shit.

Derek." He fumbled his phone out of his pocket, barely catching it before it hit the floor. Bryan frantically scrolled through his contacts, missing Derek's name on the first pass. Blowing sweaty bangs from his eyes, he willed his trembling hands to cooperate and finally pulled up the number. His feet shifted restlessly as he waited for the call to connect.

The phone rang four times before going to voicemail.

He hung up and tried again. "C'mon, c'mon. Pick up the phone." He almost wept with relief when it was answered. "Derek. Thank goodness you're okay."

"Bryan? What…."

"Where are you?"

"Why do you want to know that?"

"Derek, this is serious. Tell me where you are."

"I'm at home. Why?"

"When did you get there?"

"What's with all these questions?"

"Please, Derek. Tell me when you left the store."

"Right after you guys left. Our conversation about the Chippendale got me thinking about the past. I came home to…."

"I'm sorry, but we don't have time for this. You need to get in your car and drive away as fast as you can."

Derek laughed. "Are you trying to get rid of me so you can get the Chippendale?"

"No." Bryan's eyes flicked to the television. Derek's shop was now completely consumed by flames. "I need you to listen to me. Something's been following Max and me. It's killing everyone we talk to."

"Hang on a minute. I hear a noise out back."

"Derek!" Bryan screamed. "Derek. You have to get out of there." Bryan looked at Max in horror when muted footsteps and the sounds of doors opening and closing came through the speaker.

"Derek!" Bryan screamed again.

"Hey, I'm back. There must have been a stray animal or something. It looks like it's gone now."

"Please listen to me. Get in your car and get out of there as fast as you can."

"What the hell? It sounds like someone's trying to break down the back door."

The sound of shattering glass was loud through the speaker.

"Run, Derek. Now. Use the front door. Don't stop for anything. Just go. Your life depends on it."

"So dramatic." Derek chuckled. "It's probably just some kid."

"I'm not freaking kidding with this!" Bryan screamed. "Get the hell out of there before you get yourself killed."

"All right, already. I'm going. You better have a good explanation for this, Galway."

Bryan gripped the phone tightly as he listened to the sound of running feet, then a car door opening. There was a clatter when the phone was tossed on the dash before the engine roared to life. He exhaled a relieved breath when Derek started driving, the sound of the vehicle accelerating was like sweet music to his ears.

Bryan grinned at Max. "He got away. I wasn't too late."

Bryan dropped the phone when the sound of tires screeching and a loud crash came through the speaker.

"What the hell is that thing?"

There was another crash, then the line went dead.

"Derek!" Sickness spread through Bryan's system. He hurriedly dialed, hanging up when the call went to voicemail. He tried again. Then a third time before giving up. He looked helplessly at Max. "We have to find him. We can't let him die."

Max pointed at the gap in the hotel room's drapes, which showed the sun had already risen. "I can't go out there. We'll have to wait until dark."

"He'll be dead by then." Bryan glared at the offending sunrise, angered by its deadly effect on vampires. He picked up his phone and shoved it in his pocket, then rushed toward the door. "I'll have to go after him by myself."

Strong arms wrapped around him, preventing him from reaching the door. "You're not going anywhere without me."

"I don't have a choice. Let me go."

"No. You can't face the minion on your own."

"Watch me." Bryan kicked back, smashing his heels against Max's shins, which only made him hiss and hold Bryan tighter.

"Stop that."

"Derek can't fight that thing. He needs my help." Bryan pulled on his power, feeling horrible at the thought of using it against his mate, but Max was leaving him no choice.

Max shook him. Hard. "Don't you dare use your magic against me."

"Please, Max. He's going to die."

"And so will you if you go after it by yourself." He shook Bryan again. "Is that what you want? Are you trying to kill both of us?"

Bryan stilled. "What are you talking about?"

Max spun him around and shoved his back against the door. "You can't beat that thing on your own. When it kills you, and it will, because you're not thinking rationally,

I'll die as well. And if for some reason I don't, I'll wish I had, because I can't live without my mate."

Blood drained from Bryan's face at the thought of something happening to Max. Then Derek's frightened voice filled his mind. "I can't let him die. Not like that." Bryan fisted his hands in Max's shirt. "Please. You have to let me help him."

"Bryan. Mate. It's already too late. There's nothing you can do now except get yourself killed as well." Max pulled him close, tucking Bryan's face into his shoulder, his harsh breaths burning the back of Bryan's neck. "Please. I can't let you go out there. I can't have you die. Who am I without my mate?"

It was the desperate fear in Max's voice that finally broke him. Bryan grabbed him tightly around the waist, unable to believe he'd a been willing to risk his mate's life for a virtual stranger. He whispered, "I'm so sorry. Please forgive me. I wasn't thinking."

Max squeezed tighter. "There's nothing to forgive. Protecting people is what you do." He pulled back and cupped Bryan's neck, pressing their foreheads together. "Just try to remember, you can't save everyone. No matter how much you want to."

"It's just, it's our fault the minion found him. He's dead because of us."

"I know. And I'm sorry for that." Max tucked Bryan's face into his neck again. "You did everything you could."

"It wasn't enough." Bryan rested his weight against Max and let his familiar scent soothe the raw edges of his emotions. "Promise me we'll stop that thing before it kills anyone else."

"You have my word that we'll destroy it the first chance we get."

They held each other close, drawing strength and comfort, while the sun rose higher in the sky.

Chapter Sixteen

The car screeched to a stop. "What in the hell is that thing?" With Bryan's warning ringing in his ears, Derek threw open the car door and took off down the alley as if his life depended on it. And if his eyes hadn't been deceiving him, it truly did.

Derek ran as quickly as he could to distance himself from the sounds of breaking glass and the screech of tearing metal as the red-eyed creature destroyed his vehicle. But it was the pounding steps chasing him down the alley that had him lengthening his stride to go faster. Never had a hundred yards seemed so far. As he felt the thing chasing him begin to close the gap that separated them, Derek put on another burst of speed, never more grateful he'd inherited his father's long legs than he was at that moment.

Straining with every ounce of his body, he burst from the alley and ran into the street, sliding across the hood of a car that was unable to stop in time to avoid hitting him. Derek fell awkwardly to the pavement, banging his elbow but somehow managing to protect his head. Rolling to his feet, he ignored the cacophony of honking horns and angry curses and kept running.

Derek wove through the traffic, raising his hand to cover his eyes from the morning sun glinting off the sea of chrome and tinted windows he was trying to navigate. Seeing a gap, he raced toward the other side of the street. He'd just started crossing the last lane of traffic when the car he went to run past suddenly slammed on its brakes. Not having time to adjust, he clipped its bumper, the impact knocking him to the ground.

Derek pushed himself to his feet, holding his throbbing knee. Looking back, he saw the red-eyed monster run out of the shadowed alley into the sunlit street, screaming when the sun's rays fell fully on it. Covering its eyes, it turned and ran back toward the shade between the buildings, not seeing the truck barreling down on it.

"Yes." Derek punched the air when the truck hit it, smashing the creature's body into the side of a building. "Take that, you little bastard."

Derek put his hands on his hips and gingerly walked down the middle of two lanes of vehicles as he tried to get his breathing under control. Yells across the street had him twisting to look. Ice coated his veins when the creature stood up, its dislocated arm jerking into place before it twisted its head and turned fiery red eyes in Derek's direction. It started toward him but stopped before it reached the brightly lit street. Baring its sharp teeth at Derek, it slipped back into the shadows.

He stared into the dim alley, his fists clenching when two crimson spots appeared in the dark. Keeping his eyes on the alley, Derek walked backward down the middle of the street, fear tangling his insides when the red eyes followed his movements.

He looked at the sun rising in the sky, then at the long shadows on the ground. That thing was going to run out of dark places to hide eventually. All Derek had to do was keep moving until the sun banished all the shade. Then he would do whatever was necessary to flee the city.

Praying to the Goddess for strength, he turned and began a staggering run down the middle of the street, cupping his injured knee every few steps. The slowly heating pavement scraped against the soft skin of his feet. Grimacing at the blisters he could feel forming, Derek really wished he'd had time to put on his shoes.

Red eyes watched from the dark as the man disappeared from sight. He breathed deep, a toothy grin filling his face when he caught the man's scent. He kept to the shadows as he chased his prey, following the traces of fresh blood smudged on the ground.

* * *

Night finally comes…

Steam swirled around Bryan when he left the bathroom, following him as he walked toward his bed. Giving his hair a final swipe, he tossed the damp towel on the bedspread and shoved the bag holding his dirty clothes to the bottom of his overnighter. He pulled out a fresh set, then let the towel wrapped around his waist fall to the floor. Pretending to ignore the eyes burning into him, Bryan slowly dressed, grinning when he heard the quick intake of breath behind him. Until he remembered the panic in Derek's voice.

No longer in the mood to tease Max, Bryan pulled on the rest of his clothes with efficient precision, then picked up the wet towels and returned them to the bathroom. He took a moment to run a hand through his damp hair to smooth out the few tangles he always had at the back. Leaving the bathroom, he was halfway across the room before he realized Max was on the phone.

"Have it here in the next hour. I'll pay extra for the inconvenience," Max dropped his phone to the bed and began rummaging through his own duffel.

"What was that about?"

"I'm having something delivered. We can pick it up at the front desk on our way out." Max pulled an item out of his bag and tossed it at Bryan. "Put this on."

Bryan grimaced when he caught the Kevlar vest. Taking one look at Max's grim expression, he sighed and pulled it over his head, then tightened the straps. "Where are we going?"

"To take care of the minion like I promised. We can't afford to have it follow us any longer." Max held up a gun to Bryan. "Do you know how to use this?"

Bryan shook his head. "If I tried, I'd probably shoot you." He blinked. "Accidently, of course."

Max snorted. "Of course." He shoved the gun in his coat pocket.

Bryan frowned at the slight bulge in the sleek leather jacket. "Do you really think that's going to help?"

Max shrugged. "It might. Especially since it's loaded with bullets designed to neutralize paranormals."

Bryan gasped. "Those were made illegal a hundred years ago."

Max lifted an eyebrow. "Your point?"

"Other than it being against the law? Those bullets could kill you. Why would you carry something like that around?"

"You never know when it might come in handy." Max smirked. "Don't worry, I promise not to shoot you."

"You idiot. I'm not worried about that." Bryan marched across the room and shoved Max. "You're stupid to carry around something that could kill you? What if someone gets a hold of your gun?" He shoved him again. "Don't you know that most shooting deaths are caused by the owner's own weapon?"

"Please. No one has ever relieved me of my weapon. That's not going to change today." He stepped out of Bryan's reach. "Grab your gear. I want us to relocate to another hotel."

Bryan narrowed his eyes. "You better not get shot or I'll…I'll shoot you myself." He stomped over to his bed and started jamming everything into his bag. His aggravation at the unnecessary risk Max was taking overriding his normal compulsion for neatness.

"Bryan, relax. Everything will be fine."

Before he could respond, the phone on Max's bed rang. Roman's name lit up the display.

Answering it, Max said, "Roman, I've got you on speaker."

"Good. I need to speak with both of you. I just got off the phone with the Chief. He called to tell me that two days ago, Trux and his personal guards walked out of the morgue."

Bryan sucked in a breath. "Could you repeat that, Roman? I'm not sure I heard you correctly."

"Trux and his men climbed off their autopsy beds, killed the medical examiner and his assistants, then walked out the front door."

"Why didn't he tell you about this when he called earlier?" Max asked.

"He has been otherwise distracted. A number of his men were killed when they attempted to waylay the corpses. A wake was scheduled for the fallen officers earlier today."

Something in Roman's tone had alarm bells ringing. "You said the wake was scheduled? Did it get cancelled?" The agitated hiss that burst from the speaker raised the fine hairs on the back of Bryan's neck. He shared a tense look with Max while they waited for Roman to continue.

"Partway through the proceedings, the officers rose from their caskets and walked out of the funeral home."

"Holy shit," Bryan exclaimed. "Did anybody get hurt?"

"No. The Chief and his officers kept everyone back. They tried shooting the bodies, but the bullets had no effect."

"It sounds like the demon is amassing an army," Max said, his voice grim.

"That is my fear."

"Did anyone see where they went?" Max asked.

"They did not. The officers in attendance had their hands full dealing with the crowd."

"It's probably a good thing they didn't try to follow them. They wouldn't have been able to defend themselves if they were attacked," Bryan said.

"Agreed. Any attempts by the police to find them will only bring about more deaths. I have advised the Chief that we will take care of the problem. To that end, I have called Gideon and Carlos back from New York to assist."

"I bet Carlos was pleased about that."

"Ecstatic. Sophia, on the other hand, would like me to send him back as soon as possible. It seems that in the short time he was there, he had removed some of the more annoying sycophants from Court."

Bryan could easily believe that.

"If you need us, Bryan and I can head home right away."

"Not yet. I want you both to find out where the undead are hiding."

"We'll begin looking immediately."

"Good." There was a pause before Roman continued. *"There is one more thing I need you to do. The Chief's lead detective, Officer Davenport, has footage of you and Bryan entering three businesses yesterday that have now become crime scenes. Two of them are being investigated for suspicious deaths and the other for arson. The Chief would like you to speak with him as soon as possible."*

Bryan stood up straight. "Is he accusing us of the crimes?"

"Not at all. You two are the last ones to see the victims alive. They require your statements as part of their official investigations."

"I spoke with the detective a short while ago," Max said. "I've already made arrangements to meet with him tomorrow evening."

"Why are you not giving your statements tonight?"

"Bryan and I have something to take care of first."

"More important than assisting the detective?"

"Yes." Bryan shivered under the fierceness of Max's gaze. "We're going hunting."

* * *

Bryan followed Max out of the hotel lobby, quickening his steps to keep up with his faster pace as they headed toward their vehicle. "You told Roman we're going to hunt for the demon's minion tonight."

Max's eyes slanted sideways. "You knew that was the plan."

"I know. But how are we going to kill it? I haven't been able to come up with a way that might work." He shook his head. "I think we should ask Gideon to help. Without access to dragon magic we won't have a chance."

"We don't need Gideon. I've come up with another way." Max patted his pocket.

Bryan eyed the square lump. "Your mysterious package?"

"Yes."

"What is it?"

"A liquid nitrogen sprayer."

Bryan squinted. "Like the kind used to burn off warts? It sprays what, an inch or two? Were you planning on squirting it in the eye?"

Max snorted. "No. I thought we could use it on this." He reached into the top of his shirt and pulled up a chain, letting the object hanging from it dangle in front of him. Light from the streetlights shone on it, illuminating the red sparks that flickered under its surface.

"Holy crap. That's one of Gideon's scales." Bryan reached out and stroked it reverently with his fingertip. "How did you get it?"

"Carlos gave it to me for protection." Max held the chain out further so that the fiery diamond shape spun slowly in the air. "We're going to freeze it with the liquid nitrogen, then stab the minion with it."

Bryan cupped his hand under the dangling scarlet, the residual magic in the scale tickling his palm. "Dragon magic and cold. Max, you're a freaking genius."

A pink flush highlighted the sharp ridges of Max's cheekbones. "Any half-intelligent person could have come up with it."

"I'm not so sure of that." Bryan reluctantly pulled his hand away. "Just in case this brilliant idea of yours doesn't work, do you have a backup plan?"

"We throw everything we have at it, then run like hell."

"Deal."

Max's laughter followed him to the SUV.

Bryan buckled up his seat belt, then shifted sideways in his seat. "Where do you want to start looking?"

Max shoulder checked as he pulled out of the parking space. "I thought we'd start at Marie's Occult Shoppe. The minion might have left a trail we can track."

"I assume you'll also want to go to Hank's," Bryan paused to swallow, "and Derek's?"

"I can check out the antique store by myself."

The depth of understanding in Max's voice warmed some of the chill Bryan had been feeling ever since Derek's death. He shook his head. "Thanks for the offer, but we agreed to stay together. Until we take care of this thing, neither of us goes anywhere alone."

"All right." Max gave him a small smile before pulling into the street.

Bryan ducked his head under the yellow police tape Max held up as they broke into the living area at the back of the shop. He sucked in a sharp breath when he stepped across the threshold and saw the damage to what had obviously been a well-kept and welcoming home.

"What exactly are we looking for?"

"Anything out of the ordinary."

Bryan frowned. "Like what?"

"I don't know. But there'll be a trace of something left behind. We just need to find it."

Max strode past him and crouched next to the scorch marks burned into the floor. Bryan joined him, opening up his magical senses. He whistled softly. "Marie put up one hell of a fight."

"So it would seem." Max stood, his narrowed eyes looking around the small room. He stepped over shattered fragments of porcelain to investigate the burn marks marring the walls. Brushing his fingers over them, he turned and scanned the rest of the room before frowning. "Something's off."

"What do you mean?"

Ignoring Bryan, Max strode the length of the wall, continuing down the perpendicular side when he reached the corner. He strode past the beaded curtain covering the doorway that broke up the wall on that side, then came to a stop in the center of the room. He put his hands on his hips and glared at the first wall. "The dimensions in here don't match the outside."

"They don't?" Bryan looked around. "How can you possibly tell that?"

"I just can," Max said absently.

Right, Bryan thought. Probably some kind of vampire mojo. He watched curiously as Max walked over to the flower-patterned wall, which only had minor damage. He studied it for a moment, then leaned in and breathed deeply, his nostrils flaring slightly. Something Bryan didn't understand flashed in his eyes. Max immediately began pushing against the paneling, his nimble fingers moving swiftly across the surface as he tested new sections every few inches.

Bryan moved to stand next to him. "What are you looking for?"

"A hidden latch. I can sense an opening behind this wall." A moment later, his fingers skated across a bouquet of pink lilies. He paused, then went back and pressed firmly against the lightly tinted petals. There was a soft click and then a section of the wall moved. Max's eye flicked to Bryan's before he slipped his fingers between the slight separation and pulled. The panel swung open to reveal a small storage area behind it.

Bryan flicked his fingers and conjured up a mage light before following Max into the small space that was filled to overflowing with an assortment of mystical and religious objects.

"Whoa." Bryan spun in a circle, his eyes widening as he took in the entirety of the room's contents. "Max, some of this stuff carries its own magical signature. This is probably where Marie stored the book."

Hearing only a grunt, Bryan turned to see Max crouched in front of a recessed spot in the corner. He was once again pressing his fingers against the wall.

"You think there's another hiding spot?"

"I'm sure of it." Something clicked. There was a quiet whirr as a panel slid to the side, revealing dank darkness behind it. Bryan crouched next to Max and sent his orb into the empty space. The globe's light revealed a narrow, curved passageway that sloped downward. He sent his light along the path, but was unable to make out many details before it went around the corner and faded from sight.

When he magicked up another orb, the softly pulsing light reflected off of something partially buried in the dirt. Before Bryan could move, Max dug in with his fingers and plucked up a necklace.

"Someone was hiding here. The scent of their fear is still thick in the air," Max said, running the delicate chain through his fingers. He rubbed his thumb over the attached heart pendant then held it up to Bryan.

Leaning over, Bryan read the faint script. "Angela. Who's that?"

"Marie's granddaughter."

"Do you think she was hiding here when the minion attacked Marie?"

"More than likely. She helped Marie out in the shop. At the first sign of trouble, Marie would have made her leave." Max stood and dusted off his knees. "If the minion sensed her presence, we need to find her." Before it does, was left unsaid.

Bryan tilted his head as he studied the narrow confines of the tunnel. "I won't fit in there." He looked at Max's broad chest and shoulders. "And you definitely won't. We need another way to search for her." He grimaced. "I just don't know what that is."

"If we don't have a way to find her, then we're going to have to kill the minion as quickly as possible. It'll be the only way to keep her safe." Max strode out of the room. "Let's go. We've still got more places to check out."

Bryan slid the secret tunnel's door closed, then followed after his mate. In his hurry, he forgot to extinguish the magically powered orb he'd sent into the tunnel.

Far down the passageway, the globe pulsed as it drifted along the narrow tunnel, slowly increasing in size as it absorbed the remnants of power lingering in the darkness. It flickered, growing brighter as it was pulled forward, magic calling to magic; its awareness growing as it travelled.

Max slammed the door of the SUV and gripped tightly to the steering wheel, which groaned under the force of his hold. Damn it. He didn't want to be the one to tell Roman that Angela was in danger. Or possibly dead. The soft-spoken whimsical girl held a special place in the Prince's heart.

"Maybe you shouldn't squeeze the steering wheel so hard. If you rip it off, it'll be difficult to get around corners."

Max glared at Bryan, whose teasing smile fell from his face. Shit. Max opened his mouth to apologize when his phone dinged with an incoming message. A second later, so did Bryan's.

Bryan pulled out his phone first, confusion covering his face when he read the message. "What in the world?"

Max grabbed his off the dash, his eyes widening when he read the summons.

"Priestess Apolline is waiting on your attendance." A second message contained the address.

"Who is Priestess Apolline?" Bryan asked.

"I have no idea. I've never heard of her."

"Should we go see what she wants?"

"No. We don't have time for any side trips. We need to find the minion."

"Okay." Bryan set his phone down, then picked it back up when it dinged again.

"Do not delay."

Bryan frowned at his phone, then turned back to Max. "Maybe we should make the time. She seems pretty insistent."

"I don't take orders from someone I don't know."

"You might want to make an exception this time." Bryan wiggled his phone. "These are burners. How did she get our numbers?"

"That's a very good question." Max slammed the SUV in gear and rocketed into the street, ignoring Bryan's shout and the screeching tires and blaring horns from the people he'd just cut off.

He had no idea how Apolline had their numbers. He'd be sure to find out when he met the lady.

Chapter Seventeen

First meeting with Apolline…

Bryan turned from the portrait he'd been examining when the young girl stepped into the room. "The Priestess will see you now."

Bryan's shoulder brushed against Max's as they followed the girl down a narrow hallway to the back of the converted home. As they got closer to the room at the end, his magic flared in a reflexive response to a rival power. He leaned over and spoke under his breath. "Be careful. Whoever this is, she's very powerful."

Max nodded and quickened his pace, placing himself slightly before Bryan. Rolling his eyes, Bryan formed a protective barrier around Max, then stepped up beside him and jabbed his elbow into his ribs. "Together. Remember?"

Max grunted, which Bryan took as agreement.

Their escort stopped in front of a heavily beaded curtain. She parted the strands and gestured them inside. "Please take a seat. Priestess Apolline will join you shortly."

Bryan and Max stepped into a small room that was unfurnished except for a small table and three chairs. The starkness surprised him. He'd been expecting the room to be filled with the accoutrements that would normally be used by a spiritual practitioner.

Jingling from another curtained doorway heralded the arrival of Apolline, who paused on the threshold before gracefully walking over to the table.

"Excuse me, Priestess," Max said, stepping into her path, "I have a couple of questions for you."

Sidestepping him, Apolline finished walking to the table and sat down, then motioned to the two seats across from her.

Max strode to the table and glared down at her. "We're not sitting until I get some answers. Now, who are you and how did you get our numbers?"

In response, her hand again gracefully invited them to sit down.

Seeing that the only way they'd get her to talk to them was to do as the Priestess wished, Bryan elbowed Max and shook his head before he could say anything else. When Max's eyes narrowed, Bryan grabbed hold of his hand and pulled him to the chairs, tugging on his arm to get him to sit. Max dropped heavily into his seat, and crossed his arms, glaring equally between Bryan and Apolline.

Ignoring his fuming mate, Bryan turned to Apolline, who set her clasped hands on the table and looked back and forth between them. Or so Bryan assumed. It was hard to tell through the dark tinted glasses she was wearing.

After a long, tension-filled silence, where Bryan kept an eye on Max, worried he would explode if the priestess didn't get on with it, Apolline removed her glasses and laid them on the table. He barely stifled his gasp when she lifted her eyelids and revealed milky orbs, the pupils and iris completely covered by opaque whiteness.

She fixed her blind gaze first on Bryan, then on Max, before shaking her head. "This should not be. My vision has failed me." Apolline stood from her chair. "You must leave and return when you are ready."

Bryan stood as well. "That's it? What the hell? You told us to come here."

Her finger pointed at Bryan. "Guilt hinders you. Until there is forgiveness, you will be incomplete."

"Forgiveness?' Bryan's face screwed up in confusion. "Who do I need to forgive?"

Ignoring him, Apolline turned to Max, his heated glare making no impression on her. "You must learn to trust. Else all will be lost."

"I trust just fine," Max said, rising from his chair. "Except for you. I don't know what you're trying to pull here, lady, but I want some answers."

"Heed my words." Apolline's melodic voice carried a sharp edge. "Until you do as I've spoken, you will be closed to the message from the Universe." She turned her back and walked toward the curtain, pausing to speak over her shoulder. "You will soon come to a crossroads. Choose wisely, or that which is broken will never be mended." With those parting words, Apolline departed, leaving confused silence behind her.

"What the hell just happened?" Bryan asked.

"I don't know."

"Why would she refuse to talk to us after ordering us to come to her? That doesn't make any sense."

"No, it doesn't." Max glared at the gently swaying beads. "But we've wasted enough time. We need to get back to our hunt." He strode from the room, the echoing thumps of his footsteps an indicator of his annoyance.

Bryan groaned at the thought of being trapped inside the vehicle with a cranky vampire. He just knew it was going to be a long night. As he followed Max, he glanced behind himself more than once, sure he could feel blind eyes on him, weighing and judging.

Bryan tapped his fingers on the dash as Apolline's words kept running through his head. He could own the guilt she'd accused him of. After breaking the bond between Max and himself, how could he not feel that way? He also wondered if Max would ever learn to trust him. He was doing his damnedest to convince him, but his mate was nothing if not stubborn.

"Could you please stop that. I'm trying to think."

Bryan's fingers froze. "Sorry. I always fidget when I'm thinking."

"Or nervous."

Bryan slowly panned to the left. "Excuse me?"

"You fidget when you're nervous. Or when you're worried."

He shifted in his seat to see Max better. "How do you know that?"

"Because I have eyes in my head." He shot Bryan a look he couldn't decipher. "I'm not as oblivious as you think."

"I know you're not. I just didn't think, I mean, I didn't know, uhm…."

"You didn't realize I watched you as often as you watched me."

"Something like that." Bryan hoped the heat burning in his face wasn't visible. Max's smirk killed that notion.

Clearing his throat, Bryan asked, "Changing the subject, are we going to Hank's place now?"

"No. I think we might have more luck finding a trail at the antique store."

"Even after the fire?"

"Because of it." Max's eyes flicked toward Bryan. "I think the minion was angry when it didn't find Derek. I'm counting on its anger making it careless."

"You think it burned down the antique store because it was having a temper tantrum?"

"Yes."

Bryan's phone rang. Pulling it from his pocket, he frowned at the display. Showing the screen to Max, he answered. "Hey, Sandi. What's up?"

"I need you to come home."

"I can't right now. I'm in the middle of something with Max."

"You have to. I need your help."

Bryan's eyebrows lifted. He glanced over at Max, surprised to see him glaring at him. What was that about? He turned back to the phone when Lysander's voice rose.

"Did you hear me, Bryan? I need you to come home right away."

"For what?"

Tommy's missing. You have to come back to help me find him."

Bryan flinched when Max swore, then had to brace his hand on the dash when the vehicle swerved into a parking lot, cutting off two lanes of traffic. The noise from the angry drivers pounding on their horns drowned out his brother's next words.

Max brought the SUV to a screeching halt, then got out, slamming the door with enough force to rock the vehicle. Bryan scrambled to undo his seat belt so he could go after him, but the stupid thing was jammed. By the time he'd managed to free himself, Max was gone.

His brother's panicked voice jolted him from looking for his mate. Scrabbling around on the floor, he snatched up his phone and pressed it to his ear.

"Bryan. Answer me. Bryan."

"Sorry. I'm here."

"Did you guys get in an accident?"

"No."

"It sure sounded like it. Are you okay?"

"I'm fine. Nothing happened."

"Then what was all the noise?"

"Max was in a hurry to park."

"He was? Why?"

Wasn't that the question of the hour. To his brother he said, "He saw an open spot and didn't want someone else to get it."

"Okay. As long as you're all right."

"I am." He couldn't say the same for his mate. He glanced at the surrounding buildings but didn't see Max anywhere. That damn vampire better have a good reason for taking off on Bryan like that. "What were you saying about Tommy?"

"He's missing. Richie just got a call from the Conference Director in New York. When Tommy didn't show up for his presentation, they went looking for him. Somebody destroyed his room." Lysander sniffed, before whispering, *"They found blood, Bryan. Someone hurt my Tommy."*

"I'm so sorry, Sandi."

"You have to help me find him."

"I can't." Bryan again looked for Max, then gave up with a sigh. "Max and I are searching for the minion. I can't walk out on him."

"Max, I'm sorry to call off your hunt, but I really need Bryan's help."

"He's not here. I think he got out of the vehicle to give us some privacy." Bryan's eyes narrowed as he began to suspect the reason for Max's hasty departure. Surely, he wasn't that insecure about Bryan's feelings. Was he?

"Oh. Okay. Then please let him know I need you to come home right away."

The thought of Max chasing the minion by himself made Bryan's blood run cold. "Sorry, but there's no way I'm leaving Max on his own. Not even for you, Sandi. Not this time."

"Then what am I supposed to do?"

"You could always ask Roman for help."

Silence.

"You know he'd drop everything for you."

Still nothing.

"And with his connections, he can probably find Tommy faster than me."

"I'm such an idiot."

Bryan snickered.

"I'm so used to going to you, I didn't even think of asking Roman."

"He's probably dying to help."

Lysander's sigh was loud in Bryan's ear. *"And is probably hurt that I didn't go to him first."*

"It's possible. But you know he'll forgive you."

"That's not the point. I have to do better by my mate. Always going to you for help isn't fair. To Roman or to Max." He sighed again. *"Sorry for trying to take you away from him."*

"It's okay. I get it. But mates should come first. Even before brothers."

A heavy groan sounded in Bryan's ear. *"I guess I wasn't ready to let you go.*

"I understand. Trust me, I like being the one you come to. But we really need to stop."

"I know." Another sigh. *"Growing up sucks."*

"That it does. But think of the rewards."

Lysander laughed in his ear. *"True."*

"Go talk to Roman. Call me when you guys find Tommy."

"I will. You should find Max and let him know he comes first. It's past time he heard that."

"I'm going to do that right now. Later." Bryan smiled wistfully when he put his phone away. He'd miss being the person his brother depended on, but the torch should have been passed to Roman months ago.

Now, if only his cranky vampire would come back, he could tell Max what was really in his heart. Bryan got out of the vehicle and leaned against the door, once again searching the darkness for movement. He'd give Max five more minutes. If he wasn't back by then, Bryan was going to track him down and drag him back. Like a caveman. He grinned as he imagined Max's look of surprise if he did.

* * *

Max rounded the corner of the building and came to a stop, not sure if he was angry with Bryan, Lysander, or himself. He looked back at the vehicle, his heart aching when he saw his mate still on the phone with his brother instead of following him. Which was stupid. Bryan always put Lysander before everyone else. And he always would. Even if Max had convinced himself otherwise.

But could he really be blamed? At every challenge, Bryan had shown he'd had Max's back, supporting and protecting him in whatever way he could. Max had thought it meant something. But it hadn't been about him at all. That was just the kind of man Bryan was.

Max stomped down to the end of the building, not wanting to be mad at his Consort. It wasn't Lysander's fault Bryan was conditioned to put his needs first. Or that Bryan couldn't say no to him. And just because Max had finally begun to trust in Bryan as a mate, he shouldn't be mad at Lysander for his part in showing him the truth. That when it came down to the two of them, Max would always come in second. His heart cracked a little more at the thought.

Max sighed, his steps slowing. He couldn't even be angry with Bryan. The man was only being true to his nature. His loyalty to those he cared about was endless. One of the many reasons Max respected him. And why his heart felt shredded now. He leaned his head on the side of the building, swallowing down his hurt at not being as important to his Bloodmate as Bryan was to him.

He only allowed himself a few minutes to pout. And yes, he could admit that's what he was doing. Then he pushed away from the brick wall. They had things to do and no more time to waste on foolish emotions like self pity. Burying his hurt and his hopes for what-ifs, Max headed back to the vehicle. When he saw Bryan worriedly pacing next to it, he raced over to him, wincing when his sudden appearance startled his mate, causing him to bang his elbow against the side mirror.

"What's wrong?"

Bryan rubbed his elbow and gave Max a look he couldn't interpret. "I was worried about you."

Max squinted. "Why?"

"Because you took off." Bryan glared at him. "We agreed to stay together. That means you don't get to run off and leave me behind."

Grimacing, Max said, "You're right. Sorry. I needed a minute." He walked around the front of the SUV and opened his door. Speaking across the roof, he asked, "When is the Consort expecting you?"

"He's not."

"That must mean you're heading straight to the airport? Get in. I'll have you there as quickly as possible."

"I don't need to go to the airport?"

Max frowned. "Then how are you going to get to New York? Oh. Gideon must be taking you."

Bryan shook his head. "I'm not going to New York."

"Won't it be easier to search for Tommy if you're there?"

"If I was looking for him, yes, but I'm not."

"Why not?"

"I told Lysander I needed to stay with you. He's going to get Roman to help him."

"You did?"

"You sound surprised." Bryan's eyes narrowed. "Is that why you took off in a snit?"

"Excuse me?" Max drew himself up. "I was not in a snit."

"You were too." Bryan came around to his side of the vehicle and punched him in the chest. "You're such an idiot."

Max crossed his arms. "Is that right?"

"You thought I was putting Lysander before you."

"Because you always do."

"Not this time."

"Why not?"

Bryan looked at him like he was stupid. "Because you're my mate."

Max grunted, wishing that actually meant something. "Get in. I'll drive you home."

"I already said I'm staying with you."

"That's not necessary. I know your brother needs you."

"Would you listen to me." Bryan's finger jabbed his chest. "I said I'm putting you first."

He slapped Bryan's hand aside. "You never put me first. Why start now?" Max was caught off guard when Bryan shoved him against the door, fisting his hair to hold him in place.

"You should have come first, Max. Always. And I'm sorry that you didn't."

Max spun them around and pinned Bryan against the door, ready to argue some more. He froze when he saw his mate's eyes, hardly daring to believe the message in them.

Bryan's expression softened. "It's okay, Max. I understand. One day you'll believe. Until then, I'll believe enough for both of us." The patient understanding on his face was too much for Max's unsteady emotions. He could hear the moment his tightly held control snapped.

Gripping Bryan's biceps, Max smashed their mouths together. Bryan's gasp of surprise allowed him entry, which he readily took advantage of. He pulled his mate closer as he ate at his mouth, groaning when his fangs scraped the tender flesh on the inside of Bryan's mouth. The small sip of blood ignited his system, speeding up his heart. He sucked greedily on the small wound, gasping as an electrical current ran through his body. His hair lifted, whipping around his head like coiled lightning.

Bryan began struggling in his arms. Max pulled back to let him go, but stopped, his eyebrow lifting when Bryan growled. His mate quickly climbed his body and wrapped his legs around Max's waist, before he shoved his hands into Max's electrically charged hair and forcefully pulled his head down. Eager lips fastened onto his, ravaging his mouth. Their tongues twined as Bryan delved deep, grunting loudly as he licked his way around Max's mouth.

When Bryan's tongue brushed against his fang one time too many, Max's dominant nature took over. Tearing his mouth free, he waited until Bryan opened his eyes and gave Max his full attention. Never breaking eye contact, Max slowly leaned in and pulled Bryan's plump bottom lip between his teeth. His tongue toyed with the captured flesh before he bit down, moaning when the magically charged blood spilled into his mouth. Bryan jerked. The smell of his release filled Max's senses, sending his own need into overdrive.

He ground himself against Bryan as he continued to suck on the small wound, unable to get enough of his mate's electrifying blood. His hips bucked faster as his passion rose, the feeling better than anything he'd experienced before. He groaned when Bryan hardened against him, grinding faster as he searched for release. He needed just a bit more to send him over. When Bryan tilted his head, Max tucked his face into his neck and bit down. Bryan shuddered. The fragrance of fresh seed scented the air.

That was all it took. Max's body shook from the force of his release. Crushing Bryan against the vehicle, he held on tight as he rode the waves of his climax, hungrily swallowing the blood spilling into his mouth.

Max's hips gradually slowed, thrusting one final time before stopping. He leaned heavily against Bryan, his trembling limbs unsteady in the aftermath of his explosive release. Jeers and honking from a passing vehicle penetrated his consciousness, reminding him of where they were. Groaning, he pulled back from Bryan's neck and licked the wound closed. "We shouldn't be doing this here," he said hoarsely. Contrary to his words, he didn't move away, instead tracing his fingertips from his mate's hair to his cheek, then moving behind his ear, before running them down his neck to his collarbone. When his hand finally came to a rest on Bryan's heart, he waited until Bryan's heartbeat slowed before dropping his arms. Bryan grabbed onto him before he could step back.

"Not yet." Bryan locked his legs around Max's waist and rested his head on his shoulder. "I've been waiting for this for so long."

Max wrapped his arms around him and held him close. He rubbed his cheek against Bryan's hair and breathed deeply, drawing in the soul-soothing scent of his mate. The ache he'd been carrying for so long dissipated, peace and contentment taking its place. The shield Max had built to protect his heart pulsed, hairline cracks fracturing its surface. When Bryan slid his hands under Max's jacket and fisted the back of his shirt to pull him closer, the barrier weakened further. His mate's contented sigh as he snuggled in caused the first fragment to loosen and fall.

Max tucked his face into Bryan's neck, a small smile crossing his face when he felt the next piece break free.

***

A quick magical cleanup later and they were on their way to Hank's shop. Bryan was reading his messages when the SUV took a hard right, knocking his arm into the door. His eyes flew to Max. "What's going on?"

"Change of plans. I want a word with Apolline."

Before he could ask what about, Bryan's phone chirped with an incoming text. Glancing at the screen, he sucked in a sharp breath at the one-word message. "Holy shit. Drive faster, Max. Apolline's in trouble."

Chapter Eighteen

Bryan rushed into the house, Max hot on his heels. He skidded to a stop when he saw the minion crouched over Apolline's still form. "Get away from her, you bastard." Magic surged. With a motion of his hand, he peeled it off Apolline's body and hurled it across the room. He got his first look at the minion when it pushed itself off the floor and turned its fiery red eyes on Bryan.

"Holy shit. Peter?"

The thing that had once been an Elder gnashed its blood-stained teeth and charged. Bryan threw out his arm and sent the minion flying. It smashed into the rear wall with enough force it busted through the paneling and vanished from sight.

"Apolline." Bryan raced across the room and slid to his knees beside her. He took a quick inventory of her injuries, blowing out a relieved breath when the Priestess slowly opened her sightless eyes. "Are you all right?"

"I'm not sure." She raised a trembling hand to her head. When she struggled to sit up, Bryan placed his hand behind her back to assist. She gasped and dug her nails into his bicep.

"I'm sorry. I didn't mean to hurt you."

"It returns."

Ice filled his veins. Before Bryan could react, Max cried out behind him. He heard the sound of Max's body falling to the floor. A spray of warmth hit the back of his neck. Bryan leapt to his feet and spun around, horrified to see Peter sprawled over his mate, chewing ravenously on Max's neck.

"Get away from him." Magic rushed from his hand, tearing the minion off his mate and hurling it across the room, where it crashed into one of the house's support beams. Before it could rise, Bryan swept all the furniture in the room toward it, burying it beneath hundreds of pounds of wood and metal.

Bryan dropped next to Max, who had his hand clamped over his neck, trying to stem the gushing blood. Barely holding back a scream, Bryan placed his hands over Max's, panic rising when the flowing red didn't slow. He leaned over, baring his neck. "Bite me, Max. You're not healing fast enough. You need my blood."

"N…no time." The broken words scraped painfully across his heart. "F…fight." Blood dribbled from Max's mouth. He lifted a trembling arm, holding it up to Bryan. The blood covering his hand ran down the chain he held loosely in his fist, dripping off the crimson dragon scale dangling beneath it.

Bryan shook his head, fear for his mate squeezing his lungs. "You need to feed. Please, Max. You're bleeding out."

The chain was shoved in his face. "K…kill n…now." More blood bubbled up, running down Max's chin in an ever-growing stream.

Bryan wrapped his hand around Max's, squeezing it before taking hold of the chain. He lifted his other hand from where it was keeping pressure on Max's neck wound. Terror filled him when the blood flow increased. He fumbled blindly in Max's pocket for the sprayer. Yanking the sprayer free, Bryan stood and dashed tears from his eyes. "You better not die on me, you stubborn jackass." Hearing a noise behind him, he whipped around, shocked to see the minion had broken free of the barricade. Overly large teeth grinned at him.

Forcing his trembling hands to cooperate, Bryan kept one eye on Peter as he pulled the trigger, spraying liquid nitrogen liberally on the dragon scale until it was covered in a thick layer of frost. As fast as he was, Peter was almost on him by the time he was done.

Dropping the sprayer, Bryan screamed, "Die, you rotting bastard." Magic surged, condensing the air around the diamond-shaped missile and sending it hurtling toward the minion.

The hoarfrost coated projectile slammed into one of Peter's demon-fired eyes. A cloud of mist exploded around his head, his piercing scream loud enough to pop Bryan's ears. Peter dropped to the floor.

Bryan waited, watching closely, but Peter didn't move to get up again.

Gasping in relief, he fell to the floor next to Max, cutting him off when he struggled to speak. "I don't want to hear it. You feed right freaking now." Bryan thrust his wrist against Max's teeth, tearing the delicate skin. "Drink, asshole, before you finish bleeding to death."

He dropped his head, giving thanks to the Goddess when fangs pierced his skin and he felt the pressure of Max's mouth pulling on his blood. He started when he felt a spark of connection and quickly reached for it, but it faded before he could grab hold.

"The head," Apolline cried. "You must burn the head."

Turning to look, Bryan's eyes widened when he saw Peter's hands twitch.

Max's mouth pulled away from his arm. "Tear off first," he slurred, before latching back onto Bryan's wrist.

Nodding, Bryan called up his power. He wrapped Peter's body and head in separate bands of air, then wrenched them violently apart. The head flew through the air, hit the wall with a splat, then bounced along the floor before coming to a rolling stop. Its remaining eye opened, the crimson orb rolling until it focused on Bryan. He cried out when he felt the demon push against the barrier protecting his mind, its unworldly evil fracturing his mental shield. He quickly added another layer of protection, desperately trying to hold the demon back.

Feeling his shield start to give, Bryan called up an enormous fireball and launched it at Peter's head at the same time his shield shattered.

The demon surged into his mind.

Bryan and the head both screamed, torturous agony filling the unnatural connection between them. Struggling against the force trying to take control of all that he was, Bryan made his fire burn hotter, pushing until the flames turned purple. Black spots appeared before his eyes as the crushing force in his head expanded, shoving him to the side. He cried out, fighting back until he created a small pocket of space. Bryan pushed through the unrelenting pain burning through his mind to give what he knew would be his final effort. Using the last of his flagging strength, he let his remaining power rush out. The flames turned white.

The head exploded, disintegrating into ash which floated gently through the air, falling to cover the crimson dragon scale laying on the floor.

The demon disappeared from his mind. Bryan sank back on his heels, swaying as he blinked to clear the red fog covering his vision. When that didn't help, he raised a trembling hand and rubbed his eyes, smearing blood-tinged ash across his face. At a sound from Max, he looked at his mate and smiled when he saw his healing neck.

Bryan slowly toppled to the side. As the cool comfort of oblivion rolled over him, he heard a melodic voice whispering in the distance. "Sleep, child. Your work is done." Letting go, Bryan allowed himself to sink into the depths.

* * *

Bryan jerked upright, his heart racing as he scanned the room, only slowing when he saw Max leaning against the wall with his arms crossed over his chest.

"You're okay."

Max raised an eyebrow. "There's nothing wrong with me. You're the one lounging around in bed." His lip twitched, stopping Bryan's angry response before it could form.

Until he noticed how pale Max was. Throwing off the covers, he slid from the bed and staggered over to his mate. "You asshole. Why didn't you let me heal you first? You almost bled out before I could get back to you."

"You needed to kill the minion."

"Screw that. I needed to help my mate."

"The minion was your priority. You made the right choice."

Bryan fisted his hands in Max's shirt and pulled himself up to eye level. "You are my priority. You, Max. Not some demon-possessed Elder."

"Not in this case."

"In every case," Bryan yelled. "I could have dealt with it after I healed you. I was almost too late to save you."

"I didn't know it was there."

Bryan dropped to his heels, his brow wrinkling. "What are you talking about?"

"Just that. I didn't feel it sneaking up on me. My survival instincts have been honed for centuries, Bryan, and I couldn't sense it. Your protective shield didn't even slow it down." Max took him by the shoulders. "Do you understand? If it could break through your magic that easily, nobody would have been able to defend against it."

"I'm sure Lysander…."

Max shook his head. "Even with as strong as Lysander is, he couldn't have stopped it either. Not with the demon powering it. We had no choice but to kill it when it was weakened by the dragon magic."

Bryan heard the logic but didn't care. His mate had almost died when he could have prevented it. "Gideon would have helped if we'd…."

Max cut him off again. "How many more people would the minion have killed if we'd let it get away? It had to be done right then, no matter the cost."

"Your death is not a price I'm willing to pay. I will never risk you like that again, no matter what you say." He pressed an angry kiss on Max's mouth.

Max pulled back and smiled gently at him, covering Bryan's fists with his hands. "You did the right thing."

"I don't care." He refused to let Max's smile diffuse his anger.

"I'm proud of you, mate."

Poof. The anger was gone. "You are?"

"More than you could ever imagine."

"Damn you," Bryan collapsed against his chest, all his fight gone. "Please don't ask me to do something like that again. My heart can't take it."

"I'll try my best."

Bryan would hold him to that.

They separated when Apolline walked into the room. The Priestess graced both of them with a smile as she walked to the small table set against the wall. Bryan rushed over to pull out her chair. "Thank you."

"You're welcome. How are you feeling?"

"I am quite recovered." She set her hand on his wrist. "Thank you for coming to my rescue."

Bryan covered her hand with his. "Thanks aren't necessary. I'm just grateful we got here in time." Bryan hesitated before asking, "I, uh, didn't see your assistant earlier. Do you know where she is?"

"Betsy had to leave early today. She is safe at home." She smiled brightly at him, her milky-white eyes seeming to peer into his soul. "I am proud of both of you for passing your first challenge."

Bryan exchanged a surprised look with Max before turning back to Apolline. "Killing the minion?"

Apolline shook her head. "You put your mate first."

Bryan's shoulders slumped. "I'm sorry to disappoint you, but I didn't. I wanted to, but Max insisted that I deal with the minion first."

"Not then. When you chose your mate over your brother's friend."

"Tommy?" Bryan's brow creased. "That was nothing."

"To the contrary, it was everything."

"It wasn't, not really. Lysander has lots of people who can help him. He didn't need me."

"Yet he turned to you first." She smiled serenely at him.

"Well, yeah. But…."

Max interrupted. "Bryan, when was the last time you told him no?"

"It was when, no, I think it was…," Bryan frowned, racking his brain. Surely, there was one time he hadn't run to Lysander's side.

"Don't worry about it." Max rested his hand on Bryan's shoulder. "Your brother is the most important person in your world. It's natural for you to be there for him."

Bryan shook his head. "You're wrong. I'll always want the best for Lysander, but he's not the most important person in my world. You are."

"I am?"

"Yes. And it's about damn time you knew it." Bryan put his hand on Max's chest. "It should have always been you. I was so busy being responsible for everything and everyone else that I didn't realize how badly I was hurting you. How badly I was hurting us." His other hand joined the first. "I won't ever do that again. I hope one day you'll be able to forgive me for my stupidity."

Max hauled Bryan close, whispering in his ear. "I forgave you long ago. It's taking me a bit longer to get over being angry with you, but that's mostly gone too."

Bryan took in a stuttering breath as Max's words lifted a weight off his soul.

A lighthearted laugh filled the air. As one, they turned to Apolline. "You are very close to completing your second challenge."

"Which is what?" Bryan asked.

"You must learn to forgive."

"You said that before. But who? My mother?" Bryan shook his head. "I'm sorry. But I don't think I will ever forgive her. She's caused the death of too many innocents."

"You need to forgive yourself. There can be no moving forward until you do."

"Oh." Bryan swallowed hard. "That."

"Your guilt is closing you off from all the Goddess has to offer. This cannot continue."

"I'll work on it." Bryan squirmed under her penetrating look. For all that Apolline was technically blind, she sure didn't act like it.

"See that you do." Apolline directed her attention to Max. "As for you, Max Fraser, Second to the great Prince Roman Greystone, leader of the vampire covens of North American. How long will it take for you to trust your mate?"

"I do trust him." Max scowled.

"To some degree, perhaps," she said, arching her eyebrow, "but not with your whole heart. Until you can bare your soul, with complete trust and faith in your mate, you will be closed off from all that awaits you."

"And what is that?"

"When you are ready, the Universe will answer." Apolline stood, her blind gaze landing on them. "Be warned. If you do not pass your final challenges, your failure will lead to the end of everything."

Before Bryan could ask what she meant by that, Apolline turned and headed toward the doorway.

"Wait," Max called out, "I still want to know how you got our numbers."

Apolline smiled over her shoulder. "It is a simple enough task when one is blessed by the Goddess."

She walked out of the room.

Clearly, their time with her was over.

* * *

"Apolline sure sounds a lot like Lysander when he has a premonition."

"I noticed." Max's fingers tapped on the steering wheel, an annoyed expression on his face.

"I'm sorry you don't trust me yet, Max," Bryan said. "I understand why. Believe me. I'd do anything for that moment back."

Max pulled the SUV into the nearest parking spot. Turning off the ignition, he turned sideways in his seat.

"This is exactly what Apolline was talking about. You need to let go of your guilt."

"I'm working on it."

"Work harder. Did you make a mistake when you damaged our mating link? Yes. Did you compound it by keeping it a secret? Absolutely. Did you hurt me and damage my ability to trust? Also, yes." Max reached for Bryan's hand. "I told you I understood how it happened. I can almost understand why you kept it a secret. Almost."

"But…,"

"But you need to stop. Apolline was right. Holding onto your guilt serves no purpose. It only helps the demon. I know you didn't do any of the above through malicious intent."

"Of course, I didn't. I was just being stupid."

"Yes, you were." Max chuckled at Bryan's offended gasp. "But we'll work it out." He held up his thumb and finger an inch apart. "I'm this close to letting go of my own issues."

"Really?" Bryan's heart gave a leap. That was better than he'd hoped.

"Yes. It'd probably go faster if we talked it out." Max's face scrunched with distaste.

Bryan snorted. "Possibly. But once we go back to the mansion, we won't have a moment to ourselves to try." He shook his head. "It's too bad we destroyed your Bayou getaway. Nobody would have disturbed us there."

Max started the SUV and slammed it into gear.

"What's wrong now?"

"I know the perfect place to go." He pressed hard on the accelerator.

* * *

Max pulled into his parking spot and turned the key. The ensuing silence was broken only by the ticking of the cooling engine.

"You brought me to Darkness?"

"This is where we first met. Can you think of a better place to start over?"

Bryan's lips curved. "Actually, I can't." He looked out the windows. "The construction company has done an amazing job fixing all the damage."

Max leaned forward to look at the upper level, pleased to see the addition he'd asked for was complete. "It looks like it's ready for us to move in the moment we've finished dealing with Ruth and the demon."

"You're asking me to move in with you?"

Max slid his eyes sideways. "You're my mate, aren't you?" Bryan's slow answering grin erased the last of his doubts.

He climbed out of the vehicle and went around to Bryan's side. Opening the door, Max held out his hand. "Would you like to come up and see what I've done with the place? We'll be able to talk here without any interruptions. For as long as we need."

"I'd love to." Bryan grinned and let Max help him from the vehicle. "And maybe we can get to know one another better, too. You know, by not talking."

"That sounds like an excellent idea." Max grinned back. "Come on. Let's see if we can get it right this time."

He led Bryan through the back security door into the dark deserted building, then pulled him up the stairs. Anticipation filled him. After almost a year, he would finally get the chance to bond with his Bloodmate. And he had no doubts that they would succeed. Mostly because neither of them would be leaving the apartment until they had their Goddess markings. No matter how many times they had to try. His mouth spread in a wolfish grin at the thought.

* * *

Many hours of conversation later…

Bryan tilted his head and arched his back, trying to get the annoying vampire to pick up the pace. "Now, Max. Bite me now."

The infuriating asshole slowed down even more.

"Move, damn you." He locked his legs behind Max's back and lifted his hips, pulling him in tighter. There. Finally. He rocked them together, chasing his release. Bryan was right on the edge when Max grabbed his hips, stopping his movements. Bryan groaned in frustration.

"Why are you doing this?"

"I want to savor the moment, not race to the end." Max thrust forward and hit Bryan's sweet spot, lighting up all his nerve endings. "Trust me. It'll be better this way."

"It'll be better if you move, damn it."

Max grinned and pressed forward a bit more. Sparks flashed behind Bryan's eyes. He arched, wanting to feel that again. Max's hands clamped down on his hips, holding him still.

"Stop being an ass and let me finish already."

Max smirked. "Is that any way to speak to your fated mate?"

Bryan sucked in a breath, realization hitting him. They were actually going to do this. After months of torturing himself with guilt and weeks of Max's anger, they had finally reached this point.

"Now you understand," Max said softly, unhooking Bryan's legs and letting them fall to the bed. He braced himself over Bryan's chest, all signs of humor gone. "This is the big one. There's no turning back after I bite you this time. Are you prepared to be tied to me for eternity?"

Bryan blinked back the moisture that suddenly filled his eyes. "I've never been more ready for anything in my entire life," Bryan croaked. "Please don't make me wait any longer."

Max's face softened in a way it never did. "I won't." Propping himself on his right arm, he slashed a lengthened nail across the left side of his chest, opening a long, deep gash. As the blood started to drip from the wound, he spoke the ancient vampire bonding ritual. "Do you freely agree to become my True Bloodmate, forging our souls into one, as fated by the Goddess, bonded together through eternity?"

Bryan's acceptance had barely left his mouth before Max put his hand behind Bryan's head and lifted it to press his mouth to the bleeding wound. Bryan groaned when Max's blood hit his tongue. The spicy flavor tasted more luxurious than the finest champagne and bubbled in his veins like froth overflowing the bottle. Bryan was distantly aware of Max biting deep into his neck but was more focused on getting as much of that effervescent goodness as possible. Swallowing again, he jerked when the bubbles popping in his veins turned into lightning that burned through his system.

Max tore his mouth free with a yell and arched his back, driving deeper into Bryan. He had to brace his arms against the headboard when Max's hips rocked forward in a fast, bruising pace. Another burst of liquid fire rushed through Bryan's body. He let go of the headboard and grabbed Max around the neck as the surge rushed through his veins before exploding with a force that almost drove them apart.

His magic flared to life, pouring from him to surround his mate. Max's mouth opened in shocked surprise when he was encased in a whirlwind of wild magic. Bryan tried to pull it back, clawing at the sparkling strands, but the magic refused to do his bidding. The power blazed, spinning higher and faster, around and through his mate with a will of its own. Max's head tipped back as streams of magic burst from his open mouth and outstretched hands.

Bryan held tight to Max as the magic swirled, the air coming alive with the crackling energy. Gold and silver streams wrapped around them, binding them together, until Bryan didn't know where he ended and Max began.

The torrent of swelling magic finally crescendoed, exploding with a deafening boom that shattered the windows. Max collapsed limply in Bryan's hold.

"Holy crap. That was intense."

It took Bryan a moment to realize Max wasn't breathing.

* * *

Lysander ducked under the fist and motioned upward with his arm, sending his assailant flying. The airborne vampire executed a nifty aerodynamic spin with a few unnecessary twists before landing in a three-point crouch. Freaking showoff.

Carlos grinned. "Not bad. Next time don't let me get so close before taking the offensive."

"Whatever you say." Lysander dropped back into his fighting stance, then nodded at Carlos. "Let's try that again."

As Carlos rushed forward, a tsunami-like wave of magic swept through the mansion, knocking them both to the ground and tumbling them across the mat until they crashed into the wall. Lysander was preparing to defend against the attack when he realized what was happening. Laughing, he grinned at a wild-eyed Carlos, who had landed in a crumpled heap next to him.

"Is that what I think it is?"

"It sure is."

Carlos climbed to his feet and brushed off his pants. "Aren't they supposed to be hunting the minion?"

"They must have found a way to work out their problems."

"It's about fucking time. I was starting to think those two would never pull their heads out of their asses."

Lysander snorted. "Me, too."

"Does this mean we're going after the demon now?"

"Yes." Lysander's face grew serious. "I was hoping they'd find the relic, but now that Bryan and Max have mated, we can't wait any longer. It's time to finish this."

"Then playtime is over." Carlos walked to the center of the mat and dropped into a fighting stance, his hands in guard position. "Prepare yourself. Starting now, we train for real."

* * *

Bryan raised his interlocked hands over his head and brought them down with a teeth-shuddering crash against Max's chest. "Beat, damn you," he swore at his mate's heart before resuming chest compressions. "You better not die on me, asshole," he raged, sweat dripping off his forehead onto Max's cheek. Bryan watched as it slowly trickled down to his ear. Wait a minute. Was that a twitch? He watched closely as he continued with the compressions. Holy shit. It was. He pushed down on Max's chest with renewed vigor.

Max groaned, knocking Bryan's hands away. "Why are you trying to crush my chest?"

"I'm trying to save your life."

"It doesn't need saving." Max glared accusingly at Bryan before shoving him off to sprawl next to him. "Seriously. Why were you hitting me?"

"I thought you were dead. Your heart wasn't beating."

Max closed his eyes and rubbed his chest. "I think your magic stopped it."

"I'm sorry. I don't know what happened. I just lost control of it."

"It probably had something to do with this." Max reached out and blindly placed his palm on Bryan's chest.

"What are you talking about…oh," Bryan looked at the mark that was revealed when Max's hand dropped away. "I didn't realize," he whispered, running his finger along the colorful lines that swirled around two triangles that connected at the point, forming a mirror image of each other. "What do you think it means?"

Max opened his eyes and looked at the mark Bryan couldn't stop touching. Bracing himself on an elbow, Max brought his face closer, frowning at the design. "It reminds me of an ancient hourglass. In the middle of a windstorm."

Bryan looked at the symbol again. "It kind of does, doesn't it? I wonder why?"

Max flopped back. "I'm sure we'll find out when She's ready for us to know."

Bryan traced his fingers over the swirling lines again. They'd been touched by the Goddess. He reached out a trembling hand and brushed aside Max's hair to touch the matching symbol on his chest. Which was when realization came. "Max," he whispered, "we're True-mated. We actually did it."

Max looked at Bryan, then down at his own chest, then back to the symbol on Bryan's chest, before smiling. "That we did, Bloodmate." He pulled Bryan down to lay on top of him. "I think that calls for a celebration." He waggled his eyebrows.

Laughing, Bryan attacked his mouth, more than ready to get started on the festivities.

Chapter Nineteen

Arriving back at the Galway Mansion…

"I'm glad you guys are back."

Bryan locked his arms around his brother. "Me too. Even if it was only a few days, I missed seeing everyone."

"You've been through so much, I'm sure it seemed like a lot longer."

"You have no idea."

"I might have an idea." Lysander laughed and pounded him on the back. "Congratulations on your mating, Bryan. I'm so happy for you."

Bryan stepped back and grinned. "Thanks. I'm pretty happy for me too."

Lysander snorted. "I bet. You can tell me all about it later."

Bryan's eyes widened, flicking first to Max then back to his brother. "Uh, that's a hard no."

Lysander's face screwed up. "Not that. I meant how you guys finally worked it out."

"Oh." Bryan cleared his throat. "I knew that."

"Did not, you ass. I can't believe you thought I was asking about that."

"It was an honest mistake. Can you blame me?" Bryan pointed at Max. "I mean, look at him."

"Stop talking." Lysander slapped his palms over his ears. "You're my brother, for crying out loud. I don't want to be thinking about you doing that."

"You're the one who asked." Bryan snickered when Lysander gave him the finger. Awkward moment over. Until he opened his big mouth. "Has there been any word on Tommy yet?"

The laughter faded from his brother's face when he shook his head. "Marcus has his entire coven out looking, but they haven't found anything yet."

"I'm sorry, Sandi."

"What if they can't find him?"

"They will."

"You don't know that."

"You're right, I don't. What I do know is that Tommy's a resourceful guy. If anybody can get out of trouble, it's him."

"I guess. He's had a lot of practice with that."

"Exactly. I have no doubt he'll find a way out of whatever he's gotten himself into and be back home with you in no time. You just have to keep the faith, little brother."

"I'll try."

Bryan grabbed Max's hand when Roman pulled Lysander into his arms. Marcus had better find Tommy soon or Bryan was going to drag Max to New York so they could look for him themselves.

* * *

Bryan walked into the game room with Max, a smile breaking over his face when he saw his best friends. He hurried over and pulled them into a three-way-hug. "Am I ever glad to see you guys. When did you get here?"

"Yesterday. We headed back the minute we got your text."

"And the guys following you?"

Nick snickered. "We wrapped them up in a bow and handed them to Roman. They're locked up in the Council dungeons. At least for now."

"Oh?"

"Yeah. Some General called Roman and said he's going to take them off of his hands."

"I'm glad that's sorted out."

Alex bumped Bryan's shoulder. "Appreciate you letting us help out. Nick and I haven't had that much fun since school."

"Thanks for getting them off our backs. Did they give you any trouble?"

"Us?" Alex asked. "Surely you jest."

Bryan laughed, smacking him in the arm. "Don't be an ass."

"Speaking of…," Nick started.

"Which we're not." Alex pushed Nick back, giving him a look Bryan couldn't interpret.

"Fine. Am I at least allowed to ask about the angry vampire who's trying to kill us with his eyes?"

"Who? Max?" Bryan swung around to see his mate glowering at the three of them. *"What's with the look? It's just Alex and Nick."*

"I don't like them touching you."

"You're going to have to get over that. They're my best friends so we hug each other a lot."

Max grunted. *"Perhaps that can change."*

"Or you can realize they're not a threat and get used to it." Wanting to reassure his disgruntled mate, Bryan walked

over to Max and grabbed his hand, before grinning at his friends. "Guys, good news. Max and I managed to fix our bond. We're officially Bloodmates."

Alex and Nick looked at each other and smirked. "Oh, we're quite aware. The shockwave of magic when it happened knocked us off our feet."

Bryan's cheeks burned. He'd had no idea. But he should have expected something like that when the windows of the apartment blew out.

"Your brother's been answering calls all day from panicked magic-users." Alex snickered. "I hope you've outgrown your shyness, Bryan, because everybody knows your business now."

"Shit."

"It's good they know you're mine. They will know not to go near you." The satisfaction in Max's tone could not be missed.

"I think everybody knew that anyway."

"It never hurts to be sure."

"Possessive much?"

Max started to laugh, Bryan's elbow shot to the ribs not concerning him in the least

* * *

Roman set down his phone and smiled at Lysander. "Marcus says he has a lead on Tommy. He will call back the moment he finds him."

"Thank the Goddess." Lysander fell onto his chair with a thump. "I was about ready to go look for him myself."

"I am aware. Marcus is having our room prepared."

"You knew?" Lysander blinked at his mate. "He is? Holy crap," he said, jumping up. "When do we leave?"

"We will depart the moment you are ready. Bryan and Max can look after the mansion and coven now that they have returned."

"Great." Lysander started toward the door but paused halfway across the room. He turned back to Roman. "Should we even be going? We're preparing for war."

Roman walked over and took his hand. "While I have complete faith in Marcus, Tommy is your friend and brother. You must do what is best for you."

"I don't know what that is. My heart wants to go, but my head is saying I need to stay here."

"What would Tommy say?"

Lysander's shoulders slumped. "He'd want me to stay and protect everyone and prepare for the upcoming battle."

Roman's finger tipped his chin up. "I will support whatever you wish to do."

Lysander squeezed his eyes shut, his mind filled with all the terrible things that could be happening to his best friend. Forcing the images to the side, he whispered, "Are you sure Marcus can find him?"

Roman's arms wrapped around him and pulled him in close. "I promise. He will leave no stone unturned."

"Please ask him to hurry."

"I will, beloved. I will make sure he calls in hourly with reports."

Lysander shook his head. "I'd rather him spend his time searching. Just ask him to call the minute he knows something."

"I will." Roman kissed the top of his head. "I am proud of you. This was not an easy decision to make."

"No. I hope Tommy will understand."

"You know he will."

He did. Tommy would be the first to kick his ass if Lysander had chosen to put him before everyone else. It still didn't make his decision any easier. Being a responsible adult really did suck.

* * *

Daily training in preparation for the final battle…

Carlos picked himself off the ground. "What the hell's the matter with you?"

Lysander shook out his hands, preparing himself for the vampire's next charge. "Nothing. Let's go."

"I'm serious."

Lysander stood and put his hands on his hips. "I said there's nothing wrong. I'm just trying to get ready. Which would be easier if you'd stop screwing around."

"That's bullshit. You've been in a pissy mood since we started."

"Stop being a baby." He flexed his hands. "Are we doing this or not?"

Carlos' eyes narrowed. Then he vanished. Lysander threw up a shield to stop the blur rushing toward him, but he was too slow. The impact of Carlos crashing into him drove him into the wall. He landed on the ground with a jolt. Shit. That one hurt.

Crawling to his knees, Lysander waved his hand and sent Carlos skyward before he could come at him a second time. Lysander gingerly climbed the rest of the way to his feet. He wiggled his jaw and rotated his shoulders. Good. Nothing was broken. Even if it felt like it. Ignoring the yelling from the asshole floating along the ceiling like a balloon, he stretched out the kinks in his back and cracked his neck. Personal protective shields were all well and good at preventing serious injury, but impacts still jarred the body.

"Hey. You. Jerkface. Get me the fuck down from here."

Lysander flipped him off. "Not until you stop being an asshole."

"I'm not the one acting like an asshole, Consort. Put me down before I get angry."

Lysander tipped his head back, wondering how much trouble he'd be in if he tied a rope around the vampire's ankle, took him outside, and flew him like a kite. There was a stiff breeze today. He could probably get some good distance with him. He turned to the door. He should invite the kids. They'd think it was great fun.

"Consort!" Carlos yelled, "If you don't put me down right fucking now, I'm telling Max what you did."

Lysander whipped around. "You wouldn't dare."

"Try me."

"You promised to keep your mouth shut."

"And you said you'd stop being a dick." Carlos put his hands on his hips, which caused his body to tilt to the side.

The sight of him clawing at the air to right himself almost brought a smile to Lysander's face. Almost. He thought seriously about leaving Carlos up there. It would serve him right for being such an ass.

"Final warning, Consort. Bring me down or I'll tell both of them about your spying fetish."

"You're an asshole."

"Right back at you."

"You want down? Fine." Lysander snapped his fingers. Carlos dropped like a stone. The jarring crash when Carlos landed did bring a smile to his face.

Rolling onto his back with a groan, Carlos flipped him off. "Fucker. You'll pay for that."

"Whatever." Lysander strode toward the door but was cut off before he could make his escape.

"What's going on, Sandi?"

"Nothing." He stepped to the side to go around his brother, but Bryan blocked him again.

"Try again. What I just saw was completely uncalled for."

Lysander threw up his hands. "He annoyed me. Okay. Can I go now?" He shoved Bryan out of the way and managed two steps before he was tackled to the ground.

"Get the hell off of me." He let his magic rise.

Bryan smacked the back of his head. "Don't you dare use your magic against me." Bryan rolled Lysander over and pinned his arms to the floor. "Now tell me what the hell's going on."

"I already did, asshole."

"Carlos isn't the problem, Sandi. You are."

"There's nothing wrong with me."

"You're being cruel for no reason. That's not like you."

"It's not my fault he's a stupid dumbass. Forgive me if I don't want to deal with his crap today."

Bryan tilted his head. "Are you angry because of Mother? I saw you fighting with her earlier."

"I hate that woman," Lysander yelled. "She's walking around bossing the staff like she's not a prisoner. After everything she's done, why does she get to do whatever she wants? Huh. How come she's alive and Father had to die? It's not fair." Wetness streaked down his cheeks. "I hate her, Bryan. I wish she wasn't here."

"Do you want me to send her back to prison?"

Lysander blinked back his angry tears. "You can't. We gave our word. If we break it now, nobody will trust us again."

"What do you want me to do?"

"Nothing. There's nothing you can do."

"Sandi," Bryan said patiently, compassion filling his voice, "I really don't think this has anything to do with Mother. Is all this anger because of Tommy?"

"Maybe. I don't know. Marcus hasn't called back. My best friend is alone out there somewhere, scared, and probably hurting, and I'm here doing my freaking duty instead of looking for him."

"Tommy will understand. He'd be the first to tell you you're doing the right thing."

"I don't care," Lysander shouted. "I should be with him. What if the demon gets his hands on him? What then, Bryan? He could get eaten and I'd never see him again."

"Shit. I didn't realize." Bryan moved further back so he could pull him into a hug. "I'm scared of the demon too, little brother."

"What if we can't defeat it, Bryan?" Lysander's voice was clogged with tears. "I hear screams in my sleep every night. So much horror and death." He shuddered as memories of blood covering the earth and glowing red eyes flashed in his mind. "What if we're not enough?"

"We have to believe we are. Otherwise, we're destined to fail."

"Beloved. Why did you not tell me?"

"Roman." Lysander pushed at Bryan. "Let me up." When Bryan moved off of him, he scrambled up and rushed to his mate who pulled him in close. "I'm sorry. I didn't want to bother you."

"You could never be a bother. You should know that."

"I do know that. It just seemed silly to waste your time because of some stupid dreams."

"I was aware your sleep was restless but thought it was worry over Tommy. Forgive me for not checking further."

"Only if you forgive me for blocking my thoughts." Lysander hung his head. "I would have said something but I hate feeling like a coward because I'm afraid of my dreams. I had no idea how much they were stressing me out."

Roman tipped his chin. "This is more than that. The anger I could feel earlier was not like you. It felt unnatural."

A gasp sounded behind him. Lysander looked over his shoulder, his eyes widening when he saw the serious look on Bryan's face. "What is it?"

"Lysander, when did the dreams first start?"

He frowned, thinking back. "I don't know. A week. Maybe a little more."

"Which is about when we first encountered the minion. I mean, Peter."

"Yeah." Lysander nodded. "I think they started the day you almost got arrested."

"I could be wrong, but I think the demon is manipulating your dreams and sending you the visions."

Lysander shook his head. "That's impossible. I always have my shields up. It shouldn't be able to do that."

"I know it shouldn't. That doesn't mean it isn't." Bryan's face hardened. "And if that's the case, we need to find a way to block it."

"I'm using the mental shields you taught me. If it can get through those, how can we stop it?"

Bryan frowned. "I'm not sure. Maybe it'll help if I also put a shield around your mind."

"What if that doesn't work?" Lysander buried his face into Roman's chest. "What if we can't keep him out?"

"Then we keep trying." Bryan's hand landed on his shoulder. "No stupid demon is going to hurt my baby brother."

Lysander pulled away from Roman and stomped a few feet away before coming back. "This is unbelievable. I've been so scared and angry, thinking I was a cowardly weakling, and all along that freaking demon has been messing with my mind." He froze, nausea rolling through him. "If the demon can control me, you could all be in danger from me," he whispered. "I need to leave before I hurt anyone." He started backing away.

Bryan darted forward and grabbed him. "Stop. I don't think it has that much influence over you."

"Bryan's right," Roman said. "During your waking hours, you are more alert. It would be difficult to influence you without your knowledge. While you sleep is when you are at your most vulnerable. Ideas can be planted in your dreams so subtly you would not suspect the thoughts were not your own."

"You're both wrong. It is affecting me. Just look at what I did to Carlos." He turned to the vampire who had joined them. "I'm sorry for taking my anger out on you. For some reason you just really got under my skin today and I lashed out."

"Don't worry about it." Carlos winked. "It's not the first time I've annoyed you. It definitely won't be the last." He barked out a laugh. "Though it was the first time I've been hung up like a pinata."

"Balloon."

"I'm sorry, what?"

"Not a pinata. I hung you up like a balloon. I wanted to take you outside and fly you like a kite for the kids."

Carlos' eyes rounded before a laugh escaped. "Can you imagine what Gideon would think if he came home and saw me flying at the end of a string?"

"He'd wonder why you were having a party without him." Gideon strolled into the training room.

"Hey. You're back." Carlos sauntered over to his mate, who smiled and tossed an arm over his shoulders.

"I am. Now, what was this about the Consort turning you into a kite."

"He's having a rough day. That fucking demon is getting into his dreams."

Gideon turned to Lysander. "You have your mental shields up?"

"All the time. But they're not strong enough to block it."

"That's not good. We need to find a way to keep it out."

"I'm going to try adding my shield to Lysander's," Bryan said. "We're hoping that might be enough to protect him."

Gideon nodded. "That might work." Turning to Lysander he asked, "Would you allow me access into your mind to add another layer of protection? I understand this may be an imposition, but we cannot allow the demon to gain control of you."

"If you can keep it out of my head, you can have access to whatever you want."

"Thank you. I'd also like to speak with my parents. They may have a better idea of how to stop it."

"Their assistance would be most welcome." Roman tipped his head respectfully. "It relieves my mind to know my Consort is being watched over by the King and Queen of Dragonkind."

"It is our pleasure, Prince. Your Consort is important to all of us."

Lysander smiled. "Thanks, Gideon. I'm really glad you made it back in time to help."

"Speaking of that, what did your father want to talk to you about anyway?" Carlos asked. "You left in such a hurry this morning I didn't get a chance to ask."

"He wanted to let me know Randal has gone missing. He would like us to keep our eyes open for him."

"Why is he worried about him? You dragons are always running off on your own."

"He was worried Randal might try to harm you."

"Me?" Carlos scoffed. "As if."

"I've explained to my father the many steps we've taken to ensure your safety. He's no longer concerned." His eyes sparkled. "Though I might have overlooked the kite-flying gambit."

Carlos snorted. "Yeah. I guess the only way to stop that is to keep this on, even if it does interfere with our training." He pulled Gideon's mating talisman from his pocket and slipped it over his head."

"I said I was sorry, asshole."

For some reason, Carlos' laughter made Lysander feel less scared.

* * *

Gideon pulled his hands from Lysander's head. "There you go, Consort. I've done what I can."

Lysander leaned back in Roman's arms with a sigh. Other than a small tingle inside his head, he didn't feel any different. "You have a light touch. I barely felt you."

"Good. I tried to be as least invasive as possible."

Lysander squinted. "What did you do? It feels different than what I'm used to."

"I overlaid the shields you and Bryan put up, reinforcing the whole. That should be enough to block the demon from accessing your thoughts."

"I hope so. I'd love to get a full night's sleep."

Gideon smiled. "On that note, we'll take our leave. Pleasant dreams, Consort." He nodded at Roman. "Prince."

Bryan stepped closer and touched his arm. "I'll be just down the hall if you need me."

"That's not necessary. Roman is with me. You should be with your mate."

"If you insist." The joy on his brother's smile made Lysander smile.

He watched the men leave Roman's and his private suite, filled with hope for the coming night. Mostly. Underlying it was a sense of dread that the demon would still manage to break through. He didn't know what he would do if it did.

"It will be fine, beloved."

"Will it?"

"I have faith in your combined abilities."

"I do too. I just can't help worrying about what we'll do if this doesn't work?"

"If it does not, we will keep trying until we find a way. That demon cannot have you. You are mine."

The calm assuredness in Roman's tone washed over him, a soothing balm that coated his rising panic. "Okay." Lysander gripped his hand tight. "Promise you'll wake me if I have a bad dream."

"I will watch over your every moment, beloved. Rest easy, knowing you are in my care."

Lysander smiled and let himself be led off to bed.

* * *

Lysander rushed toward the Dragon Queen as quickly as he could, but his legs felt weighted, as though he was wading through gelatin. "Sophia. No." He watched helplessly, his arms extended, as the Queen fell lifeless to the ground. Mocking laughter bombarded his eardrums.

"She is only the first."

Lysander spun around, searching for his enemy. The scene shifted, showing a city street where Tommy waved happily at him.

"Ell, there you are. I've been looking everywhere for you." He began running toward Lysander, not seeing the danger in the shadows.

"No. Go back, Tommy. Please go back."

Too late. The darkness rose up, engulfing his best friend.

"Tommy!" Lysander screamed, red filling his vision as the laughter boomed again.

"Lysander. Beloved. You must wake."

"Get away from him, you bastard. Hold on, Tommy. I'm coming." Lysander strained to reach his friend, but something had a hold of him. He lashed out with his power, breaking free of the restraints, and rushed toward the cloud of darkness that covered his friend."

"You are too late. He is mine now."

"You can't have him," Lysander screamed, hurling bolts of lightning toward the voice.

"Sandi! Wake up."

Something pulled at him again, stopping him from helping his friend. Magic swirled around him. He lifted his hand.

"Consort. Enough. You will wake up right now!"

Lysander bolted up. "Max. What are you doing in my bedroom?" His eyes flicked around the room, opening wide when he saw that his brother, Gideon, and Carlos were also standing around the bed. "What are all of you doing here?"

"I could not wake you, beloved. They came to help."

Lysander turned to his mate and gasped. "What happened to your face?"

"It is nothing."

But it wasn't. The black mark burned into the stark whiteness of Roman's cheek could only have been caused by magic. "It's not nothing. I'm so sorry. I didn't mean to hurt you."

"It was not your fault. You were caught in a nightmare." Roman gave a small smile. "Next time I will know to duck."

"There won't be a next time, even if that means I never sleep again." Lysander reached for his mate. "Please forgive me."

Roman pulled him close. "There is nothing to forgive. I got slightly singed when a bolt came too close. It is almost healed now, so no harm has been done."

"Still. You know I would never hurt you."

"I do." Roman smiled. "You were trying to help your friend. I believe I got in the way."

Lysander jerked back. "Tommy. That bastard has Tommy." He spun toward Gideon. "He killed Sophia. I'm so sorry. I tried to save her, but he killed your mother before I could reach her."

Gideon paled. "The demon killed my mother?"

Carlos caught Gideon when his knees buckled. "Hey. Before you freak out, do that dragon speaking thing and check in with your parents. The Consort was dreaming. It might not have been real."

A dream? Lysander blinked. It had seemed so real. He kept his eyes locked on Gideon, blowing out a relieved breath when the dragon smiled.

"It's okay. Mother is fine. Very worried about you, Consort, but she is unharmed."

"Then the demon doesn't have Tommy?"

"No." Gideon shook his head. "It's using your fear for your loved ones against you. To weaken you. And us." He looked around the room. "Mother is most concerned that the demon had such a tight hold on the Consort. We must find a way to block it."

"Agreed." Roman's concern flowed to Lysander through their link. "Does the Queen have any suggestions on how that might be accomplished?"

"Not yet. She and Father are going to check the Archives. They'll let us know if they find anything."

"Why is it going after me?" Lysander asked. "Is it because it knows I'm the weakest link?"

"The Liberator is the center. If he falls, chaos and darkness shall prevail."

The cavernous resonance in his brother's voice was alarming. But not as much as the vacant look in his eyes.

Chapter Twenty

"That's good, Clancy. Now, if you make a small adjustment to the weave here, you can create a focused concussive blast, which is best when fighting in a confined area," Bryan said.

"I think I've got it, sir. Thank you."

"Excellent. Practice the enhancement with your group until they've perfected it. We want to avoid any magical fallout from harming our allies."

Clancy's eyes widened at whatever he saw over Bryan's shoulder. Leaning in, he whispered, "I think your brother wants you. And he's looking particularly determined."

Bryan looked around the fully occupied training area, realizing he was trapped. He'd managed to avoid Lysander for most of the day, but his brother was nothing if not perseverant. And he'd timed his ambush well. "Thanks for the heads up."

"You're welcome." His eyes widened further. "I'll, uh, just take my trainees over there." He pointed to the far side of the room, then quickly hustled his group of magic-users clear of the impending explosion.

"What the hell was all that about earlier this morning?"

"Hey, Lysander. How are you feeling?" Bryan pasted an innocent smile on his face.

"Don't try and pull that crap with me." Lysander jabbed him in the chest. "I want to know why my brother's suddenly speaking like the Oracle of Delphi.

Bryan sighed. "It's because of a book."

"A book?"

"Yeah. Max and I think a book transferred its knowledge to me."

"How?"

"I'm not really sure. It was when we were asking about the relic. The shop owner brought out a book. I was trying to analyze its magical signature and well, things get a bit foggy after that, but it seems to have shoved information into my head."

"What the hell, Bryan? You didn't think to mention it before now?"

Bryan winced, his shoulders tightening uncomfortably. "To be honest, I kind of forgot about it."

"Are you freaking kidding me?" Lysander yelled. "A book possesses you and you forgot about it?"

"I've been a little distracted lately. There's been a lot going on."

Lysander shoved him back a step. "You're blaming sex-brain for why you didn't tell us you were possessed by a book?"

Bryan pushed him back. "It didn't possess me. It just transferred its knowledge to me."

"Yes. That's much better. An inanimate object accessed your brain without your permission. But you didn't think it was necessary to warn us." He paused, then squinted. "Does this knowledge know how to stop the demon?"

"Maybe." He shrugged. "I'm not really sure."

"You're not sure." Lysander said flatly.

Bryan shook his head. "It doesn't work like that. The information just kind of comes to me on its own."

"Well, that's just crap." Lysander poked him in the chest again. "What if it happens in the middle of a battle? Did you even think of that? You were completely checked out. Not there, Bryan. For minutes. Long enough to get killed if it happened in the wrong place."

"I trust you and Max to look after me." The look that came over his brother's face made him take a hasty step backward.

"Yes," Lysander hissed, stalking him. "Let's just talk about Max, shall we. Where was he when this mysterious book possessed my brother?"

"Stop. Neither of us could have seen it coming. It just happened."

"Then why didn't he mention it? Both of you idiots could have jeopardized everything by keeping silent. What if the book is working for our enemies?"

"I don't think it's evil. It's just information."

"You didn't think at all. Neither of you." Lysander spun in a circle. "Where is that mate of yours? I want a word with him."

"You leave Max alone. We did nothing wrong." Which was the wrong thing to say. Bryan braced himself for the explosion he could see building on his brother's face.

"Beloved. What's wrong? I could feel your anger from the other side of the mansion."

Bryan blew out a breath of relief at the timely interruption. Catching Max's eyes as he and Roman hurried toward them, he mentally sent a warning through their link.

Lysander turned to Roman, jabbing his finger in Bryan's direction. "Did you know Bryan was possessed by some magical book?"

He nodded. "Max just informed me of that fact."

"Did he?" Lysander's eyes glinted dangerously. "And did he also tell you why we didn't know about this sooner?"

Max answered, completely stone faced. "My apologies, Consort. I have been a little distracted by sex-brain lately."

Bryan choked, then clapped a hand over his mouth as he spun around. This would be a bad time to laugh. A really bad time.

The snicker escaped his best efforts to hold it back.

"You're both idiots."

"Beloved, there is nothing to worry about."

"Yes, there is. Bryan could be in danger from that book."

"My old friend Marie would not have done anything to harm one of my family."

"Let's just ask her, shall we."

"We can't." Bryan turned back. "Peter killed her."

"Shit." Lysander rested his hand on Roman's arm. "She was your friend?"

"For a long time. I will miss our talks."

"I'm so sorry for your loss."

"Thank you, beloved." Roman patted his hand.

Lysander gave his arm a gentle squeeze then turned to Bryan. "What happened to Marie's book?"

"We think her granddaughter escaped with it, Consort," Max said, coming to stand next to Bryan.

"And where is she?"

"We don't know."

Lysander's eyes narrowed dangerously. "What do you mean, you don't know?"

"Just that," Bryan said. "She fled down an escape tunnel. It was too narrow for us to chase after her."

"So you've been possessed by a book and nobody knows a damn thing about it except for the person you let get away."

"I told you, I'm not possessed."

"We don't know that for sure." Lysander pointed his finger at Max. "You better find Marie's granddaughter and that damn book. I want some answers."

"We'll search for it the first chance we get."

"See that you do." Lysander gave Roman's hand a final squeeze, then stomped from the room.

The door slamming behind Lysander as he exited brought all activity to a standstill. The trainees looked around nervously before resuming their lessons when nothing further happened.

Roman tipped his head. "If you will excuse me, I have news that will improve my beloved's mood."

"Like what?" Bryan asked, doubting anything could make his brother happy right now.

"Tommy has been located."

Except for that.

* * *

Tommy arrives at the Galway Mansion…

"Marcus. It is good to see you, old friend."

"You as well."

"Tommy." Lysander rushed down the steps past Roman and Marcus to pull his friend into a hug. He got his first inkling something was wrong when Tommy's arms remained at his sides.

"Hey, Ell."

Lysander let go when Tommy leaned away. "I've been so worried about you."

"I'm fine." Tommy wouldn't meet his eyes, instead keeping them trained over Lysander's shoulder.

"I can see that you're not. What happened?"

Tommy's jaw clenched but he didn't respond.

"Tommy?"

"Let it go, Ell"

"But…."

Tommy held up his hand. "Please. I don't want to talk about it."

"All right," Lysander said slowly. "I'll leave it alone."

"Thank you." Tommy pointed to the door. "Can I go in?"

"Of course," Lysander answered quietly, stepping out of his way. "Your suite has been prepared. Let me know if there's anything you need."

"Sure." Still not making eye contact, Tommy moved past him and made his way up the steps and into the house. He never looked back.

As soon as he was sure his friend was out of earshot, Lysander turned to Marcus. "What happened to him?"

"I'm sorry, Consort. It's not my place to tell."

Lysander stepped closer to the visiting vampire. "I'm his best friend. I want to know what happened to him."

"Beloved…,"

"Don't you beloved me. Did you see him, Roman? He wouldn't even look at me."

"I saw." Roman took his hand, pulling him away from Marcus. "You need to give him time and space."

"Did Marcus tell you what happened?"

"No. And I will not invade Tommy's privacy by asking."

"How can I help him if I don't know what's wrong?"

"By being there. Everyone processes trauma in their own way and on their own schedule." Roman pulled him close. "Tommy knows that he is loved. When he is ready, he will come to you." Roman kissed his hair before murmuring, "He will need your strength when it is time to grieve."

"Grieve?"

"Yes. His soul cries out in pain and sorrow. I fear your Tommy has lost something of great value."

A tear trickled down Lysander's face. "What happened to you, brother?"

He stared at the empty doorway knowing he had no choice but to wait until Tommy came to him. So, that's what he'd do. For now.

* * *

Training, training, training…

"Lysander. You need to focus. That is the third time you have dropped your guard." Roman towered over where he lay in a crumpled heap on the exercise mat. "If you are unable to give your full attention to your training, perhaps it would be best if we stopped."

"No. We need to keep working if we're going to be ready." He hauled himself laboriously to his feet, muttering, "Maybe if you didn't move so damned fast, I could see you coming."

"Is that your plan, Consort? To ask your enemies to slow down to accommodate your sluggish reflexes?" Max asked as he walked by.

"Screw you, Max. I'd like to see you do any better." Fire sparked from his fingertips. One more word and he'd let the vampire have it.

"We are done for the day," Roman said. "Max, gather everyone outside. I would like to speak with them after I have finished fighting with my beloved."

"Yes, Prince." Chuckling, Max strode away, shooing the pockets of training enforcers and magic-users from the room.

Fuming, Lysander turned on his mate. "I said we needed to keep going. We don't have time to take a break."

"And yet, if we do not, we will burn everyone out. That will lead to careless mistakes that could get them hurt. Or worse."

"I think you're worrying over nothing. So I dropped my guard a couple of times." He shrugged. "I'll pay closer attention next time."

"That is exactly my point. You do not make mistakes of this nature. When you are alert and focused, you are unstoppable." Roman tugged gently on his hand. "I know you are not sleeping. It is taking a toll."

Lysander flinched, Roman's understanding expression nearly his undoing. But he dug in his heels, refusing to back down. "We have to keep practicing. I'll try harder. I promise. But we can't stop now."

"Beloved, it is not just you. Tension is building in everyone. If they are not given an opportunity to rest and recharge, someone is going to get hurt."

"They'll get hurt worse if they're not ready to face our enemies."

"If they do not have a break, they will have nothing left with which to fight. We need to allow them some down time."

"Then we'll quit an hour early today."

Roman shook his head. "I want everyone to participate in a recreational activity together. It will clear all of our minds and renew our focus."

"No, Roman. We don't know how much time we have. We can't waste it playing around. Call everyone back. We need to keep training."

Roman cupped his cheek. "Beloved, talk to me. I do not understand this need to drive yourself and everyone else into the ground."

Lysander swallowed. "It's coming for me. I can feel it. I have to be ready."

"And we will be."

"You don't understand." Lysander gripped the front of Roman's shirt. "I can't sleep, Roman. Its eyes follow me everywhere. If this goes on much longer, I won't be capable of fighting. We need to be ready now."

"I wish we could protect you from this."

"I know. But you can't." He touched Roman's face. "I'm worried I'll hurt you again."

"The other was my fault. I did not realize how firmly the demon had you in its grip." Roman's voice hardened. "I will not make that mistake again."

""And that's another thing. You don't have time to spend it worrying about me. You and Max should be focused on coordinating our allies and working out battle strategies."

"Beloved, you are my first priority."

"But I can't be right now. Everything else needs to come first." Lysander picked at a button on Roman's shirt, then whispered, "I don't know if I'm strong enough to face it."

He was abruptly crushed against his mate's chest. Roman's rich muskiness flooded his body, soothing his soul. The coiled tension he'd been carrying for what seemed like forever, slowly released. He let himself go boneless, knowing Roman would hold him up.

"You forget that we are stronger together. As you take strength from me, so do I from you," Roman said. "You are not alone in this. Do not take it all on your shoulders."

Lysander made a noise of agreement and continued breathing in his mate.

They stood holding each other for a few minutes, with Roman running his long fingers through Lysander's hair, soothing him further. Sooner than Lysander was ready for, Roman stepped back. "It is time to speak with the others."

Lysander sighed. "Is this really necessary?"

"Trust me. A few hours of pleasure today will benefit everyone. You will see the difference when we resume our training sessions tomorrow."

Knowing when he was beat, Lysander could only give in. "Fine. If you think it will help, let's go play."

Roman's smile brought forth a small one of his own. It would be interesting to see what his mate considered recreational activity.

* * *

Bryan's mouth dropped open. "You want us to play hide-and-seek? Now?"

"I do. As soon as the children join us, we will begin."

Bryan turned to his mate and whispered. "Did Lysander hit him too hard in the head?"

"Roman is fine. The Consort gave him no challenge today. He was the one who took too many blows to the head."

"Really? I saw him working with you last week. His defensive skills were great. Especially the way he compensated for your speed."

"That was last week. As of now, he will be a liability when we engage our enemies."

"Hey."

Ignoring Lysander, Bryan frowned at Max. "I don't understand. He's training harder than I've ever seen."

"Training that is worthless since he has lost all focus. His carelessness will get himself or someone else killed."

"I can hear you, asshole."

"Then pay attention to what I'm saying. It may save someone's life. Including yours."

Bryan walked over to his brother. "Are you really struggling that much?"

"I guess." Lysander looked down and toed the grass. "Roman thinks it's because I'm pushing too hard. He's probably right." Lysander's shoulders dropped. "Not being able to sleep isn't helping."

Bryan's stomach clenched at the defeated look on his brother's face. "I'm sorry we couldn't do more. Gideon and I are still looking for a way to block the demon." He put his hand on his brother's shoulder. "Don't give up hope. I know we'll figure it out."

"Sure." Lysander pulled back with a fake smile that hurt Bryan's heart. "But hey, since we're playing hide-and-seek, you want to make it interesting?"

Playing along, Bryan smirked. "I might. Same stakes as when we were kids?"

"Of course."

"You're on." He punched his brother in the arm. "But this time, I won't let you win."

Lysander punched him back. "Asshole. You never let me win. I kicked your ass fair and square."

"You keep telling yourself that, but we both know the truth." Bryan flicked him on the nose then ducked behind Max, laughing when his mate crossed his arms and raised a challenging eyebrow. Lysander's hand stopped mid-air.

"Chicken." Lysander's nose wrinkled. "You won't always have your mate to hide behind."

A huge grin spread across Bryan's face when he realized Lysander was wrong. Max would always be there. Bryan knew that down to his soul.

As if knowing what he was thinking, Lysander gave him a real smile this time. One that got brighter when Roman joined them.

"Max, please have some of your enforcers spread around the perimeter to keep an eye on the children."

"It's already taken care of, Prince. The property boundary lights have also been turned on."

"Excellent. I expect anyone not standing guard to join in."

"The enforcers have already drawn straws."

Roman frowned, "With the losers having to play?"

Max shook his head and grinned. "Everyone was looking forward to playing. The enforcers that pulled the short straws are the ones on guard duty."

"I see." Roman gave Lysander a look Bryan couldn't interpret.

"Hush," Lysander said, elbowing Roman in the ribs. "So, how is this supposed to work? The vampires and the wolf pups can see in the dark. With your advanced hearing and the pups' sense of smell, the magic-users don't stand a chance. Are we going to mix up the teams?"

Roman shook his head. "I am sure the magic-users can find a way around our abilities. It only requires some creative thinking."

Lysander tilted his head, frowning at his mate. "This feels a lot like the stealth training we were working on a few days ago."

"Does it? What a strange coincidence."

"You said we were taking a break."

Bryan choked back a laugh at the disgruntled look on his brother's face. Trust Roman to find a way to get his brother to play while still giving him an opportunity to develop his fighting skills.

"And so we are." Eyes twinkling, Roman held out his hand. "Come, beloved. We will hide behind that tree and count to one hundred. You and I are It."

* * *

Happy squeals from the children interspersed with excited yips from the pups playing in their shifted forms filled the night air. Bryan led Max down the path to his secret hideaway, pulling him through a break in the hedge few knew about. Sneaking past the groundskeeper's house, they reached the mighty oak tree he'd loved playing under as a child. He led Max beneath its low sweeping branches to the far side of the large trunk, then sat on one of the exposed roots. tugging Max down beside him.

"Why'd you bring us all the way out here? The children are on the other side of the property."

"I didn't feel much like playing hide and seek. Well, I don't want to seek, but I have no problem hiding." He waggled his eyebrows.

Max chuckled. "Is that right? What evil idea is brewing in that head of yours?"

Bryan pushed him to the ground and straddled his waist. "Let me give you a clue."

The laughter in Max's kisses tasted sweeter than the strawberries he had for lunch.

* * *

"Someone's coming." Max rolled off Bryan and stood, pulling up the zipper on his pants.

Bryan squeezed his eyes shut and pounded his fists on the ground. Damn it. Why now? They'd just been getting to the good stuff. He groaned quietly when his brother's voice carried on the breeze.

"I'm sure I saw them heading this way. They have to be around here somewhere."

"Why are you so determined to locate your brother? We passed six enforcers and three magic-users we could have found."

"Because I want to win our bet."

"And this wager is of such great value, we will let the others win so that your brother will lose?"

"Exactly."

Bryan shook his head. His brother was such an asshole.

"What could possibly be worth giving up a victory?"

"Apple pie."

"Pardon me."

Lysander's joyful laugh was good to hear. Even if it meant he was going to lose his birthday pie once his brother broke through the hedge. Sighing, Bryan rolled to his knees and let Max pull him to his feet.

"Mrs. Smith always makes us a special treat for our birthday. Winner gets to eat the loser's pie."

"I do not understand. You can have pie any day of the week."

"But it wouldn't taste as good."

The sound of muffled footsteps drew nearer. Next came the rustling of clothes getting caught on branches as his brother and Roman pushed through the hedge. Bryan gave Max a rueful smile, wishing they'd managed a few more minutes together before being discovered. Alone time had been in short supply since they'd gotten back.

The rustling sounds stopped, letting Bryan know Lysander and Roman had made it through the hedge and were now on the other side of the tree. Even though it was foolish, Bryan crossed his fingers and whispered the chant he'd always used as a child. "You can't see us, you can't hear, look right past us, we're not near."

"Ready or not, here we come, Bryan."

He rolled his eyes when Lysander stepped around the tree trunk. "How did you find us so quickly?"

Lysander came to a halt, his head moving back and forth. "Huh. That's strange. I thought for sure he'd be here."

"Don't be a jerk. I know you can see me."

Roman glanced around. "I'm not sure what you saw, but I do not sense anyone in the area."

He didn't? But they were standing right here. Bryan's head snapped over to Max, who was frowning at Roman.

"Weird. I could have sworn they came this way. It must have been a rabbit or something."

"Hey," Bryan shouted, waving his arms wildly. "We're standing right here."

Roman smirked. "It seems you will be getting only one pie this year."

"Damn it. I always win." Lysander kicked at the tree, narrowly missing Bryan's shin. "I bet it's that damn Max's fault. He's much sneakier than Bryan."

"Which is one of the qualities that makes him an exceptional Second."

"And super annoying."

Roman snorted. "That as well. Come, beloved. Let us find the others we passed earlier. Victory will still be yours."

"Fine." Lysander gave the tree one last kick, then ducked under the branches. "But I really wanted that pie."

"I will ensure one is prepared especially for you when you are victorious."

"You will? Let's hurry. We need to catch your enforcers before they get away."

Roman and Lysander's laughter faded as they moved out of earshot.

"What the hell just happened? Were they gaslighting us?"

Max's brow creased as he processed the last few minutes. "Roman would not do that."

"Then why couldn't they see us?"

"I don't know." Max's eyes narrowed as he turned to Bryan. "What did you do?"

"What do you mean, what did I do? I didn't do anything."

"You hid us from them somehow."

"I couldn't have."

"I think you did. There's no other explanation."

"I'm telling you I didn't. This has nothing to do with me." Bryan began pacing in front of the tree.

Max felt bad to keep pushing, but something told him solving this puzzle was of utmost importance. Stepping in front of Bryan, he took hold of his shoulders. "Stop for a minute. We need to think this through."

"Think what through, Max?" Bryan threw his hands in the air. "They couldn't see us. Either they're conning us or we're somehow invisible."

"I can see you just fine. There is something else at work here." He ran the sequence of events through his mind again, knowing he was missing something. Then it hit. "I could feel your magic when they got close. What were you thinking?"

"I still don't understand how you can do that."

"Don't worry about it right now. Just answer the question. What were you thinking about when you first heard them?"

"Nothing. How many times do I have to say that?"

"Are you sure?" Max squeezed his shoulders. "Think hard. This is important."

Bryan gave a long-suffering sigh before his brow creased in thought. "Nope. There's nothing. Well, except for a silly chant I always said as a kid."

This was it. Max knew it. "What was the chant?"

Bryan shrugged, his cheeks flushing. "It's stupid really. Just a wish that nobody would see us. It's not like it ever worked."

"This time it did."

"Come on, Max. You can't seriously be suggesting I made us invisible."

"No. But you may have convinced their minds we were."

"Mind control isn't a thing." Bryan pushed him back. "There has to be another explanation for what happened. One grounded in reality."

"Does there?" Max tapped Bryan's chest over his Goddess mark. "Or does this explain everything?"

"No." Bryan shook his head, backing away. "Do you have any idea how dangerous a power like that would be? It has to have been something else."

Max's heart clenched at the fear pouring off his mate. "You need to calm down."

"I can't calm down. You don't understand. If I was able to tamper with Roman's mind, nobody would be safe from me. I could do it to anyone. Even you." His eyes went wide with horror.

Max froze. The idea that someone could alter his thoughts had Max's lizard brain shrieking in terror. Would he even be able to tell if it was happening? His protective instincts flared in response to his fear. He needed to get away from the threat.

"Max?"

What if it had already happened? Were his thoughts even his own? Was any of this real or was he living his mate's reality? He lurched to a stop. Did he even have a mate or was that only a trick of the mind too?

"Max. Please don't run from me."

The mate bond burned, Bryan's distress breaking through his panic-clouded thoughts. He jolted back to awareness and looked around for his mate. Bryan was standing ten feet away with his arms wrapped around himself, the misery on his face enough to break Max's heart. Damn it. He could kick himself for doing that to his mate. He rushed over to Bryan and gathered him in his arms.

"I'm sorry. Please forgive me," Max said.

"It's okay. I understand. I'd be afraid of me too. Oh, no." Bryan started struggling to get away. "You have to let me go."

Max held him tighter, but was barely able to hold on when Bryan thrashed harder. "Stop. You're going to hurt yourself."

"Better me than you." Bryan went limp, surprising Max into loosening his hold. Bryan quickly moved out of reach. "Please, Max. Get away from me before I hurt you."

"You're not going to hurt me."

"You don't know that. Look what I did to my brother. He didn't know we were here. My own brother and he couldn't see me. And Roman. Even with his enhanced senses, he couldn't feel us."

"Once you reverse what you did, everything will be fine."

"Until I do it again. When does it end, Max? When I mess with everyone's minds and take over the world. Who could stop me?"

"I would."

"Not if I controlled you too."

Panic rose, but only for a moment as a half-forgotten legend passed through his mind. "I don't think you can," he murmured.

"What?"

Max smiled at his worried mate. "I don't think you can deliberately harm me. Our mate bond won't allow it."

"It won't?" Hope sparked in Bryan's eyes.

"No. But we should test it to make sure."

"Oh, no." Bryan shook his head and took a step back. "I'm not going to do that."

Max darted forward and grabbed Bryan's hand before he could get away. "You have to. It's the only way to know for sure."

"I don't want to. The thought of messing with your mind…just no. I won't do it."

"It'll be fine. Trust me." Max picked up Bryan's other hand. "Please."

Bryan stopped trying to get free and stared into his eyes. Max pushed his confidence and belief in Bryan through their mate bond. Eventually, he nodded. "Fine. But don't blame me for making you cluck like a chicken."

That startled a laugh out of him. "Give it your best shot, oh mighty mage."

Bryan gave him the stink eye before closing them. Max could feel the buzz of his power as it covered his body like a warm blanket, bringing him the same feeling of comfort that his mate did.

One of Bryan's eyes popped open. "Feel anything?"

"Just your magic."

"There's no compulsion to cluck?"

"Nope. Did you want to try again?"

In answer, Bryan closed his eye. The magic flowing around Max increased until the air sparkled.

"Still nothing?" Bryan asked, opening both eyes. He looked intently into Max's face. "Not even to bark?"

"Nothing." He cupped Bryan's face. "Your magic will not hurt me. Ever."

"But it can hurt everyone else."

"You won't let it." Of this, Max was sure. "You, of everyone, knows the price of tampering with people." He cocked an eyebrow.

"Like our Bloodmate bond," Bryan whispered.

"Exactly. Because of that, you will be more cautious to prevent something similar from happening again." He smirked. "Besides, do you honestly believe the Goddess would grant you this ability if you couldn't be trusted?"

Bryan covered the spot on his chest where he'd been marked. "Do you really think that?

Max nodded. "I really do. And like the Goddess, there's no one I trust more than you."

Bryan's mouth dropped open. Before he could say any of the thousand thoughts Max could see in his eyes, a bell sounded, calling everyone back to the house.

"It looks like the game is over. We need to go back."

Bryan's hand squeezed his. "And I need to fix whatever I did to Lysander and Roman. If I can."

If Max knew anything about his mate, it was that Bryan wouldn't rest until he'd reversed the damage he'd accidentally caused.

Bryan gripped tight to Max's hand when they neared the crowd gathered on the side lawn. The next few minutes should prove to be very interesting.

"There you guys are." Carlos gave them a thumb's up. "Looks like you're the winners."

"Who are you talking to?" Lysander asked.

"There's no need to be a sore loser just because your brother beat you."

Lysander laughed. "Bryan didn't beat me. I think he and Max snuck off somewhere instead of playing with the rest of us."

Carlos squinted at Bryan. "How hard did he hit his head earlier?"

"It's not that," Bryan said. "I accidentally…."

Lysander shoved the vampire. "Seriously, Carlos. Who are you talking to?"

"Your brother, idiot. He's standing right in front of you."

Lysander glanced around. "No, he's not. Roman, can you see Bryan?"

"No, beloved. Neither Max nor Bryan have returned yet."

Carlos' eyes flicked between Roman and Lysander, looking at them like they were crazy.

Sighing, Bryan placed his hand on his brother's shoulder.

Lysander jumped back. "Who just touched me?" He waved his hands in front of him, smacking Bryan before he could duck out of the way. "Show yourself right now."

Carlos whistled. "He really can't see you. How the fuck did you manage that?"

"I'll tell you as soon as I fix this." Hoping this worked, Bryan wished for Lysander and Roman to be able to see Max and him again.

"Bryan, you asshole." The punch caught him in the shoulder. "Why would you play a dirty trick like that? I thought Carlos was screwing with me. Or I was going crazy."

"Sorry. It wasn't intentional."

"Max, why would you and Bryan torment my mate?" Roman frowned at them.

Looking around at the curious crowd, Bryan cleared his throat. "Could we please take this inside? What I have to say should be kept between us."

"I hope by between us, you also mean me and Gideon?" Carlos said.

"Yes. And Jackson." Bryan grimaced. "We should probably include Edgar as well."

"Then this is a Council matter," Roman stated. "We will gather in my office after I am done here." He raised his voice to be heard over the crowd. "Eric, please bring Casey and the pups to me."

Everyone waited until the men herded the excited pups over to Roman. He smiled fondly when they sat at attention at his feet. "Well played, pups. You did your Alpha proud. I'll be sure to tell him how skillful you all were the next time I speak with him."

The beaming grins, whether wolf or child, lifted the spirits of everyone gathered.

Roman continued. "Since Max and Bryan have been disqualified for not following the rules, the wolf team, led by Eric and Casey, are the winners and will receive the prize for tonight's event."

Bryan clapped his hands over his ears to drown out the excited cheers, yips, and howls. And the catcalls shouted at him and Max by the enforcers.

Roman held up his hands and waited for everyone to settle down before speaking again. "Mrs. Smith has a special treat waiting for the winners." He winked at Lysander. "I believe it is apple pie."

Bryan's laughter at his brother's downcast expression was drowned out by the next round of cheering from the pups."

Chapter Twenty-One

"Could you repeat that."

Bryan flinched at the anger in Edgar's voice. "I said…."

"Oh, I heard what you said. How dare you interfere with my Prince's mind?"

"I told you, it was an accident."

"I'll accident you the next time I see you."

"Enough, Edgar. No permanent harm was done. There is no need for such anger."

"But, Prince…."

"Bryan cannot be blamed if he was unaware of this ability."

"Until he does it again."

"Trust me, you don't have to worry about that." The mere thought of it made Bryan nauseous.

"What if you have another accident?"

Max held up his hand when Bryan went to answer. "Bryan's power doesn't affect me. I will make sure he doesn't try to take over the world," He winked at Bryan, who grinned back, never more thankful than now that he'd earned Max's trust. Without it, this conversation could have gone very badly.

"And who's going to…." Muffled sounds of a scuffle came over the phone. *"Give me that phone back."*

"Let it go, Edgar. You heard Roman. He's fine. There's nothing to be angry about."

"I'll decide that, not some fur-brained neanderthal…."

Jackson's voice raised over Edgar's curses. *"Thanks for the update, guys. You'll have to excuse us. I need to run the cranky out of my mate."*

"If running doesn't work, you could always try fu….".

Jackson's laughter cut Carlos off. *"I'm sure I'll do that anyway. Talk later."* He ended the call, cutting off Edgar's new round of cursing.

Bryan chuckled, then turned to smile at Roman. "Thank you for supporting me. I was worried you were going to be furious."

Roman folded his hands on the desk. "While I understand you had no way of knowing what you were capable of, I will admit that this new power of yours leaves me unsettled. Fearful even. I will not be alone in that."

Bryan swallowed hard. "I know."

"There will be those who will want to destroy it." He paused, looking at Bryan with sympathy.

"By destroying me."

"Yes. Or by trying to control you. They will then attempt to destroy you when controlling you does not work."

Bryan nodded. "I've thought of all of this. And I understand the fear my power will cause. That's why I'm never going to use it again."

"That would be best." Roman glanced around the room. "We will also keep knowledge of it between ourselves."

"I'd like to ask Mother to protect this information the same way we did for Melissa," Gideon said. "Which means I'll need to tell my parents."

Roman frowned. "How do you think they will react?"

"I'm not sure. Hopefully they'll be okay with it."

"And if they're not?" Lysander asked. "Who's going to protect Bryan if they decide he's too dangerous to live?"

Max growled. "I'll deal with anyone who thinks they can threaten my mate."

"Settle down, tiger." Carlos rolled his eyes. "We'll all protect him."

Roman tipped his head at Bryan. "The final decision must be yours. Are you agreeable to Gideon informing the King and Queen of Dragons of your newfound ability?"

He gave a helpless shrug. "I don't really have a choice. Not if I want Sophia's help."

"Then it is settled. Gideon, I know this may put you in an uncomfortable position, but please let us know if there are any concerns when you speak to your parents. If they act adversely to this information, we will need to take steps to protect Bryan from them."

Gideon's brow creased. "I'll let you know, but I seriously doubt my parents would want to harm him."

"You cannot predict how anyone will react if they feel threatened. An ability to alter their thoughts is not something that will be taken lightly."

That sparked an idea. "Maybe Sophia could bind my power."

"Would you really want to do that?" Lysander asked. "The Goddess gifted you this ability for a reason."

"I'm afraid of what I could do. I don't want to take any chances of messing with someone's mind again. Especially not by accident."

"I can discuss it with her and let you know," Gideon said.

"Thank you." Bryan slumped back in his chair, glad the explanations and decisions were over. And that nobody wanted to lock him up. Or kill him.

"Hold off on that request please, Gideon." Lysander turned to Bryan, the expression on his face sending chills down his spine. He was already shaking his head before Lysander got the first word out. "I need you to use your power on me."

Bryan jumped out of his chair, sending it flying backward. "No." He slashed his hand through the air. "Did you hear nothing I said? I will not use it. Never again. And especially not on you."

"Bryan…."

"No, Sandi. I mean it. The subject is closed."

"Just hear me out. I have an idea." He spoke quickly. After no more than a few words, Bryan stopped shaking his head and began to pay attention. A minute later, he picked up his chair and slowly sat down. Before long, he was fully engaged in the conversation, throwing out ideas of his own. His excitement rose as he realized this might be the solution they'd been looking for.

* * *

Bryan reached for Lysander's hands, then paused, flexing his fingers for the umpteenth time. Max bumped his shoulder and placed a hand on his lower back, his touch immediately settling Bryan's nerves.

"Relax." The husky word tickled the insides of his ear. "You've got this."

Nodding, Bryan pushed his worry to the side and decisively grabbed his brother's hands. "Okay. It'll be just like we talked about. I won't be touching your thoughts, just altering the shield protecting your mind so anyone searching for you won't be able to find you."

"Except for Roman. You can't shut me off from him." His brother smiled at his mate who was standing next to them. "I've grown used to him talking in my head."

Bryan nodded. "I'll make sure Roman has access to you." He blew out another breath.

Lysander tightened his fingers around Bryan's and smiled. "Don't be scared. I trust you."

"I'm worried I'll change something by accident."

"I'm not. You're too careful for that."

"But…."

"Bryan. stop worrying so much. I know I'm asking a lot, but there's nobody I trust more than you." A throat clearing beside them made him grin. "Except for Roman, of course."

"Of course." Bryan inhaled deep, then exhaled slowly. "Okay. Here I go." He closed his eyes and felt his way along the link Lysander had established between them. Not paying attention to any of the stray thoughts that flickered around him, Bryan approached the hub of Lysander's consciousness and painstakingly built the strongest shield he was capable of. Once it was in place, he used his new magic to make his brother invisible to anyone but Roman and himself. When he was satisfied with what he'd done, he slowly withdrew.

Lysander blinked then smiled at him. "You're getting good at that."

"What?"

"Shielding my mind. I barely felt your touch."

"Great." Bryan waved that off. "How do you feel?"

"Fine." He looked up at his mate. "Mind-speak with me so I can reassure Bryan everything's okay before he explodes."

Bryan watched closely, his heart slowing to its normal pace when he realized they were having a silent exchange, their mating link not damaged in the least by his actions.

Gideon shouted and grabbed his head. "Mother. Not so loud." He was vaguely aware of everyone looking at him but his mother's distress was taking all of his attention.

"Gideon. You must find the Consort. I fear something terrible has happened to him."

Gideon's eyes flicked to Lysander. "The Consort is fine, Mother."

"Are you sure? I can't feel him anymore."

"Feel him?" Gideon's eyebrows shot up. "You formed a link with him? Without him knowing?"

"Once I became aware of his existence, the connection developed on its own. I feel him the same way I feel you. But now our link is gone. Are you certain he's all right?"

"Yes. I'm looking right at him."

"Then why can't I feel him?"

"Bryan enhanced the shield around his mind."

"With this new power."

"Yes." He winced when she started yelling. "Don't be upset, Mother. We were all a part of this decision."

"Bryan promised not to use his power on anyone."

"He didn't actually use it on Lysander, only on the protection around his mind. He made it, and therefore, Lysander, invisible to everyone." Silence. He waited a beat, then two more before she responded.

"Impressive. Your Father and I wouldn't have thought of that."

Gideon smiled reassuringly at everyone staring worriedly at him. "Nor I. They are very creative in their thinking."

"I agree. I am most thankful the Consort isn't hurt. When the connection vanished, I assumed he'd been killed."

"He's very much alive."

"Thank the Goddess. If he had died, everything would have been lost."

"What does that mean?" Silence. "Mother. Damn it. Answer me." When she continued to ignore him, he gave up, realizing she wasn't going to respond.

Lysander cleared his throat. "I gather your mother was able to sense me?"

"Yes," Gideon nodded. "Through your bloodline connection. When Bryan did his thing, it cut off the link. She thought you'd been killed."

"That must have worried her.

"I had no idea she could yell that loudly."

Bryan snickered. "Sorry about that. I didn't realize she had a connection to Sandi."

"Neither did I." Gideon turned to Lysander. "You may want to have Bryan give her access again. Having a direct connection to the Queen of Dragons could be very advantageous."

"I'll think about it." Lysander smiled at Bryan. "If your new shield worked to block the Queen, that gives me hope it'll also work for the demon."

"There is but one way to know for sure," Roman said. "It is time for everyone to leave so that Lysander can get some much overdue sleep."

Bryan leaned over and hugged his brother. "Pleasant dreams, Sandi."

"Thanks." Lysander squeezed him tight, whispering in his ear, "I really hope this works. I've been praying for a good night's sleep for weeks."

"I hope it works too." Giving him a last squeeze, Bryan nodded at Roman, grabbed Max's hand, then followed everyone out of the room.

* * *

Bryan didn't have time to brace himself before the body hurtling toward him tackled him to the ground. "What the hell, Sandi? Get off of me." He pushed him away, groaning at the knee that caught him in the ribs when his brother scrambled off.

"Sorry. Sorry." Lysander grabbed Bryan's hands and pulled him to his feet. "I just couldn't wait to tell you."

"It worked then?"

"It did." Lysander grinned, then jumped at him again, long arms wrapping around his neck. "Thank you so much. You have no idea how worried I've been."

Bryan squeezed him back. "We were all worried. You were so full of anger, you were becoming a different person," Bryan whispered in his ear. "I'm so glad to have my brother back."

"It's good to be back." Lysander sniffed. "I'm sorry for how I've been acting. It was just so hard holding back the anger. I wanted to yell all the time. Especially at Carlos. He took the brunt of my temper."

"Don't worry about him. He understands better than all of us what you were going through."

"Still. I'm glad that's over."

"Me too."

"Me, as well," Max said, appearing out of nowhere. "Now that you've had some sleep, it's time to step up your training, Consort. You've fallen far behind the others."

Bryan grinned when Lysander groaned.

"You, as well, Bryan. Both of you will be working with the enforcers today."

The smile dropped off his face. Was Max for real?

Like he knew what Bryan was thinking, Max nodded and gave them an evil grin. "I told them not to take it easy on you." He clapped his hands. "Move it before I make you do laps."

Shit. He was serious. They looked at each other, then back at Max, who raised his eyebrow and tapped his watch in warning. They started running toward the enforcer training area, neither of them daring to look back.

* * *

Lysander rolled to his stomach on the floor and groaned. "I think your mate broke me."

Bryan grunted from his place next to him. He had his arm draped over his eyes, appreciating how comfortable the soft carpet felt to his over-used muscles. He might just stay here for the next twenty-four hours, which was about how long it would take for his legs to stop shaking.

"I don't understand how burpees and running suicides are going to help us fight the demon."

"Me either, but Max is an expert when it comes to training and battle readiness. If he felt they were necessary, he must have a good reason." Bryan flexed his toes and stretched his spine, groaning loudly when he felt the pull in all his overused muscles. "Shit. Even my skin hurts."

He lifted his arm off his eyes when Roman and Max snickered, then scowled when he saw Max's huge grin. "You ass. You tortured us on purpose."

"A conditioned body means a conditioned mind. You and the Consort will need both in the upcoming battle."

"As soon as I can move, I'm lighting your mate on fire." Lysander threatened.

Bryan flipped off Max before covering his eyes again. "I'll help you." Damn vampire. Bryan would get him back for this. Once he could move.

Footsteps sounded in the doorway. "Bryan, I would like to speak with you."

Groaning, he rolled to his side, then pushed off the floor. "What is it now, Mother?"

"I would like to pay my respects to your father."

Bryan frowned. "I don't recall you ever going to his burial vault before."

"Because I didn't." Charlotte pursed her lips. "I could not forgive him for being unfaithful and having a child with another woman." Her eyes drifted to Lysander, who immediately stilled.

"And now that you know the truth, you're willing to visit him." Bryan shook his head. "I should've expected nothing less from you."

"If you were in a proper relationship, you would understand. A betrayal of that magnitude is not easily swept aside."

"My Bloodmate bond with Max is stronger than any arranged marriage. I will never be in doubt of his feelings or his loyalty."

"And yet, it brings you no advantage."

"I'm not going to discuss this with you, Mother." Bryan waved to the window. "Go and make your peace with Father. If you've forgotten where the family tomb is, the caretaker can assist you."

Bryan wondered at the glare she directed at Max, which was returned by his mate. About the time Bryan thought he'd have to step in, Max enlightened him.

"The enforcers have been instructed to not allow your mother beyond the confines of the mansion."

"And the reason for that?"

"So we can keep an eye on her. You may trust her to keep her word, but I do not."

Bryan sighed. "Can you please ask your enforcers to let her out?"

"Only if she has an escort. The tomb is distant enough for her to get up to all kinds of mischief." He turned accusing eyes on Charlotte. "Or to set up secret meetings. Isn't that right, madam?"

"Your concerns are invalid. I wish only to have a private word with my husband."

Lysander pushed himself off the floor. "Why don't we all go? I haven't talked to dad in a while."

"Beloved, I can take you another time."

"No," Lysander said, glancing at Bryan from the corner of his eye. "It needs to be now."

Bryan raised an eyebrow. He received a nod in return, confirming Lysander had seen something. "Sure. Let's all go. It's time I introduced Max to Father anyway."

"How lovely." Charlotte's sarcasm could not be missed. "Perhaps we should be on our way. It would be a shame if the vampires were still outside at dawn." The scornful look she turned on Max and Roman belied her words.

* * *

"Thank you for taking me to see your father. After hearing the stories you and your brother shared, it makes me regret that I never had the chance to meet him."

Bryan smiled at Max. "I wish he could have met you too. And Roman. He'd be thrilled his boys found their forever mates."

Max returned his smile, then hissed and dropped into a fighting stance. His eyes scanned their surroundings. "Someone's coming."

Looking around frantically, Bryan asked, "Where? I didn't feel anything come through the shield."

"Max," Roman yelled behind him. "Prepare for attack. Something is headed this way."

"I can't see anything," Bryan yelled to be heard over the sudden clamor. "How do you know?"

Streams of orange fire shot from the clouds, heralding the arrival of a green dragon.

"Shit." Bryan reflexively ducked. "Who in the hell is that?"

"Randal, you betraying bastard." Gideon rushed past Bryan and Max and jumped into the air, changing into his red dragon form mid-leap. He arrowed toward the green dragon, who trumpeted in challenge before turning on his wing and shooting upward, disappearing into the night sky.

"Bryan, look out." Lysander's warning had him ducking in time to avoid the incoming fireball. Looking for the source of the attack, he scowled when Ruth stepped out of a shadow-filled arch that had materialized in the middle of the lawn.

"Ruth, you traitorous bitch. How dare you attack my home?"

Bryan tuned out his mother's angry words, instead watching the figure that stepped out of the arch behind

Ruth. It looked like Jillian, but there was something about her that set his nerves on edge. Fear momentarily immobilized him when he realized what it was.

"Jillian? How could you betray me like this?" Charlotte called out.

Shaking off his paralysis, Bryan yelled, "That's not Jillian. It's the demon."

"Son of a bitch," Lysander cursed when he and Roman moved up beside him. "How the hell do we fight it?"

Burning orbs of red turned on Lysander. An inhuman snarl twisted Jillian's mouth. ***"Liberator."***

"Why is it looking at me?" Lysander asked.

Not knowing what else to do, Bryan erected his strongest shield around their group, praying it would be enough.

"How have you hidden yourself?"

"Liberator?" Charlotte turned to Lysander in horror. "Dear Goddess. I didn't realize."

Movement from Ruth caught Bryan's eye.

"Look out." He pushed his mother to the side. Ruth's ball of flame passed harmlessly between them. He turned back to the demon in time to see its arm arch over its head, a flaming spear in its hand."

"If you will not heed, you will die," the demon roared, launching the spear at his brother.

Bryan threw up his hands and sent a wave of air toward the incoming missile to knock it off its trajectory. He watched in horror as the spear tore through his magic like a hot knife through butter, its flight unaffected. "Lysander, get down."

"No!" Charlotte was a streak of movement as she rushed past Bryan and threw herself in front of Lysander, taking the spear in her back.

"Mother." Lysander was propelled backward when her body crashed into him, both of them falling to the ground. "Bryan! Help us."

Before he could move, Gideon dropped from the sky and shot blue flames toward the demon, encasing it in ice. It turned its head toward him and slowly lifted its arm, frozen shards dropping to the ground. Gideon blasted it with another wave of icy blue fire. This time it froze in place.

Bryan rushed forward and flung a fireball at Ruth, knocking her back a few feet. Her return fire hit his shield, then broke through, missing him by inches. Shit. He prepared to launch another volley when her red eyes flashed. She waved her hand. A cloud of darkness covered the area. When it cleared, Ruth and the demon were gone.

Lysander propped his mother on her side and brushed her pale blonde hair from her face. "Why, Mother," he sobbed. "I thought you hated me. Why did you save me?"

"Liberator…forgive…didn't know." She coughed, blood spraying from her mouth.

"What is the Liberator?" Lysander pulled his shirt over his head and wadded into a ball. He reached around and pressed it against her wound, trying not to jar the spear embedded in her back.

"John…loved…boys…proud." She gurgled, coughing again. A gush of blood rushed from her mouth.

Lysander looked up when Bryan dropped to his knees next to them. "Mrs. Davies is on her way."

"Do you hear that, Mother? Help is coming. You just have to hold on a bit longer."

"John…coming." Charlotte raised a hand to something only she could see, her blood-stained mouth curling up at the corners.

"Mother. No."

Charlotte took a last rattling breath, then fell still.

"Mother!" Lysander yanked the spear from her back and tossed it to the side, not seeing how the grass blackened and smoked around the tip. He rolled Charlotte to her back, then began pumping her chest with both hands. "You don't get to die. You hear me, Mother. Breathe, damn it. You have to breathe." He kept up the compressions until spots danced across his vision. He cursed everyone who tried stopping him, snarling like an enraged animal. He only stopped when Bryan tackled him and knocked him off her body, then locked his arms around him.

"She's gone, Sandi," Bryan said, his voice hoarse and broken. "You have to let her go."

"I can still save her. I know I can."

"It's too late. She's with Father now." Wetness ran down his cheek, falling onto Lysander's hair.

Lysander fisted his hands in the back of Bryan's shirt, crying angry tears into his shoulder for the mother he had both loved and hated. Moments later, their mates were with them, offering support and comfort while he and Bryan grieved.

* * *

"How are you feeling?"

Bryan turned away from the window and waited as Max walked over to him. "I'm not really sure. My emotions are all over the place." He looked over at his brother, who was sitting on Roman's lap with his head leaning against his chest. Lysander nodded every so often at whatever Roman was saying to him. Lowering his voice, Bryan said, "To be honest, I'm more worried about Lysander. He's hurting so much. Even though he tried to convince himself he hated her, at the end of the day, Charlotte was still the only mother he'd ever known."

"Which is unfortunate."

"Yeah." Bryan sighed. "It doesn't help that he blames himself for her death. He had a feeling we all needed to be outside but he didn't know it would result in Mother dying. The guilt is eating him alive."

"Roman will help him through it. My concern is for you. I can feel that your mind is in turmoil."

Bryan gave him a wobbly smile, then buried his face in Max's chest when his arm encircled Bryan's waist and pulled him close. He soaked up the comforting waves of support Max sent through their link, which helped to dull the sharpest edges of his grief. Heaving a big sigh, Bryan hoped Max could make sense of his jumbled thoughts.

"I'm so confused about how I should feel. On one hand, I'm angry at the power-driven woman who made our life hell and hurt so many people. On the other, I'm heartbroken that the doting mother who used to sing me to sleep is dead."

"I cannot picture Charlotte singing."

Bryan gave a watery laugh. "I know. It's hard to imagine. But she really was wonderful when I was a child. She was always singing and laughing about something." Max's disbelief flowed through their link. "I'm serious. She was a completely different person back then. One who loved Father and me very much."

Max grunted. "Tell me one of your fondest memories."

Bryan grinned when the perfect moment flashed in his mind. "Father and I were making her a Mother's Day breakfast. French Toast with bacon and sliced oranges. We had just finished assembling the tray. Father had the canister of icing sugar and was sprinkling it on her breakfast when Mother came through the door behind him and startled him. He spun around so quickly the sugar flew everywhere, but mostly on Mother."

"She must have been furious."

Bryan shook his head. "She laughed, Max. She laughed so hard, I thought she'd never stop. Then she grabbed a piece of French Toast off the plate and threw it at Father. We made such a horrible mess that day. The kitchen was a disaster. When the cook came in to check on the noise, she found us lying on the floor, covered in syrup and sugar, laughing like loons. Father even had a piece of bread stuck in his hair. Eventually, Father scooped Mother up and said we'd all go out for breakfast after we'd cleaned up. I could hear her laughing all the way to their room. They didn't come out for hours."

"What could have made her change so much?"

"She loved my father with all her heart. I think the thought of him being unfaithful broke something in her. After Lysander came home, she turned into a cold, angry woman who didn't laugh or sing anymore. She and Father fought constantly. Power became her obsession." He looked up at Max. "I'd always wondered what I'd done to make her stop loving me."

"You were a child. None of what happened was your fault."

"I know that now, but for years I did think it was because of something I did. It's part of the reason I let her get away with so much. Once I came of age and took over the clan, I could have sent her away."

"But you didn't."

"No." Bryan shook his head. "I couldn't bear the thought of how disappointed Father would be if I made her leave. And I tried to protect Lysander as much as I could." He sighed. "And, well, Lysander might not have been the only one hoping for his mother's love."

"I'm sorry she couldn't be that for you. But understanding what changed her doesn't excuse her actions or the harm she caused."

"Maybe if I'd acted sooner, it would have knocked her off the course she was on."

"What ifs serve no purpose. They only undermine your confidence and distract you from your responsibilities."

"I know." Trust Max to bring out the tough love. "I hate who she became. Part of me is relieved she is gone." Bryan's voice trailed off.

"And you feel guilty about that?"

"How could I not? She was my mother and I'm thankful we don't have to deal with her anymore." He sucked in a shaky breath, his voice breaking as he finished. "And I miss her, Max. I miss that horrible, cold, angry woman, who cared only about power because that same woman once loved me as a child and sang silly songs to me. Now she's gone and I'll never get the chance to tell her that I finally understand and that a part of me still loved her."

"I think she knew." Max rested his cheek on Bryan's hair. "She did come to you when she had nowhere else to go."

"Maybe." Bryan was sure that had been mostly out of desperation.

"She also saved Lysander in the end. She may have cared more than anyone realized. Including herself."

"I'm not sure if she was saving Lysander or this Liberator."

"The end result is the same, so it doesn't matter."

"I guess." He looked over at a pained noise from his brother. "Lysander's a mess. He hated her and loved her and hates himself for loving her."

"As do you." Max's words shocked him into stillness. "I can feel it, though you try to bury it. Tell me something. Did you ever grieve for the mother you lost as a child?"

Bryan frowned. "Why would I? Mother wasn't dead."

"Your mother may have been alive, but the caring mother of your childhood was not. Did you ever grieve the loss of the mother who loved you?"

"No," he whispered.

"I didn't think so." Max put his hands on his shoulders and smiled down at him. "Let me take this burden from you. I will hate the woman your mother became so that you can mourn the mother of your childhood. Share your best memories with your brother. Show him the mother he never got a chance to meet."

"What good will that do?"

"It will free you both from guilt. And might be the way to find forgiveness. You have a good heart, as does your brother. But this misplaced guilt and self-hatred is a burden neither of you needs to carry." His fingers tightened. "At the very least, talking with him might help him deal with the memory of his mother dying in his arms."

"Shit. I never even thought of that. Poor Sandi. He's gone through so much lately."

"He's tougher than any of us realize." He looked over Bryan's shoulder and nodded. Bryan could only assume

Roman had signaled him. "Take him somewhere private and talk with him. Give yourselves a chance to remember and mourn. Roman and I will make the final arrangements for Charlotte."

Bryan squeezed Max's hand. "Everything was such a tangled mess in my head. Thanks for helping make sense of it all."

"Thank you for allowing me in." He tapped Bryan's chest. "Sometimes you hold parts of yourself back."

"I'm so…."

Max shook his head. "Don't apologize. You've always had to be the strong one. It's hard to put that down."

"I don't mean to keep you out."

"We're still a work in progress. We'll find our way." He smiled at Bryan. "But for now, help your brother. Then, together, we will right Charlotte's wrongs and balance the scales. That will bring both of you peace and close this chapter so we can all move forward."

Bryan stared into his mate's eyes as Max's unconditional support and belief in Bryan flowed through their bond. The blossoming love he felt filtered back through their link, obviously surprising Max from the way his eyes widened. Bryan smiled and gave Max's hand a squeeze before pulling away and walking over to his brother.

Running his thumbs under Lysander's eyes to dry his cheeks, Bryan asked, "Did I ever tell you about the time Father and I tried making breakfast for Mother?"

"No," Lysander said, wiping his arm across his face. He got to his feet at Bryan's gentle urging.

"Then let me tell you about it now." Bryan led his red-eyed brother through the French doors and out to the center of the garden, holding his hand and telling his story as they walked.

It was hours before Roman and Max came to find them. Hours of soul-baring conversation, sharing their greatest fears, their hopes, and reliving their memories, both good and bad. Hours in which Bryan realized he wasn't just starting to love Max. No. He was head over heels for the strong warrior vampire with the steadfast heart

Chapter Twenty-Two

The day of Charlotte's funeral…

Bryan and Lysander talked quietly as they walked down the gravel path toward the gazebo where the rest of the men were waiting for them. They'd set up their mother's coffin under the shelter to allow the household staff an opportunity to pay their respects. When they arrived, Bryan touched Lysander's arm and tipped his head toward the couple he needed to speak with. Lysander nodded and headed toward Roman while Bryan made his way over to Gideon and Carlos.

"Please accept my condolences on your loss," Gideon said.

"Thank you." Bryan touched his jacket pocket, then pulled out a cloth -wrapped object. Handing it to Carlos, Bryan said, "I'm returning this so you can keep your promise to your mate."

Carlos unfolded the handkerchief, smiling when he saw the vibrant red scale. "Thank you." Turning to his mate, Carlos opened the top three buttons of Gideon's dress shirt, then reached in and set the scale in the spot it had been taken from. "Here you go, dragon. Back where it belongs. Just like I promised."

"Thank you, treasure." Gideon's fingers gently brushed Carlos' cheekbones before he bowed his head at Bryan. "And thank you, as well. I wish it could have done more to protect your mother."

"None of us expected the demon," Bryan said. He paused, then decided to share the thought that had been rolling through his mind. "But I don't think the scale was intended to protect her from that. Something makes me think it was meant to keep her safe so she'd be able to save Lysander when the time came."

"You really think that?"

"I do. It feels right somehow."

"Interesting. I didn't even consider that."

"Neither did I. At first. But Mother was correct in thinking she had enemies in the household. Without the protection from your scale, I'm not sure she would have survived as long as she did. Your gift to her is why I still have my brother. I'll never be able to thank you enough for that."

Gideon smiled. "Lysander is precious to us all. If I had any part in keeping him safe, it was worth whatever small sacrifice I had to make."

Bryan tipped his head at Gideon. Heat settled at his back. Looking over his shoulder, he smiled at Max, leaning into his mate when Max's hand landed on his hip.

"Are you almost ready to begin?" Max asked.

"Yes. It's time to reunite Mother with Father."

Bryan took his position across from his brother. Max was behind him, paired with Roman. Bringing up the rear were Gideon and Carlos. The six of them, flanked by Jackson and Edgar, would be carrying Charlotte to her final resting place. At a signal from Bryan, the men lifted the coffin off the platform it was resting on and started down the long, graveled path that led to the family burial tomb.

Bryan shifted his grip on the handle when they came to a stop before the tomb and waited for Edgar to open the door. Once Edgar moved to the side, they walked up the two stone steps, and in synchronization, the six of them placed Charlotte's casket in her final resting place. The other men took a respectful step back as Bryan stared blankly at the flower strewn lid, years of memories flashing through his mind.

He didn't know how long he'd been lost in his thoughts when Max bumped him and whispered, "Did you want us to step out while you say goodbye?"

He quickly shook his head and gripped Max's hand. "Please stay." With a glance at his waiting brother, Bryan cleared his throat and said his farewells.

"Mother, I'm sorry we couldn't save you. I could never have imagined you'd sacrifice yourself for another, so I'm extremely grateful that you saved Sandi's life. I would have been lost without my brother. This doesn't make up for the way you always treated him, but it does help to balance the scales." He licked his dry lips. "We talked. Lysander and I. I told him what you used to be like when I was young. It's something I'd never spoken about before but it was good to be able to share those memories with him. It made me realize I'd never stopped loving the mother of my childhood and that I'd always hoped you'd somehow find your way back to being that person. But you never did."

He stopped, only starting again when Max gently nudged him.

"I've tried but I can't find it in my heart to forgive you for everything you've done since Lysander joined our family. Thankfully, the responsibility for that is not mine. I hope, now that you're with Father again, you'll find the peace you could never find with us." He reached out and laid his hand on the casket. "Goodbye, Mother. May the Goddess watch over you and keep you safe." He took a step back and nodded to his brother.

Lysander stepped forward. "I'm sorry you never saw past your pain to love the people around you, especially your sons. We tried our best to love you, but you finally drove us away. Something I think you regretted at the end."

He touched one of the flowers on the casket's lid and gently stroked its petals. "I know how hard it must have been to lose the one person who was your entire world. I can't imagine living on without Roman, so I understand the pain you must have suffered. But not your anger. There's nothing Roman could do that would turn me against him the way you turned on my father. I think one day I'll be able to forgive you for the way you treated me, but I'll never forgive you for what you did to Father and Bryan. Neither of them deserved that."

'Neither did you, Sandi."

Lysander waved Bryan to silence before continuing. "I hope you'll be happy now that you're back with Father and know the truth. Tell him I love him and miss him every day." He stepped back, then forward again. "I almost forgot. Thank you for saving my life." Moving back again, he grabbed Roman's hand and looked at Bryan. "I'm done. Is there anything else we need to do or can we go now?"

"We can leave unless anyone else would like to say something."

When the rest of the gathered men shook their heads, Lysander pulled Roman toward the doorway. He stopped just before they crossed the threshold. "Bryan, you need to come here."

"What is it? Did you have something else to say?"

"No. Just come here."

Concerned by the strange tone in his voice, Bryan rushed to his side.

"Look." Lysander pointed to an alcove set next to the entrance. Inside the niche was a stone box engraved with the family crest. An envelope was propped against it. Leaning over Lysander's shoulder, Bryan sucked in a breath when he saw his father's handwriting. He reached out a trembling hand and picked up the envelope addressed to him.

"I didn't know this was here," Bryan mused. "I've come and talked to Father numerous times and never once saw it. I don't understand how I could have missed it all these years."

"I sense dragon magic," Gideon said. "The box was most likely hidden. Until now."

"But why?" Lysander turned around and plucked the envelope from Bryan's numb fingers. "Why would Father have left a note here and not in his office?"

Bryan took the envelope back. "There's only one way to find out." Slitting it open, he pulled out a single sheet of paper. Swallowing around the lump in his throat, Bryan read aloud John Galway's final words to his beloved sons.

My dearest sons. If you're reading this, it means your mother and I have both left this world, turning responsibility for the Galway Great Task over to the two of you. In this box, you will find....

Bryan sucked in a breath when a word jumped out at him.

"What is it? What did he say?" Lysander asked, coming to read over his shoulder.

In this box, you will find a relic. It has been passed from father to son since our great ancestor, Silas Galway, was first tasked with its care by the Father of Dragons.

To aid in this task, the Father of Dragons created a dimensional pocket to hide the relic and keep it safe until it can fulfill its purpose. The box is accessible only to those of our bloodline and makes itself known to the new caretakers when it is time for them to take up the burden that has been put upon us. With the relic, comes this message from the Father of Dragons

"When the malevolent shadow darkens the earth and hope is all but lost, the Chosen shall gather and shed their life upon the stone. Thus, they shall converge and the Liberator will set them free."

Lysander, my dearest boy, I pray I am wrong, but I believe this message is for you. Knowing what will be asked of you is almost more than I can bear. Know that if I could have spared you this burden, I would have. My one comfort is knowing you have your brother to lean on.

Bryan, you were a shining star from the moment you were born. Your unstinting care of others, even at an early age, was nothing short of awe inspiring. My soul will rest easy knowing you will not hesitate to offer your strength and protection to your brother as his destiny unfolds.

The great task that was long ago set upon our family now falls to the two of you. It is with heavy heart that I pass the Platter of Unification, and all it entails, into your care. Knowing your brave and pure hearts, my greatest fear, yet proudest moment, will be when you eagerly take up the gauntlet to prevent the foreordained shadow from swallowing the earth

Know that there has never been a father more proud of his sons than I am of the two of you. Or one who has loved his sons more.

Hold faith in the Goddess until we meet again in the next life,

Dad.

"Son of a bitch. The relic's been here all along."

The annoyance in Carlos' voice made Bryan snort. He exchanged a watery smile with his brother. "Somehow, I feel we should have expected this."

"After everything, we really should have." Lysander wiped his arm across his eyes. "Father always was full of surprises."

Carlos nudged Bryan. "Open the damn box. Let's see what all the fuss was about."

Lysander reached into the alcove, grunting when he lifted out the stone box and set it on the table that was used to hold gifts for the departed. Sharing a quick look with Bryan, he removed the stone lid, then reached in and lifted out the relic, carefully setting it on the table for everyone to see.

Bryan leaned in, transfixed by the pentagonal disc that shimmered with an opalescent sheen, its surface covered with detailed carvings that had to have been an ancient craftsman's greatest work.

He held his breath as his eyes roamed over the small hollows that had been formed in each of the five sections. They were joined by a groove carved around the perimeter of the stone. Smaller lines led from each of the five sides to a larger depression in the center, which sparkled with a magical signature he couldn't identify.

"The Platter of Unification," Bryan murmured, buzzing sounding loudly in his ears.

"I wonder why it's called that?" Lysander said.

"I'm not sure." Bryan leaned closer, his eyes locked onto the notches that had been cut into the base of the stone on each of the five sides. Reaching out his hand, he rubbed his fingers over the smooth indentations. Were these supposed to be hand grips? The buzzing in his mind increased. Yes, he was sure that's what they were. He started when someone bumped his arm.

"Bryan, are you even listening to me?"

He blinked at his brother. "What?"

Lysander stared at him intently for a moment before his eyes flared in surprise. "Never mind. Go back to what you were doing."

Bryan nodded, rubbing his fingers over the small opening again. The buzzing in his ears sounded louder, drowning out the chatter around him. As if from a distance, he watched his hand grab onto the edge of the stone, his fingers sliding perfectly into the grooved indentation. "These are for holding it," he murmured. The buzzing faded away. Shaking his head to clear the fog clouding his thoughts, Bryan raised his eyes to see everyone staring at him. He blinked, then looked at the stone again. "The platter needs to be held by a representative from every community."

Lysander leaned in to get a closer look at the disc. "I think you're right. There are symbols carved into each side." He pointed to the first one. "This one looks like a wolf's head. That must be for the shifters." He ran his fingertips over the other symbols. "The pentagram symbol must be for magic-users and the long fangs for vampires. These look like wings. Would that be for dragons?" His forehead creased as he looked at Gideon. "Shouldn't dragons be with the shifters?"

"Not necessarily," Roman said. "Dragons are a special kind of magic. It stands to reason that they are in a category of their own."

Gideon nodded. "Roman is correct. Throughout our history, dragons have always been considered a separate classification, regardless of the fact we are shifters."

"I guess that makes sense," Lysander said as he touched the last symbol. "And this must be for humans. Which means we need to take one with us into the final battle." A calculating look that set off Bryan's alarms crossed his face. "And I know just who to ask."

* * *

Stephan crossed his arms and glared at Lysander and Bryan. "No. I will not let you take my mate into battle."

"We need someone who's human," Lysander said. "I know Richie will agree. And since you'll be there, you can keep an eye on him to make sure he's safe."

"He'll be safer if he stays here."

"Except that I need him to come with us."

"No, Consort. I will not allow it."

"But Stephan…."

"I'll do it," said a quiet voice behind them.

Lysander spun around "Tommy. How are you doing?"

"I'm fine."

Bryan could see he was anything but.

Tommy gestured toward the glowering vampire. "Leave Richie and Stephan alone. If you need a human that badly, I'll come with you."

"That's okay, Tommy. I know you have other things to do." Lysander turned back to Stephan and smiled brightly. "Once Stephan thinks about it, he'll realize Richie joining us in the final battle is a good thing. He'll fight harder with his mate beside him than he would if Richie stayed behind."

"Are you out of your mind?" Tommy yelled, spinning Lysander around. "Richie is an artist with a sensitive soul. You can't expose him to the ugliness of battle. It would destroy everything that makes him special."

"You're worrying over nothing," Lysander said dismissively. "Richie's stronger than you're giving him credit for. He'll be fine."

"I don't care how strong he is." Tommy gave Lysander a look of disgust. "I can't believe you would even think of asking this of him. I thought you cared about him more than that."

"I love Richie as much as I love you. But I need him to come with us so we can save the world."

"Well, you can't have him." Tommy pointed his finger at Lysander. "I'm going with you and there's nothing you can do to stop me. Just let me know when it's time to leave." Tommy crashed against Lysander's shoulder when he walked past him and stomped down the hall until he reached his room. The sound of his door slamming shut echoed loudly through the corridor.

Lysander smiled at Stephan. "I guess we won't need Richie after all."

"Like that was ever going to happen. Have a good day, Consort." The door slammed in his face.

Lysander grinned at the closed door. "Damn. I had no idea Stephan had such a temper."

"You ass. You never had any intention of taking Richie. You were after Tommy all along," Bryan said.

"I have no idea what you're talking about."

"Don't play dumb with me. You completely manipulated the situation. And Tommy."

"I had no choice. Tommy's been avoiding me ever since he got here. I knew if I asked him outright, he'd refuse."

"But he'd step in to protect Richie." Bryan shook his head. "You shouldn't manipulate your friends like that."

"Tommy hasn't been himself since he came here. He refuses to talk to anyone and insists on being left on his own. That's not good for him. I'll do whatever is necessary to break him out of the prison he's locked himself into."

"Even if that means taking him into battle."

"Even then. Tommy needs something powerful to remind him of who he is. A fight against a demon should give him that."

"I hope you know what you're doing."

"Trust me. Tommy needs to save someone in order to save himself."

* * *

The final days of preparation…

Bryan stalked outside in search of a way to diffuse his anger. Looking around, he saw most of the newly arrived clans were hard at work learning the battle weaves he'd developed. Except for Helen and her clan. He ground his teeth, his frustration rising again because of the woman's blind stupidity.

Deciding against working with the magic-users, Bryan joined a group of sparring enforcers. Physical combat was just what he needed to take the edge off. He lifted his hands into a defensive position, then wiggled his fingers at one of the female enforcers from Marcus' coven, goading her to come at him.

* * *

Thrown to the ground for the fourth time, Bryan thought maybe he'd just stay there. The grass under his cheek was cool, soothing the sting where the enforcer had gotten under his guard. A foot nudged his hip.

"Go away. I don't want to fight you anymore."

Laughter filled the air. "From what I saw, you weren't fighting at all. You looked more like a rag doll being tossed around by an angry lioness."

Groaning, Bryan rolled over, wishing he had the energy to punch his brother. "What do you want?" Mocking eyes stared down at him.

"You know you shouldn't fight when you're angry."

"It seemed like a good idea at the time."

Lysander snorted, then held out his hand to help Bryan up. "I take it Helen's clan isn't coming."

"No." Bryan slowly got to his feet. "And she's convinced three other clans not to join us." He stretched his back and cracked his neck, then adjusted his jaw. Good. Nothing seemed broken.

"Don't those idiots know what we're facing?"

"Helen's managed to convince them that we're lying." Bryan looked around the yard where all the training stations had been moved to accommodate the increased numbers as more covens and clans had arrived. "Hopefully, the ones who've joined us will be enough."

"Roman said there are a couple more covens on their way. And Alpha Clint and Jackson should be here with the wolf packs tomorrow."

"Thank goodness. We'll need whatever wolves they've managed to round up when it's time to fight." He leaned over to brush off his pants, grimacing when he saw the grass stains ground into his knees. "Who's going to be leading the Denver pack while Alpha Clint is with us?"

Lysander snorted. "Jackson said they had a Beta challenge so the Betas could fight for ranking position. You'd never guess who came in as number one."

Based on the laughter in his brother's eyes, there could only be one choice. "Mary."

"You got it. She completely dominated the other Betas. I guess Clint wanted to bring her to fight beside him, but Jackson told him to leave her in charge of the pack."

"I almost wish she'd come with them."

"Why?"

"Stephanie refused to go home to the General and will be fighting with the enforcers. If those two ever teamed up, nobody would be able to stand against them."

"No kidding. I've seen Stephanie spar. Mary must be just as fierce."

"And then some." Bryan put his hands on his hips and let his eyes roam over the amassed fighters, looking for his mate.

"What's Max's plan with the wolves?"

"Once everyone gets here, he's going to separate them into mixed teams so they can learn to work together."

"That should be interesting. I don't think shifters and vampires have ever battled on the same side. Especially not with magic-users."

"They'll have no choice but to get used to it," growled a voice behind them.

Bryan spun around. "Max. I didn't see you out here."

"That's because you were too busy letting an enforcer toss you around." Max crossed his arms, glowering at

Bryan. "You've been taught better than that. Where was your head?"

Bryan grimaced. "I might have been angry and not thinking straight."

"Which is not an excuse. You need to be smarter. I can't have my mate getting hurt because he's being reckless."

"You're right. I know better. It's just that Helen's managed to convince more clans not to join us. I needed a way to work off my anger."

"A series of suicides should clear your head."

Lysander started laughing.

Max turned his head. "Suicides are always more effective with competition. It's good of you to volunteer to join him, Consort."

Before Lysander could utter the retort that was sure to give them extra rounds, Dychelle ran into the yard, screaming for someone to help.

"What is she saying?" Bryan asked

Max squinted. "Something about the baby."

Lysander gave a loud gasp and went tearing across the lawn. "Nico. Get down from there."

Bryan looked up, his heart stopping when he saw the baby floating outside the upper story window.

"Holy fuck," Carlos yelled from across the yard. "Somebody needs to get that kid down."

"I've got him." Bryan ran toward Lysander, who was underneath the floating baby, keeping pace with his movements. Once Bryan got close, he wove a net of air and tossed it at his nephew, stopping his upward motion. Bryan felt Max come up behind him as he carefully tightened the magical net and began pulling Nico to safety.

Bryan grinned at his nephew's happy chortles as he pulled him closer. "You little rascal. You almost gave us all heart attacks." He reached out to grab him. Nico screeched in excitement and waved his chubby arms in the air. Bryan felt his magic snap before it rebounded at him.

"No," he yelled, diving forward, just missing the baby, who shot upward, out of his reach. Bryan sent another web of air toward him, but it dispersed before it reached him. "He's blocking my magic. I can't catch him."

"I'll get him," Lysander yelled.

Bryan felt when his brother released his magic. Nico kept moving upward.

"He's stopping me too," Lysander cried. "Somebody, do something."

Carlos' voice rang out. "Gideon, get your ass out here. You need to rescue the baby." He skidded to a stop next to Bryan and Lysander. "How in the hell is he doing that? I thought magic-users didn't get their powers until puberty."

"They don't." Bryan kept an eye on his floating nephew and tossed up a web of magic to try capturing him again. The net dissipated before it reached Nico.

A red dragon suddenly flew past them as Gideon raced to the rescue. Bryan held his breath when Gideon reached his nephew, his arms reaching out to encircle the infant. There was a loud pop, then Nico vanished, reappearing behind the dragon. Gideon executed a tight turn and tried grabbing him again. Nico's body veered wildly to the side, baby screams of laughter filling the air.

"What the fuck? Did that kid just translocate?"

"I think so," Bryan whispered, staring disbelievingly at his nephew, who kept popping out of sight and zipping away any time Gideon came near.

"Bryan, do something. Nico's going to get hurt."

He looked helplessly at his brother, then back at the flying baby. "I don't know how to stop him."

"There has to be something you can do," Lysander cried, darting forward as he tried to grab Nico when he went whizzing past them before shooting up in the air again.

"Stop," Max yelled, the power in his voice vibrating Bryan's eardrums.

Bryan blew out a breath when Nico slowed enough for Gideon to catch him and pull him into his chest. "Thank the Goddess. Gideon got him." Bryan grabbed Lysander around the waist, laughing in joyful relief.

It took him a moment to realize his brother wasn't moving. At all. "Sandi?" He stepped back, his eyes widening when he saw that Lysander was frozen in place with his face turned upward. "What the hell?"

He took another step back, choking when he realized Roman wasn't moving either. Spinning in a circle, he saw everyone on the lawn was stationary, like a garden of statues. Everyone except for Carlos, that is. Seriously, what the hell was going on?

Bryan rushed over when Gideon landed on the grass with Nico held safely in his arms. Footsteps sounded behind him before a hand landed on his shoulder. Bryan reached up and squeezed Max's hand, thankful he hadn't been frozen like everyone else.

"How the fuck did you freeze everyone?" Carlos asked.

"I'm not sure." Bryan glanced around at the motionless bodies, with no clue as to how he'd done this.

"Not you. Max."

Bryan squinted at Carlos. "Max couldn't have done this. Maybe Gideon did something so he could catch Nico."

Gideon shook his head as he held out the baby. "Sorry. It wasn't me."

Bryan took his nephew from the dragon. "He's not moving either. How is this possible?"

"Maybe you should ask your mate," Carlos said. "He's that one that froze everyone."

"I did not. Only someone with magic could have done this." Max crossed his arms and glared accusingly at Bryan and Gideon. "One of you had to do this."

"I know," Bryan said. "I just don't know how it happened."

Carlos rolled his eyes. "I already told you. Max did this."

"I did not."

"Then explain why you aren't frozen like the rest of them," Carlos said.

"Why aren't you?" Max shot back.

"Because magic can't touch me when I'm wearing my talisman." He pulled it from the top of his shirt to prove his point.

"Just like it doesn't affect Gideon," Bryan mused aloud. "And I'm pretty sure I didn't freeze anyone." A faint buzzing sounded in his mind. Bryan glanced down at his wrist and saw that the second hand on his father's old watch wasn't moving. "Or time," he whispered, raising his eyes to Max.

"Stop looking at me like that," Max said, taking a step back.

"I think you stopped time. Look." Bryan shoved his wrist in Max's face.

Max pushed his wrist away. "That means nothing. You obviously forgot to wind it."

"I wound it this morning and it was working perfectly." Bryan rubbed his thumb over the face of the watch as his mind flipped through the sequence of events from the moment Dychelle first called for help. The answer hit him like a bolt of lightning. "Holy crap. Carlos is right. It really was you," he breathed.

"No, it wasn't. Why won't you listen to me?"

Bryan quickly grabbed his mate's hand, stopping his backward movement. "Max, think about it. Nothing we did to catch Nico worked. Until you yelled at him to stop. And everything did. Including time."

"You can't be serious." Max tugged his hand free.

Bryan immediately grabbed onto his shirt. "Nothing else makes sense. It had to have been you."

"If Max somehow managed to stop time, he needs to restart it before we get too far out of sync with the rest of the world," Gideon said.

"Unless he stopped the whole world." Bryan's eyes widened at the thought.

Carlos whistled. "Do you think that's possible?"

"I didn't stop time," Max yelled.

Ignoring him, Bryan answered Carlos. "I'm not sure if Max affected the whole world, but I know a way to check." Bryan smiled at his glaring mate, patting him reassuringly on the back, then walked in a straight line away from everyone. Keeping a close eye on his watch, he came to a stop when the second hand started moving. He turned back to the others, surprised at how far away they were. Waving his arms in the air, he shouted, "My watch works over here." He jogged back to the others. "How far do you think that was, one hundred yards? One fifty?"

Gideon nodded. "About that." He turned to Max. "Can you please unfreeze everyone. We need to discuss this new ability and figure out how to work it into our plans."

Max threw his hands in the air. "You've all lost your minds if you think I did this."

"I know it seems unbelievable, but there really is no other explanation." Bryan put his hand on Max's chest when it looked like he was ready to argue some more. "Perhaps this is your gift from the Goddess."

Max stilled. "The Goddess?"

Bryan nodded.

"You really think I was given the ability to stop time?"

"I do." Bryan tapped Max's chest. "Which would explain the hourglass symbol."

Max blinked, then rested his hand over Bryan's fingers on his chest. "Damn." He looked around at the motionless bodies. "If you're right, I'd better fix this. Do you have any idea of how I do that?"

"I'm not sure." Bryan looked around as well, then shrugged. "Maybe you just need to tell them to move."

"Wait," Carlos said, an evil grin on his face. "Before you do that, does anyone have a black marker? I want to give the Consort a mustache."

That surprised a laugh out of Bryan. "Lysander will kick your ass if you mess with him."

"Like I care. I owe him for being such a dick lately."

"Leave him alone, treasure." Gideon tossed an arm over his mate's shoulder. "We need to get everyone moving so we can make plans." He gave Max and Bryan a pointed look. "I think all of the Goddess' pieces are now in play. It's time to find that demon."

His words had a sobering effect on all of them.

* * *

After a few false starts and some coaching from Bryan, Max was finally able to unfreeze time and get everyone back to normal. Other than a few suspicious looks from the enforcers, Lysander, and Roman, nobody seemed aware anything had happened. While Max had been doing that, Gideon had set a binding on Nico's powers. Bryan was hoping dragon magic would be more effective on his nephew than his magic had been.

Once they calmed Dychelle and got her and Nico back to the nursery, they gathered in Roman's office to discuss the new development.

"I will admit to finding these new powers of yours discomforting," Roman said. "I am unused to being at the mercy of magic I cannot overcome."

"I'm sorry, my Prince."

"It's not your fault, Max. Nor is it Bryan's. I know you can both be trusted with the gifts you were given."

Bryan grimaced. "Trust me, I'd give my power back if I could."

"No." Lysander shook his head. "You have them for a reason. And Roman's right. You and Max are probably the only ones who can be trusted not to abuse these powers." Lysander tilted his head. "I wonder if there's a way to use Max's new power to trap the demon."

"What are you thinking?" Bryan asked.

Lysander tapped a folder on the desk. "Mother gave us information for all the hidden locations the Elders used. Since we have the relic and you and Max now have your Goddess powers, we should start checking them out. The demon has to be in one of them."

Bryan cleared his throat. "I hate to point this out, but we don't know how the relic works."

Lysander shrugged. "We know we need five people to hold it, which we have. I'm sure we can figure out the rest."

"You can't assume the information will just pop into our heads.

Lysander gave him a dry look. "Are you sure? Perhaps you should ask that book."

Bryan flipped him off. "It doesn't work like that and you know it."

"This might be one of those times it does. Come on, Bryan. We know the relic is a weapon designed to fight a demon. We need to find it and destroy it before it kills anyone else."

"The smart thing to do is figure out how the relic works before we go demon hunting."

"How? By fooling around with it here?" Lysander shook his head. "I don't want to put anyone at risk using unknown magic on the estate's grounds. We need to take the relic to the demon."

Bryan crouched in front of his brother. "I know how badly you want this over, but we can't run into danger and hope for the best. Too much is riding on our success. We need more time to get ready.

"We might not have time to wait."

"Unless something else happens, I don't think we have a choice. Max needs to learn how to control his powers, and everyone else is still getting used to working together. Going after the demon before we're ready could jeopardize everything we've been working toward."

Lysander gripped the arms of his chair so tightly his fingers turned white. "I know we should wait. Trust me, I'm as aware of the risks as you are. But I can feel that we're running out of time. If we don't act soon, it might be too late."

"What have you seen?"

"Nothing exact. Just vague impressions. But enough to know something bad is coming." He dropped his head.

"I really wish we could just be told what we need to do so we can get on with it already."

Bryan peeled Lysander's hands off the chair's arms and held them tightly. "You know She can't do that. Not without jeopardizing the balance that prevents everything from falling into chaos." Bryan leaned his forehead against his brother's. "All we can do is put our trust in the Goddess and have faith we'll be in the right place at the right time."

"Like we always do." Lysander whispered.

"Like we always do," Bryan repeated.

* * *

Strategy meeting after another long day of training…

"The enforcers are still unable to locate where the undead are hiding," Max said. "Unless we manage to follow one of them, I don't think we'll find them. Not with the demon shielding them."

"I'll let the Chief know." Roman sat back and clasped his hands. "How is your control coming along?"

Max held out his hand, tipping it back and forth. "It's improving. Magic is more difficult than you would think."

Lysander snickered. "Tell me about it. Do you have any idea how many times I almost blew up Bryan when I was learning?"

"Seven at last count. I have grey hairs from that time."

Lysander squinted at his head. "I didn't think vampires could get grey hairs."

"We can't."

Lysander's eyes narrowed, then he flipped Max off.

"Stop teasing him." Bryan elbowed Max before answering Roman. "Max's control is fine. There won't be any issues with him freezing our fighters by mistake."

"Good. That brings us one step closer to being prepared." Roman turned to Marcus and Clint. "And the training with the vampire and shifter teams? How is that progressing?"

"Better than I anticipated," said Marcus. "The wolves have proven to be fierce and wily fighters. The enforcers are coming up with some creative ways to work with that."

Clint grinned. "And the enforcers' greater speed has forced the wolves to become more attuned to their instincts, which has improved their reflexes and made them more agile in their thinking."

"I agree," Jackson said. "Working with the enforcers has been extremely beneficial in developing the fighting skills of the younger wolves. The packs will be better protected when we send their wolves back as fully trained Betas."

"I am pleased that what we are doing here will help strengthen the packs." Roman glanced between Clint and Jackson. "I will admit to being surprised by the number of wolves you were able to gather, especially after the devastating losses the packs suffered."

"After what was done to them, they all wanted a chance to fight. I had to enforce a minimum age of seventeen or we would have been overrun by juvenile wolves," Clint said.

"The desire to vanquish the enemy is strong in both vampires and wolves."

"Extremely."

Roman looked at Bryan. "And the magic-users? Are they ready?"

"I believe so. They've been practicing the modified weaves. With Nick and Alex leading them, they should have no trouble holding the perimeter."

Roman's phone rang. Glancing at the screen, he held up his finger. "Please excuse me, I need to take this." Answering the call, he said, "Chief, how can I help you?"

Max stiffened when he heard the Chief's words. At Bryan's questioning look, he used their mind link to fill him in, noting that everyone else was paying close attention to Roman's conversation.

"Have your men pull back and cordon off the area at least three blocks out. We will be there as fast as we can." Roman set his phone on his desk.

"What's happened now?" Lysander asked.

"A few hours ago, the dead began walking out of funeral homes, morgues, and breaking out of tombs in the cemeteries. A city-wide advisory has gone out informing everyone to stay inside and not interfere or confront them." He paused.

"What else?" Lysander asked.

"The horde of undead have been steadily working their way to the Port, killing and enthralling any who cross their path. They are amassing in vast numbers at the warehouses."

"The demon is mobilizing its forces," Max said.

Roman nodded. "Whether we are ready or not, we are out of time. Gentlemen, gather your teams and meet in the parking garage. We leave in thirty minutes."

Chapter Twenty-Three

Bryan stood with Alex and Nick in the parking garage, going over an adjustment he wanted them to make in the protective barriers around the battle site when Lysander joined them.

"Bryan, I need to speak with you privately for a minute."

"Can it wait until I'm done?"

"No. It needs to be now."

"All right." Bryan smiled at his friends. "If you'll excuse me, I'll finish explaining in a bit."

"No worries. I think we've got it." Nick lifted an eyebrow at Alex, who nodded. "Go do whatever you need to do. We'll make sure the clans are in place with the modified spell."

"Thanks." He bumped fists with his friends then followed his brother. Lysander led him away from the gathered fighters to the other side of the garage where Roman and Max were waiting.

Bryan glanced between Max on Roman, tensing at the grim looks on their faces. "What's going on?"

"You need to use your power to shield everyone's minds from the demon," Lysander said.

Bryan reared back. “What? No. I told you I wouldn’t use my power on anyone again.”

“If we go in there unprotected, the demon will be able to take control of everyone. And that will be it. Game over. We can’t let that happen.”

“You can’t ask me to tamper with people’s minds.”

“We’re not. We want you to protect their minds, nothing else.”

“That’s still tampering. Do you have any idea of what could go wrong if I tried?”

Lysander shook his head. “Not really.”

“Neither do I,” Bryan said, crossing his arms.

“But we do know what will happen if you don’t.”

Bryan glared. “Don’t try to guilt me in this.” He stomped away a few feet then came back. “Did you even consider what could happen to me if I tried? You know there’s always a price for using magic against another.” He waved his arm indicating the full garage. “With this many people, my soul would be tarnished beyond redemption. Is that what you want for me?”

“No. But I don’t think that will happen.”

“But you can’t know for sure that it wouldn’t.”

“You’re right. I don’t.”

“Exactly,” Bryan said, thinking that would be the end of it. He should have known better.

“But you know I’d never ask you to do anything that would harm your soul.” Lysander reached for his hand. “And I know that this won’t.” He slapped a hand over his heart. “I know it here.”

Bryan shook his head. “I’m sorry. I can’t do it. It’s too much.”

Max stepped forward and took his hand from Lysander, holding it between his own. “We do not ask this lightly. We all understand your worry. Especially me.”

"Then why, Max. Why would you ask me to do this?" Bryan whispered.

"Because we can think of no other way to protect everyone."

"But…"

Lysander jumped in. "Bryan, I think this is the reason you were granted this power. You're the only one who can keep us from falling under the demon's control."

"I know that. But you don't understand." Bryan tried pulling his hand free, but Max refused to let go. "If I do what you ask, I could destroy their minds. Or change who they are. I could erase their entire being. I would be worse than the demon." He covered his mouth with his free hand, bile rising at the thought of everything that could go wrong.

Max pulled his hand away from his mouth and threaded their fingers together. "We're not asking you to do anything invasive. You will not have to enter anyone's mind. I promise."

Bryan blinked. "I won't?"

"No," Lysander said, touching his arm, "we've thought of a way around that. Instead of putting up a shield in everyone's mind to make them invisible like you did with me, we want you to plant a suggestion that they can't hear the demon."

Bryan frowned. "I don't understand."

"We're hoping if you tell them to ignore the demon's words, it will protect them from falling under its spell. And if you send the message as a suggestion that will fade over time, it won't permanently affect them."

"That's still brainwashing."

"No, it's not," said Lysander. "It's no different than if you spoke to everyone out loud, except that you'd be sending the idea directly to their minds." Lysander smiled reassuringly. "We don't expect it to work on everyone, but it should help protect most of us. I discussed it with Sophia. She's the one who proposed this option."

"It still feels like I'm controlling their minds."

"No more than you would do by giving them orders as Head of the Clan," Max said. "In fact, as Clan Leader, you have more control over their actions than what we are asking of you now." Max smiled gently at him. "But this is a decision only you can make. Which option places less of a burden on your soul?"

Bryan looked from his mate to Roman, whose face held nothing but compassion, before going back to Lysander.

"Do you really think the Goddess won't punish me for tampering with everyone's minds?"

"Do you really think the Goddess would punish you for saving her people using the gift she gave you?" Lysander countered.

"I hate arguing with you."

Lysander snorted. "I know. But this is the best plan. You're not putting anyone under a compulsion. You're planting a suggestion that they ignore the demon. If we dared to tell anyone of your abilities to ask for their permission, I'm sure most would accept."

Bryan tried to find another option but couldn't think of any other way to protect everyone. Sighing, he nodded. "I'll try. But I'm kicking all your asses if you're wrong."

Max squeezed his hand. "I will be first in line."

Clinging tight to Max's hand, Bryan closed his eyes. He imagined thousands of butterflies, all programmed with the directive to ignore the demon's words. He wiggled his fingers, sending tendrils of magic throughout the crowded garage. Thousands of thought butterflies fluttered above everyone's heads, carrying the message he'd given them. They set down on every person, popping out of metaphysical existence once their task was complete. The hum of talking voices paused momentarily before starting up again, with no one the wiser that Bryan's suggestion had been planted in their minds.

Bryan opened his eyes and looked at Roman. "How do you feel?"

"As I always do. I assume you protected my mind as well?"

"Yes. Do you feel any different? Compelled in any way?"

"I feel the same as always." Roman tipped his head toward Bryan. "The power to affect lives is a heavy burden I understand well. You have my respect and gratitude for those you have saved this day."

Bryan swallowed through a suddenly tight throat. "Thanks, Roman." He leaned into the hand Max settled on the small of his back.

Roman nodded, then looked over the crowd. "It appears everyone is ready. Do you have the relic?"

Lysander patted the backpack slung over his arm. "Right here."

"Then we had best be on our way. The Chief is waiting."

* * *

The officer moved the barrier to the side and waved them through. SUV after SUV drove through the opening as their combined forces travelled along the deserted streets until they reached the predetermined staging area where they would hand out final assignments. Bryan held tight to his brother's hand on one side and Max's on the other. Today, the long months of struggle against the remaining Elder and the demon who wanted to destroy their world would finally come to an end. They would either be victorious or they would fail. Either way, none of them would ever be the same.

* * *

Bryan knew he was being ridiculous in repeating the instructions he'd already given at least two other times but he couldn't seem to help himself. Ignoring the patient smirks Alex and Nick exchanged, he again told them how he wanted them to deploy the magic-users. "Set everyone up around the perimeter to power the shield. One of Marcus' enforcers, Johan, will be leading the group of vampires protecting the magic-users. If anything manages to break through the barrier, they'll deal with it. If they can't, do whatever is necessary to stop it. You can't allow any of the undead to escape into the city"

"We won't," Nick said. "While we're looking after that, who's going to be protecting you?"

"Lysander and I will provide cover for our group. Max also has a team of enforcers surrounding us." Bryan nudged his concerned friend. "Don't worry. We'll also have Carlos and Gideon with us. Nothing will be able to get through them."

"Fair enough. Just keep your head down, Galway. I don't want to lose any friends today."

"You and Alex watch your backs as well." Bryan pulled his friends into a group hug, praying they would all come through the upcoming battle safely. "Now go get the perimeter locked down."

Alex bumped fists. "See you on the other side." He grabbed Nick's arm and dragged him over to the waiting vehicles that were driving the magic-users to the edge of the cordoned off area.

Bryan turned when Max walked up to him. "Are the enforcers ready to go?"

"Yes. Eric and his team will be with us. Stephan will be in charge of the enforcers facing the undead." Max smirked. "He's looking forward to tearing off some heads. The thought of anything harming his mate has brought forth an anger I didn't know he was capable of."

Bryan grimaced. "Lysander may have inadvertently caused that."

"So I understand."

"Did I hear my name?" Lysander asked as he and Roman joined them.

"Stephan is riled up. Your visit left him wanting to destroy the demon's minions."

Lysander winced. "He's still angry? I didn't mean to do that. Do you think I should talk to him?"

"He will be fine," Roman said. "Stephan has not had a mate to protect before. The thought of our Bloodmate being in danger brings out the beast in all of us. Your talk may have started the process but the anger he feels towards the enemy would be the same either way."

"Even though Richie is safe at the mansion?"

"Even then. As long as the demon is loose in our world, the threat to his mate is real."

"Are you sure I shouldn't apologize? I don't want him to stay mad at me."

"All will be fine. Once he's shed the blood of our enemy to protect his mate, he will return to his normal demeanor."

"What do you guys want me to do?" Tommy asked, coming to stand behind Lysander, his eyes darting back and forth as he watched everyone get ready.

"Stay next to me and Roman as much as you can," Lysander said. "It might get a little crazy the closer we get to the demon. Do you have any weapons to defend yourself with if we're separated?"

"Sure do." Tommy patted his jacket pocket. "Max gave me a gun and this knife." He pulled the blade from a sheath tied to his leg. It looked more like a small sword than a knife to Bryan. "He said to cut off the head if one of those things comes near me."

Lysander looked him over then pointed. "What's that strapped to your shoulder?"

Tommy grinned for the first time. "This here is Betsy," he said, pulling a recurve bow from behind his back.

Bryan whistled. "You know how to use that thing?"

"Sure do. State Champ. I figured it might come in handy for fighting zombies."

"Uh, we're not actually fighting zombies."

"Yes, you are. All of them are walking dead. From what I hear, they kill and eat their victims, then those bodies also rise from the dead to do the same. Sounds like a typical zombie to me."

Bryan thought it over, then nodded. "I guess it does. Well, undead, minions, or zombies, the only way to kill them is by cutting off their heads and burning them before they can get back up."

"Which is why I have this." Tommy pulled something from the holster tied to his other leg. "Max equipped all of us with mini flamethrowers."

Bryan squinted at what was basically a strong lighter. "Is that going to be powerful enough?"

"It should be. I only need to set the hair on fire. Once that's going, the rest is history."

Bryan turned to Max. "Did you arm the vampires with flamethrowers too?"

"Yes. Since the magic-users were needed elsewhere, I had to improvise."

"As long as Tommy can defend himself, improvise whatever you want." Lysander tossed his arm over Tommy's shoulders. "When we find the demon, we'll use the relic like I explained to you and end this."

"All you told me is that I needed to hold onto the section marked with the symbol for humans. What happens then?"

"Uhm, well, I don't actually know."

"What do you mean you don't know?"

When Lysander looked at Bryan for help, he held up his hands, then zipped his lips shut.

Lysander glared. "You're an asshole."

Tommy looked back and forth between them. "What's going on?"

"Here's the thing. We don't know exactly how it works." Lysander winced when Tommy shouted and pushed him back.

"Are you freaking kidding me? We're running through a hoard of angry man-eating zombies to face off against a demon and all we have is a fancy stone dinner plate that nobody knows how to use. What are we supposed to do? Throw it at him?"

"I'm sure there's more to it than that."

"Well, that's just great." Tommy held out his hand. "Max, I'm going to need another flamethrower."

Bryan held back a snicker when Max immediately reached into his cargo pants and pulled one out.

"Tommy…," Lysander started, but was cut off when Jackson and Edgar called out to them as they ran across the tarmac.

"Eric said everyone's almost ready to go."

"And the newly arrived vampires? No issues with them being teamed with the wolves?" Roman asked.

"Nope." Jackson's eyes danced. "In fact, there's some heavy wagering going on between the vampires and wolf shifters."

"What would they be betting on?" Lysander asked.

"They're having a competition about who can kill the most minions," Edgar said drolly.

"Who is your money on?" Roman asked.

"The vampires, of course."

"Hey," Jackson said, "I thought we agreed on the wolves."

"We did. Then I decided I'd rather win."

Bryan nudged Max. "Who did you bet on?"

"Why would you think I placed a wager?"

"Please." Bryan rolled his eyes. "You were a soldier. It's in your blood."

Max smirked. "I bet on Tommy."

Tommy's mouth dropped open. "You did? Why would you bet on me?"

"I've seen you use a bow."

Bryan could only laugh at Tommy's dumbfounded expression. He started to ask how he could get in on the betting when a siren pierced the sultry evening air.

The gathered fighters fell silent, their preparations halting as they turned toward the noise. The wailing of the klaxon faded, the resulting stillness broken by the sound of a dog barking. It was joined by another, then another. The low hum of conversation restarted. The shriek of the siren again cut through the night, stopping all activity as everyone turned to Roman, who nodded grimly at Jackson. "It's time. Call them out."

Jackson's powerful voice sounded above the din. "Team Leaders, assemble your groups. We leave on my mark." He looked at everyone around him. "Are we ready?"

Bryan drew in a deep breath, making eye contact with Lysander. Seeing only determination on his face, he said, "We're good, Jackson."

Nodding, Jackson raised his head, shouting. "Teams. Move out."

Moments later, the staging area was empty. The fading echoes of running footsteps the only indication they'd ever been there.

* * *

They were half a block from the warehouse when they ran into their first resistance.

The vampires and wolf shifters sped forward to intercept and engage with the walking dead. Bryan sent more power through the modified shield he and Lysander had erected, hoping the modified weave would be enough to counteract the demon's magic. At the very least, he hoped it would slow the enemy long enough for the enforcers to eliminate them before they could break through.

Bryan was surprised by how quickly the paired wolves and vampires dispatched the opposing forces. But not even they came close to the number taken out by Tommy, whose bowstring sang a song of death as arrow after arrow found their mark.

"Damn, Tommy. That's amazing," Bryan said, sending a fireball towards one of Tommy's victims. "How soon before you run out of arrows?"

Tommy grinned. "Never. I had Nick magic me up a perpetually filling quiver." He shot an arrow over Bryan's shoulder, then spun and dropped to his knee, shooting off three more in quick succession. The four zombies creeping up on their flank fell, one arrow skewering two of them together. Bryan quickly torched the bodies before they could rise.

They continued their slow progress forward.

After what seemed like eons, the door to the warehouse was finally in sight. Bryan flicked his sweaty bangs to the side as he fired off another volley of fireballs. His magical reserves were starting to run low. If they didn't break through soon, he'd have nothing left when they faced the demon. Even Tommy was flagging as the horde of undead continued to stream through the opening up ahead.

"I can't keep this up much longer," Bryan yelled.

"Me either. We need to put them down faster," Lysander cried. "Gideon, do you have enough fire left to take all of them out at once?"

"I think so."

"As soon as we disengage from the enemy, you're up."

"Yes, Consort."

Bryan sent another wave of flame toward the open doorway. "Max, call your enforcers back. Jackson, same for the shifters. We need our fighters out of range before Gideon starts flaming."

Bryan covered his ears when Max raised his voice loud enough to be heard over the cacophony. At his command, the enforcers began separating from the minions, retreating to the safety of the shield. Jackson raised his head, the song of the Alpha calling to the wolves. The wolf shifters began streaming toward them, hamstringing zombies along the way.

"Lysander, expand the shield to hold everyone. I'll keep the minions back until everyone's inside." Bryan spread his hands, sending a wave of air across the battlefield to push the zombies back. The enforcers who had been guarding the retreating fighters began falling back.

Bryan kept the minions pushed back until everyone had made it to safety. Conserving his remaining energy, he released the weaves of air that had been hindering the undead from attacking. The shield was immediately swarmed. As the minions pushed against the barrier, the demon magic that powered them began to weaken the protective covering.

As more of the undead covered the shield, the cumulative effect of the demon's taint began to thin sections of the barrier to be almost nonexistent. Arms and legs started to break through. The vampires quickly wrenched the appendages from the bodies, lit them on fire, then tossed them back into the heaving mass surrounding them.

"We're being overrun," Max yelled as he grabbed at a body that had managed to climb up the side of the shield and partially work itself through. He yanked it free and tossed it back into the crowd. "It might be time for me to freeze them in place

"No. You'd give away our advantage," Bryan shouted, blasting a group of bodies off the top of the barrier. "Hurry, Gideon. There's too many for us to hold back much longer."

"Shifting now." Dragon magic swirled around them.

"You better watch your back, dragon. I don't need some asshole tearing your wings off." Carlos shouted.

"You worry too much, treasure. I'll be fine." Fragments of dusty cement kicked up when Gideon took to the air. A moment later, frosty-blue ice fire obscured the battlefield. It took three passes to slow the enemy and a fourth to freeze the last minion in place. Once he was done, Gideon hovered overhead, waiting for them to proceed.

Bryan scanned the frozen panorama, searching for any signs of movement but Gideon's ice-fire had done its job. Everything looked like they were clear to proceed, but his nerves were pinging. "Did that seem too easy?"

Tommy lowered his bow. "What do you mean, too easy? We've been fighting them off for hours. And they just about overran us."

"Until Gideon stopped them. And the demon knows he's with us." Bryan kept looking around, knowing something was wrong. "It would have accounted for him."

"I agree," said Max, standing back-to-back with him, his eyes darting back and forth. "That felt like a test of our abilities. Or a diversion. Be prepared. The demon's real attack is still to come."

"What else does he have besides the minions?" Lysander asked.

"That," yelled Tommy, the twang of his bow sounding as he shot arrows at the shadow that streaked toward them through the night sky.

"Gideon, behind you." Carlos' yell of warning rang through the night, but he was a moment too late. Claws raked down Gideon's back, tearing through the delicate membranes of his wings. His agonized roar filled the sky as he clumsily beat his wings, trying to stay aloft, but the damage done to him was too great. Gideon careened through the air before spiraling down to the concrete with a bone breaking crash.

"Damn it. I warned him." Carlos passed through the shield, then raced across the concrete, clambering up and down frozen minions until he reached his injured mate. "Shift, dragon."

Pain-filled roars filled the air.

"I don't care how much it fucking hurts. Shift now."

A triumphant cry came from the green dragon's throat. He blew out fire, covering Carlos and Gideon with orange flames. Carlos' voice rose over the whooshing fury of the inferno. "Randal, you fucking bastard. I'm going to kill you when I get my hands on you." More fire poured over them in response.

"Shouldn't we be helping them?" Tommy asked, shooting another arrow toward the dragon. It bounced harmlessly off the dragon's scales.

"Fire can't hurt them. And Gideon will be fine once he shifts," Bryan yelled to be heard over the dragon's roars coming from overhead. "We're the ones in trouble. The shield won't protect us from dragon fire."

"It won't? What the hell are we supposed to do?"

Bryan wished he had an answer.

Gideon's pained cries were heartbreaking but Bryan didn't dare take his eyes off the green dragon to check on him. The dragon hovered over Carlos and Gideon, his head swiveling back and forth as if weighing his options. Bryan's breath stalled when the triangular green head suddenly locked on them, its eyes flashing red. "Shit. He's going to attack. Sandi, with me."

Bryan shot lightning at the dragon streaking toward them. Lysander sent up fireballs at the same time. Their combined efforts worked to distract the dragon, who overshot its mark, its fire hitting the side of the warehouse. Shrieking in anger, the green dragon dropped its wing and executed a sharp turn. It gave a cry of triumph before it shot toward them, orange flames lighting up the sky.

"He's coming back," Edgar cried. "Somebody better do something."

Damn it. How were they supposed to stop a demon-possessed dragon? Buzzing filled his mind, the answer suddenly there. Thrusting out a hand to Tommy, Bryan shouted, "Give me a couple of arrows."

When Tommy handed them over, Bryan passed his fingers over the arrowheads, not questioning where the knowledge for this particular weave came from. Giving them back, he yelled, "Aim for where the wing attaches to the back. There's a small divot below the first wing joint."

Tommy drew his bow, narrowing his eyes as he sighted down the arrow. "I can't hit it from this angle."

"I know." Bryan swallowed hard. "I'll get you your shot." Not giving himself time to think, Bryan bolted, running at a right angle to the direction the dragon was coming from.

"What the hell are you doing?" Lysander screamed. "Get back here before you get yourself killed."

Too late. He was committed now.

He vaulted over a frozen minion, his feet hitting a patch of ice when he landed that sent him into a skidding slide. His arms flailing, Bryan crashed into an ice statue which spun him around. Unable to recover, he fell to the ground and slid forward until he bumped into another frozen minion. Flames passed over his head, narrowly missing him. Sizzling came from the ice where the fire hit, a cloud of ice fog rising up.

Rolling to his back, Bryan fired lightning bolts at the shrieking dragon, who veered to the side, his next volley of flames missing Bryan and sending up another cloud of mist. Using the thickened fog as cover, Bryan scrambled sideways, then regained his feet and sprinted as fast as he could across the treacherous icy landscape.

"Bryan Galway. Get your ass back here."

Bryan ignored Lysander and jumped over a couple of frozen bodies as he headed toward a distant metal storage container.

Cursing from multiple mouths reached his ears. He heard the sound of rushing air, then Max was running beside him. "What in the hell do you think you're doing?"

"No time to explain." Bryan looked over his shoulder and ran faster, the dragon closer than he'd expected. "Shit. He's going to catch us." The words had barely left his mouth before Max grabbed his arm and took off. Wind whistled in Bryan's ears as his feet left the ground.

Dragon fire fell harmlessly to the ground behind them.

A loud high pitch screech sounded from overhead. Max slowed their headlong rush enough for Bryan to get his feet under him and look back. The green dragon wobbled in the air as it frantically beat its wings, its motion impeded on one side by the arrow embedded in his back. The dragon roared before clumsily straightening out and coming toward them in a lurching flight, fire streaming continuously from its mouth.

Damn it. Would nothing stop that thing? As if in answer, the challenging roar of a furious dragon cut through the night. Gideon's red form streaked through the air and crashed into the green, sending it into a spin. Before it could recover, Gideon's red dragon swooped down and embedded his claws in the smaller green dragon's back before carrying it off into the night.

"Are you out of your freaking mind?" A hard body slammed into him, Max's hold the only thing keeping him upright. "What would possess you to run from a dragon? Do you have a freaking death wish?"

"Hey, Sandi."

"Don't you hey Sandi me." Lysander shoved him. "What the hell, Bryan? You could have been killed."

"Tommy needed a clear shot," Bryan said, pretending a calm he most definitely did not feel. "I gave it to him."

"You almost got yourself flambéed, asshole." Lysander pushed him back again. "What am I supposed to do if you get killed?" His voice cracked on the last word.

Bryan grabbed him and pulled him close. "I'm sorry," he gasped into Lysander's ear. "I didn't think about that. I just acted."

"Damn straight you didn't think. I can't lose my only brother, you jerk."

"I know. I'm sorry."

"Don't be sorry. Just don't do something that stupid again."

"I make no promises."

Lysander snorted, wiping his face on Bryan's shoulder.

Bryan pushed him back and looked at his shoulder. "Gross. Did you really have to do that?"

"Yes, asshole. Remember that next time you feel like doing something idiotic."

Bryan flipped him off.

"If you guys are done, can we kill the demon now?" Tommy asked.

Bryan nodded, then jerked when a pulse of anger hit him through his link with Max. Spinning around, he met the livid eyes of his mate.

"How dare you sacrifice yourself like that?"

"I had no choice."

"One of the enforcers could have distracted the dragon."

"There wasn't time to explain," Bryan said. "Not without the dragon turning his flame on everyone."

"Even so. There had to have been another way than putting yourself at risk."

"There wasn't." Bryan stepped closer to Max. "And even if there was, I wouldn't put someone else in danger to save myself. You should know that."

"All I know is my mate could have died, which is unacceptable. Never again."

"I can't promise that."

"Then promise you will not do it without me. We will face danger together or not at all."

"You can't put yourself in danger because of me," Bryan cried.

"Don't do anything stupid and I won't have to." Max crossed his arms.

Bryan glared at him and his damn vampire logic, then shook his head ruefully. "I'm sorry, Max. Not for distracting the dragon, because I had no choice in that, but I am sorry for worrying you."

"So stubborn." Max pulled him close. "I don't like it, but caring for others is one of your great strengths." He glowered. "And one of your greatest weaknesses."

"What else could I have done?"

"As I said before. Next time, I will go with you."

"Okay." Bryan pressed his forehead to Max's. Not knowing how this night would end, and wanting to ensure Max was in no doubt about his feelings, Bryan opened his heart wide and let everything he felt for his mate flow through their link. Max's anger faded. Bryan sighed and closed his eyes when he felt the powerful waves of love, tempered with determination to keep him safe, that came back to him. He let the vastness of Max's feelings wrap around him, gathering them into his soul as he drew strength for the challenges still to be faced.

Tommy cleared his throat. "Can we go now or do you guys need another minute?"

Bryan snorted when Max mentally said, *"Tommy is almost as annoying as Lysander."*

"That he is." Turning to Tommy, Bryan said, "Yes. We're done."

"About damn time. Let's go find that freaking demon."

Max's amused laughter echoed in his head. Shooting him a grin, Bryan mentally reaffirmed his promise. They would finish this. Together.

Chapter Twenty-Four

They made their way to the warehouse's open overhead door without further mishap. At a signal from Max, Marcus and his team of vampires and wolves split in half, silently running down the left and right sides of the warehouse to cover any other exits.

Eric's team lined up to either side of the entrance. At Max's nod, they disappeared through the opening to set up a perimeter inside the building. When Eric didn't sound an alarm, Max motioned the rest of them forward, with the enforcers taking point.

Bryan crept along the long row of racking, attempting to walk as silently as Max. Despite his best efforts, his foot still occasionally scraped against the cement, sounding loud in the quiet warehouse.

Ahead of him, Max hissed and came to a sudden stop. Bryan stumbled to a halt then had to brace himself when Lysander ran into his back. Peering over Max's shoulder, Bryan stiffened when Ruth stepped out of a patch of darkness. The enforcers immediately moved forward and set up a wall of protection against the threat.

When Bryan went to move past Max, he found his way blocked. He put his hand on his mate's arm and pushed it down. "You need to let me pass. Ruth is my responsibility to deal with, not the enforcers'." Max's jaw tightened, but he nodded and stepped to the side, letting Bryan pass. Bryan walked up to enforcers, who separated at a signal from Max and allowed him through. Bryan quickly threw a web of magic over the Elder. Once he had her secured, he asked, "Where's the demon, Ruth?"

Ruth's head slowly turned, her crimson gaze burning through the darkness. When her eyes locked on him, her mouth twisted into a horrifying grin. Bryan's binding magic disintegrated and rebounded on him.

"Shit. She broke my hold."

"Let me try." Lysander jostled him when he moved to stand beside Bryan.

"It won't work. The demon is blocking our magic."

Lysander ignored him and raised his hand. Whatever he sent to Ruth held enough power to make Bryan's hair stand on end, but the only effect it had on the demon-controlled Elder was to turn her attention to him.

"Liberator. We've been waiting for you." Her words held an eerie echo of two voices speaking as one.

"And I've been looking for you, bitch. Where's that asshole demon hiding?"

Bryan elbowed his brother in the side. Hard. "Maybe don't anger them," he hissed.

"Like it matters. They already want to kill us."

"Still." He tensed when Ruth's hand raised and instinctively sent a wave of air hurtling toward her. Nobody was more surprised than him when it swept her backward and smashed her into the wall at the far end of the warehouse. The booming crash when she hit rattled the highest windows and sent clouds of dust into the air. Ruth's body slid down the wall and landed in a crumpled heap on the floor. She didn't get back up.

"That…that shouldn't have happened," Bryan muttered. "Ruth should have seen that coming and blocked it easily."

"She might not have been the one driving the bus," Carlos offered.

"We don't have time to worry about it," Lysander said. "The demon obviously knows where we are, so there's no sense in us sneaking around." He turned to Carlos. "Tell Gideon we're going to need him right away."

"Give me a second." Moments later, Carlos snorted. "He's on his way. The idiot dragon's been toying with Randal while he waited for us to get into position. He says he has a grand entrance planned. We should hurry. I don't want to miss it."

"You heard him. Let's move it, people." Jackson took point from the enforcers and led the way in a zigzag pattern, running them under and between the long rows of racking.

Faster than Bryan had expected, considering the indirect route Jackson had taken, they reached the center of the warehouse and came out into the middle of a nightmare.

Jillian was sitting on a gold-plated chair, surrounded by minions that stared at them with an eerie calm. Bryan fought to keep his eyes on her, but the constant motion of her rippling skin and the wavering alien aura surrounding her were nausea inducing. Swallowing hard to keep his stomach in place, Bryan finally turned his head so he could keep an eye on the demon with his peripheral vision. This gave him a clear view of Ruth, who was looking a little worse for wear after her run-in with the wall. She stood on the demon's right, her vacant eyes jerking as she tracked their movements.

But the true horror stood next to Ruth. Bryan swallowed, in real danger of losing the contents of his stomach on the floor, when his mother turned toward them, a sibilant hiss escaping her mouth.

"Holy fuck. What the hell's Charlotte doing here?"

"Charlotte is gone. That is nothing more than an abomination which must be destroyed," Roman said. "I suggest we let the enforcers deal with it."

"Yeah," Bryan said weakly, unable to tear his eyes off the creature that wore the face of his mother. "That's probably best."

"You are foolish to challenge me." The demon stood, its unworldly voice disconcerting coming from Jillian's mouth. ***"You will die for your insolence."***

"The only one dying today is you," Lysander taunted.

"Liberator. Long have I waited for this moment." The demon's harsh laugh raised the hairs on the back of Bryan's neck. He had to look away again when the shifting movements in Jillian's skin increased, as if the demon was trying to escape the prison of her flesh. ***"Kneel before your Master."***

"I have no Master," Lysander yelled before whispering from the side of his mouth. "He is talking to me, right?"

"Pretty sure," Tommy whispered back.

"You cannot defy me." The demon's outraged roar shook the building's foundations. The enforcers eyed the roof warily. ***"Bow before me. Now!"***

"No."

The demon reared back. ***"Your mind is closed. How can this be?"*** Glowing red eyes passed over them, then back, jerking to a stop on Bryan, whose stomach clenched when a hideous smile, full of overly large teeth, marred the delicacy of Jillian's features. ***"You are aware. Prepare to suffer for their defiance."***

The demon clamped its mental claws into his brain. Bryan cried out and grabbed his head before falling to his knees.

"Bryan, what's happening?" Lysander's voice came from a distance.

"Demon…head," he gasped as he fell to the side, not feeling when his body hit the floor.

"Shit. The demon's got him. We have to stop it."

"How?" Carlos asked from the end of a long tunnel. "Bryan's the only one who can do that."

Bryan was vaguely aware of being pulled against a hard chest. Max's fury rolled through their mate link, momentarily pushing back the demon's attack. "Max," he gasped, "help me."

"Fight it, Bryan. Use your power to stop it."

"Trying." Bryan pushed against the molten claws digging through his mind, bands of black fire scorching as fiery tendrils wove a net around all that he was. He pulled on his link to Max, his mate's fierce love giving him the strength to fight back. He worked furiously, tugging on the black lines and rolling them into a knotted ball, as he slowly regained control of his mind. Just as he was gathering the last of the ebony vines, the demon surged into his mind.

"You shall not escape me."

Bryan lost his grip on the slippery tendrils. Triumphant laughter filled his mind as the knotted ball of darkness he'd painstakingly gathered exploded. Oozing inkiness, pulsing with scarlet, covered his awareness. His screams echoed through the warehouse as the black vines burned through his mind.

"Fight, damn you. You are mine. Not his." Max's voice faded as the demon's presence filled him, sweeping aside all else.

Laughter sounded again. Bryan whimpered as molten hooks dragged through his thoughts.

"You are both mine."

Max's cry of pain sliced through the darkness shrouding Bryan's mind, his agony spilling down their mate-bond and pushing against the dark fog. Holes formed in the roiling black clouds bringing a moment of clarity. Max. Desperate to protect his mate, Bryan renewed his struggles, fragmenting the clouds further.

The demon's roar shook the earth. The storm rolled back, stronger than before. Helpless against the surge, Bryan sank to his core, its pulsing gold buffering him from the black madness consuming him. He gathered himself for one final push, knowing failure would mean the death of his mate. Drawing on the power of his core, Bryan used all that he was and thrust out, shredding the inky darkness into fluttering streamers that he expelled from his mind.

Bryan gasped out a breath and painfully drew air into his oxygen deprived lungs. Rolling to his side, he coughed, spitting bile onto the concrete. Bryan pressed his shaking arms to the floor and slowly raised his body into a sitting position. Blinking to clear the sweat from his eyes, he looked through a haze at the concerned faces staring down at him. "I'm fine," he rasped. "I got free."

His brother's eyes widened at the same time long fingers wrapped around Bryan's neck. The strong digits tightened, closing around his throat with agonizing slowness. "Max. Stop," Bryan wheezed as his breath was cut off. He thrashed wildly, twisting his body as he tried to stop his mate from choking him. Max's fingers tightened further. Bryan's feet drummed on the ground as he clawed at the hands that were strangling him. Black spots filled his vision.

"Do something, Roman. He's going to kill Bryan."

"I cannot break Max's hold."

"Then tear off his hands. Hurry, Roman. He's strangling Bryan."

Darkness rolled over Bryan as he began sliding into the depths. His last thoughts were of his mate and how Max's part in Bryan's death would break him. His soul wept knowing his mate would be driven insane by an all-consuming grief before he followed Bryan into the arms of the Goddess.

No! He couldn't let that happen. Bryan forced himself to hang on, refusing to let Max die. Not like that. He had to save him from the demon, who could not have him. Max was his!

Red rolled over Bryan's vision. But not from the demon this time. No, this was the cleansing heat of pure rage that rose up, scouring away all vestiges of the demon and unlocking a reserve of power he'd been unaware of.

Bryan sent his newfound power exploding outward in a fury driven golden wave. Glass shattered when the windows blew outward. The steel racks holding pallets groaned under the strain, the metal twisting and rivets popping, before dropping their loads to the ground.

Sightless, Bryan stood, power pouring from him with the blinding radiance of the sun. "You will not touch him. He is mine!" he screamed, his eardrums bursting from the ferocity of his yell. Raising his hands, he sent his magic to seek out and destroy the dark pockets of wrongness that surrounded him. There. And there. Flicking his fingers, he sent a whip of lightning behind his back, grim satisfaction filling him when the patch of red-tinted black was obliterated.

He moved forward, dealing death with no more than a thought and the slightest motion of his hand. He turned toward the largest patch of darkness, ready to send it into the ether.

"Enough, Bryan. Pull it back."

Shaking off the hold that was tugging at him, he raised his hand, preparing to dispel the evil blackness staining the earth.

"Please, Bryan. Mate. No more. You've done enough."

Stilling, he cocked his head. He knew that voice. Arms wrapped around his waist. A warm body settled against his back.

"That's it," crooned a husky voice. "Come back to me, mate. I need you."

His magic receded in a rush, taking his strength with it. Bryan's knees gave out. He was caught and carefully lowered to the ground. Warm hands caressed his face. He blinked the spots from his vision until he was able to look into the worried eyes of his mate. "Max," he breathed.

"There you are." A smile spread across Max's face. "I knew you could do it."

Bryan reached up a trembling hand to touch him. "Are you okay?"

"I'm fine."

"I was so worried the demon would take you from me."

"It tried." Max stroked his cheek with his thumb. "Thank you for saving me."

"I had to. You're my mate."

Max's eyes warmed. "And you are mine." He rose to his feet and held out his hand. "Can you stand? We need to finish this."

"Yeah." Bryan let Max pull him up, then support his weight when his knees wobbled. He glanced around, wincing when he saw the tumbled bodies strewn around the warehouse. Only Roman, Carlos, and Lysander were still on their feet. "Damn. Did I do that?"

"Yeah." Max held him tighter. "You were putting out so much power it was hard to stand against it."

"Did I hurt anyone?"

"Not on our side," Lysander said as he and Roman walked over. "But whatever you did took out most of the minions."

Bryan recalled his magic hunting shadows. More than there should have been. "Are you sure no one on our side got hurt? I zapped a lot more than I remember being here."

"We're all fine." Carlos said as he joined them, Tommy limping after him. "There were a lot more undead hiding in the rafters. They're pretty much dust now."

"I don't understand how I did that," Bryan mused.

"Me either." Lysander pulled him into a one-arm hug. "I just know you scared the crap out of me again."

"Sorry." Bryan thumped him on the back then stepped back. "Where's the demon now?"

Lysander's face twisted. "When you turned into a sun, it grabbed Ruth and vanished."

"Shit. Does that mean we have to search for it again?"

"Fools. I am not so easily vanquished."

Bryan spun around in time to see the demon and Ruth step from the shadows. "Max. Now."

Max thrust out his hand, yelling, "Stop." Ruth and the demon became motionless.

"It worked. Holy crap. It actually worked," Lysander said, punching Bryan in the shoulder.

"Uh, guys. Take another look."

Bryan turned to Tommy in confusion, then looked back when he heard Carlos cursing.

Bryan's blood ran cold when the demon's eyes flashed and its hand started to rise. "Again, Max. Hurry."

Max's voice thundered through the warehouse. "Stop!"

The demon froze. They waited tensely, but it didn't move again.

Bryan turned to Carlos. "Where the hell is Gideon? You said he'd be here."

Something crashed through the remains of the roof. Bryan jumped back when the green dragon slammed into the ground. Gideon dropped through the hole and flew over them, pouring a cascade of icy-blue fire over Ruth and the demon. When he stopped, an inch of ice covered them.

"Again, Gideon. Make it as thick as you can." Only when the ice was six inches thick was Bryan satisfied. "That should be good enough. Roman, where's the relic? It's time."

"Here." Roman reached into the backpack he'd been carrying for Lysander and pulled out the stone platter.

"Everyone, take hold at your assigned spots." Bryan kept one eye on the demon as he waited for them to take their positions around the platter.

Tommy, Jackson, Roman, and the now shifted Gideon, placed their hands in the special grips built into the platter. Lysander reached toward the magic-user slot, then paused.

"Why'd you stop?" Bryan asked.

"I don't think it's supposed to be me."

"What are you talking about? You're the strongest magic-user around."

"After your little display, I'm not sure that I am."

"Whatever. Grab the handle."

"No," Lysander said, backing away. "It doesn't feel right."

"What are you doing?" Bryan glanced over to the demon. Still frozen. "Grab onto the platter before I kick your ass. We don't have time to waste."

"I think it's supposed to be you, Bryan."

He jerked. "Me? Are you sure?"

Lysander nodded. "You're the one who completes the five. You, Bryan, not me."

"Shit. I hope you're right about this." Bryan quickly slid his hand into the grooves underneath the platter and took a firm hold.

Nothing happened.

"Umm, shouldn't it be doing something?" Tommy asked.

"It should." Bryan looked at his brother. "Are you sure it's supposed to be me?"

"You are the last of the five." Lysander peered over Bryan's shoulder and pointed to the channel that edged the relic. "There's something about this groove. It's there for a reason. What would it be used for?"

Tommy tilted his head. "The way the lines lead off of it toward the middle, it looks like it was designed for something to flow through it."

"Probably blood," Edgar said. "Most ceremonies call for the shedding of blood."

Lysander blinked. "I think Father's note said something about that. Read it again, Bryan."

Bryan reached into his back pocket and pulled out the letter. Carefully smoothing it open, he found the part Lysander was talking about and read it aloud. "When the malevolent shadow darkens the earth and hope is all but lost, the Chosen shall gather and shed their life upon the stone. Thus, they shall converge and the Liberator will set them free."

"I don't know about the rest of you, but I'm not letting you kill me on this rock." Tommy pulled his hand free and took a step back.

"There is no need to die," Roman said. "Blood is life. Life is blood. All we need to do is shed our blood upon the stone. A small amount is probably all that is necessary."

"Are you sure?" Tommy asked doubtfully. "The note says shed their life."

"This will be all that is required. Trust me."

Tommy looked at him sideways, then stepped forward, reaching for the stone. "How do we do it?"

"Like this." Edgar held up his hand, one of his nails longer than the others. "Give me your hand."

Tommy eyed him suspiciously but held it obediently out. Edgar grabbed hold and slashed across Tommy's palm. Ignoring his curses, Edgar held his hand over the small hollow marked with the symbol for humanity. Tommy's dripping blood quickly filled the small indentation and started running along the groove around the perimeter.

Edgar held Tommy's palm to his mouth and licked the wound closed, grinning when Tommy snatched his hand back. "Who's next?"

In short order, the shallow channel around the edge of the stone was filled and everyone had resumed holding the relic. Bryan tightened his grip, watching closely as the blood trembled. It pulsed, then began to flow from the outer ring, traveling down the small spokes that led to the larger indentation in the center. A faint chime rang in the air. The blood started to glow. Bryan tensed in anticipation.

Nothing further happened.

"Now what?" Tommy asked. "Does it need more blood?"

"I'm not sure." Bryan ran over the words from his father again. Something was tickling at his brain.

Carlos's head jerked sideways. "The demon's starting to break free. Gideon, hit it again."

Bryan turned his head away when Gideon breathed ice-fire and covered the demon, stopping its movements.

"Cool," Tommy said. "I didn't know you could do that in human form."

Gideon grinned and waggled his eyebrows.

"We need to figure this out quickly," Lysander said. "Come on, people. What do we know?"

"You set us free," said Tommy. 'But how?" He frowned at the stone. "Why is all the blood in the middle? Oh. I know. Maybe you need it to paint symbols on us."

Lysander screwed up his face. "I hope not."

"The note called this the Platter of Unification," Roman said. "It must require more than the combination of our blood, though I cannot imagine what that would be."

"Look." Edgar pointed to the center of the stone. "Another symbol just appeared."

Bryan blinked when the symbol Edgar was pointing at began to glow. The world fell from beneath his feet as he focused on it, his vision tunneling until all he could see were the three wavy lines of glowing red. Buzzing sounded in his ears. The words from his father's message floated across the landscape of his mind. They blended with the red lines, spinning around and around, faster and faster. He fell to his knees, caught in a whirling kaleidoscope, drowning in a vortex of light and words. It reached its crescendo, spitting him into the universe to fly among the stars. The answer, when it flashed into his mind with sparkling clarity, catapulted him from the heavens, sending him crashing back to Earth.

Falling sideways, he called out. "It's you, Sandi. You're the one."

Lysander slid his arms under Bryan's and lifted him to his feet. "What happened? One minute we're talking, then the next you're on the ground babbling nonsense."

Bryan turned, stumbling into Lysander. He patted his chest. "You're the Liberator."

Lysander's eyebrows shot up. "Are you sure you didn't hit your head?"

Ignoring him, Bryan waved excitedly at the stone. "Those lines. Spirit. This is what you were born for."

"What are you…."

"You need to link us, Sandi. You're the only one with the power to do that."

Lysander eyed the crazy man who looked like his brother. "Maybe you should sit down."

Bryan grabbed him by the biceps and shook him. "Listen to me. You have to connect our powers. It's going to take all of them to defeat the demon. Unite us so you can destroy it." He stepped back and held out his hand. "I know this is the way. Trust me."

Lysander didn't hesitate in reaching for Bryan's hand, easily putting his trust in his older brother as he'd always done.

Bryan pulled him back to the others and took his place around the stone relic. He squeezed Lysander's hand, his faith in him shining from his eyes. "Link with me, Sandi, like you have before. But this time, bring in the others."

Lysander took a deep breath and closed his eyes. He started by following the familiar connection he had with his brother until he reached Bryan's core. He pulled loose a thin strand of his brother's golden essence and tied it around his wrist. Next, he followed the glowing line permanently connecting his soul to Roman's, taking a moment when he was surrounded by the radiance of Roman's love to draw strength from the ancient vampire for the task ahead of him. He carefully pulled a strand from Roman's center and tied it next to Bryan's. He then moved on to Tommy. Or tried to. He gently pushed, but his friend was locked down, resisting his efforts to get inside.

Not wanting to force his way, Lysander whispered, "Let me in, Tommy."

"I can't." Tommy's anguish hurt Lysander's heart. "You'll see."

"I promise not to look."

"Ell, please. I can't…you will…."

"I won't poke around. Pinky swear, Tommy. You'll always be safe with me."

There was a slight easing, so Lysander carefully slipped inside. True to his word, he turned a blind eye to Tommy's thoughts, seeking only his core. He faltered when he saw the tear. A small piece was missing from his best friend's center, sparkling gossamer light trickling from the wound. Oh, Tommy. What happened? Immeasurable sorrow nearly drove him to his knees from Tommy's soul crying out its agony and pain to the universe.

Lysander swore and moved closer. Gently stroking the edges of the horrific wound, he promised, "I'll make this right, brother. I'll help you heal. You are not alone." A tendril of Tommy's inner light reached for him. Carefully pulling on the strand, he tied it next to Roman's. "I'll return it," he promised. "You will not suffer further loss." The core pulsed weakly, its pain softer, as if it understood and knew he would honor his word.

Lysander sent a plea to the Goddess to look after his friend, then flowed out of Tommy and into the Alpha.

The wildness inside Jackson was a shock. Lysander stood a moment surrounded by the crackling energy, amazed at Jackson's strength and ability to temper the aggressive beast that resided inside him. When he reached Jackson's center, angry vines lashed around the inner mass. Tentatively reaching out his hand, he jerked when a strand leapt at him and attached itself to his wrist. He moved it to the other side of Roman's, away from Tommy's, whose soul was too wounded to deal with the Alpha's ferocity.

Pulling gently on the lines leading off of him, he quickly flowed over to Gideon, eager to meet with the dragon again. This time he was prepared and didn't allow himself to be distracted by the galactic universe encapsulated within the Dragon Prince, instead heading directly toward his powerful core.

As he neared the massive red and blue sphere at Gideon's center, he found the dragon waiting for him. He bowed, awestruck, as before, by the majesty of the ancient beast.

"Greetings, Ancient One."

"Welcome, child. I have been waiting for you."

"You knew I was coming?"

"This moment was written in the stars."

Lysander stared at him in shock, then bowed again. He took a step toward the immense red-blue orb, pulsing with life and magic. As he got closer, it pulled at him, streamers of his magic drawn toward it like scarves in a wind. He jerked back, his magic swirling around him, agitated by the magnetic pull of Gideon's core. He stared helplessly at the turbulent sphere, not daring to go nearer for fear he'd be captured by the overwhelming vastness of its power.

Turning to the dragon, he asked, "Can you help?"

In response, the ancient beast reached out and grabbed a handful of threads from the pulsing core. "Watch." His black-tipped claws wove a masterful weave. "Do you see?"

Lysander nodded. The dragon fluttered his claws, dispersing the magic. He reached and grabbed a single strand, handing the thread to Lysander. Sliding the other strands off his arm, Lysander concentrated, copying the weave he'd been shown. Finished, he held it up. The dragon used the tip of a claw to make a minor adjustment, then nodded.

"Now, child. The demon awakes."

Lysander thrust his hand outward. Magic unleashed, a beam of light bursting into the warehouse with a sonic boom. Lysander braced to hold himself steady as the torrent rushed through him. Ancient stars and comets holding the mysteries of the universe streamed forward, carrying hints of earth and untamed spirit. Flows of copper, holding the fierceness of an ancient warrior wound around the constellations, while sparks flickered to life, shining with the purity of a human soul. Weaving it all together were golden strands of lighting-filled magic.

Lysander held strong as a doorway formed, shining as bright as the noonday sun. Acting on instinct, he pointed his free hand to the demon hidden in Jillian's body. Crooking his finger, he tugged and pulled the malevolent red and black spirit free, then flicked it toward the glowing door. The dark shadow hit with a loud thunderclap of noise. White light exploded, magic going supernova. A loud chime filled the air. The doorway vanished.

Lysander blinked the spots from his eyes. "Where did it go?"

"To a place of emptiness." The ancient beast bowed his head. "You have done well, fledgling. Know that we are proud of you."

Lysander spun toward the dragon, his magic sparkling around him. "Fledgling? Does that mean I can turn into a dragon?"

"Perhaps one day. When you are ready." The dragon gave him a gentle push and sent him through the constellations until he landed back into his body with a jarring thump. Everything faded as he sank into darkness.

Bryan rolled over, then grabbed his head, groaning at the drum pounding in his brain. He waited a minute until the beats subsided then pushed himself to his knees. His heart stuttered when he saw Max lying motionless next to him. Diving at his mate, he frantically ran his hands over Max's body, searching for a heartbeat. "Max. Max."

He jerked back when Max shot upright, then he lunged forward, tackling his poor mate to the ground. "You're okay. Thank the Goddess. You're alive."

"I'm fine." Max's strong arms wrapped around Bryan.

"What happened?"

"It got a little wild at the end. When everything exploded, I shielded you from the worst of the damage."

"You did what?" Bryan popped him in the chest. "Don't do that again. What if you'd been hurt? Look after yourself next time."

Max smiled and took hold of his fist. "I will always stand between you and danger. Always."

Bryan lost himself in his mate's eyes, feeling Max's determination to protect him from all harm. Smiling warmly at him, Bryan shared his thankfulness that they'd survived and his joy in being able to spend forever with the other half of his soul. "I'll always be there for you too," Bryan whispered.

"As it should be between mates."

Bryan buried his head in Max's chest, part of him a little surprised that he was still alive to experience this. And thankful beyond measure that he could.

"Lysander. Beloved, please. You must wake up."

Roman's distress had Bryan scrambling off of Max and rushing over to where he was crouched over Lysander's still form.

Bryan dropped to the ground next to his brother. "What's wrong with him?'

"He's not breathing."

"Shit." Bryan leaned over Lysander to start chest compressions when Lysander sucked in a sharp breath and jerked up, kneeing Bryan in the ribs. He fell sideways in a graceless sprawl. "Damn it, Sandi. Why do you always do that?"

"Sorry."

Bryan sat up, rubbing his side. "Don't apologize. You can knee me anytime you want. I'm just glad you're all right."

"Why wouldn't I be?"

"Your heart stopped beating, beloved." Roman pulled Lysander into his lap. "I fear you have shortened my life by a century. You must not do that again."

Lysander patted Roman's chest. "Sorry about that. I didn't mean to worry you." He turned to Bryan. "I'm assuming it worked."

"And then some." Bryan climbed to his feet and looked around. The destruction caused by the blast was considerable. Any racks that had still been standing had been blown aside. One of the walls was nothing more than rubble and the roof was completely gone, exposing the night sky that was starting to get lighter. "Thanks for not destroying the world."

Lysander snorted and climbed off of Roman's lap. "The dragon showed me what to do. He would have made sure that didn't happen." His brow creased. "I think he called me fledgling."

Gideon's sharp gasp drew their attention to where he was climbing over a pile of cartons. Carlos popped up behind him and threw a steel girder across the warehouse. Gideon hurried over. "What did my dragon say?"

"He said they were proud of me. Then he called me fledgling." He looked at Gideon. "Does that mean I'm a dragon?"

"I'm not sure. Maybe. I'll have to ask Mother. She might know."

"It will have to wait until we get this mess cleaned up," Edgar said as he and Jackson joined them, a bedraggled Tommy stumbling along behind them. "Is everyone all right?"

"We're good." Bryan looked around and noticed Ruth pushing herself to her feet. He flicked his fingers, binding her powers before she could escape. He tensed, waiting for her to break his weave, but she only struggled helplessly against the bonds, unable to escape with her demon-infused powers gone. "I have Ruth. What should we do with her?"

"Gideon and I can take her for a ride," Carlos offered. "I'm sure there's a volcano around here somewhere that we can drop her into."

"Sorry. As tempting as that sounds, I can't let you do that."

"I don't see why not. It's the least of what she deserves."

Bryan shook his head. "Now that the battle is over, we need to treat all life as precious. Even if they're a treacherous magic-user who was prepared to feed us all to a demon."

"I think you're making a mistake to keep her alive. Given half a chance, she'll betray you again."

"I know. But we have to start somewhere," Bryan said as he looked around the warehouse. "There has been enough death. We'll find another way to punish Ruth for her crimes."

Max spoke up. "I'll have Eric take charge of her when he reports in. We can lock her up in the dungeon with Jillian's father."

"Good idea. She'll be safe there until we have time to deal with her."

"Speaking of Jillian, has anyone seen her?" Lysander asked, looking around. "I thought she was standing near Ruth?"

"She was. Let's see if we can find her. Or her body." Bryan started moving crushed cartons to the side.

They'd barely begun the search when Marcus and his team of enforcers and wolves raced into the building. At a signal from the coven leader, they fanned out and looked warily around. Marcus continued across the warehouse until he reached Roman. "It's good to see you alive."

"You as well, my friend."

"I'll admit to being worried for your safety when the roof blew off."

"As you can see, we are fine. What took you so long to come in?"

"I'm not sure what was going on in here, but the entire place was covered by some kind of silver barrier. It only came down a few moments ago." He looked around, whistling softly. "You guys made quite the mess in here."

"It could not be helped."

"It never can with you. What do you need us to do?"

Roman glanced at Max, then looked at the toppled racking and frowned. "Eric and his team have yet to report in. I fear something may have happened to them."

"We'll begin searching immediately."

"I would appreciate that."

Bryan stepped up. "Could you keep your eyes open for a young woman? If you do find her, be careful. She may be dangerous."

Marcus' eyebrows shot up. "How dangerous?"

"As in, keep back and send someone to get me so that I can deal with her."

"We'll keep our eyes open and let you know if we find her." Marcus tipped his head to Roman, then called out to his team. "You heard the Prince. Start searching through the rubble for our missing people."

They continued looking for Jillian in the piles of broken timber and cinder blocks along the near side of the warehouse. When they found any ex-minions who hadn't been destroyed by Bryan's sun power, they carried them to the wall near the entrance and laid them out. The number of bodies they were digging up was surprising. Setting down another one, Bryan sent a quick prayer to the Goddess to look after them, then wiped an arm across his sweaty face and headed back to the section he and Max were searching.

Bryan was stretched out, pulling a carton off the pile when he stumbled, falling to one knee. His overhead mage-light fell on a glittering object that reflected the light. Pushing debris to the side, he sucked in a breath when he recognized the large signet ring his mother always wore. The one they'd left on her body when they'd laid her to rest. He began feverishly digging in the rubble.

"Max. Come help me."

Max was instantly by his side. Between them, they had Charlotte's body uncovered in no time. Bryan lifted her free of the debris and set her carefully down on a clear spot on the floor. He took hold of one of her hands and looked at the ragged and dirty fingernails, knowing his mother would be appalled by their condition. He rubbed his thumb over a black smear, wiping the stain away.

A strangled sound behind him alerted him to his brother's presence a moment before Lysander fell to his knees next to him. Lysander reached out a shaky hand to push Charlotte's hair back from her face.

"We can't leave her here, Bryan."

"We won't."

"Let me have her," Roman said quietly from behind them. "I'll have one of the enforcers take her home."

"Can you have them ask Mrs. Davies to clean Mother up?" Bryan asked. "I can't put her back with Father in this condition."

"I will ensure she is looked after. You have my word."

"Prince, we found them." Bryan looked up to see Marcus speeding toward them. "Eric and his team were buried when the outer wall collapsed. We're digging them out now."

"Is anyone seriously injured?"

"Not so far. A couple of broken bones. Nothing that can't be healed."

"What about the wolves that were with them?" Jackson asked, walking over, his forehead creased with concern. "And my brother?"

"They're fine. The enforcers protected them from serious harm." He smirked at Roman. "Your crusade to bring harmony among the communities is working."

"Which is good. The events of today should clearly demonstrate that we are stronger when we work together."

Marcus shook his head, smiling ruefully. "I would never have expected vampires, wolves, and magic-users to fight together. This would not have happened under the previous Council.

"Which is what made us vulnerable in the first place." Roman stopped, then frowned. "I wonder."

"About what," Marcus asked when Roman didn't continue.

"It's possible the demon may have been manipulating the Elders longer than we thought."

"But that would mean this began centuries ago and not a few decades like you thought."

"Time has no meaning to a demon."

Marcus frowned, then nodded. "That would explain why some of the ancient laws were put into place. In particular, the ones that weakened us."

"Indeed."

Marcus whistled. "Then it's fortunate you and your Consort met. If you hadn't rebelled and mated, we would not be standing here."

"Give your thanks to the Goddess. We are no more than her soldiers fighting to maintain order in the universe."

Marcus froze, then said quietly, "It's kind of scary when you think about it."

"That it is. But the rewards are without parallel."

"If you say so."

"I do." Roman put his hand on Marcus's shoulder. "Daylight is approaching and there is much to be done."

Marcus smiled. "Then I'd better get back to digging out your missing people."

"Thank you. Please send Eric to me when all of his team is accounted for."

"Yes, Prince." Bowing to Roman, Marcus raced off to the other side of the warehouse.

"I'm glad Eric is okay," Lysander said, getting to his feet. "Casey would've been devastated if anything happened to him."

"As would I." Roman crouched to pick up Charlotte's body.

Once he saw that Roman had his mother's body firmly in his hold, Bryan looked over to the pile of debris where he'd found his mother, sighing when he saw how much was left to go through. "I don't know if Jillian could have survived being buried under this. Maybe we're wasting our time." Regardless of his words, he got up and walked over to pull another piece of bent steel off the pile he'd been digging through.

"We promised Richard we'd bring her back so we need to keep looking." Lysander rushed over to help Bryan lift a large beam off the pile. "What are we going to do with her if we find her alive?"

"She should be locked in a cage next to Ruth," Carlos said, lifting a huge section of wall and tossing it to the side.

Lysander shook his head. "Whatever the demon did is not her fault."

"But what she did with the Elders is."

"But how much of that was her choice? With Mother involved, Jillian may have been caught in the middle of her manipulations and scheming."

"Or she might have been playing a game of her own," Carlos countered.

"Possibly. Or she might have been a victim who was just trying to survive."

"She might have been all of that or none," Bryan said. "Let's focus on finding her first. After being possessed by the demon, there might not be enough left of her mind to worry about it."

Lysander paused in the midst of shifting a carton. "I think a part of her was still aware." He winced. "But only a very small part."

Bryan stood and wiped a hand across his brow. "If that's the case, we'll help her as much as we can. If Jillian somehow recovers, we can decide what to do with her then."

"What the hell's the matter with you two. She's not some innocent girl. She's a viper who got into more trouble than she expected."

"I know she's a horrible person," Bryan said, "but that doesn't mean she's a criminal. We're not going to pass judgement on her until she is well enough to defend her actions."

"Have it your way. But don't blame me when she stabs you in your sleep."

Bryan was cut off before he could respond.

"I found her," Tommy shouted. "And she's still breathing."

Bryan rushed over with Carlos and Lysander. Kneeling beside her, he quickly checked her over but didn't see any external injuries aside from some bruises and minor cuts. Internally was a different story. She lay unmoving, her open eyes vacant. Bryan called her name numerous times and clapped his hands in her face, but Jillian was completely unresponsive. He dropped his head and sighed. Jillian was no threat to anyone. Not anymore.

"Fuck," Carlos breathed behind him. "What did that demon do to her? Can she even be fixed?"

"I have no idea. All I know is we have to try." Bryan went to lift her body.

"I've got her," Carlos said, pushing him to the side. He lifted Jillian, cradling her in his arms. "Gideon and I can fly her to the mansion while you guys finish up here."

Bryan narrowed his eyes at Carlos. "Can I trust her with you?"

Carlos nodded. "You can. I know I didn't sound concerned about her earlier." He looked down at the broken girl in his arms. "It's different somehow, seeing her like this. Whatever her faults, she didn't deserve this."

"No, she didn't. If she's able to come back from this, she won't be the same person. Only time will tell if it's for better or worse."

"Let's hope it's for the better." Carlos looked around the wreckage of the warehouse. "This is going to take a while to go through. It might be easier if Gideon just burned everything."

Bryan shook his head. "We need to keep looking for bodies so we can return them to the people who loved them. We already destroyed too many of them getting in here and fighting the demon."

"We didn't have much choice."

"I know. But that won't bring any comfort to the families."

"Don't take everything on yourself, Bryan. You're not responsible for the actions of the demon. Just turn the dead over to the police. They can contact the families. You've done enough."

"I suppose. Somehow this doesn't feel like a victory."

"War never does." Carlos nudged him with his shoulder. "Gideon's waiting for me. We'll see you back at the mansion."

"Sure," Bryan said absently, looking around at the devastation that was the result of the Council's greed and need for power. A need which had made them susceptible to the lies of a demon. The number of bodies he could see on the concrete outside was mind-numbing. And what had happened here was only the tip of the iceberg. It would take decades for all of the communities to recover from the demon's attempt to take over the world.

Kicking a piece of rebar out of his way, he wondered if it wouldn't be easier to take Carlos' suggestion and purge everything with dragon fire. Then he shook his head. The dead deserved better than they'd been given. And so did the living.

Victory tasted bitter when so much had been lost.

* * *

In a grotto, hidden deep in the bayou, a large stone lay forgotten and partially buried under a layer of mud and grass. The large triangular head of a cottonmouth bumped its surface, its long tongue flicking out to test the air before it coiled around the stone and settled into place.

A pinpoint of red sparked to life. The snake lifted its head, hissing in agitation. The tiny dot spread, growing brighter as it pushed against the darkness of the cavern. Sensing danger, the snake began unwinding its body to slither away.

The stone flared with a burst of crimson fire, leaving behind a large patch of scorched earth, devoid of life, before it settled into a steady glowing red, inky ribbons of darkness moving unceasingly beneath its surface. The stone's light dimmed further until only a central spark remained, pulsing softly in the shadows. Waiting, until it was time to wake again.

Epilogue

Bryan poured a hefty dose of whisky in each of the tumblers he'd laid out on Roman's desk, then picked up his glass. "I had intended to propose a toast to celebrate our victory, but it doesn't seem appropriate somehow. Even though we achieved the impossible and saved the world from the demon, too much was lost for it to feel like a win."

"Sometimes all you can do is be thankful for those you have managed to save," said Roman, picking up two glasses and handing one to Lysander. "There is no true winner when it comes to war."

"No. There really isn't." Bryan motioned to the tumblers, then stepped to the side when the rest of the men came up and got a glass before returning to their seats. Once everyone was settled, he said, "I think we should take a moment to remember everyone who was lost." The room grew quiet. Bryan sent a silent plea to the Goddess asking her to watch over the souls of everyone who had passed on to the next life.

After a bit, Bryan cleared his throat. "As difficult and as heartbreaking as the last few months have been, we did manage to bring all of our communities together and use our combined strengths to vanquish the demon. And that is something worth acknowledging." Holding up his glass, he said, "To the Goddess for showing us the way and to all those who helped us save our world." He took a sip of his drink, with everyone else following suit.

Lysander set his glass on the desk "We should be proud of what we've accomplished so far. It took a lot to get where we are right now."

"Yes," said Roman, putting his glass beside Lysander's. "We make a formidable team. Which is good. There is still much to be done to rebuild and strengthen the paranormal communities."

"If last night was any indication of what it's going to be like hanging around with you guys, I'm willing to give up my seat on the Paranormal Council," Carlos said.

Lysander grinned. "As if you'd let Gideon go into danger on his own. Face it, you're stuck with us for the rest of your life."

Carlos shuddered dramatically. "That's a scary thought."

"Indeed," said Roman dryly.

Muted laughter filled the room.

Tommy pushed up from the couch and walked over to the desk. Staring into the depths of his glass for a moment, he drank what remained then set it down before giving Lysander and Bryan a sad smile. "Thank you for letting me join you. Getting the chance to be a hero helped."

"Whenever you're ready, Tommy, I'm here for you," Lysander said quietly.

"I know. Soon. I promise." He retook his place on the couch next to Jinx, who made a production out of stretching each leg before leisurely curling up on his lap. Tommy sank his hand deep into his fur and started scratching him. Jinx's loud purrs filled the silence that had fallen over the group.

Bryan tossed back the last of his drink then set his glass on the desk. He picked up the decanter to refill it, splashing more into Roman's and Lysander's glasses, then looked over at Tommy who shook his head. Setting down the decanter, he said, "I wish we could have saved the relic. After all those centuries of our ancestors protecting it from harm, we managed to destroy it in less than a week."

Lysander snorted. "I know. But I don't think it matters."

"Why do you say that?"

"I think it was only a tool. Something to show us the way." He looked at Bryan. "The knowledge of what we did is still inside my head."

"Does that mean if another demon tries to take over the world, we'll be able to stop it?" Tommy asked.

"Not…exactly. This demon wasn't able to manifest fully since it was trapped in Jillian's living body. That limited its capabilities."

"That was limited? Shit. We're doomed if another one breaks through."

"Maybe not. All of us have special abilities. Even you, Tommy. Your talent with a bow is extraordinary. I think once the rest of us learn more about our powers and develop our skills to your level, we'll have everything we need to stop another demon from taking over our world."

"Even without the relic?"

"Even then. If nothing else, what we've learned will give us a chance. Which might be all that we need."

"Hopefully, we'll never have to find out."

"I think we can all agree to that." Bryan raised his glass again. "Today we saved our world. Tomorrow we'll start rebuilding our communities, making them strong, and teaching them to live together in harmony. Once we have achieved that, nothing will be able to stand against us."

Jinx's loud purrs filled the room. The Goddess agreed.

Epilogue Part Two

Warning. This is a setup for the next series. Read only if you wish to continue on to the next story arc…

Bryan's phone rang. Setting down his glass, he glanced at the screen, frowning when he saw it was the front gate. "Hey Joe. What's up?"

"Sir, I have a young wolf wishing to speak with you. Shall I let him in?"

"Did he say which pack he was from?"

"He says he didn't grow up in a pack."

"Oh? Did he tell you what he wanted?"

"No, sir. He just said he needed to speak with you."

"All right, let him in. Please ask Albert to bring him to Roman's office."

"Yes, sir."

Bryan hung up. "Why would a wolf want to talk to me?' he asked Jackson.

"I'm not sure. I'm more concerned by the fact he wasn't raised in a pack. Wolves have a tendency to go feral if they're left on their own."

"He'd better not be planning to cause any trouble," Lysander said. "We deserve some peace and quiet after the last few months."

"Agreed," Carlos said, hopping up from his chair. "Gideon and I are planning to lock ourselves in our room before we have to take that idiot Randal back home." He scowled at his mate. "Are you sure we can't leave him in the dungeon? It's the least he deserves for being such an asshole."

"Sorry, treasure. The King said we needed to bring him back."

"What did your mother say?"

Gideon laughed. "Mother wants us to take our time. It seems the Court is a much quieter place without him."

"Excellent advice. Remind me to bring her flowers the next time we see her."

"She would love that."

Max crossed his arms. "I don't like a wolf showing up at our door right now. The timing is suspicious."

"I agree. I fear this wolf brings nothing but trouble." Roman came around his desk and stood next to Max. "Eric, send for more guards."

"At once, Prince."

Tommy snickered. "You guys might want to chill out. Security said it was a young wolf. You're going to terrify him with all this posturing."

"I fail to see the problem," Roman said.

Tommy rolled his eyes.

A knock on the door stopped further conversation.

"Enter," Roman called out.

Albert opened the door. "Sir, I have a Mr. Hobbes wishing to speak with Mr. Galway."

"I told you to call me Jory." A lanky young wolf with messy blond hair, faded jeans, and a scuffed leather jacket strolled into the room. He came to an abrupt stop when he saw everyone staring at him. Then he rolled his eyes. "You can all relax. I'm not here to cause trouble. Jeesh."

Shaking his head, he wandered over to the bar and started poking around in the cupboards. "Anyone mind if I have a drink? It's a lot hotter outside than I expected."

Bryan raised his eyebrow at the wolf's boldness, then followed after him, closing the cupboard doors he'd left open. "What can I get you?"

"Water would be great. I must have sweated a bucket running here."

Bryan pulled a bottle from the cooler and handed it over. He waited as the young man drained the bottle, then handed him another. "How can I help you?"

Jory wiped his hand across his mouth. Bryan handed him a napkin, which he looked at blankly before shoving in his pocket. "You're Bryan Galway?"

"I am."

"Great. I need you to help me find someone."

Bryan squinted. "Why did you come to me?"

"Mom said you'd be able to help."

"And where is your mother?"

The wolf's face scrunched up as he blinked furiously. A single tear still managed to fall, leaving a trail in the dust covering his face. He wiped his arm across his face, leaving streaks of dirt behind. Sighing, Bryan handed him another napkin, which joined the first in Jory's pocket.

"My condolences on your loss," Bryan said.

Jory sniffed. "She's not dead, just missing."

"I see. You want me to help you find her?"

He shook his head. "She always told me she was going to leave when I came of age." Jory shrugged, his eyes glossy with unshed tears. "I just didn't expect her to actually do it."

"I'm sorry that happened to you."

"It's fine." Bryan could see it was anything but. "So, can you help me?"

"It depends. Who are you looking for?"

"My brother." Jory reached into his pocket and pulled out a tattered photo, which he handed to Bryan.

Bryan sucked in a breath when he looked at the picture of a young boy wearing a red baseball cap. A boy he knew well. Looking across the room, he saw the moment Jory's next words registered. And the shock and denial that followed.

"Mom said his name is Lysander. Lysander Galway."

Fin

Thank you to all of my loyal readers who stayed with me to the end of the Reforming the Paranormal Council story arc.

Now that the Paranormal Council has been established and the demon defeated, the events that started in Forbidden Bonds, Book One of Reforming the Paranormal Council, are now complete.

But that doesn't mean the story is finished.

The real work for the Paranormal Council is just beginning. Of their many tasks will be uncovering the secrets behind Lysander's birth, investigating what happened to Tommy, and discovering the reason all of them have been given such over the top powers. And how is the Father of Dragons involved?

Book One of The Paranormal Council - Legacy will be out soon. I hope you all come along for the ride.

Till next time,
Much love,

Sheri

If you enjoyed this story, please think about leaving a review at your place of purchase, Reviews really help new authors like myself attract readers. Thanks again for your support.

About the Author

Sheri is an MM Romance writer who believes that love should have no boundaries, in happy-ever-afters, that dragons are real, and in strong leading characters...oh, and bacon; there's always room for bacon.

She has been an avid reader since a young age and always had a dream to write a book. Sometimes dreams really do come true, especially if you're prepared to put in the work.

Sheri is a 1ST Dan Black Belt in Taekwondo. She lives in Alberta, Canada with her husband, two sons, four cats, and one crazy, energetic dog.

You can visit her website @ https:/www.sherieleese.com

I really appreciate you reading my book! Here's where you can find me:

Amazon author page:
https://www.amazon.com/~/e/B08HNJ6R7T
Smashwords author page:
https://www.smashwords.com/profile/view/Wikatu
Friend me on Facebook:
https://www.facebook.com/sherieleesewrites/posts/

Or you can email me directly at sheri.eleese@shaw.ca

Other Books by This Author

Please visit your favorite eBook retailer to discover other books by Sheri Eleese:

Reforming the Paranormal Council:

Forbidden Bonds - Book One
Feral Bonds - Book Two
A Paranormal Family Christmas - Book 2.5
Treasured Bonds - Book Three
Hidden Bonds - Book Four

Made in the USA
Monee, IL
19 August 2021

76065771R00243